CW00870582

WITHDRAWN
FROM
CIRCULATION

C2000 00031 8178

COUNTERPLOT

Also by Alastair MacNeill

MOONBLOOD
DOUBLE-BLIND
DAMAGE CONTROL

COUNTERPLOT

Alastair MacNeill

VICTOR GOLLANCZ
LONDON

Copyright © Alastair MacNeill

All rights reserved

The right of Alastair MacNeill to be identified as the author
of this work has been asserted by him in accordance with
the Copyright, Designs and Patents Act, 1988.

First published in Great Britain in 1999
by Victor Gollancz
An imprint of Orion Books Ltd,
Orion House, 5 Upper St Martin's Lane,
London WC2H 9EA

A CIP catalogue record for this book
is available from the British Library.

ISBN 0 575 06757 8

Typeset by Deltatype Ltd, Birkenhead, Merseyside
Printed and bound by Clays Ltd, St Ives plc

Metropolitan Borough of Stockport
Libraries
WITHDRAWN
0003181778
FROM
CIRCULATION

Prologue

Chicago

He retrieved the 12-gauge sawn-off shotgun from under the passenger seat as soon as the stolen car pulled up outside the jeweller's and slipped it barrel-down into the deep inside pocket of his battered brown leather overcoat. Then, removing a pair of sunglasses to reveal his distinctive cobalt-blue eyes, he glanced fleetingly at the two men seated in the back of the car. Both nodded silently. They were ready. It was time.

'Be careful, Frankie.'

Frankie Genno gave a reassuring smile to the woman behind the wheel. 'Always, Annie, you know that,' he replied, and traced a finger lightly down her cold, waxen cheek. Her sunken eyes were emotionless, her haggard face pallid. Her blonde hair hung lifelessly on bony, emaciated shoulders. Anne Stratton was a junkie hooked on cocaine, and totally dependent on him.

He knew that his two colleagues had serious reservations about using her as the getaway driver. Henry Drummond had already spoken to him privately about it. Henry was his only real friend, having grown up in the same run-down apartment block in the back streets of Chicago. He normally listened to Henry, but on this occasion had chosen not to heed his advice, especially as Annie had been adamant that she wanted to be in on the heist from the start. Her involvement had meant a lot to him. It had brought them closer together over the past couple of months. He almost felt that he could finally trust her. Almost. On the other hand, Julian Merill – or Jules as he preferred to be called – had been more blunt, expressing his disquiet in no uncertain terms in front of her. Julian. Jules. Either way, he didn't like the guy. Henry had suggested bringing him in at short notice after their original accomplice had been arrested in New

York for an unrelated offence. And Henry's recommendation had been good enough for Frankie.

'I'll be waiting out here for you,' Anne said softly beside him, interrupting his thoughts.

Genno cast a quizzical glance at her. Why had she said that? Stating the obvious? Nervousness? Probably. Her eyes were fixed on the St Christopher medallion secured to the dashboard. She was sweating profusely. Her hands were trembling. It was obvious that she needed another hit. Badly. He had the coke and a clean spike in his pocket. He'd let her have them once they reached the second getaway car, parked in an alleyway a few blocks from the jewellery store. Then she could shoot up and savour the subsequent rush in all its glory. But not before. She had to play by his rules. He grabbed her chin and turned her face towards him. 'Make sure you start the engine the moment you see us coming out that shop door,' he told her, and tightened his grip on her chin when she tried to pull away from him. 'Don't let me down, Annie.'

'I know what to do, Frankie,' she was quick to assure him, desperately trying to inject some much needed self-confidence into her shaky voice, and then flicked her tongue quickly across her dry, cracked lips in a vain attempt to try and moisten them. 'We've been through it enough times.'

'Just don't fuck up, that's what he means,' Merill hissed at her from the back seat.

Genno swivelled round in his seat to glare at Merill. 'If I want your input, Julian-fucking-Jules, I'll ask for it.'

'I was only—'

'Shut up!' Drummond cut sharply across Merill's protestations. His eyes went to Genno. 'Let's go, Frankie. The sooner we do it, the sooner we're outta here.'

Anne put a hand lightly on Genno's arm. 'Frankie, I love you.'

Genno just nodded in response, then slipped on a pair of black leather gloves and opened the passenger door. As he stepped out of the car, the handcuffs which were secured to the side of the belt glinted momentarily in the midday sun. Then his jacket fell back against his body and they disappeared from view again. He never went anywhere without handcuffs. To others they were his trade-mark. To him they were a practical necessity. Nothing more.

He stood over six foot tall and although only twenty years of age, he appeared older with his thick matted beard and long, uncombed coppery-brown hair which hadn't been washed for several days.

Drummond and Merill, who got out of the back of the car, were both armed with automatics, hidden from view in their jacket pockets. Drummond was carrying a holdall. Genno scanned the length of the street. Nobody appeared to be taking any notice of them. He walked the short distance to the entrance of the shop and, once in the doorway, slipped a black stocking over his face. Then, in one fluid movement, he pulled out his shotgun and swept confidently into the shop. Drummond and Merill followed close behind him. They, too, had put on black stocking masks.

One assistant behind the counter. Late sixties. Mrs Yablonsky, the owner's wife. Two customers – a couple in their early forties. Genno was in no mood for possible heroics and quickly trained the shotgun on them to dispel any such notions. 'Both of you, face down on the floor. Now!' He waited until they had obeyed him, then snarled at Merill, who had locked the front door and pulled down the blind, 'Watch them. And if they move, shoot them.'

Drummond had disappeared into the back of the shop to locate the owner, and he now returned with Yablonsky, his automatic pressed against the man's neck. 'The fucking old fool set off the panic alarm in his office before I could get to him,' he told Genno.

'Did you take care of it?' Genno demanded.

'Yeah, I got him to call the cops and tell them it was a false alarm. They're not coming out.'

'Good. Get what you can out of the display cabinets while I have a little chat to our hosts in the back office.' Genno moved behind the counter and manacled Hannah Yablonsky's hands behind her back. He then ordered Yablonsky to return to his office, and followed behind him using a terrified Hannah Yablonsky as hostage.

'Please, take what you want, just don't hurt my wife,' Yablonsky pleaded once they were inside the office, but he flinched instinctively at the sound of breaking glass as Drummond smashed one of the display cabinets in the front of the shop.

'We *will* take what we want,' Genno replied coldly, 'and that includes the consignment of diamonds you received by courier this morning. I'm reliably informed that it's worth at least two hundred grand.'

'I . . . I . . . don't know . . . what you're talking about,' Yablonsky spluttered, but his eyes darted involuntarily towards the safe in the corner of the room.

'That's where I thought they'd be,' Genno said with a triumphant

3

sneer as another glass cabinet was smashed in the front of the shop. 'Open the safe and give me the diamonds. Then we'll be on our way.'

'I . . . I . . . told you—'

'Don't fuck with me, old man!' Genno cut in furiously, and Hannah Yablonsky cried out in terror when he tightened his grip round her throat and pushed the barrel of the shotgun brutally into her neck. The jagged tip of the barrel nicked her skin and a trickle of blood seeped down her throat and stained the collar of her white blouse.

'Please, don't hurt my wife,' Yablonsky begged, clasping her hands together in a gesture of intense supplication. 'Please.'

'You've got five seconds to open the safe, or you become a widower,' Genno said disdainfully. 'One . . . two . . .'

'I'll open it, I'll open it,' Yablonsky blurted out fearfully, and scurried over to the safe, his fingers trembling as he fumbled with the coordinates of the dial. He exhaled in relief when the door opened at the first attempt. Then, taking a small velvet pouch from the safe, he held it out towards Genno. His hands were still shaking uncontrollably.

Genno pushed Hannah Yablonsky to one side with such venom that she stumbled and almost fell to the floor. He grabbed the pouch from Yablonsky and looked inside. The diamonds winked back invitingly at him in the glare of the overhead fluorescent light. He grinned to himself and stuffed the pouch into his overcoat pocket. Then, removing the handcuffs from Hannah Yablonsky, he clipped them back on to his belt. He lashed out viciously at each of them with the butt of the shotgun, and they crumpled to the floor. Unconscious, but alive. He hurried back to the front of the shop. 'I've got the diamonds, let's get outta here,' he told Drummond, who was about to shatter another display cabinet.

'Just one more,' Drummond said excitedly, then smashed the top of the cabinet and greedily snatched handfuls of jewellery and stuffed them into the holdall.

'Leave it,' Genno implored and grabbed Drummond's arm, hauling him away from the display cabinet. 'We've got more than enough as it is. Now come on, let's go.'

Drummond zipped up the holdall, ducked out from behind the counter and crossed to the front door. At that moment Merill made the mistake of turning his back on the two customers, who were still lying face down on the floor. A shot rang out, and Drummond stumbled forward into Genno. The disbelief was still in his eyes when

4

his legs buckled awkwardly underneath him and he dropped to his knees. In that split second Genno saw the automatic in the man's hand. It was already swinging towards him. Instinctively, he fired the shotgun. The blast caught the man in the shoulder, sending the weapon spinning from his grasp. It came to land near Drummond who was now lying on his stomach, his face creased in agony. He was bleeding profusely. The bullet had struck him in the small of the back. He drew on all his strength to raise his head to look up at Genno, but when he tried to speak blood bubbled into his mouth and spilled out over his lips. Then his body shuddered and he fell forward on to the carpet. He didn't move again. Genno, his face twisted with rage, raised the shotgun again and for an instant met the defiant gaze of the man who was on his knees, his bloody hand clutched against his shattered clavicle. He was furious with himself for not having made Merill frisk the customers when they first entered the shop. It hadn't even entered his mind that either of them could have been armed, such was his craving to get at the diamonds. And now his best friend was dead because of it. He pulled the trigger again. The man was hit full in the chest, knocking him back against one of the shattered display cabinets. The woman screamed in horror as she stared at the lifeless figure propped grotesquely against the front of the cabinet. Then she reached out a hand and touched his face. And screamed again when she realized he was dead.

Genno calmly removed the two spent cartridges, slipped two more into the breech, and snapped it shut once more. Then he approached the woman. 'Who is he? Your husband?'

'Gerry,' she whispered in a barely audible voice, seemingly oblivious to Genno standing next to her, gently stroking her hand over the top of his head as the tears streamed uncontrollably down her face. 'Oh God, Gerry, no. No. Please, no.'

'I said, is he your fucking husband?' Genno snarled.

'Yes,' came the reply between tormented sobs.

'In sickness and in health, until death do you part.' Genno aimed the shotgun at the woman's bowed head and squeezed the trigger.

'Sweet Jesus, no,' Merill screamed and hurried over to where Genno was staring dispassionately at the two bodies, the shotgun now hanging loosely at the side. 'You said there'd be no shooting. That's the only reason I agreed to come in on this. What the fuck is wrong with you, Genno?'

'That's good coming from you. All you had to do was watch them. And if you'd done your job properly, Henry wouldn't be dead.'

5

'You didn't need to kill them in cold blood,' Merill retorted, but there was a tone of defensiveness in his voice. He had screwed up. And he knew it.

'You want me to make it three?' Genno pushed the barrel of the shotgun into Merill's stomach.

'Drummond was right. You *are* a fucking psycho. There's no reasoning with you, is there?'

Genno looked at Drummond's body and for a fleeting moment there was hurt in his eyes. Then it was gone. 'Just get the door, Julian-fucking-Jules. And take the holdall with you. It's your responsibility now. You can manage that, can't you?'

Merill bit back his anger as Genno's sarcasm cut deep. Then, slinging the holdall over his shoulder, he unlocked the door but didn't open it. Genno paused beside Drummond's body and was about to crouch down and close his sightless eyes when he heard the approaching police siren in the distance. 'It's the fucking cops. Let's get outta here,' he shouted, and jumped nimbly over Drummond and followed Merill out into the street. He collided with Merill who had stopped dead in his tracks. 'Get into the car, for fuck's sake,' he yelled, looking around him wildly and brandishing the shotgun as horrified passers-by scrambled for cover.

'What fucking car?' Merill shrieked.

It was only then that Genno turned his attention to where the car had been parked, directly in front of the shop. It wasn't there. And the police sirens were closing in fast on them from both directions.

'Bitch!' Merill exclaimed furiously, desperately scanning the street for any sign of the car. It was nowhere in sight. 'I told you she wasn't reliable, Genno. I told you. But no, you had to go and think with your fucking dick.'

'Shut up, and look for something we can use to get outta here,' Genno snarled.

'Thanks to your bitch we're both looking, at best, at life without the possibility of parole,' Merill continued bitterly, oblivious to Genno's urgency behind him. 'At worst, we'll be on death row for the next ten fucking years.'

'You won't.' Genno shot Merill in the back from close range. He grabbed the fallen holdall, picked up Merill's automatic, then sprinted across the street towards a parked car. Although it appeared empty, he had seen a woman seated behind the wheel moments earlier. She had obviously ducked down when everyone else had run for cover. If he could take her hostage, he still had a chance of getting away.

'Drop your weapon!' an authoritative voice boomed through a megaphone.

Genno looked round without breaking his stride and saw the two patrol cars parked diagonally across the street, blocking any escape route. There were several policemen crouched down behind the open doors, their handguns trained on him. 'Drop your weapon!' the voice commanded again. Genno was only feet from the car now. He saw the petrified woman lying across the front seat, her eyes wide and uncertain. A baby was harnessed in a support chair in the back. Perfect. Now he would have two hostages. And the cops wouldn't dare shoot for fear of hitting the baby. He raised the shotgun butt to smash the driver's window. A bullet hammered into his upper arm, knocking him sideways, and the shotgun spilled from his grasp and clattered noisily on to the road, such was the silence that had now fallen on the usually busy street. Screaming in fury, and with his injured arm clutched protectively to his side, he opened fire with Merill's automatic on the two patrol cars. The police returned fire. A second bullet slammed into his ribs and he dropped down on to one knee, his face twisted in pain. The automatic slipped from his fingers and came to rest underneath the parked car. He was still desperately trying to retrieve it when he felt a vicious blow slam across his shoulder blades, knocking him off balance.

A patrolman, who had been crouched out of sight close to the car, had broken cover the moment Genno had dropped the automatic. He had lashed out with his night stick, and as Genno fell forward on to the road he placed his knee across Genno's neck to immobilize him and twisted his arms viciously behind his back. Within seconds he was joined by half a dozen colleagues. Despite struggling violently under their combined weight, Genno was quickly overpowered and a pair of handcuffs were secured tightly round his wrists. He screamed in agony as the tip of a police boot caught him in his injured ribcage. Another kick in the same spot. Harder. The pain was excruciating. He couldn't move. The side of his face was pressed firmly against the surface of the road and he could taste blood in his mouth from his lacerated lip. Fists began to systematically punch his back and sides. Helpless. Hardly able to breathe. And all the time he kept thinking of Annie . . .

'That's enough!' He vaguely heard the voice from somewhere above him. 'Get him to his feet.'

Genno gasped gratefully for air when the pressure was released from the back of his neck, then he was hauled up roughly and found himself face to face with a middle-aged man in a bland grey suit. Tie loose at the neck. The man held up his shield. 'I'm Detective Haggerty. You're Francis Genno, aren't you?' He noticed the look of surprise in Genno's eyes. 'Your girlfriend gave us a very thorough description of you.'

'Where is Annie?' Genno blurted out. 'What have you done to her?'

'She's in the patrol car back there,' Haggerty replied, stabbing his thumb over his shoulder. 'She's been very cooperative. Right from the start. Except that we were expecting you to hit the jeweller's tomorrow. That was the original plan, wasn't it? So why bring it forward twenty-four hours at such short notice? So short, in fact, that Miss Stratton didn't even have time to tip us off beforehand. That's why we weren't there to meet you when you arrived.'

'What are you talking about?' Genno demanded, spitting out the words.

'Miss Stratton's been feeding us information about the heist ever since you first hatched it,' Haggerty replied smugly. 'While you were fucking her, she was fucking you over. Life's a bitch, eh, Genno?'

'I don't believe it!' Genno snarled, struggling furiously with the two patrolmen who were holding his arms. 'Annie would never cross me. Never. She's my girl. You're lying, you bastard. You're fucking lying.'

'You keep convincing yourself of that if it'll make it any easier on your vanity. She doesn't need you any more. As you'll discover when she testifies against you in court. That was part of the deal we made with her. I think you'll find that she's got quite a lot to say as well.'

'Sir,' a younger plain-clothes policeman called out, running up to him. He shot Genno a withering look before addressing Haggerty. 'Drummond's dead. He was shot by an off-duty cop who happened to be in the shop at the time. Appears to be purely coincidental. Both the cop and his wife are dead. She was unarmed.'

'Read this piece of shit his Miranda rights, then take him away,' Haggerty hissed disdainfully at the two patrolmen, and then followed his colleague to the jeweller's shop.

Genno wasn't listening when he was Mirandized, and as he was being led towards the two patrol cars parked further up the street, all he could think about was what Haggerty had told him. He was caught in two minds. A part of him still refused to believe that Annie would ever do anything to hurt him. She loved him. It made no sense. On the other hand, what would Haggerty have to gain by lying to him? It wasn't as if they needed to prove his guilt. There were more than enough witnesses who'd seen him shoot Merill in the back. Yet he still found it incomprehensible that Annie could have turned on him. Not his Annie.

'There's your junkie screw, Genno. So, what do you think of her, now that you know she set you up from the start?' one of the patrolmen scoffed, shaking Genno's arm roughly to get his attention.

Genno turned his head to look at Anne Stratton seated in the back of the nearest patrol car. She looked away before their eyes could meet. It was at that moment he knew she had betrayed him. A fury rose inside him unlike any sensation he had ever experienced in his life. It seemed to give him a flash of inhuman strength and, bursting free from the vice-like grip on either arm, he stumbled towards the patrol car, his movement hindered by his manacled hands. She shrunk back in terror when he pressed his face up against the back window. 'You sold me out, Annie. You fucking sold me out,' he screamed, as a mixture of blood and saliva escaped from his lips and spattered the closed window. Hands grabbed him roughly from behind and he struggled maniacally as the two patrolmen dragged him away from the police car. Another patrolman rushed to their aid, and although an arm was locked savagely round his throat, he still managed to scream at her, 'You're dead, Annie. D'you hear me, dead . . .'

One

'Have you seen my math book, Mom?'

'Why don't you try searching the ruins of that bomb blast you call a bedroom?' Sarah Johnson called back to her fifteen-year-old daughter, without looking up from the morning paper she was reading at the kitchen table.

'Very funny, Mom,' Lea Johnson retorted, as she passed the open door and disappeared up the stairs to her bedroom.

Sarah poured herself a second cup of coffee and then studied the shares page, as she did every morning. Minor gains. Acceptable losses. She would scrutinize the market in more detail at work later that morning. At thirty-six, she was the newest, and youngest, partner in Morgan Beech, a firm of independent financial advisers with a set of plush offices on Loyola Avenue in the Central Business District area of New Orleans. Yet, unlike many of her colleagues, she wasn't an Ivy Leaguer and had no university degree to her name. She had started out as a secretary and, within three years, had worked her way up to become the personal assistant to one of the senior partners. Having witnessed at first hand her astute financial acumen, he had suggested that she attend night school, knowing she wanted to further her career within the firm. Five years later she had been offered a junior partnership in the firm, replacing the senior partner who had initially been so keen to see her better herself. The irony hadn't been lost on her and although saddened to see him leave, she had known at the same time that she couldn't allow sentimentality to cloud her own advancement.

'Sarah, have you seen my car keys?'

'Does this look like Lost Property?' Sarah replied tersely, lowering the newspaper to give her husband a sharp look as he hovered in the doorway.

'Hey, I was only asking.' Bob Johnson raised his hands in a

defensive gesture. 'Well, have you?' he continued, when she turned her attention back to the financial section.

'No!'

'OK. OK. I'll go and find them myself.' A frown creased his forehead. 'Are you all right? You seem a bit . . . stressed out this morning. It's not your time—'

'No, it's not my time of the month,' Sarah cut in angrily. 'You can be a real patronizing son-of-a-bitch at times, Bob, d'you know that?'

'Well, excuse me for being concerned about my wife,' came the caustic reply.

'We've been married for sixteen years now. That's one hundred and ninety-two months for those of us who have trouble with our calculations. And you still haven't the faintest idea when I have my monthly period, do you?'

'If you're like this now, I sure as hell don't want to know,' Bob replied disdainfully and walked off.

Sarah carefully closed the newspaper, folded it neatly in half, then slapped it down angrily on the table. There could be no hiding the fact that their marriage was on the rocks. The problems had first started when she had agreed to look over the books of his troubled real estate company, with a view to tightening overheads. But instead she had found major inconsistencies: all transactions personally handled by his partner which, in turn, had been audited by the company's accountant. So either the accountant was incompetent, or else he was working in league with Bob's partner to slowly bleed the company dry. Her professional advice to her husband had been to hand the books over to the police, and by the end of the week both his partner and the accountant had been taken into custody, charged with over a dozen counts of embezzlement. The trial had painted Bob as a naive, guileless businessman and although his partner and accountant were given custodial sentences, it had all but destroyed his own reputation within the New Orleans business community. Bob hadn't been the same again after that and, though he had never said it so many words, she knew he held her partly responsible for his current plight. If she hadn't found any discrepancies in the company's books, he wouldn't have been subjected to such public humiliation.

Yet worse was to come for Sarah when, earlier that month, she first met Renée Mercier, Bob's new secretary. He had told Sarah that he'd been forced to hire her at short notice after his last secretary had walked out on him, unable to deal with the pressure of the scandal which still surrounded the company. Renée Mercier wore the kind of miniskirt that didn't so much ride up her thighs as gallop at an alarming pace. She had legs of the type normally seen only on the packets of expensive stockings, high heels that seemed to defy every law of gravity, and big hair held in place with enough spray to open another hole in the ozone layer. The peroxide blonde hair had particularly stuck in her mind. What woman in her mid-twenties had big hair these days? It just wasn't fashionable any more – which only seemed to further cheapen her already tarty appearance.

Sarah had convinced herself that Renée Mercier was having an affair with Bob from the numerous sly, covetous looks his secretary had given him at work that morning. Not that Sarah had any proof to back up her suspicions. Just instinct. And intuition. But it also answered some of the persistent doubts she'd had at the back of her mind for the past few months. Doubts which had first surfaced when Bob had begun to come home late on week nights, claiming that he had to catch up on his paperwork at the office. She could count on one hand the number of times Bob had worked late in all the years they had been married. Then there had been the time when, a few months back, he had told her he would be entertaining a client at Brennan's restaurant, one of the most exclusive eateries in the city, only for her to ring up in an emergency and discover that he wasn't there. Furthermore, he hadn't even reserved a table. She had never mentioned the incident to him, but it had added to her suspicions.

The day after she met Renée Mercier she had taken the decision to have a private detective follow her husband and report his movements back to her. It was the only way of putting her mind at rest. He had rung her at work the previous day to say that his investigation was now complete. She had agreed to meet him at his office later that morning . . .

'Mom, where's Dad?' Lea asked in exasperation from the doorway. 'I'm going to be late for school.'

'Looking for his car keys, I think,' Sarah told her, coming out of her reverie.

'How could he lose his car keys?'

'Have you found your math book?' Sarah asked, raising her eyebrows as a faint smile touched her lips.

Lea grinned sheepishly, then pulled out the chair opposite her mother and sat down. Sarah could see so much of herself in Lea at that age – the feisty, independent streak; the single-minded determination. And in her appearance. Lea certainly had her mother's beauty. The classical cheekbones and full lips. The slim, petite figure, and exquisite, silky blonde hair that fell delicately on to her slender shoulders. Not that Sarah was blonde any more. She had been a brunette for most of her adult life. She'd kept her hair long until her late twenties, but had finally decided to cut it short to give herself a more professional appearance at work. Now she could never imagine growing it long again, despite Lea's repeated attempts to try and get her to change her mind.

'Dad, hurry up!' Lea called out irritably over her shoulder.

'I'd be a lot quicker if you helped me look for my car keys,' he shouted back to her from the adjoining room.

'Yeah, right,' Lea muttered scornfully, as if the mere thought of going to his aid was beneath her. 'What's wrong with Dad?' she asked her mother, her face suddenly serious. 'He's always losing things. OK, so I misplaced my math book, but at least I found it. He seems to lose something every day.'

'Whenever my father lost anything around the house, my mother would always just say that he was a man and therefore didn't know any better,' Sarah said with a wistful smile.

'Yeah, but then Dad's not a man . . .' Lea trailed off and gave a quick shrug when she saw the look of mock surprise on her mother's face. 'You know what I mean?'

'No,' Sarah replied. 'Unless you know something I don't.'

'He's my dad. I don't see him as . . . well, you know . . .'

'Ah, I think I understand,' Sarah said, feigning a serious expression as she nodded to herself. 'Your dad's just your dad. But Johnny Depp, now he's a man.'

'Ah, Mom,' Lea protested as her cheeks flushed.

Sarah smiled, knowing that Lea had a crush on Johnny Depp. She sat back in her chair and folded her arms across her chest. 'So if your dad's not a man, does that mean I'm not a woman either?'

'Aw, c'mon, Mom, you're twisting my words. Of course Dad's a man . . .'

'I'm relieved to hear it,' Bob Johnson announced from the doorway, then raised his hand and jangled his car keys. 'Found them.'

'And where were they?' Sarah asked.

'In the pocket of the suit I wore yesterday,' came the sheepish reply.

'Maybe there was something in what Gran said after all,' Lea replied with a knowing smile in her mother's direction. She had always referred to Sarah's parents as 'Gran' and 'Grandpa' even though she had never met them – both had died before she was born.

'Why do I get the feeling this is a dig at me?' Bob patted Lea lightly on the shoulder. 'Come on, *ange*, let's get you to school.'

'See you later, Mom,' Lea said, kissing her mother on the lips before leaving the kitchen.

'I'm going to be working late again tonight,' Bob announced as he was about to follow Lea into the hall. His words almost sounded like an afterthought.

'Ah-ha,' Sarah muttered indifferently.

'I'm sorry, Sarah, but I've got to put in these extra hours now that I'm running the company by myself.'

Well that's certainly a new excuse, if nothing else, she thought contemptuously to herself.

'You know the company's been in trouble ever since the trial,' he continued, 'but I'm determined to make a go of it.'

And I also know that the financial damage is irreparable. Six months at the most, then the liquidators will move in and close you down. She had told him as much when she'd audited the company's books after the trial. At the time he seemed to have accepted it. Now, suddenly, he was determined to put up a fight to save the company. Not that she believed a word of it. If only he put as much effort into trying to save their marriage . . . She was fighting a losing battle, and she knew it. Yet despite his faults, she still loved him. So what did that say about her? She chose not to answer that.

'Don't bother cooking anything for me tonight,' Bob told her. 'I'll get a take-out and eat it at work.'

'So when will you be home?' Sarah asked, hating herself for keeping up the pretence of not knowing what was going on between him and . . . *that* woman. It was all so hollow. And pointless. But she still did it. Every time. Again, she chose not to think about what that said about her.

'I honestly couldn't say. Depends on the work. It's best if I call you later this afternoon. I'll have a better idea then of when I'll be back.' Bob kissed her lightly on the cheek. 'You have a good day now, y'hear?'

'Oh, I'm sure I will,' Sarah muttered meaningfully to herself, but Bob had already left the room.

*

14

When Sarah had first decided to hire a private detective she realized that she didn't know the first thing about these people or their profession. Common sense told her to select one from the *Yellow Pages*. But how could she be sure they would be reliable? Or discreet? With this in mind, she chose instead to contact the company's security adviser, whom she'd had dealings with in the past, to seek his professional advice without letting on why she needed the services of a private detective. He had been very helpful and suggested several names to her. All ex-cops he'd worked with during his time as a detective with the New Orleans Police Department. She had picked the first name on the list: Derek Farlowe.

Looking back on that first meeting, she hadn't really known what to expect when she'd arrived at Farlowe's office on Canal Street. Somewhere, tucked away in the back of her mind, she had imagined he would look like Humphrey Bogart, or a young Robert Mitchum. But any stereotypical illusion she may have harboured had been quickly dispelled. He was corpulent, bald, and wore a shapeless white linen suit that hadn't seen an iron for a very long time. If ever. An empty box of Dunkin' Donuts had lain open on his desk. Nevertheless, any initial reservations she may have had about his abilities were soon banished, not only by his competent manner but also by his capacity to put her at her ease and make her open up to him. As he had told her, the more he knew about Bob, the more he would be able to tell her once his investigation was complete . . .

'Ah, good morning, Mrs Johnson,' Farlowe said genially when his secretary showed Sarah into his office. He hauled himself out of his padded chair and shook her hand briefly. 'Would you care for some coffee?'

'Not for me, thank you,' Sarah replied, noticing that he was wearing the same crumpled suit he'd worn at their last meeting. Was it his only suit? Did it matter? She dismissed the trivial thought.

'I'll have my usual,' Farlowe told his secretary, who then withdrew from the room, closing the door behind her. He dabbed his fleshy jowls with a damp handkerchief before wiping it across his sweating forehead. 'Damn this heat. I've lived in New Orleans all my life and I've still never got used to it.' Like many locals, he pronounced it 'Nu Awrlins'. He patted his ample girth. 'Then again, carrying around this kind of surplus weight doesn't help any either. Please, won't you sit down?'

'What have you got for me?' Sarah asked.

'Straight to the point. I like that,' Farlowe said, easing himself back down into his chair, which creaked ominously under his weight. 'You'd be surprised at how many of my clients will talk about absolutely anything rather than hear what I have to tell them. And more often than not their fears are totally unfounded. It's a psychiatrist's paradise in here.'

'Your time is my money. I don't intend to waste either.'

'Ah, the voice of the financial adviser,' Farlowe said with a faint chuckle, and then clapped his hands together when his secretary entered carrying a tray with a mug of steaming black coffee and a couple of jam doughnuts on a side plate. 'Are you sure you won't join me, Mrs Johnson?' he asked after his secretary had placed the tray on the desk.

'Positive,' Sarah replied, a trace of irritability creeping into her voice for the first time. She just wanted to get to the truth. The waiting was playing havoc with her nerves. She watched the secretary leave the room, and as the door closed she turned back to Farlowe. 'So, was I right? Is my husband fucking . . . that bitch?'

Farlowe's hand froze as he was about to pick up a doughnut and his eyes flickered towards Sarah. He was momentarily caught off guard not so much by her gritty language but rather by the sheer venom in her voice. Turning his attention back to the tray, he selected a doughnut, bit it in half, then opened the top drawer of his desk and removed a folder which he placed in front of him. 'Yes, I'm afraid you were right,' he announced after swallowing his food. 'Your husband is having an affair with Ms Mercier. I'm very sorry.'

'Why should you be sorry?' Sarah retorted bitterly, as she struggled to come to terms with the mixture of hurt and anger which threatened to engulf her. 'You were just doing your job.' She gestured to the folder in front of him. 'Is that the evidence?'

'Yes.'

'Photographs?'

'Photographs, as well as a comprehensive timetable of his movements over the past week,' Farlowe told her.

'May I see?' Sarah asked. Farlowe pushed the folder across the desk to her. She opened it, ignored the sheets of typewritten text, and slit open the sealed manila envelope to get at the incriminating photographs. Most had been taken outside an apartment block she didn't recognize. An unmistakable sense of intimacy between Bob and Renée Mercier came across in the photographs. A look. A gesture. A touch. 'Where were these taken?' she asked.

'Outside Ms Mercier's apartment.'

'And where is that?'

'It's all documented in there,' Farlowe said, indicating the folder in her lap. 'If it's any consolation, I know how you must be feeling right now.'

'No, it's not,' Sarah retorted brusquely, then tossed the folder angrily on to the desk. 'You're a voyeur, Mr Farlowe. You watch the anguish of others from the safety of a camera lens. That doesn't make you an expert on my feelings, or those of anyone else who comes in here seeking your help. You're paid to do a job. Nothing more. So please don't patronize me.'

'I wasn't being patronizing, Mrs Johnson. I turned in my badge when I discovered that my wife was having an affair – with my partner of fifteen years. I foolishly thought that he was my best friend. Then, to add insult to injury, she walked out on me to go and live with him. They're still together as far as I know. Believe me, I do know how you must be feeling right now.'

'I'm sorry, I had no idea,' Sarah said softly, furious with herself for allowing her emotions to surface so easily. It was essential that she keep her feelings in check, especially in front of outsiders. 'Do you want me to pay you now?'

'That's entirely up to you. I can just as easily forward the invoice to your workplace once you've had a chance to read the folder.'

'No, I'd prefer to pay now.'

'As you wish,' Farlowe replied. He then handed her an envelope which she opened, and after satisfying herself that the costs incurred matched the figures he had quoted her at their last meeting, she removed her chequebook from her bag and wrote out a cheque for the full amount. 'Thank you,' he said, taking it from her. 'I just wish I could have put your mind at rest about your husband's infidelity. I am sorry.'

Sarah picked up the folder and got to her feet. 'My mind is at rest, Mr Farlowe. I've got nothing to feel guilty about. I'm not the one who's been unfaithful.'

Farlowe watched her leave, then pushed the other half of the doughnut into his mouth and turned his attention to the battered diary on his desk to check on his next appointment of the day.

Sarah somehow managed to retain her composure, at least outwardly, until she was safely alone in the corridor. A sudden nausea hit her with the force of a tidal wave and she had to grab on to a wooden bench to steady herself when she felt her legs buckle underneath her. She was sweating. She felt sick. Physically sick. She could taste the excess saliva rise up her throat and into her mouth. For an instant she thought she was going to throw up right there in the corridor. Then the nausea passed as suddenly as it had flared up and she sat down gingerly on the bench, dropped the folder on to the floor at her feet, and leaned forward with her head in her hands as she struggled to try and regain some kind of self-control. She had already resigned herself to the fact that Bob was fucking his secretary even before she'd approached Farlowe, so why had she taken the news so badly when her suspicions had finally been confirmed? Maybe that was the difference – before, they had only been suspicions. Which still meant that she could have been wrong. Not any more. All the evidence was there in black and white. She'd told Farlowe her mind was at rest. Lie. She'd told him she had nothing to feel guilty about. Lie. It was only now that the questions began to take root in her mind. How long had he been screwing her? Was she the first? If not, how many had there been before her? Then she began to challenge her own role in the whole sordid affair. Suppressed guilt. Why had he needed to seek solace in an extramarital affair? Had she become too wrapped up in her own career to even notice his needs? Was she lousy in bed? Had she failed him as a wife? Did he still love her? Was the marriage over?

'Excuse me, are you all right?'

She looked up to find an elderly man standing in front of her, a concerned frown on his face. Where had he come from? She hadn't seen or heard him approach. 'I'm all right, thank you,' she said brusquely, and then quickly retrieved the folder from the floor.

'Are you sure?'

'Do you want it in writing?' came the acerbic riposte.

He shook his head to himself and walked off. She instantly regretted her outburst and for a moment she was tempted to call out after him to apologize for her abrupt and abrasive hostility towards him. But the thought quickly dissipated within the confines of her troubled mind. There was no point. He wouldn't have understood anyway. He was a *man*.

She rode the elevator to the lobby and slipped on her sunglasses before emerging into the bright sunlight. Farlowe was right. The heat was stifling at that time of year. Mid nineties. Not that it had ever bothered her. She spent most of her day behind a desk in a temperature-controlled, air-conditioned office with the blinds drawn to block out the reflection of the sun on the computer screen. And at weekends she was usually too busy catching up on her paperwork to indulge in the hedonism of the sun-worshipper. Yet she could still remember a time when she'd had a tan that was the envy of the whole office. A time before she became a junior partner in the firm. When she still had time on her hands to enjoy the simple pleasures of life. Time spent with her family – her daughter, her husband.

She got into her car, started up the engine and pulled away from the kerb. The lights changed to amber as she approached the intersection of Canal and St Charles. She slowed the car to a halt and watched the green streetcar emerge from St Charles and turn up Canal, heading towards the picturesque Garden District. She and Bob had met on a streetcar. Packed at rush hour. The streetcar had pulled away before she could get to the stop and board it. She could still remember chasing after it, trying desperately to grab on to the rail. Then, from within the cluster of commuters crammed round the opening at the rear, an outstretched hand appeared, gesturing to her to grasp it before the streetcar gathered speed and left her behind. She did. A strong, powerful grip pulled her on board, despite the muttered complaints of those already cramped inside. The hand had pulled her clear of the doorway. That's when she had first seen him. A knight in shining armour. *Her* knight in shining armour. A smile. A word of gratitude. A conversation started. A date arranged before she had reached her stop. *Good days. Innocent days.* The armour had certainly tarnished since then . . .

A blast from a car horn startled her out of her thoughts and she noticed the lights had changed back to green. She pulled away, heading downtown to the Central Business District. Her eyes flickered to the folder on the passenger seat beside her. Now that she had proof, what was her next move? Confront Bob with the evidence. That seemed the most logical step. Then what? Ask him to stop seeing the bitch? *Ask?* Like hell she would. She had to go on the offensive. She would *tell* him! Order. Demand. Insist. Threaten, even. He had to make a choice. And what if he called her bluff? Where would that leave her? Where would that leave Lea? Above all else, Sarah desperately wanted to protect Lea from any potential recriminations from either side. It certainly wasn't her intention to turn Lea against her father. She was *their* daughter. And despite his other failings, Bob had always been there for Lea when she'd needed him. A good father, but a lousy husband. And what if he agreed not to see Renée Mercier again? The damage had already been done. Could she ever trust him again? If not, what kind of foundation was that to try and rebuild a marriage? Trust? That was a good word, considering the skeletons of her own past. She pushed the thought quickly from her mind. She was getting sidetracked. This was about Bob. Not her. Did she even want to rebuild the marriage? She left the question unanswered. Better that way. Give herself time to consider the options, because in her current frame of mind the bastard could go to hell and take that sleazy bitch with him for all she cared . . .

Sarah parked, as usual, in her designated spot in the underground car park, picked up her bag and the folder from the passenger seat, then got out of the car and absently returned the security guard's friendly wave as she strode briskly to the elevator. She rode the elevator to the offices of Morgan Beech on the twelfth floor and emerged into a pastel-coloured corridor and walked the short distance to her own office. She slipped in unnoticed through a side door, then sat down behind her desk, switched on the computer, and phoned her secretary in the outer office to let her know she'd arrived. She liked Louise Atchison. Early twenties. Vivacious, bubbly, efficient and hard-working. She and Bob had recently attended Louise's wedding. Her husband seemed pleasant enough, but Sarah had secretly thought that Louise could have done a lot better for herself. She laughed out loud, only it came out more like a snort of derision. You're a fine one to talk about husbands, she thought disdainfully to herself.

'I take it you don't like the dress?' Louise said from the doorway, arms extended. There was a faint smile on her lips.

'Pardon?' Sarah replied in surprise, noticing Louise for the first time.

'You seemed to laugh just as I came in. I thought maybe you didn't approve of the dress. I admit it is a bit on the short side—'

'It looks great on you,' Sarah interjected. 'And anyway, you've got the legs to get away with it. No, I wasn't laughing at you. Just a private joke.'

'Right,' Louise replied, but with a hint of uncertainty in her voice which seemed to imply that she'd never had a private joke of her own. Which was probably true, given her ebullient personality. She would have wanted to share it with everyone in the office. 'I thought you'd like to know there's someone outside to see you,' she added, stabbing a thumb over her shoulder in the direction of the interconnecting door, which she had already discreetly closed behind her. 'He's been waiting for the past half an hour.'

'I thought I didn't have any appointments scheduled for this morning,' Sarah said with a frown.

'He doesn't have an appointment . . . as such. But he did say that you'd want to see him as soon as you got in.'

'Oh, he did, did he? And just what's he selling?' Sarah asked suspiciously.

'I don't know, but I'd buy it.' Louise gave her a knowing smile. 'He's real cute.'

'Honeymoon worn off already, has it?'

Louise chuckled as her cheeks flushed. 'Just window-shopping, that's all.'

'Pity some people can't just stick to that,' Sarah said bitterly.

'I guess,' Louise said hesitantly, caught unawares by Sarah's sudden mood swing.

'What's his name?' Sarah asked, furious with herself for allowing her emotions to surface again so easily.

'Jack Taylor.'

'Can't say I know him.'

'He said you wouldn't know him, but that you knew a colleague of his. Ted Lomax.'

'Oh my God,' Sarah gasped in horror and clasped a hand to her mouth as the blood drained from her face.

'Sarah, are you all right?' Louise took a hesitant step towards her.

Sarah slowly lowered her hand from her mouth. Then she clamped her hands together tightly on the desk in an attempt to stop them trembling. 'Ted Lomax is a name from the past,' she said in a shaky voice. 'A long time ago. I just didn't expect to hear it again.'

'Look, if you don't want to see this man, I'll have security throw him out. No problem.'

'I appreciate the offer,' Sarah said with a weak smile, 'but I'm afraid it's not that easy. Show him in.'

'Are you sure?'

'I'm sure.'

Louise stared uneasily at Sarah, the concern obvious in her eyes, then reluctantly opened the interconnecting door and asked the man to come in. The concern turned to suspicion as she stepped aside to let him pass, her eyes never leaving his face.

'Thank you, Louise,' Sarah said. 'Hold all my calls. I don't care who it is, I don't want to be interrupted.'

'Sure.' Louise withdrew from the room and closed the door behind her.

'Mrs Johnson, my name's Jack Taylor. I'm with the United States Marshals Service.'

Sarah took the slimline black wallet that he extended towards her. It contained his shield. She estimated him to be in his late thirties. Louise was right, he was ... well, Sarah preferred good-looking to cute. Animals were cute. Then the thought was gone. His presence, rather than his appearance, was her main concern. She handed the wallet back to him. 'Deputy Marshal Lomax assured me after I came to New Orleans that he would only contact me if it was absolutely necessary. That was part of the deal. I haven't heard from him since then. But he did say at the time that if for any reason he couldn't speak to me, he would make sure that whoever did contact me would have a letter of authorization from him to say that they were acting on his instructions.'

'May I?' Taylor said, indicating the soft, padded chair in front of the desk. Sarah nodded absently. Taylor sat down, placing an attaché case on the floor beside the chair. 'Ted Lomax is dead,' he said bluntly. 'He was murdered.'

Sarah inhaled sharply but kept her eyes focused on Taylor's face. 'Are you my new case officer?' she asked, more out of hope than belief. Even if he was, she knew he still had no reason to contact her unnecessarily. Not unless something was wrong. Something that directly concerned her.

'For the moment, I suppose you could say I am.' Taylor put the attaché case on to his knees, opened it and removed a thick, dog-eared folder. Then he closed the case and replaced it once more at the side of the chair. 'But I'm not actually attached to the Witness Security Program,' he continued, 'at least not any more. I've been with Internal Affairs for the last few years now. I'm part of the team investigating the circumstances surrounding his murder. And as a result of our findings so far, we have every reason to believe that your life could now be in danger. Which is why I'm here.'

It was only then that Sarah, almost reluctantly, lowered her eyes from Taylor's face to the folder in his lap. She recognized it straight away. Which was hardly surprising. She had seen it enough times after Lomax had been assigned as her case officer all those years ago. The words CONFIDENTIAL INFORMATION – AUTHORIZED PERSONNEL ONLY were printed boldly across the top of the folder. Then, in the centre, were the words FILE NAME. Beside it, in Lomax's distinctive handwriting, was written: *Anne Stratton*.

In that moment she instinctively knew that the once secure life she thought she'd had as Sarah Johnson, wife and mother, could never be the same again . . .

Two

'Mom, what are you doing home so early?' Lea asked in surprise from the doorway of the living room. She still had her school bag in her hand. Her eyes went to Taylor seated in the armchair by the window, but didn't query his presence.

'There's something I need to discuss with you and your father,' Sarah replied softly to her daughter.

'You've been crying,' Lea said anxiously, noticing that her mother's eyes were red and raw. She entered the room and crouched down beside her mother, taking her hand gently in hers. 'Mom, what's going on? And who's he?'

'This is Mr Taylor. He's a . . . business associate,' Sarah told her, but there was little conviction in her voice.

'You haven't been fired, have you?'

Sarah laughed quickly, then leaned forward and kissed her daughter lightly on the forehead. 'No, sweetheart, I haven't been fired. I only wish it were that simple.'

'I don't understand,' Lea said with a confused frown.

'Wait till your dad gets here. Then I'll explain everything. He shouldn't be long now.' Sarah squeezed Lea's hand. 'Be patient, sweetheart. Please.'

Lea retreated to the couch where she stared silently at the carpet, arms folded tightly across her chest, until her father arrived. He paused in the doorway, noticed Lea's defensive posture, then entered the room and, after casting a cursory glance at Taylor, focused his attention on Sarah. 'You called me at work this morning and told me to meet you back at the house when Lea returned home from school. But when I asked why, you refused to say any more over the phone. I tried to call you back at your office. You weren't there. I rang the house. You weren't here either. I even rang the school to make sure that Lea was safe. You've had me really worried, d'you know that? I think you owe me an explanation, don't you?'

'Go easy on your wife, Mr Johnson,' Taylor interceded. 'It hasn't been easy for her either.'

'Excuse me?' Bob retorted indignantly. 'And just who the hell are you?'

'His name's Jack Taylor,' Sarah told her husband in a soft, hollow voice. 'He's with the Marshals Service.'

'You're a cop?' Lea said, a mixture of surprise and uncertainty in her voice.

'I'm a bit like the Arnold Schwarzenegger character in *Eraser*, only without the muscles and the on-screen charisma,' Taylor said with a quick smile. It was a line he sometimes used to try and help diffuse tension. This time it didn't work.

'I don't like his movies,' Lea replied bluntly.

'I saw it,' Bob said. 'Witness Protection, right?'

'Uh-huh, although I'm not actually affiliated to that department any more. But you're right though. My presence here today is directly related to the WITSEC Program.'

'WITSEC?' Lea queried.

'Witness Security. Or Witness Protection, as your father called it. It's the same thing.'

'You still haven't told us what the Witness Protection Program's got to do with any of us,' Bob demanded.

'Me,' Sarah said in a barely audible voice.

'You?' Bob replied in bewilderment. 'What are you talking about? I don't understand.'

'I'm part of the WITSEC Program, Bob. I always thought . . . hoped . . . I could keep it from you and Lea. I was wrong.'

Bob sat down slowly on the edge of the armchair behind him. 'What . . . are you . . . trying to say, Sarah?' he asked hesitantly, struggling to understand what was going on. It made no sense to him.

'That I'm not who you think I am,' she replied.

'Mom, you're scaring me,' Lea said uneasily.

'*Ange*, I think you should go to your room,' Bob told her.

'I want Lea to stay,' Sarah said resolutely. 'She's got as much right to know the truth as you do.'

'And just what is the truth?' Bob wanted to know.

'That my real name isn't Sarah. Nor was my maiden name Wendell. And I don't come from Ohio. In fact, I've never set foot in

Ohio in my life. Everything I've ever told you about myself before I arrived in New Orleans was all part of a detailed cover story, made up for me by the Marshals Service when I joined the WITSEC Program.'

'So you're saying . . .' Bob trailed off, unable to voice his disbelief.

'That I've been living a lie for the past sixteen years,' Sarah finished the sentence for him. 'I guess I always knew there was a chance that my past would return to haunt me. I prayed it wouldn't. Every day. Every night. Without fail. Only it didn't work. So much for the power of prayer.'

'So . . . then . . . who *are* you?' Bob asked at length, voicing the first seemingly logical question that came to mind.

'My real name's Anne Stratton. I grew up in the slums of Chicago. It was a violent neighbourhood. I had violent friends. A lifetime away from what I now have here with you and Lea. And that's why I've never told you the truth about my past. What purpose would it have served?'

'You've been lying to me—'

'Yes, I've been lying to you,' Sarah cut in angrily across Bob's words. But the anger was targeted solely at herself. 'There was never going to be a good time to tell you the truth about myself. I knew that from the moment I first met you. And what you didn't know couldn't hurt you.'

'Until now.'

'I always hoped I could keep the truth under wraps. It was a calculated risk. I got it wrong.'

'Why did you have to change your identity? Did you do something bad?'

All eyes turned to Lea. She had been momentarily forgotten during the sharp exchange between Sarah and Bob. 'Your mother didn't do anything bad, Lea,' Taylor replied before Sarah had a chance to respond.

Sarah shot Taylor a withering look before addressing Lea's question herself. 'I got involved with some bad people when I was in my late teens, sweetheart. One, in particular. His name was Frankie Genno. He and I were . . . well, kinda close.'

'You mean he was your boyfriend?' Lea clarified.

'I guess he was, although I never really thought of him that way. He filled a need I had in my life at the time.'

'What kind of need?' Bob demanded.

'Drugs,' Sarah replied sharply, her voice hardening. 'I was a junkie.

He was my dealer. I couldn't have survived without him. It was that simple. OK?' She looked down at her feet, trying desperately to marshal her thoughts, and when she spoke again she had regained her composure. 'I was busted twice for possession. The first time I got off with a verbal warning. The second time I was looking at a custodial sentence. I was willing to do anything to stay out of jail. I knew the cops had been looking to take Frankie down for some years, especially as he had close connections to organized crime, but they never had anything to use against him. So I agreed to cut a deal with them. I'd give them Frankie, in return for dropping the charges against me. He was planning a heist on a jewellery shop around that time, so the cops told me to get involved in the action so I could give them constant feedback on what was going on. Frankie brought in a couple of ex-cons to add muscle to the operation. I was the driver. The cops told me to wait until the three of them had gone into the shop, then drive off. The police would then move in and arrest them, and it would look as if I'd been arrested trying to escape to deflect any suspicion away from me. The cops thought they had every angle covered. But they overlooked one factor – Frankie's paranoia. He brought the operation forward by twenty-four hours. Except that he only told us at the last possible moment and I didn't have a chance to tip off the police. I dropped them off at the jeweller's, as planned, and the moment they were inside I drove to the nearest payphone and called the cops.

'But it all went wrong long before the police got there. There was an off-duty detective in the shop with his wife. He shot one of the ex-cons, who happened to be Frankie's best friend. Frankie, in turn, shot the cop and his wife in cold blood. Killed them both. When the police did arrive, the other ex-con wanted to surrender. Frankie shot him in the back. Frankie was then wounded in a firefight with the cops and taken into custody. By that time he knew I'd sold him out, and he vowed to kill me. That really shook me up because I knew Frankie never made idle threats. That way he ensured his peers took him seriously. So the cops came up with another deal – if I agreed to testify against Frankie and tell them everything I knew about his connections to organized crime in Chicago, they'd give me a new identity under the WITSEC Program. It was also my one chance to get away from my futile existence in Chicago and start a new life. I went through detox and came out clean before the trial started.

'Frankie was offered a deal to reduce his sentence if he turned state's evidence and testified against his senior contacts in the Mob.

He never betrayed them. Which is why the Mob have left him alone in prison all these years. The so-called code of honour among thieves. He was given life without the possibility of parole. My own testimony helped to put several members of the Chicago Mafia behind bars, but the prize scalp, as far as the authorities were concerned, was Manny Pannetta, the nephew of the local capo. He was in overall charge of narcotics distribution in Chicago. Naturally, the Mob weren't too pleased with me for testifying against them. Especially Manny's brother. Or so I was told by the Marshals Service at the time.

'Immediately after the trial I was put into the WITSEC Program, my name was changed to Sarah Wendell, and all details of my previous identity were purged from the system so that I couldn't be traced to my new location here in New Orleans.'

There. It had been said. The truth was finally out. Only it didn't make Sarah feel any better. She certainly didn't feel as if a weight had been magically lifted off her shoulders. Maybe she'd lived with her secret too long for that kind of clichéd reaction. Or maybe the circumstances surrounding it dictated the gravity of her emotions. It was then she noticed the tears on Lea's cheeks. She had been so absorbed in her own past that she had failed to notice her daughter's reaction to what she had been saying. But it was more than just the tears. The hurt was evident in her eyes. So much hurt. Sarah desperately wanted to rush over and hug Lea tightly to her. Comfort her. Protect her. But she knew better than to do that. She was the one who'd caused the hurt in the first place. And that cut deepest of all . . .

'Lea, I'm sorry,' she whispered and felt the tears well up in her own eyes. 'I'm so sorry, sweetheart. I only ever wanted to shield you from the truth. That's why I never told you. But you know something, I wouldn't change any of it for all the riches in the world, because had it turned out differently, you wouldn't be here now. And I can't imagine my life without you.'

'I wish it *had* turned out differently,' Lea shot back, the anguish breaking through her small voice as a new shower of tears began to stream down her face, 'because right now I don't even know who you are any more. You've been lying to me all my life. All my life!'

'I can understand your resentment—'

'Don't patronize me on top of everything else,' Lea cut in furiously. 'You can't begin to understand my resentment. Why didn't you just go somewhere else? God, I wish I'd never been born.' She turned and fled the room. 'I wish I'd never been born,' she shrieked again as she bounded up the stairs, and moments later came the sound of her bedroom door being slammed shut behind her.

'Oh dear God, what have I done?' Sarah whispered, tormented, as she wiped her tears away. But she made no move to go after her daughter. It would only make matters worse. She would go to Lea later, after she'd had a chance to vent her confused emotions in the privacy of her own room. Her eyes went to Bob, who was still sitting on the edge of the armchair, his elbows now resting on his knees as he stared at the floor. 'Aren't you going to have a go at me as well?'

'Do I need to? I think Lea put it pretty succinctly, don't you?' Bob said, slowly raising his head to look at her. 'There will be time for recriminations later. Right now, I want to know why you had to tell us about your past life. I assume it has something to do with the brother of this gangster you helped put behind bars. Has he found out your new identity?'

'Both Manny and his brother, Carlo, are dead. Manny died less than a week after he was imprisoned. Rumour has it the capo ordered the hit himself. Carlo died about a year later. No, this has nothing to do with organized crime. They washed their hands of me a long time ago.'

'How can you be so sure?' Bob asked.

'Because the FBI have a reliable source inside the Chicago Mafia,' Taylor told him. 'The Mob have no interest in Sarah any more.'

'Then who has?' Bob pressed. 'This Frankie Genno?'

'I think you should explain,' Sarah said to Taylor. 'This is your investigation, after all.'

Taylor shifted in his chair to address Bob. 'Your wife's original case officer was Ted Lomax. He made all the arrangements to change her identity after the trial and relocate her to New Orleans. She hasn't had any contact with him for over twelve years. But then, that's hardly surprising considering how successful her new life has been out here.

'A couple of months ago my department – Internal Affairs – instigated an undercover investigation after an informer claimed that sensitive WITSEC documents were being offered for sale on the black market. My partner, Keith Yallow, and I were put in charge of the case. Ted Lomax quickly became the prime suspect. But we needed to catch him in the act before we could arrest him. I don't know whether he was tipped off, or whether he was just being extra careful, but for the past month he did nothing out of the ordinary.

We were actually beginning to wonder whether we'd targeted the right person, then yesterday morning his body was found at his apartment in Chicago.' He paused to glance at the door to ensure that Lea wasn't there. Then he leaned forward, and his voice lowered when he continued, 'He'd been tortured before he died. Mutilated would probably be a more apt description. It was horrendous. We also discovered that all his confidential computer files relating to the WITSEC Program had been deleted. It is possible that he managed to do it himself before he was murdered. But having said that, the nature of his injuries was so severe that he would almost certainly have told his killers what they wanted to know just to stop the torture. The other scenario is more worrying. And, I have to admit, a lot more plausible. That his killers copied the WITSEC files on to another disk, then deleted all the evidence on the computer. As it is, it's going to take us some time to rebuild the entire program again. There were details on those files known only to Lomax, for obvious security reasons.'

'Which means that the killers could already have Sarah's confidential file in their possession?' Bob concluded.

'We have to assume that, yes,' Taylor agreed.

'And if they do, they might offer it to Genno for the right price,' Bob added.

'We have to assume that as well, yes.'

'So what happens now?' Bob asked, his voice surprisingly calm under the circumstances. But then he had already had to digest the truth about his wife's secret past; it was as if nothing more could possibly faze him.

'As with all the other state witnesses that Lomax has relocated over the years, your family will be placed under round-the-clock surveillance until the killers have been apprehended and the damage to the program can be assessed at first hand. At the moment, the surveillance is just a precaution, nothing more. What we'd like to do is move you all into a safe house where it'll be that much easier to safeguard you as a family. We do have one in the New Orleans area, about twenty minutes' drive from the city.'

'If Frankie were ever to discover my new identity, he wouldn't hesitate to hire someone to kill me,' Sarah said, breaking the sudden silence which had descended on the room. 'Or at least his mother would, assuming she's still alive.'

'She's still alive,' Taylor said grimly.

'His mother?' Bob said incredulously.

30

'Frances Genno is the sweetest, kindest woman you could ever imagine,' Sarah said, her mind going back over the years, 'except if you cross her by doing something to antagonize her little boy. Then she becomes the most malicious, vengeful monster imaginable. She adores Frankie as much as he does her. It almost destroyed her when Frankie went down for life. She had to be physically restrained when I arrived at court to testify against him. The judge had to have her ejected from the courtroom after she repeatedly shouted obscenities at me during the trial. She can be truly terrifying when provoked.'

'She's under surveillance as it is, but the problem is she could have already hired someone to carry out the hit on you – maybe even on your whole family. That's why it's imperative we get you to the safe house as soon as possible,' Taylor added.

'What would happen to Lea's schooling if she were moved into the safe house?' Bob asked. 'Would it be affected?'

'No, she could still go to school,' Taylor assured him. 'The only difference being that she would be shadowed by a protection team. Don't worry, they're trained to keep a very low profile. Only Lea would know they were watching her, assuming you chose to tell her.'

'I don't think we have to worry about Lea attending school for the next few days,' Sarah said. 'She's going to need time on her own to come to terms with everything I've unloaded on her this afternoon. Her whole world's been turned upside down in the space of a few minutes.'

'And you think mine hasn't?' Bob retorted.

'Except that you're not fifteen, Bob. She's going to need your support now more than ever. That's why I think it would be best if you were to move into the safe house with her until the situation has been resolved. I'm sure Mr Taylor can provide you with adequate protection while you're at work.'

'That's not a problem,' Taylor replied absently, but he was already eyeing Sarah uncertainly. 'Correct me if I'm wrong, Mrs Johnson, but from what you've just said it sounds as if you don't intend to join your husband and daughter at the safe house. If not, where do you intend to go?'

'You're not wrong. Actually, I'm staying right here.'

'Out of the question,' Taylor told her bluntly. 'It's too dangerous. You'd be a sitting target in here by yourself.'

'Which is exactly what I want. If an attempt is made on my life, then we'll know that Frankie has access to my new identity. It's the only way to be sure.'

'No, it's far too dangerous,' Taylor said, shaking his head.

'I'm not putting my family at risk, Mr Taylor. It's me he wants. So let him take his best shot.'

'And what if something were to go wrong and the assassin did get you?' Taylor demanded.

'I'm prepared to take my chances.' Sarah raised her hand to stop Taylor, who was about to argue the point further. 'It's not open to debate. I'm staying right here. And that's an end to it. Question is, will *you* help me?'

Stateville Correctional Center. Route 53. Joliet, Illinois. Sixty-four acres. Enclosed by a thirty-three-foot-high concrete wall. Guard towers manned round the clock by armed correctional officers. Designed to hold fifteen hundred inmates. Maximum security.

Frankie Genno sat pensively on the bunk in his cell, his back pressed against the wall, his arms wrapped round his knees which were drawn up to his chest. His appearance had changed little in the eighteen years he'd been incarcerated in Stateville. The tousled hair was still long, lapping untidily at the collar of his loose-fitting prison-issue overall, and the thick beard was still straggly and unkempt. The eyes, ice-cold and cobalt-blue, were as keen and focused as ever.

He appeared to be totally oblivious to the noise around him. It was easy for him to block out the incessant banter between inmates as they shouted to each other from their cells, many using hand-mirrors to put a face to the voice. In fact, he rarely spoke to anyone. Particularly not to any of the other cons, the vast majority of whom he regarded as being intellectually inferior to him, and therefore beneath contempt. With one notable exception – the one he called the Preacher.

Not that he had ever openly showed his disdain for his fellow inmates. It would have been courting certain disaster in a place like that. Especially for a lifer like himself. So he treated them all the same. He ignored them. And they, in the main, ignored him. But when he did have something to say, he was invariably listened to by those around him. And if it was something he specifically wanted, he normally got it for the right price. No questions asked on either side. It was basic psychology, and easy to instigate when the need arose. It had worked for the past eighteen years and he had every confidence that it would continue to work for the remainder of his sentence . . .

or for the remainder of his life, which he had long since accepted as being one and the same . . .

He had his own cell. It was one of the perks of being a model prisoner. He certainly preferred the solitude, but, having shared a cell with several different inmates for the first twelve years of his incarceration, it wouldn't have bothered him unduly if he were given another cell mate at some point in the future. He would just ignore him, like he did all the others. Fuck them, he didn't owe these bastards a damn thing. They had shared a cell. Nothing more. Only one of them had ever taken offence at his silence. A flipflop – prison slang for a recidivist – who'd always had his way sexually with previous cell mates in prisons right across the country. Or so he'd boasted, before being rushed to the infirmary with a ruptured kidney. The doctor concluded that he must have received a severe blow to the kidneys to cause that kind of internal damage. The con claimed to have fallen against the side of his bunk, even though there were no external marks on his torso to back up his story, but when he was eventually released from the prison hospital he had specifically asked to be relocated to another cellhouse. Frankie Genno had always prided himself on his ability to inflict maximum internal damage without leaving any superficial marks on his victim.

Victim. Now there was a word he could relate to under the circumstances. It's what he believed he'd been for the past eighteen years. But unlike so many of the other cons at Stateville, he'd never made himself out to be an innocent victim of an unjust judicial system. He'd admitted in court that he murdered the off-duty cop and his wife. He'd admitted in court that he murdered Julian-fucking-Jules Merill. He admitted that he was guilty and deserved to be locked up for the rest of his life. What he hadn't deserved, however, was to have been sold out by the only woman, apart from his mother, that he had ever really cared about in his whole miserable life. He had loved Annie in his own way. No question of that. And she had repaid those feelings with betrayal. *More fool you, Genno.* How many times had he said that to himself in the last eighteen years?

Now, finally, he was on the verge of getting his revenge on her for selling him out. The Preacher had done well. Or Paul Klyne, to give him his real name. Klyne, an ex-mercenary who had fought in over a dozen countries in his twenty years as a professional soldier, was the only person he had ever befriended at Stateville. He had nicknamed Klyne the 'Preacher' after Klyne had confided in him that, between contracts, he had earned his living as a con man in Miami, dressed as a priest. The authorites, who at the time had no sheet on him, had never linked him to any of the crimes. It had been a nickname they had understandably kept between themselves because, like himself, Klyne chose not to socialize with the other prisoners. But, unlike himself, Klyne relished confrontation. Whether it was deliberately provoking a fight with another con, or backtalking a prison guard, it made no difference to him. He'd been in solitary more times than Genno could remember. Not that the savage beatings he'd received in solitary had ever made the slightest bit of difference to him. He'd always maintained that he was immune to pain. He certainly had the scars, and the colourful stories, to substantiate the claims. Whether the stories were actually true, Genno had no way of knowing. But they had always sounded pretty convincing to him. Some called Klyne a psychopath. Others, a sociopath. Most just called him fucking crazy, but never to his face.

Klyne had only been on the outside for a couple of weeks when United States Deputy Marshal Ted Lomax first contacted Genno's mother, offering to sell her the classified file on Anne Stratton. She, in turn, had passed the information on to her son. He told her to contact the Preacher. Klyne was always available for work, at the right price. She'd subsequently acted as an intermediary between Klyne and Genno and it had been decided to set up a meeting with Lomax to discuss a possible deal. The price for the file was exorbitant. His mother had offered to remortgage her house, even put it up for sale. Genno would have none of it. There was another way. *Take* what they wanted from Lomax – which Klyne had done in Chicago the previous day. That much Genno knew from the news bulletins he'd seen earlier that morning.

It had been necessary for Klyne to kill Lomax to cover his tracks. Now Klyne had all of Lomax's classified files on one disk. Which translated into megabucks on the black market. Not that Genno was interested in making any money out of it. What use would it have been to him anyway? So Genno had come up with a plan of his own. He would let Klyne keep the disk. In return, Klyne would find Annie for him, and kill her. His mother had been due to meet with the Preacher earlier that morning to discuss it further . . .

'Genno, you've got a visitor,' a voice boomed from the corridor outside his cell. 'On your feet. Mommy's here.'

Correctional Officer Doug D'Amato was a veteran of Stateville.

Twelve years of unblemished service, apart from the beatings he administered with a fifteen-inch length of hose to those inmates whose transgressions had landed them in solitary confinement. D'Amato, a former drill sergeant in the Marines, firmly believed that the punishment was both warranted and beneficial to the individual concerned. He prided himself on never having used the hose on anyone who didn't deserve it. And such was his reputation for discipline that none of the inmates ever gave him any shit. Well, apart from the occasional punk, fresh off the correctional bus, who thought he could make an impression on his peers by coming out with some smart-arsed remark in front of the correctional officers. It was a mistake never repeated. D'Amato always made sure of that.

'Good afternoon, Dougie,' a female voice said quietly beside him. It brought him sharply out of his daydream, which was always the same – brandishing the hose menacingly over some hapless inmate who'd been confined to solitary. Every man to his own fantasy. 'I haven't seen you on my last couple of visits,' she continued. 'How's the family? Cheryl? And the boys?'

D'Amato gave her a broad smile. 'The family's good, Mrs Genno. Thank you.'

'Has my Frankie been behaving himself since I last saw him?'

It was always the same question every time she came to visit her son. And always the same answer. As if she didn't know. Frankie Genno had been a model inmate ever since he first arrived at Stateville. Never got involved in fights. Never backchatted the guards. Never been in solitary. Unlike his buddy, Klyne. Those two had been like chalk and cheese. Not that D'Amato had been sorry to see the back of Klyne, even though he knew he would be back behind bars again before long. 'You know Frankie always behaves himself,' he told her, 'I just wish all the other inmates were as well behaved as him. It would make life a lot easier around here.'

'If they were, you might just find yourself out of a job,' she said, touching him lightly on the chest with the tip of her finger.

Doug D'Amato had always liked Frances Genno, ever since she'd first started coming to Stateville, after selling everything she owned in Chicago and moving to a small, detached house in Joliet to be nearer her son. If he hadn't known her and had passed her in the street, his first thought would have been that she was the archetypal grandmother who always seems to pop up in those schmaltzy family adverts on TV. She was diminutive, a few inches short of five foot, with silver-grey hair coiled up in a bun on her head, glasses, and always

35

dressed in ultra-conservative clothing. That afternoon she was wearing an ankle-length floral dress, buttoned up to the neck, and a pair of white court shoes. He'd heard the stories about her trying to attack her son's ex-girlfriend when she'd testified against him in court. Fighting with the court ushers when they had tried to evict her from the courtroom. Lashing out at the DA with her umbrella on the courthouse steps after her son had been sent down for life without the possibility of parole. Hard to believe it was the same woman. He had always known her as a quietly spoken, God-fearing, well-mannered matriarch who enjoyed spoiling the guards once a fortnight with a batch of her delicious, home-baked chocolate-chip cookies. Always fresh out of the oven. The guards all secretly had a soft spot for Frances Genno.

'Your boy's here, Mrs Genno,' D'Amato announced, indicating the shuffling figure who appeared from a doorway behind the grille. A guard followed close behind him.

She crossed to the grille and sat down opposite her son. His hands were manacled together and secured to a metal ring attached to a thick leather belt around his waist.

'Hello, Ma,' Genno said, his eyes softening as he smiled at her through the grille. 'You're looking well.'

'Likewise, Francis.'

She was the only one who called him by his given name. She was the only one he let call him by his given name. He had never liked it. Not that he had ever indicated that to her. It was the name she had chosen for him at birth. And he would *never* intentionally do anything to distress his mother.

'Did you go to church this morning?' he asked, lowering his voice.

'I told you the last time I was here that I'd be going to church this morning to see the Preacher,' she chided him mildly as if he were still a child. 'I even said a special prayer of thanks to the Lord for returning her back to the fold. Justice will finally be done, Francis.'

'Did the Preacher say whether he could reach out to her?' Genno asked, effortlessly masking the disdain he felt for all his mother's religious mumbo-jumbo. It wasn't difficult to disguise his contempt. He'd had enough practice over the years. He'd decided a long time ago that if there was a heaven, and he had his doubts, he sure as hell wouldn't be going there. Not with his track record.

'He'll reach out to her, for the right price,' she said with a sweet smile. 'We've already agreed that we won't speak again until the deed is done.'

'The right price?' Genno spat angrily. 'The son-of-a-bitch is going to be making enough money out of this as it is.'

'Francis, please don't be so vulgar,' she scolded him again, this time with a disapproving shake of the head. 'The Preacher and I have already agreed a price. Half now. The other half when the deed is done.'

'Ma, where are you getting the money to pay him? I know very well that you don't have a lot—'

'Francis, that's enough,' she cut in quietly, but firmly. 'You needn't worry about the money. That's between the Preacher and myself.'

'I'm not asking you how much you're paying him. I'm asking you how you raised it at such short notice.' A sudden look of horror flashed across Genno's face. 'Jesus, you haven't sold the house, have you?'

'Don't blaspheme! No, I haven't sold the house. If you must know, I had some money put away in a long-term investment account for just such an occasion. You'd be amazed at how much it can grow over a seventeen-year period. Certainly more than enough to pay the Preacher. Satisfied? Or would you like me to go into more detail and tell you exactly how much I've saved?'

'I'm sorry, Ma. I didn't know about the investment account.'

'I saw no need to tell you. And anyway, I don't like talking about money. You know that.'

'When is the Preacher planning to make his move against her?'

'I don't know,' she told him, then added, 'and I didn't ask either. That side of it doesn't concern me. But he did assure me that he would contact me as soon as it was done. That's all I need to know.'

'It's sure been a long time coming.'

'As St Peter, Prince of the Apostles, said: "What glory is it, if, when ye be buffeted for your faults, ye shall take it patiently? But if, when ye do well, and suffer for it, ye take it patiently, this is acceptable with God." '

'I'm sure he did, Ma,' Genno replied in a bored tone.

She gave her son a 'tut-tut' of mild admonishment, then enquired, 'Is there anything you want, Francis? I'll bring it the next time I come to see you.'

'You know there's only one thing I've ever wanted since I've been in here, Ma. And I've waited eighteen years to get it. Now it's finally within reach. I tell you, it's a good feeling. A real good feeling.'

'I'll be sure to let you know as soon as I've heard from the Preacher again,' she said, and then put her finger to her lips and pressed it against the grille. 'You take care now, Francis. May God bless and keep you. Always.'

'You too, Ma.' Genno gave her a wink – unlike her, he'd never been one for sentimental gestures – then nodded to the correctional officer standing beside the interconnecting cell door. He was helped to his feet and led away. He didn't look back at his mother. He never did.

'That was a short visit today, Mrs Genno.' Doug D'Amato looked surprised as she approached him. 'You're usually one of the last to leave.'

'We said what we had to say to each other. Sometimes that's all it takes.' She gave him a quick smile. 'I'll see you next time, Dougie. Assuming you're on duty, of course. I hope so – I'll be bringing in some of those cookies that you like so much.'

'Chocolate-chip?' D'Amato asked, wetting his lips. He could feel his mouth watering already. 'I sure hope I'm around. Otherwise, I don't get a look in. Those cookies are always snapped up straight away. Do you know when will you be coming again?'

'I don't exactly know that yet,' she replied thoughtfully. 'But hopefully soon. Real soon.'

An hour? An hour and a half? Sarah had no idea how long she'd been sitting at the kitchen table. The blinds were drawn behind her. The back door was locked. Taylor had insisted on both before he accompanied Bob back to his office. A surveillance unit was already watching the house. Nobody could approach the house without being seen. Small consolation, if the assassin had a sniper rifle. But then she'd had the chance to take refuge in a safe house, and she'd refused. Not that she regretted her decision. It had already been decided that Bob and Lea would move into the safe house that evening. Bob wouldn't return to work again until the situation had been resolved. He'd only gone to his office to tidy up some loose ends. Neither would Lea go back to school. Both she and Bob had agreed that it would be far too risky. At least they had agreed on something. Then again, to give him his due, Bob hadn't reacted as she had thought he would. No tantrums. No guilt trips. Just a blank acceptance of the truth. Maybe he'd been in shock and the resentment would come later. Not that she could blame him if he did fly off the handle at her. How would she have reacted if the roles had been reversed? A marriage built on lies and deceit. If the marriage had been shaky before, now it was registering ten on the Richter scale. Was there any chance of saving it?

Absently picking up the mug of coffee in front of her, she took a sip. Her face screwed up in disgust and she spat the cold liquid back into the mug. Getting to her feet, she crossed to the sink and poured it down the plug hole. Only then did she notice the folder lying on the work surface beside the sink. She couldn't remember bringing it into the kitchen with her after Bob and Taylor had left the house. But how else would it have got there? One of the photographs was partially visible. A laughing Renée Mercier, her head turned slightly towards the hidden camera. Sarah felt as if she were laughing at her. Mocking her. She was momentarily tempted to rip the photograph to shreds, such was her contempt for *that* woman, but she quickly regained her composure and instead pushed it back into the folder. Earlier that morning she'd been ready to drive over to Bob's office, throw the folder on to his desk and demand an explanation. Watch him squirm when she asked how she could possibly ever trust him again. Trust? That certainly smacked of double standards after the events of the day. How could she confront him now about his adulterous behaviour, when she hadn't trusted him enough to tell him about her previous life? Not that his infidelity had been foremost on her mind since Jack Taylor had appeared on the scene. That was now of secondary importance. And it would remain that way until the situation with Genno had been resolved. Which was certainly easier said than done, considering that Taylor wasn't even sure whether Genno knew about Sarah's new life in New Orleans. She had to presume he did – which was why she had chosen to remain in the house. Bait. It was the only way to flush out any potential assassin. But even if they were to intercept the assassin, Genno would just hire another one to take his place. It's not as if the authorities could do anything to stop Genno. He was already serving a life sentence. What more could they do to him? These were the distressing thoughts which had been playing havoc with her already fraught emotions over the past few hours. Would setting herself up as a target actually solve anything? Taylor and his men couldn't protect the family indefinitely. Sooner or later Genno would get to her. Or her family. Assuming he knew where she was. It always came back to that. Like a vicious circle. Frankie Genno was back in her life again, just as she had always feared . . .

The sound of the toilet flushing upstairs interrupted her thoughts. Lea. It was the first sign that she'd come out of her bedroom since fleeing the living room in tears. Although she had desperately wanted to go up to Lea's room ever since Bob left the house, she'd wisely decided to give her daughter the time and space to take in what she had heard that afternoon. Let her make the first move. Whether flushing the cistern was that move was open to debate. But at least it meant that Lea had ventured out of her room. It was the excuse Sarah needed – wanted – to approach her daughter. Test the waters. Probably ice cold, she thought bitterly. Not that she could blame Lea if she felt that way. How would she have felt if her mother had . . . then again, *her* mother was an alcoholic who would have sold her own daughter for a bottle of Scotch. Which wasn't that far off the truth. One night she had overheard her mother negotiating a price with a man – there had been so many strange men at the house when she was a child – fifty dollars . . . to have sex with her daughter. She had been seven at the time. Streetwise, granted, but still only seven years old. Yet what she remembered most vividly was the extended pause between the man's abhorrent question and her mother's eventual reply. As if she was *actually* contemplating the idea. She had finally said no. But the damage had already been done. What kind of mother . . . ? Forget it, she thought resentfully. This wasn't the time to dredge up those kind of memories again. It wasn't about her mother any more. It was about her. And Lea.

She left the kitchen and paused at the foot of the stairs. Lea's bedroom door was at the top of the landing, directly opposite the stairs. She knew that Bob had been in to see Lea before he left the house and explained about Lomax's murder and the possibility that Frankie might now be in possession of her classified file, which could put all their lives in considerable danger. He had also told her about the safe house, although, as far as Sarah knew, he hadn't told her that her mother intended to stay behind. Not that Sarah could blame him.

Lea's door was ajar. Sarah decided to go up. Not a difficult decision to make. She felt knots of uncertainty twisting uncomfortably in the pit of her stomach as she slowly climbed the stairs, almost expecting the door to slam shut at any moment. But she persevered until she reached the top of the stairs. The days when she or Bob could walk into Lea's room uninvited were long gone. She was a young woman now, and deserved to be treated as such. Sarah took a deep breath to try and steady her unsettled nerves, then knocked lightly on the door. No reply. She knocked again. This time a little louder.

'Go away. I've got nothing to say to you,' Lea called out from the bedroom.

'Lea, we need to talk,' Sarah replied, but made no attempt to enter the room. 'Please may I come in?'

'It's your house, I can't stop you,' came the sharp riposte.

'You know very well that I won't come into your room without your permission.'

'You can come in . . . I guess,' came the reluctant response after a lengthy silence.

Sarah eased open the door and peered tentatively into the room. Lea was lying motionless on her bed, hands behind her head, staring at the ceiling. She entered the room and crossed to the foot of the bed. Still Lea didn't acknowledge her. Sarah sat down on the edge of the bed. It wasn't like her to be lost for words. Especially with Lea. They had always had a special rapport. Now she didn't know what to say, where to start. How to explain her deception.

'You lied to me,' Lea said in a soft, emotionless voice before Sarah could find the words to express herself. Sarah was grateful that Lea had breached the silence. Not that it made her task any easier. But at least now she had a starting point.

'Yes, I lied to you. I lied to your father. In fact, I've lied to everyone who's ever asked me anything about my life before I came to New Orleans. I'm not proud of myself for doing it, Lea. But it had to be done. It was the only way I knew to put my past behind me.'

'Except you haven't, have you?'

'I always knew there was a chance it would backfire on me. But it was a chance I had to take if I was to have any hope of making a future for myself here in New Orleans. There was certainly no future in the life I was leading in Chicago at the time.' Sarah put a hand lightly on Lea's leg. Her daughter didn't pull back from her. That was encouraging. 'And even if I had chosen to ignore the advice of the Marshals Service and decided that I did want to tell your father – or you, for that matter – the truth about my past, when would have been the right time for me to have dropped my little bombshell? If you can answer that, you're a better person than I am. I've been agonizing over that question from the moment I first knew I was in love with your father. There could never be an appropriate moment, Lea. That's what I've had to live with for the past sixteen years. And believe me, it hasn't been easy.'

'I hear what you're saying,' Lea sat up and propped her pillow against the headboard, using it as a cushion for her back. 'It still feels like a betrayal, though. All these years you've been living a lie.'

'It was a betrayal,' Sarah agreed, 'and yes, I have been living a lie. But it wasn't out of choice. It was out of necessity. Don't you see that, sweetheart?'

'I guess so,' Lea replied without much conviction.

'I can understand your scepticism. Your life's in turmoil. Your emotions are in free fall. You're angry. Confused. Resentful. Bitter. Distrustful. You feel alienated right now.' Sarah allowed a faint smile to play across her lips. 'I've been there, sweetheart. That's how I felt when they threatened to lock me up and throw away the key, if I didn't testify against Frankie. When they took away the security of the life I had back in Chicago. OK, so it wasn't much when I look back on it now, but I didn't see it like that then. I felt as if I'd been violated. And when the trial was over, they gave me a new identity and dumped me in an unfamiliar environment. All I knew about New Orleans was that they held the Mardi Gras here once a year. Nothing else. I had no friends, no family. I was utterly alone.' She wiped away a tear that escaped from the corner of her eye. 'And loneliness like that can breed the kind of constricting fear inside you that you just can't shake off, no matter how hard you try. All I did was lie awake at night, unable to sleep, not knowing what was going to happen to me from one day to the next. And that's scary. God, is that scary, especially when I also had this enduring image in my mind of Frankie screaming vengeance at me as he was dragged off to start his life sentence. I still have nightmares about it to this day. It'll never go away. Only I've come to accept it now. It's the price I've had to pay for my sins. Why would I want to share those wretched memories with the one person who means more to me than anything else in this godforsaken world? I would have done everything in my power to protect you from that part of my life. I'm sorry I couldn't manage it in the end, sweetheart. I'm so sorry.'

Tears welled up in Lea's eyes and it appeared for a moment as if she was going to respond to what her mother had said, but then she abruptly swung her legs off the bed and moved to the window. She sniffed back the tears and brushed her fingertips quickly across her eyes as she looked out across the back garden. Sarah was about to warn Lea away from the window, but before she could say anything her daughter returned to the bed and sat down. She was back in control. 'Tell me about Frankie Genno,' she said.

Sarah was surprised by the request, but quickly found her voice. 'What do you want to know about him?'

'Were you in love with him?'

Sarah pursed her lips thoughtfully as she pondered the question. 'No, I'd say in retrospect, it was more dependency than love. Frankie was, amongst other things, a dealer. He provided me with what I needed. When I needed it. Having him as a boyfriend was a bonus because I could score freely from him.'

'Did you have to pay him for it?'

'No.'

'So he got sex in return for supplying you with a fix, is that it?'

That cut deep, coming from her own daughter. But how could she be angry with Lea? It wasn't that far off the truth. 'In those days I would probably have had sex with anyone if it had meant scoring a free hit afterwards,' she replied candidly, deciding against holding back any more from Lea. 'When you're hurting, all you care about is where your next fix is coming from. Dignity is the last thing on your mind. That's what being a junkie is. You have no respect for yourself. You have no pride in your appearance. You have no self-esteem whatsoever. You're just an empty shell. Nothing else.'

'So why did you do it?' Lea asked, staring intently at her mother.

'Wrong crowd. Peer pressure. Boredom. An escape from my mother's alcoholism. Seeing no future for myself in society. It's an endless list. And each excuse as pitiful and pathetic as the last.' Sarah shook her head sadly. 'I only wish I could give you a defining reason why I ended up like that. Truth is, I don't know. And that's what makes it all the more tragic.'

'When did you stop taking drugs?'

'After Frankie was arrested. The first thing the DA did was put me into a detox programme. He needed me in some kind of coherent state when I took the stand.'

'And were you?'

'Just about. I was still very weak from doing cold turkey. To be fair to the DA, though, he did ask me whether I wanted a postponement, but by then I just wanted to get it over with and leave Chicago.'

'Have you ever regretted snitching on Genno?' Lea asked.

'No, because the alternative for me would have been jail time. I wouldn't have lasted a day in there. My only regret is not being able to tell the police when Frankie brought the heist forward by twenty-four hours. If I had, maybe I could have prevented three needless deaths. Four, if you count Henry Drummond, Frankie's best friend, who was shot in the back by the off-duty cop.'

Lea tugged absently on a loose thread in the weave of her pale cream quilt. 'Dad said that we'd be going to a safe house until this had all blown over. And that I'm going to have to miss school until further notice. This is an important year, Mom. I can't afford to fall back on my schoolwork.'

'You'll get extra tuition if necessary. Your dad and Mr Taylor are going to speak to the head this afternoon and explain the situation to him as best they can. Obviously, they can't go into too much detail.' Sarah reached out and took Lea's hand in hers. 'I'm just as concerned about your education as you are, sweetheart. Hopefully it will be resolved before long.'

'Where exactly is this safe house?'

'To be honest, I don't even know,' Sarah said with a shrug. 'Mr Taylor will be taking you there tonight.'

'Me?' Lea said, her brow furrowing uncertainty. 'What about you and Dad?'

'Your dad will be going with you,' Sarah told her. This was the part she had been dreading. 'I'm not going with you. I'm staying here.'

Lea responded by tugging her hand free from her mother's gentle grip. 'Why are you staying here?'

'Because it's the only way I'm going to find out whether Frankie does have a contract out on me. It's pointless for me to go into hiding as well. And if there is a contract, it won't be lifted until this has been resolved one way or another.'

'You could be killed!' Lea clasped her hand to her mouth as fresh tears threatened to spill down her cheeks, but there was also anger in her eyes as she glared at her mother.

'Frankie Genno ruined my life once already,' Sarah said, her voice now hard as she stared back at her daughter, all her pent-up emotions bursting to the surface. 'He's not going to do it a second time. I'm not about to start running again. So let Frankie give it his best shot. Then I'll make my move. And then we'll see who goes on the defensive.'

'What are you talking about?' Lea asked anxiously. 'Mom, what are you going to do?'

'I'm going to do everything in my power to protect my own, sweetheart. I'll see that Frankie burns in hell before I ever allow him anywhere near my family. *That* is a promise!'

Sarah left the room, closed the door behind her and returned to the living room. She knew what she had to do. Call it an insurance policy. But she had to have some kind of ammunition to use against Frankie, should he force her hand. Not that she would use it – unless he made a move against her. She couldn't, not without drawing attention to herself. There was still the chance that Frankie was unaware of her new identity. Only she couldn't afford to believe that. Not with her family being possible targets as well. After checking that Lea wasn't outside the door, or on the stairs, she removed her address book from her bag, found the telephone number she wanted, and dialled out on her cellular phone. It was answered after half a dozen rings. 'Is that Derek Farlowe?'

'Speaking.'

'Mr Farlowe, this is Sarah Johnson. With the wayward husband. I was in your office this morning. Remember?'

'Of course I remember you, Mrs Johnson. Is there a problem with the work I did for you?'

'Not at all. Tell me, do you have contacts in Joliet?'

There was a hesitant pause. 'You mean in Joliet Penitentiary?' he asked, making no attempt to mask the astonishment in his voice.

'No, I mean the town of Joliet. In Illinois.'

'I know where it is, Mrs Johnson. *The Blues Brothers* is one of my favourite films.'

'Pardon?' This time it was Sarah's turn to be dumbfounded.

'Jake Elwood? Joliet Jake? The character played by John Belushi in the film?'

'I'll take your word for it. Well, do you have any contacts there?'

'I'm afraid not. In fact, I've never been to Illinois in my life.'

'I want someone up there, in your line of work. Can you make some enquiries for me? Obviously, I'll pay you for your time. I need someone discreet, though. Very discreet.'

'What exactly is it you want them to do?' Farlowe asked.

'That's something I'd rather discuss with them. It'll be a day's work at the most. I'm prepared to pay three times . . . no, let's make that five times their standard rate, if they'll drop everything and concentrate on this.'

'You pay for the flight to Joliet, Mrs Johnson, and I'll do it myself for that kind of money. I'll even cover my own expenses while I'm there. Assuming, of course, it's something I can do. You don't specifically need a local yokel, do you?'

'A hire car and a street map, that's all you'll need.'

'Then I'm your man,' Farlowe announced. 'I can be on the next flight to Joliet, if that's what you want.'

'I was hoping you were going to say that, Mr Farlowe. At least I know your standard of work and that you're discreet.'

'You can certainly count on that, Mrs Johnson. Now tell me, what exactly is it you want me to do in Joliet?'

Three

The black shoes, polished. The black trousers, pressed. The black shirt, ironed. The white clerical collar, starched. The amiable smile – deceptive. The Preacher: Paul Klyne.

He had arrived in New Orleans on a flight from Chicago shortly after midday. It was his first trip to the Big Easy, but not his first time in the state of Louisiana. He had served two years at the Oakdale Federal Correctional Institution. It was there he had first come into contact with Etienne Pascale, a former detective with the Baton Rouge Police Department who had been jailed for an assault on his ex-wife's lover. Klyne had taken an instant dislike to Pascale and could understand why his wife had left him for another man. Yet, unlike the other prisoners who only saw Pascale as a means to satisfy their own narrow-minded retribution, he recognized the potential of having Pascale as an ally, especially with his vast network of contacts, both criminal and in law enforcement, across the south-central region of the country. So he became Pascale's self-appointed bodyguard while the disgraced cop served out a lenient six-month sentence at Oakdale. Without Klyne, Pascale would have been an easy target for every con with a grudge against the police. As it was, he walked away from Oakdale virtually unscathed. He owed his life to Klyne. Now, for the first time since Oakdale, Klyne had sought out his help. Pascale, who had settled in New Orleans after leaving jail, had assured him that he would assist in any way possible.

Pascale had booked Klyne a room under a false name in a small, undistinguished hotel on Royal Street, in the heart of the French Quarter. He had met him at Moisant Internal Airport, but Klyne had decided against going to the hotel first, preferring instead to have Pascale drive him to Kenner, a middle-class neighbourhood close to the airport. Sarah Johnson lived in Kenner. Pascale had first driven past the house, then stopped, on Klyne's instructions, two blocks

47

further on. Klyne had then got out, and told Pascale to wait for him, before heading back on foot in the direction of the house. Like many of the residences in the historic neighbourhood, the Johnsons' double-storey house had an unusually narrow façade. The reason for this was that during the nineteenth century, properties in and around New Orleans were taxed on the width of the front of the building rather than on the overall size of the structure. Known locally as 'shotgun houses', they were so named because it was said that a bullet could pass from the front to the back door without hitting a wall. The front garden was small and neatly tended, with an assortment of colourful blooms which lined a narrow concrete path leading to a set of wooden stairs which, in turn, led up to a recently swept porch. The walls, constructed of wooden slats, were painted a pastel green, with white railings enclosing the porch and second-floor balcony. The curtains had been drawn across the street-facing windows on both floors.

Klyne had first noticed the unmarked car, parked discreetly in a side street, when Pascale had driven past the house. Two occupants. Male. He was pretty sure they were marshals keeping the Johnsons' house under surveillance. They had a clear view of the house. But there had to be a blind side, making that an option for entry into the house, which was why Klyne had chosen to investigate the possibility further on foot.

His greatest asset had always been his nondescript features. He had seen police photofits of himself in the past. No two were ever alike. He had the sort of face which never attracted undue attention. And that was what he was counting on as he paused at the entrance to the side street, just out of sight of the marshals' unmarked car, but still with a clear view of the house. He opened a street map and pretended to study it, as if trying to locate his bearings, but his eyes were focused on the angle of the house to the car parked nearby. If he was going to get to Sarah Johnson, it was imperative that he knew exactly what the two-man surveillance team could see from their vantage point.

Satisfied with his findings, he folded up the map again and slipped it into his back pocket, and as he crossed the entrance to the side street he inclined his head towards the surveillance car and creased his mouth into a friendly smile of acknowledgement. Both men looked away. He took a perverse pleasure in their obvious discomfort. It also served to reinforce his initial gut feeling that they were marshals, monitoring the Johnsons' house. Then he did a quick recce of the adjacent street, on the surveillance team's blind side, before returning to where Pascale was waiting for him in the car.

He would be back. After dark. Then he would kill Sarah Johnson.

'I'm not leaving!'

'Lea, you're coming with me to the safe house, and that's an end to it,' Bob Johnson said sternly, stabbing a finger at his daughter, who was standing at the foot of the stairs, arms akimbo, eyes blazing. 'Now go upstairs and pack your things.'

'I told you, I'm not leaving,' she retorted defiantly.

'You'll do as you're told!' he shot back furiously.

'You run out if you want, but I'm not leaving Mom here on her own.'

Jack Taylor interceded before Bob could reply. 'Lea, your mother has her reasons for remaining here at the house,' he said in a placatory voice. 'I may not agree with her motives – and I know your father doesn't – but she's adamant that she's staying. She won't be on her own. I'll be with her in the house all night. There's also a surveillance team out front. Rest assured, she won't come to any harm.'

'You don't understand, do you?' Lea said with a contemptuous shake of her head. 'You can cordon off all the surrounding streets, bring in the National Guard if you want, but if my dad and I leave her now, she'll be on her own. I may still be mad as hell at her, but she is my mother. We're family, Mr Taylor. I can't just walk out on her now.'

Taylor sat down on the stairs and smiled gently at her. 'I hear what you're saying, Lea, and I respect where you're coming from, I really do.'

'But?' she said hesitantly when he fell silent.

'But your mother wouldn't want you to stay here with her. She'd only be constantly fretting over your safety. And let's face it, she's got enough to worry about as it is. You know that.'

'I know.' Lea bit her lower lip, as the vulnerability she'd been trying so hard to suppress threatened to surface. She looked down quickly at her feet. 'It's just that . . .' she trailed off with a helpless shrug.

'Yeah, I've been there too.' Taylor gave her arm a reassuring squeeze. 'You know in your heart you're right, but that doesn't make a damn bit of difference anyway. This time you've got to go with your head. Not your heart. And it hurts all the more for it, doesn't it?' Lea nodded without looking at him. 'Like I said just now, your mom won't come to any harm,' he added. 'None of you will. You have my word on that.'

'I'll go and pack,' she said in a barely audible voice, and hurried up the stairs to her bedroom.

'I'll get my stuff as well,' Bob said gruffly and went after her.

'Thanks.'

Taylor looked round in surprise to find Sarah standing in the kitchen doorway, adjacent to the stairs.

'I appreciate what you said to Lea,' Sarah continued. 'I think I'd have found it really hard to turn her away, even though I know I would have had to when it came down to it. She's right, though. I will be on my own. And that's no disrespect meant to you, or your men.'

'None taken. Don't forget, I was involved in the WITSEC Program before I joined Internal Affairs. I've relocated my fair share of families in my time. It's never easy. We're supposed to stand back and never get personally involved. Granted, it's easy if you're baby-sitting some smart-talking wiseguy who's agreed to testify against the Family. He's probably got as much blood on his hands as the defendants he's trying to help put away. But if it's an innocent family who've been caught up in something beyond their control, their anxieties do get to you after a while. We wouldn't be human if they didn't. Only we can't afford to show it. And because we don't, they think we don't care about their feelings.' He rubbed his hands over his face and shook his head slowly to himself. 'It's particularly tough on the kids. They can't take the family pets with them. They can't tell their friends where they're going. They can't even tell their own family – grandparents, aunts, uncles. But then you know that anyway. You had to leave your family behind, didn't you?'

'It was the one good thing that came out of it,' Sarah said coldly. 'I couldn't say that I was ever close to my mother. I don't even know whether she's still alive. Or perhaps I should say, I don't *care* whether she's still alive. So don't bother telling me. I really don't want to know.'

'You've also got an older brother back in Chicago, haven't you?'

'Oh, is that what he was?' she retorted contemptuously. 'I'm always reminded of that Stones song, "Mother's Little Helper", whenever I think about Raymond. He was always at her beck and call. "Raymond, get me this. Raymond, get me that. Raymond, do this. Raymond, do that." He got her all her booze. I swear if he'd had

50

more backbone and stood up to her like I did, she wouldn't have become a hopeless alcoholic. It was all so easy for her with Raymond around.'

'Sounds like the kettle calling the pot black,' Bob said from the top of the stairs, holding a suitcase in his hand. He descended to where Taylor was still sitting at the foot of the stairs. 'Genno supplied you with drugs. So what's the difference between him and your brother?'

Sarah leaned on the banister and glanced up to make sure Lea wasn't there. 'The difference being that it wasn't unnatural for Frankie to come into my bed at night.'

'You mean . . .' Bob trailed off, a look of sheer disgust washing over his face as the truth of what she was implying struck him with all the force of a sledgehammer. 'Oh . . . oh . . . my God, Sarah . . . I'm . . . I'm sorry,' he stammered. 'I had no idea.'

'Of course you didn't.' Her eyes hardened and her voice became even more scornful when she added, 'You've heard of that old adage, keeping it in the family. Well, my mother certainly took that at face value. I was Raymond's reward for being a good boy and doing all the little chores for her. Admittedly, it didn't happen very often, but it happened nevertheless. Oh yes, the Strattons were one big happy family.'

'That wasn't in your file,' Taylor said, breaking the numbing silence which had abruptly descended over them. His words sounded hollow and insensitive and from the moment they escaped his lips, he wished he'd never uttered them.

'Some things were better left unsaid at that stage of my life. If Lomax had known the truth, who knows how he might have reacted. And the last thing I wanted was to be dragged back into court again, this time to testify against my own family. What was done was done. I saw no purpose in dredging it all up again.'

'Did Genno know?' Bob asked.

'Yeah, like I confided anything to Frankie,' Sarah retorted with a derisive laugh. 'I slept with him. Period. It wasn't love. Never love.'

Bob's eyes flickered upwards when Lea emerged from her bedroom and slowly came down the stairs. 'Have you got everything you need, *ange*?'

'No,' she said, casting an accusing look in her mother's direction as she reached the bottom of the stairs.

'You know it's something I have to do, sweetheart. For me as much as for you.'

'I'm scared,' Lea said, embracing her mother.

'Me too,' Sarah replied as she gently stroked her daughter's hair.

Taylor's cellular phone rang and he was quick to answer it. He listened momentarily, then his eyes went to Sarah before saying, 'We're ready in here. In fact, we have been for ages. Where are your men? They should have been here by now.' Another pause. 'No, I'm not going to the safe house. I'm staying with Mrs Johnson.' Pause. 'Yes, she's remaining here in the house.' Pause. 'Look, I'm not discussing this with you over the phone. Your men are taking Mr Johnson and his daughter to the safe house – that is, if they ever get here. That's all that need concern you at the moment.' He exhaled irritably. 'Fuck regulations.' He winced at his own language, gave Lea a rueful grin, and mouthed 'sorry' to Sarah who was standing beside her. 'It may be your jurisdiction, but it's still my case. That makes it my call. So there's really nothing more to discuss, is there?' He rolled his eyes despairingly at Lea, who smiled back weakly at him. 'You come along by all means. I'm sure Mr Johnson and Lea would love to have your company at the safe house. But you're not hanging around here, that I can tell you now. Goodbye.' He switched of the cellphone before the caller could utter another word of protest. 'That was Deputy Marshal Robert Robideaux, my liaison here in New Orleans. He likes to play everything by the book. So, naturally, we've been banging heads ever since I got here.'

'I assume that means you don't play by the book?' Bob concluded.

'To each their own,' Taylor replied diplomatically.

'That's certainly reassuring to know,' Bob muttered.

'How long before they get here?' Sarah asked.

'They should be here within the next five to ten minutes. Seems that they got held up by some road works on the way over here.'

'You packed?' Sarah asked Lea, gesturing to the holdall by the foot of the stairs.

'I guess,' Lea replied with an indifferent shrug. 'You will ring, won't you?'

'I'll ring later tonight,' Sarah promised, 'and let you know what's going on.' She turned to Taylor. 'That will be all right, won't it?'

'All the lines at the safe house are secure, at least in theory, but you can use my cellphone as an added precaution.'

'You think the phones could be bugged?' Sarah said in surprise.

'It's highly unlikely, but we still have to take every precaution. Standard procedure.'

'So there are some things you play by the book?' Bob said with a hint of sarcasm in his voice.

'I play mostly by the book, Mr Johnson. But I'm also objective enough to know when to chance my hand. I'm a field man. I always have been. Even now, with Internal Affairs, I spend most of the time out of the office. That's how I like it. Frankly, I don't have a lot of patience for the endless red tape that comes with the job. I leave that side of things to the desk jockeys like Robideaux. Having said that, though Robideaux and I may not always agree on everything, we're still two spokes on the same wheel. As deputy federal marshals we have the same goals, only we tend to approach them from different perspectives. And as I said just now, to each their own.'

'In other words, you're a maverick,' Bob said.

'I'm an individual,' Taylor replied, and then crossed to the front door when a set of headlights swept into view through the adjacent opaque glass window. He opened the door on its chain and peered out into the street. A car was parked out front. Two occupants. Both got out. The driver was wearing a pair of faded jeans, a sweatshirt and Zephyrs baseball cap. The other one was wearing a grey suit. No tie. They climbed the steps on to the porch and held up their shields for Taylor to inspect. Only then did he remove the chain and open the door.

'We were told that you're staying here with Mrs Johnson, sir. Is that right?' the driver asked Taylor.

'That's right. You're to take Mr Johnson and Lea to the safe house. And I want confirmation once you're there. You've got the number of my cellphone, haven't you?'

'Yes, sir.' The driver turned to Bob. 'If you'd care to come with us now, sir. You too, miss.'

Bob looked at Sarah, was about to say something, but felt it inappropriate in front of the others. He followed the grey-suited deputy out on to the porch and down the path towards the waiting car.

'Miss? Please,' the driver said, gesturing towards the front door.

'It's going to be all right, sweetheart. I promise.' Sarah hugged Lea tightly to her.

'You will be careful?' Lea said in a hesitant voice.

'You can count on that.' Sarah kissed Lea on the forehead. 'Go on.'

'I'll personally drive your mother over to the safe house first thing tomorrow morning so that you guys can have breakfast together as a family,' Taylor told Lea. 'Deal?'

'Deal,' Lea said softly. Then, picking up her holdall, she left the house.

Taylor locked the door and turned back to Sarah. 'She's a pretty smart kid. Obviously takes after her mother.'

'So why am I setting myself up for a possible fall when I could have taken the easy option and gone with them to the safe house?' Sarah retorted, and then rubbed her hands wearily over her face. 'Don't answer that. Well, I guess all we can do now is wait and see what happens. I tell you, I'm real tempted to have a large bourbon right now to steady my nerves. Then again, I can't guarantee I wouldn't end up finishing the bottle. Maybe that's not such a good idea. I'll just stick to coffee. How about you? Coffee?'

'Sure, why not?' Taylor replied and followed her into the kitchen.

'It's got to be a trap,' Pascale concluded.

'You can bet it is,' Klyne replied thoughtfully, as he watched Bob and Lea Johnson being driven away from the house. It suited him to have them out of the way. They weren't targets and would only have got in his way.

'You want to abort and try again tomorrow night?' Pascale asked.

'Why would I want to do that?'

'Because it's so obviously a trap.'

'No, we do it tonight,' Klyne replied bluntly, then glanced at Pascale. 'Was that a note of apprehension I heard in your voice?'

'You mean, am I uneasy about this? Fucking right I am. I may be working on the wrong side of the law these days, but it's always been petty crime until now. You're talking about carrying out a hit here. An assassination. I'll tell you, Klyne, this is way out of my league.'

'You owe me big time from Oakdale, and you know it. And anyway, you're being well paid for your troubles.'

'So you keep telling me,' Pascale reminded him, 'except I still haven't seen so much as a dime of this wondrous payout you've been promising me ever since you first got here.'

'And as I also keep telling you, the money will come from the computer disk I've got salted away in a safe place. This hit's merely a favour for a friend. And once it's done, I can start selling the contents of the disk on the black market. That's when the big money will start rolling in.'

'And by then you'll be long gone.'

'You don't trust me, do you?' Klyne put a hand theatrically to his chest. 'You don't know how much that hurts.'

'Yeah, right,' Pascale retorted, totally missing the thrust of Klyne's veiled sarcasm.

'Don't worry, you'll get a more than generous cut of the profits. I always repay my debts.' Klyne opened the glove compartment and removed a 9mm Astra semi-automatic pistol and silencer. He slipped the silencer into the side pocket of his black jacket, and then secured the weapon in a holster concealed on his belt at the back of his trousers. 'You ready?'

Pascale wet his dry lips nervously. 'I'm ready,' he said, without sounding too convinced by his own words.

Klyne wagged a finger of warning at Pascale. 'You fuck up, and we'll both end up doing time. Only this time, you'll be on your own. No bodyguard to cover your ass every time you leave your cell. You wouldn't last a week, and you know it.'

'I told you, I'm ready,' Pascale insisted, this time more confidently. He knew he couldn't afford to make the slightest mistake. Klyne was right, he wouldn't last a week in jail. Frankly, he doubted he'd last a day. The perfect incentive to get it right first time.

'Good. Then let's go.'

'Thank God, only an hour to go,' Jess Kane exclaimed, then interlocked his fingers and cracked his knuckles. 'Ah, that's better.'

'I wish you wouldn't do that, partner,' Eddie Hungate said, pulling a face, 'you know it gives me the creeps.'

'Why else d'you think I do it?'

'Remind me to put in for a transfer tomorrow,' Kane replied. Not that he would. They had been partners for the past five years. Both were United States deputy marshals, attached to the WITSEC Program. Neither of them enjoyed stake-outs and they had been watching the Johnson house for the past seven hours.

'She's quite a looker, you know,' Hungate said, pulling a pack of cigarettes from his pocket. He lit one. Revenge. Kane, a fitness fanatic, hated smoking, especially within the confined space of a car.

'Who?' Kane replied, irritably waving the smoke away from his face.

'Sarah Johnson. I tell you, partner, I wouldn't say no.'

'She would.' Kane gestured to the cigarette between Hungate's lips. 'She doesn't smoke. Cigarettes are a real passion-killer to a non-smoker.'

'How d'you know she doesn't smoke?' Hungate asked, the cigarette bobbing up and down between his lips as he spoke.

'Unlike you, I actually made the effort to read her dossier. I didn't just drool over the photos.'

'Always the conscientious one . . .' Hungate's voice trailed off, then he removed the cigarette from his mouth and leaned forward, peering further down the road beyond the Johnsons' house.

'Over there. See him?'

'It's fucking dark out there, Eddie. What am I . . . hang on, yeah, I see somebody. He's just come out that house. His clothes are real dark, though.'

'All black. White dog collar. Ring any bells?'

'The padre we saw earlier this afternoon,' Kane replied. 'Why, d'you think it's him?'

'Could be. Looks like he's going from house to house. See, he's just disappeared up the next driveway.'

'Maybe he's collecting for the local church,' Kane suggested.

'Yeah, or delivering pamphlets. Hell, I don't know. What do we do? Intercept him before he reaches the Johnsons' house?'

'I'll call Taylor on the radio.' Kane picked up the two-way radio from the dashboard, contacted the house, and explained the situation to Taylor.

'No, let him come,' Taylor said. 'As you say, he's probably just a harmless preacher. We don't want to start ruffling feathers amongst the local clergy. This is meant to be a covert operation. I'll move Mrs Johnson upstairs as a precaution anyway. Keep the frequency open so that you can update me on his movements as he nears the house. If he's not what he seems, I want to be ready for him.'

'Will do, sir.' Kane replaced the radio on the dashboard just as the figure disappeared up the next pathway. He was still half a dozen houses away from the Johnsons' house.

'Oh, great, another local resident,' Hungate grumbled, as a man appeared from an adjoining street. He was wearing a suit and carrying a newspaper in one hand. 'How many have come down this road since we've been on duty? And every time we get the same suspicious looks. I'm surprised the cops haven't come to check us out yet.'

'Just ignore him.'

'Evening,' the man said cheerily as he drew abreast of the surveillance car. Kane, in the passenger seat, reluctantly turned his head towards the man, a forced smile on his face. The smile swiftly disappeared when he saw the Colt .38 in Pascale's hand, partially concealed by the newspaper. A suppressor was screwed on to the end of the barrel. 'Don't even think it,' Pascale hissed menacingly, when Kane made to reach for his holstered weapon. He was careful to keep his distance from the side of the car, in case the door was thrust open on to him. 'I'd like you both to use your thumb and forefinger to remove your pieces from their holsters. Butt first. And, please, do it very slowly.'

Hungate and Kane exchanged glances, knowing that Taylor could hear what was happening over the open channel. Neither of them looked at the radio as they withdrew their automatics, butt first between thumb and forefinger.

'Throw them on to the back seat,' Pascale ordered. They did as they were told and saw that the Padre was now only four houses away from the Johnsons'. Pascale took a pair of handcuffs from his pocket and tossed them into Kane's lap. It was only then that Kane noticed he was wearing surgeon's gloves. He also managed to get a better look at the face. The blond wig, false moustache and glasses were an obvious disguise. 'You, in the passenger seat, put one cuff round your left wrist, and the other one round your partner's right wrist.' Kane reluctantly did as he was told, but felt secure in the knowledge that if the gunman had wanted to kill them, he could have done it already. He only hoped he wasn't tempting fate by thinking that. 'Now, open the back door.' Hungate activated the door from a control panel beside the gear lever and Pascale got in behind them. 'Driver, remove the keys from the ignition and toss them out the window.'

The priest was now only three houses away from the Johnsons'. Pascale waited until Hungate had done as he was told, then slammed the butt of the Colt down hard on to the back of his head. He was quick to grab him by the shoulder before he could slump forward on to the steering wheel and activate the horn.

'You didn't have to knock him out!' Kane snarled, angry at his own apparent helplessness. He also wanted Taylor to know what was happening. It was all he could do now to warn him.

'He'll be just fine.' Pascale gestured to the radio on the dashboard. 'I know you'll have already contacted the house and told your colleague about the priest. Call again. Tell them he appears to be going door to door, seeking donations.' He pressed the tip of the suppressor against the back of Kane's neck. 'You heard me. Do it!'

Kane retrieved the radio from the dashboard with his free hand and had to go through the motions of pretending to open a channel to Taylor. He only hoped the gunman hadn't noticed the deception.

'Sir, it's Kane. The priest looks harmless enough. He appears to be on the donation trail.'

Kane held his breath, waiting for a reply, hoping that Taylor wouldn't give the game away. 'Where is he now?' Taylor asked.

'He just opened the gate of the neighbour's house. He's heading for the front door.'

'I want you to keep the channel open from now on and talk me through this. He may well be a harmless priest, but we can't afford to take any chances.'

Good, Kane thought. Not only would the gunman have no reason to suspect that the radio hadn't been switched off while it had been lying on the dashboard, but it also made it that much harder for him to communicate without giving his presence away to Taylor. Kane looked across at the house. It was up to Taylor now. He was on his own . . .

Taylor was seated on the stairs. Weapon drawn. Radio beside him. He'd ordered Sarah upstairs as soon as he realized that the surveillance car had been compromised – Kane and Hungate would be of no use to him now. He'd also given her the number of Robideaux's private line and instructions to tell him to send in the cavalry. Yet he knew it was already too late. He would have to deal with the bogus priest himself. One on one. He had the advantage. For the moment, at least . . .

'Sir, he's on the move again.' It was Kane on the radio. 'He's leaving the neighbouring house. Closing the gate behind him. He's coming your way.'

'Does he appear to be armed?' Taylor asked.

'Not that I can make out, sir, but he's wearing a black trench coat. He could be concealing a small arsenal under it.'

'Thanks for putting my mind at ease,' Taylor said, a taut smile twitching at the corners of his mouth. Humour in adversity. Sometimes it was all that kept him going in these kind of pressure situations. Not all his colleagues understood when he tried to explain that it was actually a form of self-discipline. He doubted Robideaux would have understood. Not that it mattered. Just as long he responded to Sarah's mayday call. He suddenly found himself having doubts about going along with her plan in the first place. But what choice did he have? She had made it abundantly clear that she wasn't going to leave, and there was no way he could have physically forced her to go to the safe house. Neither could he have left her in the house by herself, a sitting target for any would-be assassin. It was a unique situation, and one he'd never encountered before in all his years with the Marshals Service. Any other witness would have readily sought refuge at a safe house until the potential threat to their lives was over. Not Sarah Johnson. And he had to admit, he did secretly admire her for that. She wasn't just doing it for herself either. She was prepared to take a bullet to protect the future of her family, and her daughter, in particular . . .

'Sir, the priest's walking up the path towards the front door. Still no sign of any weapon.'

Kane's voice refocused Taylor's attention on the situation at hand. Not that he had let his mind wander, he was quick to tell himself. So then why the sudden guilt? He pushed these thoughts irritably from his mind. *Concentrate*. He picked up the radio and pressed it to his lips. He spoke in a whisper. 'Keep the channel open, but maintain radio silence for the time being. Let him make his play.'

He had barely replaced the radio on the stair beside him when there was a sharp rap on the door. His body tensed and he trained the 9mm Smith & Wesson on the front door. He had the perfect shot if the bogus priest was fool enough to try and kick it down. He doubted that would happen. It would leave the man overexposed. And this wasn't amateur hour. Genno had chosen wisely. A second knock. Suddenly he sensed someone behind him and glanced over his shoulder, but checked himself as he was about to aim the Smith & Wesson at the figure hovering uncertainly at the top of the stairs. Sarah looked frightened. Yet he knew there was no place for sentiment at that moment. All that concerned him was her safety. He gestured irritably with his head for her to take cover, then returned his attention to the front door.

'Sir, the priest's leaving,' Kane announced over the radio.

Taylor's eyes flickered to the radio by his feet. He knew he couldn't trust anything that Kane said. Not if he had a gun to his head.

'Sir, are you there?' Kane pressed when Taylor failed to reply. Taylor could hear the tension in his voice, as if he was being coerced into getting an answer out of him. 'Sir, can you hear me?'

Taylor picked up the radio. 'I hear you. Where is he now?'

'He's . . . walking back . . . down the path. Looks like he's leaving.' It sounded like Kane was reading out a written reply. That made sense to Taylor, especially as the gunman with Kane couldn't afford to make a sound without giving away his presence over the radio.

'So it looks like a false alarm after all,' Taylor said, forcing a nervous chuckle. But he knew it was far from over. Now he was even more on his guard, unsure from which angle the bogus priest would make his attack on the house. Front door. Back door. Side window. Conservatory. The house suddenly appeared massive. And he was one man. Not that the pedantic Robideaux would have given him any extra men to safeguard Sarah. Not stickler-for-the-rules Robideaux. What an asshole. And he'd tell him that to his face when next he saw him. *If* he saw him . . .

He was about to question Kane further over the radio when there came the sound of glass shattering. A stun grenade had been thrown through the opaque window beside the front door and had landed on the carpet at the foot of the stairs. Taylor had a split second to make a decision. Try to flee upstairs; or crouch down, close his eyes and cover his ears as best he could to minimize the effect of the flash-bang. He chose the latter option, turning his head away sharply and clamping his hands tightly over his ears in the instant before the anticipated detonation. It never came. A goddamn trap! And he had fallen for it. He was still swinging the gun round frantically towards the window when he felt the first bullet slam into the centre of his chest. A second hit him in almost the same place. He was knocked off his feet and the Smith & Wesson spun from his fingers as he stumbled back heavily against the wooden banister. *He'd failed Sarah*. It was the last, self-condemning thought he had before the darkness descended on him.

It was such a simple trick. And it worked every time. Klyne certainly thought it ingenious. But then he would, it was his cunning creation. A dummy stun grenade. Lob it through a window and the reaction was always the same. Civilians dived for cover, thinking it was a bomb. Fellow professionals would instinctively turn away to avoid the blinding flash of light and cover their ears to lessen the impact of the simultaneous explosion. Nobody ever stood their ground, weapons drawn. How often had he used that ruse in Africa over the years? Never failed him yet. No explosion, or blinding light, to disorientate him or his men. All they had to do then was rake the area with a sustained burst of gunfire, while their hapless victims cowered in fear of the flash-bang which never materialized.

He reached through the shattered window, unlatched it and pulled it open. The aperture was big enough for him to climb through. He closed the window behind him, pocketed the dummy stun grenade, then crossed to the foot of the stairs where Taylor lay face down on the carpet. Klyne kicked him hard in the ribs. No reaction. He was probably dead anyway, considering he'd been shot twice in the centre of his chest. Klyne was about to put a bullet through the back of Taylor's head for good measure, when he heard the sound of breaking glass coming from upstairs. The bitch was trying to escape. Jumping nimbly over Taylor's body, he bounded up the stairs, only pausing on the landing to get his bearings. He headed for the nearest door. He turned the handle. Locked. Stepping back, he brought the sole of his foot up savagely against the door, just beneath the handle. The lock splintered, but the door held. A second kick and the door flew open, hammering against the adjacent wall. He ran to a second closed door, which he assumed led into an en suite bathroom. It was also locked. He smashed the flimsy lock with one venomous kick.

His eyes went to the window. It was intact. Then he noticed the broken shards of glass in the basin. She'd broken a mirror. The bitch was armed. He noticed the movement out the corner of his eye and was still turning when the talcum powder was thrown directly into his face, momentarily blinding him. He fired wildly as he tried desperately to wipe the powder from his eyes. Then he screamed out in agony when Sarah stabbed a shard of glass hard into the back of his black gloved hand. The Astra slipped from his fingers and he heard it clatter noisily across the tiled floor. He cursed furiously, his vision still hampered by the talcum powder, and dropped to his haunches, patting the ground for his fallen weapon. His anguished cry tore through the whole house when Sarah caught him viciously in the groin with the tip of her boot. He collapsed into a heap on the floor, rocking back and forwards, as he cradled his genitals in his hands. Yet even through the haze of pain he knew that he had to get out. Cut his losses and get out before the bitch ran to one of her neighbours and called the cops.

He hauled himself up on to one knee. The agony was excruciating and for a horrifying moment he thought he was going to pass out. Suddenly he heard footsteps thudding towards him on the stairs. He began frantically to pat the floor around him. Where was the gun?

'Get up, shithead. Get up!' It was Pascale's voice. Hands hauled him roughly to his feet. The pain between his legs was indescribable. But he didn't fight Pascale. Christ, he needed all the help he could get. 'Good God, have mercy,' he heard Pascale mutter contemptuously under his breath as he struggled to help him towards the door. 'Walk, dammit. I'm not carrying you, *idiot*. Fucking walk. Or I'll leave you here.'

'I can't fucking walk! I can't fucking see!' Klyne snarled and gritted his teeth as another searing spasm shot through his groin.

'Then I'll kill you now.'

'What?' Klyne blurted out in horror.

'Your choice,' Pascale told him and pressed the barrel of his Colt .38 into the small of Klyne's back. 'The cops are probably on their way, as we speak. And I'm not doing time for you. So either we leave together, or I leave alone. You'd better make up your mind fast.'

'I'll walk, but you're going to have to help me,' Klyne replied, desperation in his voice.

'Then let's go.'

·Every step was unbearable. He felt as if he had already gone through the pain threshold and had now entered a new dimension of suffering. But still he moved. They reached the bottom of the stairs. He was able to see more clearly now. The front door was open. It didn't appear to have been kicked in – which probably meant that the bitch had fled, and already called for reinforcements. He was grateful to see the car parked out front. He was less grateful to see several neighbours peering apprehensively at them from behind tweaked curtains. Fuck them. They were both unrecognizable under their disguises.

Pascale pulled open the back door, shoved Klyne unceremoniously inside, then slammed it shut again and hurried round to the driver's door. He started up the car, slipped it into gear, then pulled away sharply from the kerb and disappeared around the bend in the road.

Barely thirty seconds later, the first of the back-up units that Taylor had told Sarah to call arrived on the scene. Deputy Marshal Robert Robideaux was riding shotgun in the lead car. He was totally pissed off with the situation in general, and with Jack Taylor in particular . . .

Four

'What took you so long?'

'We got here as soon as we could, Mrs Johnson,' Robideaux replied breathlessly, having jumped from the car and dashed up the path to the house when he saw the front door wide open. She estimated him to be in his mid-fifties, and the sedentary desk job would account for the extra weight he was carrying.

'Not quick enough,' she replied bitterly. 'Jack Taylor took a bullet protecting me, while you were still deciding whether to respond to my call. I don't even know if he's dead or not.'

'Not,' a voice announced behind her.

Sarah looked round and her face lit up in a broad smile, more out of relief than anything else. 'Jack, you're alive,' she exclaimed and instantly realized how stupid that sounded with him standing there on the porch. 'I saw him shoot you. I was at the top of the stairs. I thought you were dead, the way you fell. You don't even look injured.'

'Bruised, along with my ego,' Taylor replied with a grin, then he patted his chest with his fist. 'I'm wearing a protective vest under my shirt. I always do in these kind of situations. What you saw was me being knocked off my feet by the force of the bullet. I hit my head on something hard. Probably the banister. Then dreamland. What happened with you? How did you manage to shake him?'

Sarah explained briefly what had occurred in the bathroom, culminating in her fleeing down the stairs and taking refuge in a neighbour's house, where she had waited anxiously until the back-up units arrived on the scene. Then, when she had finished and the full impact of what she had just been through finally came together in her mind like some cerebral jigsaw, she started to cry. Deep, racking sobs which seemed to emanate from her very soul. There were so many different emotions struggling inside her – anger, fear, relief. And vulnerability.

Taylor was about to put a comforting arm round her, but then pulled back his hand at the last moment, deciding that she wasn't the type who would appreciate some patronizing gesture on his part. Instead, he took her arm and led her to the steps and gently, but firmly, sat her down. She buried her face in her hands as the tears continued to flow. A much-needed catharsis. Taylor walked back to where Robideaux was standing, apparently unmoved by her sudden breakdown.

'Everything that's happened here tonight will be going into my report, Taylor,' Robideaux assured him after lighting himself a cigarette. 'What were you thinking when you agreed to go along with this whole charade? It could have got you both killed.'

'She elected to remain behind at the house,' Taylor said, gesturing to where Sarah was still sobbing into her hands. 'What was I supposed to do? Leave her to the mercy of the assassin?'

'You were supposed to have made her see sense and moved her, with her family, to the safe house.'

'Then maybe you should try talking some sense into her, because it sure as hell didn't work with me,' Taylor said, and there was a faint smile on his lips as his eyes flickered towards Sarah, who had now raised her head and was staring directly at him. The tears appeared to have stopped as quickly as they had started. She managed a weak smile in return.

'I fail to see the humour in any of this,' Robideaux snapped indignantly, mistakenly thinking that Taylor was being facetious.

'Actually, you'd be surprised at how easy it is to find comfort in humour after you've just cheated death.' Taylor gently massaged his bruised chest with his middle finger. 'But then I wouldn't expect you to understand that. There's nothing about that in any of the manuals, is there? Just a load of politically correct rules and regulations that we're expected to obey at all times. Boring, Robideaux. Really boring.' He looked past Robideaux at the man approaching him. 'How are they?'

'Both had been handcuffed together and cold-decked, but they've since come round. No serious damage, but the paramedics are checking them over anyway. Just to be sure.'

'What are you talking about?' Robideaux demanded.

'I sent one of your men to check on Kane and Hungate,' Taylor told him. 'The assassin had an accomplice. He hijacked the car to make sure they couldn't step in to help me when the assassin hit the house.'

'Oh my God, this gets worse,' Robideaux said desperately and ran his hand over his thinning hair.

'Yeah, well I'll leave you to sort it out,' Taylor announced. 'I'm taking Mrs Johnson to the safe house. I think she's had enough excitement for one evening.'

'You're not going anywhere,' Robideaux told him bluntly. 'This is a major incident, Taylor. And it happened on my shift. I've already got my superior breathing down my neck, demanding answers. You're the only one who has those answers. You're staying right here until I'm satisfied you've told me everything that happened tonight.' He turned to Sarah. 'I'll have one of my men drive you to the safe house, Mrs Johnson.'

Taylor noticed the uncertainty in Sarah's eyes. He nodded at her. 'Go on. I've got it covered here. And I know you want to see Lea. I'll give you a call in the morning, see how you're all settling in.'

'Thanks, Jack. For everything.'

'It's not over, Sarah,' he replied, responding to her use of her first name. 'You know as well as I do that Genno won't give up this easily.'

'Don't worry, I've got a few surprises of my own for Frankie, now that we know he is on to me,' she said resolutely.

'Mrs Johnson, leave this to us,' Robideaux told her sternly. 'You start taking the law into your own hands and we can't protect you. You'll be on your own.'

'I have no intention of breaking the law,' she assured him. 'But if you think I'm just going to sit around waiting for Frankie's goons to regroup so that they can have another go at me, or my family, then you'd better think again.'

'And just what exactly do you intend to do?' Robideaux enquired, struggling to contain his rising anger.

'It's your job to protect me and my family. I suggest you concentrate on that. Because let's face it, you haven't exactly done a very good job of it so far.' Sarah looked at the cluster of deputy marshals standing in the vicinity. 'So which of you gentlemen is taking me to the safe house?'

None of them volunteered. Robideaux addressed the nearest deputy. 'Let Mrs Johnson pack a bag, then you take her. I want two units to go with you as back-up. One car up front. One behind.' The man issued these instructions to the other deputies around him and they headed off towards their parked vehicles, while he followed Sarah into the house.

'She's strong-willed, that one,' Robideaux mused as he watched her disappear. He ground his cigarette butt underfoot and immediately lit himself another. 'Did you get a look at the man who shot you?'

'No. He put me down before I had a chance to see his face. Sarah will probably be able to give you a description of him. It's my guess that he's military. Or, at least, ex-military.'

'Why do you say that?' Robideaux asked.

'The dummy stun grenade. The way he launched the attack. The double-tap. Two shots in rapid succession. Both in the same area. That smacks of military training to me. I could be wrong, but it's worth checking out anyway.'

'Dummy stun grenade?' Robideaux asked incredulously. Taylor explained it to him. 'Clever,' Robideaux muttered, then turned towards the house as Sarah re-emerged, carrying a holdall. 'That was quick.'

'It was already packed,' she told him. 'I didn't think I'd be here very long if Frankie was on to me.'

'I want you to give us a full statement once you reach the safe house.' Robideaux shot Taylor a scornful look. 'It seems you're the only person who actually saw the gunman.'

'He was wearing a heavy disguise. That much I did see.' She then handed a sheet of folded paper to Taylor. 'That's the alarm sequence. Will you set it after everyone's left the house?'

'Sure.'

'What should I do about the broken window?' she asked.

'There will be a uniformed cop on duty here for the rest of the night,' Robideaux assured her. 'We'll call a glazier for you in the morning.'

She took a set of keys from the pocket of her blouson and gave them to Taylor. 'They're for the house. You can bring them to me tomorrow.'

'I will.' Taylor touched her lightly on the arm. 'We'll find these men, Sarah. You have my word on that.'

She forced a quick smile, then headed off in the direction of the waiting cars.

'I'm glad you're so sure we'll nail the bad guys,' Robideaux said after the three-car convoy had driven off.

'What's the alternative?' Taylor countered.

Robideaux took a deep drag on his cigarette and blew the smoke up into the cloudless night sky. 'And if we do, what then? Maybe they'll finger Genno as the paymaster to reduce their own sentences. Only Genno is doing life without the possibility of parole. What's he got to lose? He'll just hire someone else to go after her.'

'So what are you suggesting? Having Genno iced by another con?'

A look of horror flashed across Robideaux's face and Taylor knew he'd said the wrong thing. To the wrong person. 'We're law enforcers, not vigilantes. Is that your solution, Taylor? Killing Genno?'

'No,' Taylor replied with a sigh, 'but it might be what Sarah Johnson's thinking right now.'

'If she breaks the law, she'll face the consequences. You can tell her that from me. And that's no idle threat either.'

'I know what you're thinking, Robideaux. She won't go for it. I can tell you that now.'

'How do you know what I'm thinking?'

'Because you play it by the book. That means uprooting her, and her family, giving them new identities and relocating them in another part of the country. She won't buy it. She's finished running from her past.'

'It's the only other option open to her.' Robideaux bristled.

'It's the only other option open to *you*.'

'At least I'm doing my best to try and protect her, and her family, according to the directives laid down by the Marshals Service. I wasn't the one who put her in the line of fire, was I?'

'Perish the thought.'

'Let's get this wrapped up here as soon as possible, shall we?' Robideaux said, ignoring the sarcasm. 'I'm going inside to check how much forensics still have to do. Then, once they're done, we can lock up and go back to the office where I'll expect a full written statement detailing your part in the incident here tonight.'

Taylor watched Robideaux climb the steps to the porch, where he paused to examine the shattered window before entering the hallway and disappearing up the stairs. He sat down slowly on the bottom step and noticed for the first time the crowd of inquisitive onlookers who had gathered in the street in front of the house. They were being kept back by a couple of uniformed cops, but in the main they appeared more interested in gawking from a safe distance than infringing on the actual area of investigation. But that wasn't what was troubling him. He'd had an uneasy feeling in the pit of his stomach ever since he was first alerted to the presence of the bogus priest in the street. One man to take out Sarah, and an accomplice to tackle the two deputies in the surveillance car. Genno would have known that with the murder of Ted Lomax and the subsequent theft of his computer files the Marshals Service would close ranks round all those witnesses on the list. So why just hire one man to take out Sarah? The bogus priest obviously already knew that there would only be Sarah and himself in the house when he planned the attack. Otherwise, surely he'd have brought in extra firepower to counter any larger threat from within the house? How did he know? There could only be one conceivable answer: inside information. Taylor had chosen not to say anything to Robideaux. Hell, the bastard would probably work it out for himself before long, anyway. But then, Jack Taylor couldn't afford to trust him. He couldn't afford to trust any of the local members of the Marshals Service. Not if there was a mole in the unit. But who was it?

Sarah was driven to Westwego, a small neighbourhood on the southern edge of the city, a predominantly fishing community bordering the Bayou Senette. The three cars pulled up beside a jetty and Sarah saw the black speedboat bobbing gently in the murky waters of the bayou, tethered by a rope looped round a thick wooden bollard. To her left she could make out the silhouettes of at least a dozen small shrimping boats; dark, desolate and deserted under the clear night sky.

She was helped aboard the speedboat by the deputy marshal behind the wheel, then the rope was cast off and the engine burst into life, shattering the stillness of the surroundings. A second deputy sat down beside her on the wooden seat which spanned the width of the stern. His colleague arced the speedboat away from the jetty in a 180-degree turn, then headed upriver.

'How far is it to the safe house?' she called out to the marshal beside her, above the noise of the engine.

'Not far,' came the rather gruff response.

'Are you part of the security at the house?'

'Ah-ha.' He nodded without looking at her, which was just as well since his words had been drowned out by the sound of the engine.

'Did you take my husband and daughter there earlier this evening?'

'Ah-ha,' he replied, then added, 'Your husband's real talkative.'

Sarah knew this to be true, but she wasn't sure whether the

comment had been aimed indirectly at her as well. She fell silent and soon her mind was drifting back over the dramatic events of the evening. It certainly hadn't gone as she had hoped. Or planned. But then what had she expected? It had been a calculated risk which had nearly gone horribly wrong. At least she knew now that Frankie was on to her, and she could take the necessary countermeasures. She knew exactly what to do. Though it was doubtful whether Jack Taylor would back her after the incident at the house. And she still needed him. As she had said to Lea earlier that afternoon, she would see Frankie burn in hell before she let him anywhere near her family. Admittedly, a bit dramatic at the time, but the sentiment behind her words hadn't changed since then. Not that she had any intention of having Frankie bumped off. No, she wanted him to suffer every second of every minute of every day for the rest of his life. What's more, she knew exactly how to do it. But there would be a price to pay. For her, and her family. And that's what troubled her most of all . . .

A hand on her arm startled her out of her thoughts. 'That's the safe house up ahead.'

She followed the marshal's pointing finger. At first she couldn't see anything, but as the speedboat drew closer she was able to make out the outline of the house on the riverbank. Compact. White wooden walls. Black roof. A single light was visible behind the curtains across the window overlooking the river. The vessel reduced speed and a figure emerged from the house and hurried down the grass verge towards them. She noticed the shoulder holster over his polo-neck sweater. He caught the rope tossed to him and secured it round the bollard at the foot of the wooden jetty. He held out a hand towards Sarah, who although confident that she could disembark unaided, took it all the same and jumped nimbly on to the boards. The deputy, who had been sitting beside her, retrieved her holdall from under the bench and followed her up to the house.

The door was opened for her and when she stepped inside she found herself in the kitchen. It was basic, but practical: a wooden table positioned in the centre of the room; four chairs. Cards were scattered across the table, as if a game had been interrupted and left unfinished. She wondered how many security personnel there were at the house. Probably too many, and it could get damned intrusive in such a confined space.

'Is it just the three of you out here?' she asked.

'Yeah,' replied the marshal, who had met the speedboat. His eyes went to the table. 'We were playing a few hands of poker with your husband, before the call came through to pick you up at Westwego.'

'How much has he lost?' Sarah asked suspiciously.

'Who says he lost?' the pilot of the boat said with a faint chuckle.

'That laugh for a start. And the fact that Bob's the worst poker player this side of the Milky Way.'

The three men grinned at each other. 'He hasn't lost much,' the pilot assured her. 'We haven't been playing for high stakes, anyway. None of us can afford it – not on our salaries.'

'Do you play?' one of them asked.

'Better than Bob,' she replied with a knowing smile. 'Where is he? And Lea?'

'Your daughter's in her room. She's been there since we brought them over here. Bob's in the living room, watching TV.'

'Where's Lea's room?' she asked, moving towards the door.

'I'll show you,' the pilot told her and he pushed open the door and stepped out into the hall in front of her.

'What's your name?' Sarah asked, following him.

'Ray Deacon.' He paused outside the second to last door at the end of the hall. 'I was asked to get a statement from you about what happened at the house earlier tonight.'

'Can't it wait until morning?' Sarah pleaded. 'It's been a really stressful day, as you can well imagine. I just need some downtime with my family.' She noticed the hesitation in his eyes. 'I gave a full description of the priest to one of your colleagues on the way over here in the car. That's all you need at the moment, isn't it? Surely the rest can wait until morning?'

'OK, but first thing tomorrow morning,' Deacon agreed, then indicated the door. 'This is Lea's room. As Dave said just now, she's been in there ever since we arrived. We took her some food earlier. She didn't touch it.'

'Thanks.'

'Sure. I'll leave you to it.'

'Can you tell Bob I'm here?' she called after him as he walked off.

'Will do.'

Sarah knocked tentatively on the door. No response. 'Lea?' Nothing. 'Lea?' she repeated, this time louder. Nothing. She tried the handle. The door was unlocked. She eased it open. 'Lea?' Still no reply. She opened the door fully. Lea was lying on her bed, her back to the door, oblivious to her surroundings as she listened to her portable CD player through a pair of headphones. The music was loud enough for Sarah to hear it from the doorway. Which was why Lea hadn't come out to meet her when she had first arrived at the house. She was about to cross to the bed and shake Lea's shoulder, but decided not to creep up on her without any warning. So instead she flicked the light switch on and off. Lea looked round, and then removed the headphones, switched off the music, and sat up with her back against the wall, her knees drawn up to her chest. Sarah could sense the tension between them.

'Something happened at the house, didn't it?' Lea said, staring intently at her mother. 'Otherwise you wouldn't be here. You'd still be sitting it out there with Jack the Lad, wouldn't you?'

Sarah sat at the foot of the bed. 'Yes, something did happen. Unfortunately, the guy got away.'

'But you're . . . OK?' Lea asked hesitantly.

'I'm fine,' Sarah assured her.

It was then that Bob appeared in the doorway, having been alerted to his wife's presence. 'Well?' he demanded, coming in to the room. 'What happened?'

Sarah told them what had taken place earlier at the house.

'Taylor certainly showed himself up, didn't he?' Bob snorted disparagingly after she had finished. 'You could have been killed, for God's sake.'

'Jack Taylor risked his life for me,' Sarah shot back scathingly, and got to her feet ready to confront her husband on level terms.

'Maybe he should have listened to this Robideaux guy in the first place,' Bob retorted. 'He sounds like the only one with a bit of sense in this whole damn set-up. And maybe you should have listened to him as well. What if the gunman had killed you tonight? Genno would have got his revenge. And Lea would have lost her mother. Why? All because you had to prove a point to yourself.'

'I wouldn't expect you to understand, Bob. You've never stood up to anybody, or anything, in your life. You just let everybody walk all over you. You only have to look at the current state of your business to see that.'

A look of fury flashed across Bob's face as he stepped forward, and before Sarah had a chance to react, his hand was already raised to strike her. Lea stepped quickly between her parents, her eyes riveted on her father's face. 'If you want to hit Mom, you're going to have to go through me first,' she said icily, 'so if you want to hit me, go ahead. Do it.'

'Oh my God,' Bob exclaimed in horror when he realized how close he had come to striking his wife in front of his own daughter. But would he have really done it? He sat down slowly on the wooden chair by the door. 'No,' he said, as if to answer himself. Then he looked up at Lea. 'I wouldn't have done it, *ange*. You know that. I couldn't have done it.'

Sarah slumped down on to the bed and buried her face in her trembling hands. Never before had she ever seen Bob so angry. And he had every right to be after what she had said about him. It was totally out of line, and she knew it. 'I didn't mean what I said,' she whispered, slowly raising her head to look at him. 'I'm sorry.'

'Is everything OK in here?' Deacon asked, poking his head round the door, drawn by the sound of raised voices.

'Yeah,' Bob said, getting to his feet. 'I was just leaving anyway. That game still on in the kitchen?'

'Sure, you want in again?'

'Bob, we need to talk this through,' Sarah pleaded.

'What I need is a drink,' Bob retorted bitterly. 'You guys got any booze in the house?'

'We never keep alcohol on the premises, for obvious reasons,' Deacon told him.

'Just my luck. Let's see if I can change that with the cards. Why not up the stakes while we're at it?' With that Bob left the room.

'You want me to send him back to talk to you after he's cooled down? Deacon asked Sarah.

'He'll talk when he's ready.'

'You know where I am if you need anything,' Deacon said before leaving them.

Sarah moved to the window and pushed the curtain aside with the back of her hand. A security light illuminated a small garden bordered on all sides by a hedge she estimated to be at least twelve foot high. A mesh cage stood in the shadows in the corner of the garden. It was padlocked, though she couldn't see what it contained, if anything. She let the curtain drop, and then picked up the portable CD player. 'What are you listening to?' she asked.

'You don't have to make small talk, Mom,' Lea said behind her.

'It's all I've got at the moment.' Sarah replaced the CD player on the bed, then turned to Lea. 'Your father's right. If something had happened to me earlier at the house . . .'

'It didn't,' Lea said, when her mother broke off abruptly in mid-sentence, struggling to control her frayed emotions.

'No, not this time.'

72

'What are you saying, Mom, that you're going to set yourself up as a target again? What for? You know now that Genno's on to you. It's why you stayed behind at the house tonight. Let the authorities handle it from here on in. That's their job.'

'What more can they do to him, Lea?' Sarah asked.

'We went through all this at the house earlier this afternoon. You said that you'd wait until Genno showed his hand, then make your own move against him. Does that include standing in the open with a bull's-eye painted on your forehead?'

'It involves a certain amount of risk,' was all Sarah would venture.

'Why can't you tell me what you're going to do?' Lea demanded, hands on hips.

'It's not appropriate.'

'What's that supposed to mean?'

'Lea, I'm not discussing it with you.'

'Why, because I'm just a kid and I wouldn't understand? Is that it?'

'Because I don't want to involve you any more than I already have. Is that wrong?' Sarah retorted angrily. She instantly regretted her outburst and reached out a hand towards Lea.

'Don't,' Lea said sharply, drawing away from her mother. She lay down on the bed and draped the headphones round the back of her neck. 'Just go, OK?'

'Lea, I don't want to leave it like this between us,' Sarah pleaded, but her daughter had already slipped the headphones back over her ears and switched on the music. Then she turned away from her mother, her chin resting in the cup of her palm.

Sarah had always hated to leave any situation unresolved, especially when there were negative feelings involved. And Lea knew that only too well. That hurt. Sarah wanted to pull off the headphones and make Lea talk to her. Not that it would have settled anything. She desperately wanted to keep Lea out of her machinations. And if they were to come to any sort of compromise, Lea would expect her to confide in her. That wasn't going to happen. She had to protect Lea at all costs. She only hoped Lea would come to understand that one day.

Sarah left the room and as she closed the door behind her she heard the sound of laughter coming from the kitchen. She contemplated sitting in for a few hands, if only to take her mind off Frankie for a while, but quickly dismissed the idea. She wasn't in the mood for cards. She knew she wouldn't be able to concentrate on the game, and would probably lose anyway. Bob could do that just as well for both of them. She decided instead to do a tour of the house and familiarize herself with her surroundings. The first door led into a bathroom. Standard fittings. Everything there for the short-term hermit. She moved to the next door and was about to open it when she heard the sound of a man's voice coming from inside the room. It was Bob. So he wasn't playing cards in the kitchen after all. In the past she would have just walked in on him regardless. They had never had any secrets from each other. How things had changed. A sudden thought came to her. What if he was on the phone to Renée Mercier? She put her ear to the door, hoping to listen in to what was being said. If she could just catch him . . .

'. . . you wouldn't believe. It's pretty isolated out here, but hopefully we won't be stuck in the boondocks for too long.' Pause. 'I miss you too, *chérie*, but I don't see how I can possibly get away from here. There's no way I can just sneak off without . . .'

Sarah didn't need to hear any more. *Chérie*. So that's what he called her. How *fucking* sweet! She pushed down the handle and thrust open the door. Bob was sitting on the double bed, receiver in hand. He looked round in surprise at her. She stormed over to where he was sitting, wrenched the receiver out of his hand, and slammed it down into its cradle.

'What the hell are you doing, Sarah?' Bob demanded.

'You want to whisper sweet nothings to her, that's fine by me,' she responded angrily, 'but at least have the decency to do it when I'm not in the next room.'

'Sweet nothings?' he replied, feigning a look of bewilderment. 'What the hell are you talking about, Sarah? That was Peter Hughes, the company's lawyer. I needed to clarify—'

'Do you normally call him *chérie*?' Sarah interjected scathingly. 'I know what's going on, Bob, so you can drop the act.'

'You know what's going on? Well, at least one of us does. Perhaps you'd care to enlighten me.'

His smug, patronizing tone only fuelled Sarah's rising anger and unzipping her holdall, which the deputy had left on the floor, she removed the folder and flung it on to the bed. Several of the incriminating photographs spilled out into view. His whole body language altered in an instant. His shoulders dropped, his back slumped and the sparkle of conflict in his eyes vanished, to be replaced with a look of disbelief. He slowly reached out a hand and picked up one of the photographs. 'Where did you get these?' he asked in a shaky voice.

'Does it matter?'

'You've been spying on me?' He tried to inject some anger into his voice, but only succeeded in sounding as though he was winded and trying to catch his breath. The fight had gone out of him.

'No, I hired a private detective to follow you. He only confirmed what I'd already guessed ever since the day I first met your new secretary. She wasn't very good at hiding her feelings for you.'

He opened the folder, ignored the typed report, and concentrated instead on the accompanying photographs. Each picture had its own memory for him. Only those memories were now irreparably tarnished. 'It was never anything serious, Sarah. You've got to believe that.'

'So it was physical, rather than emotional. Is that what you're trying to say?'

'Yeah, I guess you could say that,' he replied weakly.

'So you're not in love with her?'

'Hell, no,' he replied with a throaty chuckle.

'Does she know that?'

Bob frowned momentarily, then slowly shook his head. 'I never actually said it to her . . . you know. Maybe . . . she thought I did . . . I don't know.'

'Was she in love with you?'

'I guess,' he replied with equal uncertainty.

'You're pathetic, you know that?'

'Sarah, please, you've got to understand. After the trial I was really low. Depressed. I couldn't turn to you because we were having our own problems at home. Renée was there . . . for me. It just kinda . . . happened, you know? It meant nothing, you've got to believe that.' He reached a hand out towards her as if in some misguided attempt to try and bridge the psychological chasm which had opened up between them.

'Touch me and you'll be wearing that arm in a sling,' Sarah warned him in a soft, menacing voice. She didn't move.

He quickly withdrew the offending arm. 'I'm sorry. I realize that this must be a difficult time for you with everything that's already happened today.'

'And you thought that up all by yourself, did you?' she snorted contemptuously.

'What do you want me to say, Sarah?' he countered resentfully, stung by her biting sarcasm.

'What do you want to say?'

'Whatever I do say, you'll just shoot down in flames anyway. So what's the use?'

'To be honest, I'm really not interested in your excuses, or your apologies. Certainly not at the moment. I've got far more important things on my mind. But once I've got Frankie off my back, we can discuss this again. Until then, I don't want to know. I suggest that in the interim we at least try to maintain a cordial atmosphere between the two of us, if only for Lea's sake. But I'd be grateful, all the same, if you'd stay out of my way as much as possible. And I'll do the same. That way you can call her up—'

'It's over, Sarah,' he cut in, palms upturned towards her in a placatory gesture. 'I swear it's over.'

'That way you can call her up whenever you want and whisper as many sweet nothings into her ear as she can handle in a single orgasm,' she completed the sentence calmly as if he had never interrupted her.

'For God's sake, Sarah, it's over between Renée and myself. Finished. Terminated. Ended. Is there something about that you don't understand?'

'I just told you, I don't want to know about any of this until I've got my own problems sorted out.'

'I just wanted you to know, that's all.'

Sarah scooped up the photographs and replaced them in the folder, which she then handed to him. 'I suggest you pack your things, then go and find yourself somewhere to sleep.'

'But I thought . . .' he trailed off disconsolately, making a feeble gesture towards the double bed he was sitting on.

'Well, think again. While I'm here, this is going to be my room.'

'What do you mean, while you're here?' he asked suspiciously. 'You're not thinking about setting yourself up again like you did earlier this evening? You could get yourself killed next time.'

'What *I'm* thinking is that I'm tired, irritable and in desperate need of some sleep. It's been a long day and I want to go to bed. Now pack your things and get out.' She placed her holdall at the foot of the bed, as if laying claim to the territory for herself, then looked straight at him. 'Is there something about that *you* don't understand?'

Jack Taylor pushed back the swivel chair and, getting to his feet, crossed to the window and looked down on to a virtually deserted street below him. He was in the federal courthouse building on

76

Camp Street, the district office of the United States Marshals Service covering eastern Louisiana.

It was three o'clock in the morning and he was exhausted. More so mentally than physically, having just completed a written statement detailing the events of the previous evening. Robideaux had insisted it be done, together with a disclaimer stating that he had not been in collusion with either Taylor or Sarah and had known nothing about their plans beforehand. It was his way of trying to cover his own ass when the report finally landed on the chief deputy marshal's desk in the morning. Personally, Taylor thought it made him look guileless at best, incompetent at worst. The incident had occurred on his watch, and here was Robideaux professing to have only found out about it afterwards. That would certainly look good on his record! But Taylor had more pressing problems of his own to worry about. The main one being whether he would still be on the case once his superiors back at the Office of General Council in Arlington, Virginia, had been briefed on the situation. Nor did he know whether Robideaux had come up with the name of the bogus priest, or his accomplice, who had hijacked the surveillance car and taken the two deputy marshals out of the loop.

He picked up the pad and made his way down the corridor to Robideaux's office. The door was closed. He knocked. No reply. Opening the door, he peered inside. Nobody there. He closed the door behind him and went in search of the skeleton night shift he'd met briefly when he had first arrived at the courthouse, shortly after midnight. He found one of the deputy marshals glued to a computer screen in the squad room.

'How's it going?' he called out as he came into the room. 'Any luck?'

'Could be,' the marshal replied. A faint smile touched his lips when he saw the pad in Taylor's hand. 'You done writing up your report?'

'Yeah.' Taylor tossed the pad on to the desk. 'So what you got?'

'Possible name for your padre. It's being checked out as we speak.' The marshal's fingers played over the keyboard, then he brought his finger down theatrically on the final key. A face appeared on the screen. 'Name of Paul Klyne. Did time at Stateville for his part in an armed robbery over in Shreveport a couple of years back. Released earlier this year. He's a mercenary, but hasn't been abroad for a few years now.' He glanced at Taylor. 'Recognize the face?'

'Nope,' Taylor replied, staring intently at the screen, 'but then he was heavily disguised. Still, I'd stake my pension on it being him.'

'You seem very sure.'

'I told Robideaux at the time that I liked this guy either as military or ex-military.'

'We like him too, especially as he and Genno were known to hang out together at Stateville.'

'Which makes me even more certain it's him. It's a known fact that Genno rarely mixes with any of the other cons at Stateville. Keeps very much to himself.'

'As I said, Klyne's being checked out by our colleagues in Florida as we speak. Unfortunately, he doesn't have any fixed address that we know of, so we're having to check out his regular haunts, which seem to be mainly in and around the Miami area these days. So far, we haven't found him.'

'It's him. It's gotta be.' Taylor crossed to the percolator, poured some coffee into a Styrofoam cup, then eyed the unpalatable brew disconcertingly. 'Is it as bad as it looks?'

'Appearances can be deceptive. Actually, it tastes worse than it looks.'

'In that case, I think I'll give it a miss,' Taylor said, depositing the cup on the table beside the percolator. 'Where's Robideaux? I checked his office before I came here. He wasn't there.'

'He's with Chief Deputy Marshal Elworthy. They've been in the Chief's office for the past forty minutes.'

'Sounds ominous.'

'The Chief's all right. You'll see. Robideaux's the pain in the ass around here.'

'I'll take the Fifth on that,' Taylor said diplomatically, with an accompanying grin for good measure.

'Why don't you go through? Second door on the right.' The marshal tossed the pad to Taylor. 'The Chief's sure to want to hear your side of the story. Hell, you were there. You weren't running operations from the safety of your desk.'

'Doesn't anybody around here have a good word for Robideaux?' Taylor asked, surprised by the disdain in the deputy's voice.

'I believe it's my turn to take the Fifth.' The deputy marshal watched Taylor head off in the direction of Elworthy's office. 'Hey?' he called out after him and waited for Taylor to look round before adding, 'you only did what any of us would have done in your position.'

Taylor nodded grimly, then completed the short distance to Elworthy's office and knocked lightly on the rippled glass.

'Come,' a voice boomed out. Taylor opened the door, but remained in the doorway. Harlan Elworthy was in his mid-fifties: broad-shouldered, with a crew cut and a prominent acquiline nose. The reading glasses seemed out of place on the rugged face. 'You must be Jack Taylor?' he said, removing the glasses to study him more carefully.

'Yes, sir. I hope I'm not interrupting anything. I just thought you might want to read my report. I've just finished it.'

'Come in. Close the door. Sit down.' Each sentence sounded like a command.

Taylor nodded an acknowledgement to Robideaux, who was already seated in one of the leather armchairs in front of Elworthy's desk. No response. He noticed that Robideaux's normally flushed face looked decidedly pale. 'My report, sir,' Taylor said, extending the pad towards Elworthy.

'Put it on the table, son,' Elworthy told him with a vague flick of his huge hand. 'How long did it take you to write it up?'

'A couple of hours, sir,' Taylor told him.

'A couple of *wasted* hours,' Elworthy rejoined. 'The difference between Robert and me is that he's your regular desk man. It's not a criticism. Hell, he's a natural when it comes to paperwork. And that suits me just fine because I hate that side of the job. I was a field operative for over thirty years before this happened and forced me to re-evaluate my life.' It was only when Elworthy tapped the arm of his chair that Taylor realized he was in a wheelchair. 'Bullet in the spine. Paralysed from the waist down. It was either early retirement or a desk job. This is the lesser of two evils.' A smile followed. 'Seriously, though, I'd still rather be out there chasing the bad guys. But, it's not to be.' He sifted through several folders in front of him before selecting one, which he held up for Taylor to see, and then promptly tossed it back on to his desk. 'I read your file earlier. You've got an impressive track record there, son. So what on God's earth made you turn your back on a promising career in the field and join up with Internal Affairs? You guys are despised wherever you go. My people still think you're a field agent down from Washington. That was your territory, wasn't it? If they thought for one moment that they'd got IA in their midst, they'd close ranks quicker than a virgin's legs on prom night. And you could kiss this case goodbye, because they wouldn't lift a finger to help you. But, much as I dislike IA, I'm not about to make any waves for you while you're here. The contents of your file won't leave the confines of this office.'

'I appreciate that, sir.' Taylor told him.

'So why *did* you join IA?' Elworthy pressed.

'My wife wanted me out of the field and closer to home after we got married. I was offered a training position at Arlington, as you'll know from my file, but I was never cut out to put a bunch of recruits through their paces. It just wasn't me. Like you, I wanted to get back into the field. The only other opening in that area was out on the west coast. Christine's a very successful state attorney in Washington. She wasn't about to uproot and leave everything she'd built up for herself in Washington and resettle in San Francisco. And rightly so. The only alternative was IA, based in Arlington. So I took it.'

'Any regrets?' Elworthy asked.

'Life's full of regrets,' Taylor replied with a quick shrug.

'Don't worry, son, I'm not going to pry into your private life,' Elworthy assured him. 'Robert and I have already spoken about what happened with Sarah Johnson tonight. Robert's always been over-cautious, which is not a bad thing in itself. He's the voice of reason around here. And there are times when we need that. I'm more like you though. Prepared to improvise where necessary. OK, so it didn't turn out as you'd hoped, but at least now we know that Genno is on to her. How you handle the situation from here on is your affair. As long as you don't break the law or step on any toes while you're in New Orleans, you've got a free rein to handle the case as you see fit. Robert will continue as your liaison and assist you in any way he can.'

'Thank you, sir,' Taylor said, glancing at Robideaux. Not surprisingly, there was no reaction from him.

'I'm going out on a limb for you on this one, son. Don't abuse that trust or I swear I'll bury you where you fall. And you will fall, quicker than you could ever imagine was possible. Do we understand each other?'

'Yes, sir.'

'Robert, I'd like a word alone with Taylor.'

Robideaux got to his feet and left the room.

'Is he going to be all right with this?' Taylor asked, after Robideaux had closed the door behind him.

'Don't underestimate Robert. He can be a first-class pain in the ass at times, but he's a damn good deputy none the less. He'll be a district commander long before I ever get there. He plays it by the book, which includes knowing how to take orders from a superior officer. You won't have any trouble from him, although he will ensure that you complete all your paperwork before you return to Washington.' Elworthy chuckled at Taylor's mock-pained expression, then wheeled himself round from behind his desk. 'Between the two of us, what are you going to do about Genno?'

'I don't understand, sir?' Taylor said uncertainly.

'Robideaux said you'd hinted earlier tonight at getting another con to stick Genno with a shin,' Elworthy said, using the jail slang for a knife.

'I never said any such thing!' Taylor retorted indignantly. 'He sure knows how to twist a guy's words to suit himself.'

'It may be the only way, son. Have you thought of that?'

Taylor held Elworthy's questioning stare for a few moments, then got to his feet and moved to the window. He watched a taxi drive past the courthouse, the only moving vehicle in sight. His mind was racing. Was this a carefully baited trap to see how far he would go to protect Sarah? Or was Elworthy actually sanctioning murder? Was that why Elworthy had asked Robideaux to leave the room, knowing there would be no comebacks? It would be his word against that of a deputy if the conversation ever left the room. Either way, Taylor knew better than to commit himself. Not that he had a plan in mind to deal with the situation. Not as yet. He turned back to Elworthy. 'I'm the first to admit that I'll bend the rules if need be, but I won't ever break them.'

'Bend them enough times and you'll eventually break them.' Elworthy smiled in an attempt to diffuse the sudden tension in the room. 'Look, I'm not saying you should arrange to have Genno killed. What I am saying is that it's an option you may have to consider if all else fails. Problem is, you don't have many options open to you. And you'll have even less time to put them into practice, especially if you're right about Sarah Johnson not wanting to uproot and relocate under a new identity. Robideaux said you'd told him that.'

'That's the feeling I got from talking to her, but I haven't actually broached the subject with her as such. At least, not in so many words.'

'Then maybe you should – and soon,' Elworthy suggested.

'I'll be speaking to her again in the morning.'

'It's already morning,' Elworthy grumbled, looking at the wall-mounted clock behind his desk. 'I was just getting ready for bed when Robideaux called me at home. If I'm lucky I'll still get a few hours' sleep. I suggest you do the same.'

'I will. I need it.'

Elworthy wheeled himself to the door, opened it, then looked back at Taylor. 'You've heard that we've put a possible face to the priest?'

'Yes, sir. Paul Klyne. I'm pretty sure it was him at the house tonight, given his military background.'

'We've already put an APB out for him with all the law-enforcement agencies across the country. I want him found quickly, so that we can either charge him or eliminate him from the investigation.'

'It is him, sir, I'm sure of it,' Taylor said resolutely.

'Even if it is, it still won't stop Genno. He'll just find someone else to take Klyne's place. That guy's been stewing behind bars for the past eighteen years, waiting for the one chance to finally get even with Sarah Johnson. You may need to break the rules this time, son. It may be the only way to stop him before he does exact his revenge. Her life could depend on your decision. Good night.'

'Night,' Taylor replied absently after Elworthy had already disappeared out into the corridor. A lot to think about in a short space of time. Although tired, he doubted whether he would get much sleep that night . . .

Klyne awoke with a start, having fallen asleep in front of the television. For a moment he was disorientated, then remembered he was in Pascale's apartment. Footsteps approached on the bare floorboards in the hallway, and Pascale appeared in the doorway, a bag of groceries cradled in one hand. 'Hey, Klyne, how's it hanging?'

'Fuck you,' came the sharp riposte.

'Not in your condition,' Pascale said with a loud guffaw, as he put the groceries down on a small table. 'How's the hand?'

'It's hurting a bit,' Klyne replied with a shrug, but he winced when he tried to flex it. Pascale had removed the sliver of glass embedded in the back of his hand and had bandaged the wound. 'You get my stuff from the hotel?'

'Yeah, but the fuck at the desk charged me the full whack. I tried telling him you hadn't slept in the room, but he wasn't interested. I just gave him the money to shut him up. I've left your bag by the front door. You can sleep on the couch. It folds out into a bed. It's the best I can do.'

'You get the beer?' Klyne asked, gesturing to the bag on the table.

'Yeah, help yourself. I also got us a take-out. Probably cold by now. I had a few people to see while I was out.'

'I'm not hungry anyway. Throw me a beer.'

Pascale took a can from the packet and tossed it to Klyne, who leaned forward to catch it with his good hand. 'You spoken to Genno's mother yet?'

'I'll ring her first thing in the morning,' Klyne replied, then broke open the tab and took a long drink from the can. 'If we'd pulled it off, I'd have called her right away. Why wake her with bad news?'

'She's going to chew you out for fucking up, isn't she?' Pascale said, chuckling to himself, before lighting a cigarette and sitting down. 'That's why you're putting off phoning her, isn't it?'

'It's not *her* I'm worried about.'

'What d'you mean?'

Klyne drank another mouthful of beer, and then slumped back in the chair. 'I don't know how Frankie's going to take it. I really don't.'

Five

'No . . . no . . . no!' he screamed, pounding his manacled hands repeatedly on the narrow table in front of him.

'Genno!' the correctional officer yelled, then hurried over to where Genno was seated, head tilted backwards, eyes glazed, teeth bared in an animal-like snarl. The correctional officer had been taken aback by Genno's abrupt outburst. In all the time he had been at Stateville, he had never known Genno to raise his voice, let alone in front of his mother, who was sitting on the opposite side of the metal grille. 'Genno, any more shouting and you're back in your cell for the rest of the day.'

'Yeah?' Genno retorted, his voice challenging; a cold, vindictive look in his eyes.

'Yeah,' came the firm reply. He had never seen Genno in such an agitated state. It made him uneasy. Not that he showed his disquiet. You never exhibited any weakness in front of the prisoners, or they'd take full advantage of it.

Genno saw the look of anxiety on his mother's face, and glared at the officer. 'You want to back off now so that I can have some privacy to speak to my mother?'

'Then speak, don't shout.' The officer wagged a finger of warning at him, then returned to his vigil by the door.

'Francis, there was no need for that!' His mother chided him like a naughty child. 'Don't stress yourself unnecessarily. You don't want to get another peptic ulcer, do you?'

'No, definitely not!' He had a history of ulcers, going back to his childhood, and knew only too well that nervous strain was one of the main factors in bringing one on. 'I'm sorry, Ma. It's just that . . . I expected the Preacher to have fulfilled his side of the bargain. He's not going to get another chance now.'

'We don't know that, Francis.'

'It's not going to take the authorities long to put two and two together. And when they do put a name to the Preacher, he's going to have to watch his own back. You can be sure that they'll try their best to shaft him in an attempt to get at me.'

'I hear what you're saying, Francis, although I can't say that I particularly approve of the analogy.'

'Believe me, Ma, that kind of analogy goes on in here every day,' Genno said with a scornful laugh.

'I really don't wish to know that,' she bristled, screwing up her face in disgust, and wriggling her shoulders, as if trying to shake off the intrusive, ungodly image it conjured up in her mind.

'You're right, you don't.'

'What do you want me to do now?'

'Tell the Preacher to come back home.'

'I don't understand,' she said, with a confused frown. 'If there's still a chance that he can—'

'I told you, Ma, he's blown it. Big style,' Genno interjected. 'All you can do now is reach out and gather him back into the fold. Is that a better analogy for you?'

'Much better, Francis. What exactly have you got in mind?'

Genno tapped the side of his nose and gave her a winning smile. 'Leave it with me. What I will need you to do is cash in the balance of your investment account. I may need access to the money at short notice.'

'Francis, don't do anything rash.'

'I've been in here eighteen years, Ma. I learned the art of patience a long time ago. Another few days aren't going to make any difference to me. I intend to get this right.'

'Be careful.'

'Always, you know that. This isn't over, Ma. Not by a long way.'

Sarah couldn't remember how long she'd been sitting on the jetty. Certainly for a few hours. She had watched the sun come up over the bayou and had felt a pang of guilt that in all the years she had lived in New Orleans, she had never once bothered to take the time to witness such a breathtakingly beautiful sight. She had just taken it for granted, like so much else in her life. So many recriminations . . .

She hadn't slept the previous night. The double bed she had commandeered from her husband still had her holdall on it. He might as well have made use of it for all the good it had done her. Ah, but it's the principle, isn't it? she had kept telling herself. Just one of hundreds of unsettled thoughts which had swirled around in her head during those dark hours before dawn. Then again, she doubted he would have got much sleep either after she had confronted him about his affair with Renée Mercier. At least you're not referring to her as 'that bitch' any more, she thought caustically to herself. Now there's progress for you.

She had finally fled the bedroom, if only to escape her feelings of claustrophobia. In the kitchen she had found a sole marshal on duty at that hour of the morning. He was the one who had sat beside her in the speedboat. His name was Beau. On the table there was an array of electronic gadgets which, according to Beau, would ensure that nothing, or nobody, could approach the house without being detected. He had then gone on to explain how each one worked. It was the closest she had come to falling asleep all night.

·Armed with a mug of coffee, she had eagerly escaped into the garden. It was only then, when the first traces of dawn broke gently over the horizon, that she had been able to determine the precise locale of the safe house. It was built on a small island, which was little more than a spherical hump of grassland surrounded on all sides by the cold, murky waters of the bayou. There were no marshlands and no trees in the immediate vicinity. Three hundred and sixty degrees of perfect visibility, which made it impossible for any vessel to approach without being seen. She had ventured on to the jetty, where she had sat beside the moored speedboat, her bare legs dangling over the side, her feet not quite reaching the water. Beau had only interrupted her solitude once, to warn her that while fully grown alligators never ventured that far downriver, preferring to conceal themselves in the haven of swamps and marshlands located much deeper in the bayou, there were baby 'gators around which, despite being too small to drag a human underwater, could still take off a few toes if the temptation was presented to them. Her response had been to swing her legs back up on to the jetty and pull them up protectively to her chest. Beau had laughed at her reaction and returned to the house.

She was still sitting there with her legs pulled up, arms wrapped round her knees, the untouched coffee now cold in the mug beside her. Although she had since managed – as best she could – to rearrange her thoughts into a semblance of order, she had wanted to concentrate on her strategy to counter any future aggression on Frankie's part, but instead found she couldn't seem to shake off what had happened between Bob and herself the previous night. Had she been right to confront him about Renée Mercier? Wasn't there enough hostility between them already, without adding to it? Couldn't she have waited for a more suitable time? All she had done was to create even more tension between them, which would ultimately filter down to Lea. She was particularly worried about how Lea was handling the situation. It was almost as if she were blocking out the reality of what was going on around her. Holed up in her room. Headphones on, withdrawing further into herself. Uncommunicative. And when she was coaxed out of her shell, she was invariably confrontational, which only put up further barriers between mother and daughter. Bob seemed to be Lea's sole ally in all this. Not that Sarah had a problem with that. Lea needed to draw on one of them for solace. But what if she were to discover that he had been having an affair? How would that affect her already precarious emotions? A mother who'd been living a lie all her life, and a father who'd been secretly screwing his secretary? It could tilt her over the edge. Nobody to trust. Nobody to turn to for support. Sarah realized then that her struggle was now focused on two fronts. Inwardly, to protect Lea; outwardly, to neutralize Frankie. It only strengthened her resolve to keep Lea in the dark about Bob's infidelity, at least for the time being. She accepted that the truth would have to come out eventually, especially if the marriage was heading for meltdown. It was a sobering thought, and one she hadn't really contemplated until that moment. Did she want to save her marriage? Could she ever trust Bob again? Conversely, could he ever trust her again? It went both ways. A carousel of secrets and lies . . .

'Morning.'

Sarah looked round, startled by the voice, then smiled fleetingly at Ray Deacon who was standing at the end of the jetty. 'You want another coffee?' he asked, holding out a mug towards her. 'Milk. No sugar. Beau says that's how you take it.'

'Thanks,' she replied, picking up the mug beside her and tossing the unpalatable contents into the water. 'I'll try and drink this one. Where is Beau?'

'He's gone to bed. It's my shift.'

'Have you seen Bob this morning?' she asked, taking the mug of steaming coffee from him.

'He's fast asleep on the couch in the living room. You guys had a spat last night, didn't you?'

'I suppose that's one way of putting it. What about Lea? Is she up yet?'

'Could be, but her door's still closed.' Deacon crouched down beside her, a mug of black coffee cradled between his hands, and looked out over the tranquil waters of the bayou. 'I could get used to this kind of life. It's like we're in another world out here. No traffic. No noise. No nothing. Yeah, this is the business.'

'Is this your first time at the safe house?'

'It's a first for all of us. The last place got blown a couple of months back. You probably read about it in the papers. Guy called Vinnie Edwards was shot dead at a cabin on Bayou Bardeaux. It's a bit further upriver.'

'Can't say I remember,' Sarah replied, shaking her head.

'Obviously, we played it down. Made it out to be a local homicide. Vinnie was also in the WITSEC Program. He was a pit boss working at one of the Mob's casinos in Vegas. We got him to testify against the Family. Put away a couple of big heavyweights out there.'

'How long did it take the Mob to find him?'

'Three months, but then Vinnie was an asshole. Couldn't keep his mouth shout, especially after a few drinks. He didn't make it too hard for them to track him down. A couple of our guys were slightly injured in the firefight, though that never made the papers. But the end result was that we had to find ourselves another safe house. And quickly. This is it. Even more isolated than the last one.' Deacon patted her on the shoulder, then stood up. 'Don't worry, Klyne won't find this place.'

'Who's Klyne?' Sarah asked, shielding her eyes from the sun as she squinted up at him.

'You won't have heard yet, will you? Robideaux rang earlier this morning. They've put a name to the priest. Paul Klyne. Served time with Genno at Stateville. Taylor didn't recognize the mug shots, but then he did say that Klyne was wearing a disguise. We're pretty sure it's him, though. Taylor's coming out here later this morning. He's bringing the file with him so that you can have a look. You might recognize him.'

'I doubt it. I didn't exactly get a good look at his face under the disguise.'

'I heard you gave his *cojones* a wake-up call, though. Maybe we should put out an APB for a guy with a real distinctive walk.' Deacon waddled bow-legged for several steps and grinned at Sarah when she put her hand to her mouth to suppress a chuckle. 'You know, that's the first time I've seen you laugh since you got here. I know it can't be easy for you. Not for any of you.'

'You're right there,' Sarah agreed. Her cellphone, which she had earlier tucked into one of the pockets of her knee-length dungarees, began to ring. She pulled it out. 'Hello?'

'Mrs Johnson?' a voice enquired. She didn't respond. 'This is Derek Farlowe.'

Sarah cupped her hand over the mouthpiece and looked up at Deacon. 'Would you excuse me, please?' She waited until he had gone back into the house before removing her hand again. 'Sorry about that. Are you in Joliet yet?'

'I flew up last night. Charter flight. It cost a bit, I'm afraid, but you did say you wanted me to get here as soon as possible.'

'That's fine. How's it going up there?'

'I'm done.'

'You're kidding!' Sarah exclaimed in disbelief.

'It doesn't pay to kid in this line of business, Mrs Johnson. I got in at around eleven last night. Bought a street map. Hired a car. I've been up all night. But it's paid off. I got your package, as requested. It's in a locker here at the airport. I've left the key for you at the information counter. You can pick it up whenever you want.'

'You're a godsend, Mr Farlowe, do you know that?'

'For the money you're paying me, Mrs Johnson, I'll be anything you want me to be. I thought I'd better check in with you before I left. I'll tell you something, though, I'm going to sleep like a baby on the flight back to New Orleans.'

'You deserve it. We'll settle up in the next few days, if that's all right with you?'

'Yes, that will be fine,' he said.

'Thank you, Mr Farlowe. You've saved my life.'

'Well, I'd hardly go that far.'

'Believe me, you have. Thank you again. Bye.' Sarah switched off the cellphone and a faint smile of satisfaction touched her lips as she gazed across the tranquil water. 'It's my turn now, Frankie. Let's see how you like a dose of your own medicine.'

'Out of the question!'

'Surely it has to be worth a try?' Sarah replied, standing with Taylor at the foot of the jetty, out of earshot of those in the house.

'You want to go to Stateville and speak to Genno? What good would that do?'

'I could try and reason with him.'

'Oh, I'm sure that would work,' Taylor replied, shaking his head

89

in frustration. 'Chances are he wouldn't even want to see you, let alone listen while you tried to reason with him.'

'He'll speak to me all right. Don't you worry about that.'

'You seem very sure of that.'

'I know Frankie,' was all Sarah would venture.

'No, you *knew* him. Eighteen years ago. Things have changed since then.'

'Not for Frankie. He's still caught up in his own little time warp. He hasn't changed his appearance in the last eighteen years, has he? It's obvious that he's still living in the past. And I'm an integral part of that past. I'm probably the one person still capable of getting through to him.'

'How do you know about his appearance?' Taylor demanded.

'Ray Deacon told me. He heard it from a colleague in Illinois. Why, are you saying it's not true?'

'What I'm saying is that this is a nonstarter, Sarah. My superiors would never go for it. And rightly so. You'd be playing straight into Genno's hands.'

'So what do you suggest?' Sarah challenged. 'That we sit it out here until Klyne's apprehended? Then what? Wait for Frankie to send another hatchet man after me? This is a no-win situation, Jack. It *has* to be resolved.'

'There is a solution. The only practicable one as far as I can see.'

'You spirit us away in the dead of night, give us new identities, then dump us in some strange town on the other side of the country? Am I right?'

Taylor shifted uneasily on his feet and a loose wooden board creaked under his weight. 'As you said, even if we were to catch Klyne, there's no guarantee that Genno wouldn't just send somebody else after you. Your cover's been blown, Sarah. It's not safe for you, or your family, to stay in New Orleans any more. You always knew there was a chance this could happen when you joined the WITSEC Program.'

'Sure, but then I was a rehabilitated drug addict fresh out of detox. All I wanted was to put the past behind me and get out of Chicago as quickly as possible.' She held up a hand to silence him as he was about to respond. 'I hear what you're saying, Jack. I don't like it, but I also realize that it may be the only way out. What I don't want, though, is to have to drop everything at a moment's notice, then up and disappear without a trace like I did when I left Chicago. As you said, things have changed since then. I've got a successful life here now. If we do have to leave, I want the chance to put some of my affairs in order first. If only for my own peace of mind. That's why I want to meet with Frankie. It might just help give me that extra bit of time I need.'

'And how will meeting with Genno give you that time?' Taylor asked.

'That's between Frankie and me.'

'What's that supposed to mean? Have you got something on him?'

'You could say that,' Sarah conceded, with a thoughtful nod of her head.

'If you've got something on Genno—'

'It's nothing that you can use against him,' Sarah was quick to tell him. 'You've got to believe me on that.'

'Oh, I do, do I?' Taylor stubbed the rusted head of a loose nail with the tip of his shoe before looking at her again. 'It doesn't matter anyway. There won't be any meeting between you and Genno at Stateville, or anywhere else for that matter. It's not going to happen.'

'Then I'll just have to do it on my own. There's no law against me visiting an inmate in prison, is there?'

'I could easily block any meeting between you and Genno. One phone call to the warden and you wouldn't be allowed into Stateville. It would be that simple.'

'And here I thought you were on my side,' she said bitterly.

'You know I am.'

'Then prove it! Get me in to see Frankie. Just him and me. Face to face.'

'One on one?' Taylor replied in amazement, then shook his head. 'No way would the authorities go for that. Not with the history that already exists between the two of you.'

'Frankie's wrists and ankles would be manacled. I'd be perfectly safe with him.'

'It wasn't *you* I was necessarily worried about.'

'What . . . you think . . . that I'd . . .' Sarah trailed off and shook her head disdainfully. 'Credit me with a little intelligence, will you? If I attacked Frankie, which I wouldn't do anyway, I'd end up behind bars myself. Then I would be a sitting target.'

'I'd never be able to sell this to my superiors, even if I wanted to,' Taylor said at length.

Sarah remained poker-faced, although inside she felt a surge of excitement. She sensed that he was coming round to her way of thinking. 'The first thing you told me when you got here this morning was that you'd been given the all-clear to remain in charge of this case. That makes this your call, Jack. Not your superiors'. Weren't you the one who was so adamant at the house yesterday that you were your own man when it came to making decisions in the field?' Her voice softened. 'Let me speak to Frankie. It may not achieve anything, granted, but it can't hurt either, can it? It's not as if he doesn't already know my new identity. Or where I live. Or that I have a family. This is *my* life we're talking about. I have to talk to him, Jack. Please.'

'You said that you've got something on Frankie. What?' Taylor said after considering her words in thoughtful silence.

'I told you, that's between Frankie and me.'

'You want my help, Sarah, then you're going to have show some goodwill on your part as well. Whatever you tell me won't go any further than the two of us. You have my word.'

Sarah felt as though she was caught between the proverbial rock and a hard place. She sensed that he was ready to accede to her request for a meeting with Frankie. But if she were to hold out on him now, he could well turn her down. He had stuck his neck out for her once already and almost got himself killed in the process. It was time for her to repay some of the trust he had shown in her. With that thought in mind, she told him about Farlowe's trip to Joliet, without mentioning him by name, and the package he had left for her at the airport.

'You've certainly got it all worked out, haven't you?' Taylor said, when she had finished.

'Wouldn't you, if you were in my position? I've got to look out for myself.' She noticed Bob emerge from the house, pause to look around him, and then give them a hesitant wave. 'Well, Jack, what do you say? Will you set up the meeting?'

Taylor watched Bob walk slowly towards them. 'I'll see what I can do. Now, if you'll excuse me?' He acknowledged Bob with a nod as he passed him on the way back to the house.

'How's it going?' Bob asked awkwardly, pausing at the end of the jetty, careful to keep a respectful distance from her.

'Good. You?'

'Yeah, good,' he replied with a quick shrug, then added with a nervous chuckle, 'I didn't sleep too well last night, though. The couch in the living room isn't exactly my idea of comfort.'

'Well, you'd better start getting used to it,' she said incisively, and strode past him back to the house.

*

He had been half expecting it ever since he'd learnt that Klyne had botched the hit in New Orleans. Genno was summoned to see the warden at eleven o'clock that morning. The new warden. Six months into the job. He'd seen the warden from a distance, but had never actually met him before. Not that this would be a social visit. Maybe there would be Feds, or even deputy marshals, in attendance as well. What could they do? Charge him with being an accessory to attempted murder? Assuming, of course, they had any evidence against him. Then what? Go on trial? Get another ten years in jail? Yeah, that would be good. He found the whole thing ludicrous in the extreme. But they had to do their job. Not that he would admit to anything. Let them do the talking. Find out what they knew. After all, he had nothing left to lose any more . . .

'Genno, on your feet!'

He stood up. He had been sitting on a wooden chair in the outer office while he waited for the warden to see him. His hands were manacled and secured to a belt around his waist. His legs were unshackled. Officer Doug D'Amato grabbed him firmly by the arm and led him into the warden's office. There were no Feds. No deputy marshals. Just the warden. Genno felt somewhat cheated, but he pushed the thought from his mind. At least it got him out of his cell for a while. That alone had to be worth the trip.

'Francis Genno?' the warden said, consulting the folder in front of him.

Genno wanted to say 'present' like a kid hauled up before the headmaster for misbehaviour, because that's what it felt like as he stood in front of the warden. He said nothing. What was he supposed to say? Of course he was Francis Genno.

'This is the first time I've met you, Genno,' the warden said. He closed the folder, removed his glasses and sat back in his leather chair. 'I've heard a lot about you since I took over here. *The* model prisoner. Very impressive, especially for a lifer like yourself.'

'I like to keep to myself,' Genno replied with a bored shrug.

'So I believe.' The warden reached for the mug of coffee on his desk, took a sip, then put it down again. 'Tell me, Genno, how do you feel about Anne Stratton?'

So this was how he was going to play it, Genno thought. It didn't matter. He wasn't going to let anything slip. 'It was her choice to testify against me in court, but, having said that, a lot of water's passed under the bridge since then.'

'You know that she was put into the WITSEC Program after the trial, don't you?'

'I heard that, yes,' Genno conceded with a nod of the head.

'There was an attempt made on her life last night. Obviously, you wouldn't know anything about that, would you?'

'Of course not,' Genno replied, affecting surprise. 'I certainly hope the culprit was caught.'

'No, I didn't think you would,' the warden said, making no attempt to mask the sarcasm in his voice. 'It's an interesting hypothesis we've got here, Genno. Let's say for argument's sake that you'd found out her new identity, and where she now lived, and then hired someone to kill her. What measures could be taken against you if anything were to happen to her? A maximum period in solitary, perhaps? Transfer to another jail? It's all pretty tame, isn't it?'

'As you said, it's hypothetical,' Genno replied with a cold smile.

'Or you could remain here, as a known informer,' the warden concluded, returning the smile.

'I'm no informer!' Genno rejoined angrily and took a threatening step towards the warden's desk, fury now in his eyes. 'I've always abided by the code of this prison. I don't snitch. Everybody knows that.'

D'Amato grabbed Genno roughly by the arm and hauled him back to his original spot. 'You do that again, and you'll get the baton across your back,' he whispered menacingly in Genno's ear before withdrawing to the door again.

'I don't have to tell you, of all people, just how quickly a rumour can spread through this facility, Genno,' the warden continued, 'and it's even more persuasive if the original source happens to be one of my senior correctional officers. Someone like Officer D'Amato, for instance. The inmates tend to listen to him.'

'I had nothing to do with the attempt on Annie's life,' Genno insisted furiously. 'Why won't you believe me?'

'Because you're a felon, Genno. And felons lie. It's in their nature.' The warden sat forward and clasped his hands together on the desk. 'I'm not the only one who thinks your fingerprints are all over this whole affair. The Marshals Service like you for it as well. So does Anne Stratton, for that matter. In fact, she's so convinced it's you that she's put in a request to visit you here in person, presumably hoping to try and reason with you. Frankly, I think she's wasting her time.'

'Annie's . . . coming here?' Genno said in astonishment.

'It's up to you whether you want to see her. I certainly can't force you. It's your decision.'

Genno was baffled. Why was Annie travelling all the way up from New Orleans to see him? What did she hope to achieve? He would just deny having had anything to do with the attempt on her life the previous day. Surely she knew that? Another thought came to him. Did she have something on him? Yet the more he thought about it, the more he was ready to dismiss the idea out of hand. He'd been locked up for all these years. It wasn't as if he'd done anything she could use against him. No, chances were, she was going to try and reason with him, as the warden had suggested. Yeah, that made sense.

'Well, do you want to see her or not?' the warden demanded.

'Sure, I'll see her,' Genno replied, careful to suppress the mounting excitement he felt inside him.

'I'll let the Marshals Service know of your decision. That's all.'

'Let's go, Genno,' D'Amato said, opening the door.

'I had nothing to do with the attempt on her life last night,' Genno said, moving towards the warden's desk again. 'I want you to know that.'

The warden, who had already turned his attention back to the paperwork on his desk, looked up slowly at Genno, his eyes narrowing suspiciously behind his glasses. 'Then you'd better pray that nothing else happens to her, because if it does, I'll make sure that you're branded an informer and leave you to the mercy of the other inmates.'

Genno shrugged off D'Amato's hand angrily when he tried to grab his arm, and leaned over the warden's desk. 'You've got no fucking right—'

'Get him out of here,' the warden cut in irritably, glaring at D'Amato, who grabbed Genno by the arm and roughly hauled him out into the corridor. Genno was still railing vehemently against the injustice of the warden's threats against him when D'Amato closed the office door behind them. Once clear of the office, D'Amato shoved Genno forward with such force that he stumbled, lost his balance and fell heavily to the tiled floor. He was still struggling to get on to his knees when the first blow of the baton slammed excruciatingly into the small of his back.

'I was wondering when you'd come round to that way of thinking.'

'What are saying, that you suspected Klyne had a contact in this office right from the start?' Robideaux asked Taylor.

'How else would he have known about the location of the surveillance car, or that I was alone in the house with Sarah?' Taylor countered, and then looked at Elworthy who was seated pensively behind his desk. The chief deputy marshal remained silent.

'Then why didn't you voice your suspicions earlier?' Robideaux demanded.

'To whom?'

'I am your liaison officer here in New Orleans,' Robideaux reminded him.

'You could also have been Klyne's inside man for all I knew. I couldn't take the chance of confiding my suspicions to you.'

'That's preposterous. I was never a suspect.'

'Weren't you?' Taylor asked, turning to Elworthy for support.

'You never suspected me, did you, sir?' Robideaux protested.

'Why should you be treated any differently, Robert?' Elworthy raised a hand to placate him. 'I've already had a thorough check done on you. You're clean. That's why you're here. This can't go any further than the three of us, at least not until the results of the investigation are known.'

'Who's handling the investigation?' Robideaux asked, knowing that Elworthy was only doing what he would have done in the same circumstances. But it still irked him that he could ever have been considered a suspect. It also wounded him after all his years of dedicated service, but he would never let those emotions surface in front of a superior.

'It has to be handled independently. That's why I called in the local cops earlier this morning. They're doing covert checks on all those deputies who have, or had, access to this case. I'm convinced that's where we'll find our snitch. Hopefully, they'll have something for me before long. We need to plug this leak quickly before any more damage can be done to the good name of this department.'

'What about the safe house? Could that have been compromised as well?' Robideaux asked, with a hint of unease in his voice.

'No, each part of this operation has been compartmentalized,' Elworthy assured him. 'Its location is known only to those deputies who were assigned to guard the Johnsons while they're staying there. And none of them knew of Sarah Johnson before they were brought in last night, at very short notice, I might add, to take the Johnson family to the safe house. And similarly, those deputies detailed to watch the Johnsons' house don't know the location of the new safe house. That way, if there is a breach of security, the knock-on effect will be minimal.'

'I guess that's one way of putting it,' Taylor said, and instinctively traced the tip of his finger lightly over the two bruises on his chest where the bullets had slammed into his body armour. He knew only too well that it could have been a very different outcome had Klyne chosen a head shot instead. It was a sobering thought, but one which he didn't dwell on for very long.

'You saw Sarah Johnson this morning, didn't you? How's she bearing up?' Elworthy asked Taylor.

'Pretty well, all considering.'

'Did she get that charter flight to Stateville at midday?'

'Yes, sir, she did. I appreciate you setting it up so quickly.'

'It helps to have contacts in the right places,' Elworthy replied.

'What charter flight?' Robideaux looked from Taylor to Elworthy. 'Am I missing something?'

'Sarah Johnson's on her way to Joliet to speak to Genno,' Elworthy told him. 'Jack cleared it with me this morning. I don't see that it can do any harm.'

'Why wasn't I informed of this?' Robideaux demanded, glaring at Taylor.

'You weren't around,' Taylor said.

'I've been here *all* morning.' Robideaux turned to Elworthy. 'Sir, if I'm supposed to be Taylor's liaison while he's in New Orleans, then I feel it's only right that he should go through me if he wants something done. I knew nothing about the charter flight until you mentioned it.'

Elworthy gave Taylor a suspicious look. 'You told me on the phone this morning that you couldn't get hold of Robert. If he was in the building, he would have been contactable. You didn't even try and get hold of him before you rang me, did you?'

'If I'd gone through Robideaux, Sarah would still be sitting at the safe house waiting for a reply. I had to take the initiative. That's why I rang you directly. I knew I'd get a quicker response that way.'

'That's not the way it works down here, son. You want something, you go through Robert. You don't go over his head and come to me. We have a chain of command in place here. We all use it. I expect you to do the same. Is that clear?'

'Like I said, sir—'

'*Is that clear?*' Elworthy interjected, purposely stressing each word for maximum effect.

'Yes, sir. Perfectly clear.'

'As I said to you last night, this is your case and you call the shots. But should you require our help, you go through Robert. Bear that in mind, because if you pull another stunt like this you'll be on the next flight back to Washington. And your superiors will be left in no doubt whatsoever why I kicked you out of my city.'

Taylor sensed that Robideaux was watching him, enjoying his obvious discomfort. He chose not to give Robideaux the satisfaction of meeting his haughty stare.

The telephone rang. Elworthy was quick to answer it. 'Yes, speaking,' he said, then his eyebrows furrowed questioningly as he listened in silence. 'Well, I'll be damned,' he exclaimed at length. 'To be honest, he's the one person I wouldn't have suspected.' Pause. 'How much?' he blurted out, and then shook his head to himself as he raked his free hand over his cropped hair. 'It sounds like he's been doing a few more deals on the side as well. Has he been taken into custody?' Another pause and his expression became increasingly grim. 'So you've got no idea where's he's gone?' Pause. 'I'll have my men check out all his known haunts, but I doubt whether he'd go to any of them. He's no fool.' Pause. 'I appreciate you letting me know so quickly. When can I expect to receive a full report from you?' Pause. 'Thank you. Obviously, I'll keep you informed of any new developments at this end.'

'Have the local cops found your mole?' Taylor asked after Elworthy had replaced the receiver.

'Found him, then lost him. He managed to escape through a window at the back of his house, after the cops had found a secret stash of money under a floorboard in his bedroom. He obviously didn't have time to grab it before he fled. They're talking about something in the region of thirty grand, but they won't know for sure until they've counted it. They also found a notebook, with Genno's name in it. Five grand had been written beside the name. Obviously the pay-off for passing on the inside information to Klyne, or this mysterious second man.'

'Who was it?' Robideaux asked.

'Eddie Hungate.'

'But he got whacked first in the car,' Robideaux said. 'If he was in league with Klyne, surely it would have made more sense to whack Kane and have Hungate speak to Taylor on the radio.'

'Which is obviously why they decided to do it that way, to deflect suspicion away from him in the event of any subsequent investigation,' Taylor concluded.

'And to heap further suspicion on Kane,' Elworthy added, 'two deposits were put in his account in the last couple of days. A thousand dollars two days ago. Another thousand earlier today. Both in cash. Untraceable. He was being set up as the patsy. And the cops would have fallen for it as well, had they not found Hungate's secret stash at his house.'

'You need to find him quickly,' Taylor said. 'He obviously knows the identity of Klyne's accomplice. And if they know he's on the lam, they're also going to go after him, to silence him before the authorities can get to him.'

'Don't I know,' Elworthy said despondently. 'I just hope Sarah Johnson has more luck when she gets to Joliet than we're having here at the moment.'

'I wouldn't count on it, sir,' Taylor said grimly.

'Neither would I, son.' Elworthy exhaled deeply. 'Neither would I.'

Six

'Mrs Johnson?'

Sarah, who was sitting in an otherwise empty waiting room where she had been taken after being cleared to enter the correctional facility, looked up from the dog-eared magazine she had been absently flicking through to help pass the time. The uniformed figure seemed to fill the whole doorway. Cropped hair. Lantern jaw. Well-toned physique. He reminded her of the stereotypical sadistic guard – and there was always one – in those prison movies on late-night TV. The one who invariably got his comeuppance at the end. Then his mouth broadened in a friendly smile and in that instant his whole face softened and she suddenly felt guilty for her initial perception of him. Then again, what better place to feel guilty, she thought to herself.

'Yes, I'm Sarah Johnson,' she said, getting to her feet.

'I'm Officer Doug D'Amato,' he said, extending a hand towards her. She took his hand tentatively. It instantly engulfed her own, but she found his grip gentle, though firm. 'The warden asked me to escort you to where you'll be meeting Frankie Genno, then bring you back here again once you're through.'

'Escort? As in *bodyguard*?'

'Don't worry, Mrs Johnson, you won't be exposed to any of the other prisoners while you're here. It's lock-down at the moment, anyway. You won't be going anywhere near the cells.'

'That's a relief. I had visions of having to walk the gauntlet between the cells.'

'In a maximum security facility for male prisoners?' D'Amato chuckled softly to himself. 'You've been watching too many movies. Mrs Johnson.'

Sarah felt her cheeks flush as she thought back to her first impression of him.

'Many of the men incarcerated here are exceedingly dangerous,' D'Amato said, his voice now serious. 'They've committed the sort of crimes that you couldn't imagine even in your worst nightmares. It is essential that you stay with me at *all* times, and do not go anywhere without my express authorization. This facility is a maze of corridors. It's not difficult to get lost in here. I still do, on occasion, and I've been here for the past twelve years. Do as you are told, and *don't* go wandering off by yourself. I cannot emphasize that enough, Mrs Johnson. But as long as you remember that, you'll be fine.'

'Consider me your second shadow from now on,' Sarah assured him.

She walked in silence beside D'Amato and found herself thinking back over the day, ever since Taylor had informed her that the warden at Stateville had provisionally approved her request to visit Genno – assuming that Genno agreed to meet with her. But she never had any doubt of that. She knew Frankie wouldn't throw up the chance to see her again. Not after all those years of planning his revenge against her. Taylor had arranged the charter flight for her. She had no idea whether the six-seater Cessna Crusader belonged to the Marshals Service, and the pilot hadn't enlightened her further during the flight. The Cessna had touched down at Joliet Park District Airport and a correctional officer from Stateville had been on hand to drive her to the prison. She knew that the pilot had instructions to refuel, then wait for her at the airport until she was ready to return to New Orleans. The more she had thought about it, the more certain she was that it was a federal plane, despite the lack of any telltale markings on its fuselage. Once she reached Stateville, she had passed through a metal detector, and had been given a thorough body-search by a female officer. It had been both uncomfortable and degrading, but she had understood the necessity for such a procedure, given the pervasive menace of narcotics not only at Stateville but at every state penitentiary in the country. As visitors devised increasingly elaborate methods to outwit the authorities and smuggle in drugs, prison guards had to be ever more vigilant. Or so Taylor had told her when he explained the procedures she would be expected to comply with once she arrived at Stateville.

'We're here,' D'Amato said.

'Sorry?' she replied, and then gave him a quick smile. 'I was miles away.'

'I can understand that. It helps to block out the reality of this place.' D'Amato gestured to a closed metal door, with a small window in the upper centre. 'This is one of the visiting rooms. Normally, someone like Genno wouldn't be allowed to see anyone in here. But don't worry, you'll be quite safe from him.'

'Do I go in and wait for him?' she asked hesitantly.

'He's already there.'

'Oh, my God,' Sarah exclaimed, and instinctively took a step away from the door.

'Are you all right?'

'Yes,' she replied irritably, angry at herself for her overreaction. It was just that she hadn't expected Genno to be there. Then again, what difference did it make? She was damned if she going in smelling of fear. Because if she did, he would pick up the scent very quickly. And that would defeat the whole purpose of her visit. She had to get a grip on her emotions. Fast.

'His ankles are shackled and his wrists are manacled to the table which, in turn, is bolted to the floor,' D'Amato told her. 'He can't get out of the chair without our assistance. So don't worry, he can't touch you. There's an officer with him at the moment. We'll both remain in the corridor while you're in there. There's a panic button concealed under the table. If, at any time, you feel uncomfortable and want out, press the buzzer once and we'll open the door straight away. The same goes once you've finished. Just tap the buzzer once. Are you ready to go in?'

'Yes,' she said, and then took a couple of deep breaths. 'I'm ready.'

D'Amato activated the door and pushed it open. The correctional officer inside the room looked from D'Amato to Sarah, then slipped past them into the corridor. 'You sure you're going to be OK?' D'Amato asked her.

'I'll be fine. Thanks.'

'Don't forget, just tap the buzzer once when you want out.'

She felt a ball of uncertainty in the pit of her stomach and wanted to step tentatively into the room. But she knew she had to appear confident. When she had first devised this plan, she'd had no problem with her own convictions. Except that you were seven hundred miles away at the time, she reminded herself. He thinks you're playing by his rules. But you're not. And that gives you the psychological edge. Utilize it to maximum effect. Because if you don't, he will! Now get in there . . .

She tightened her grip on the attaché case she was carrying and, head up, strode purposefully into the room. The door closed behind her. The room was small. Claustrophobic and uninviting. It had a concrete floor and white windowless walls. A single light hung from the ceiling. There was a table and two chairs. One occupied.

It was only then that she looked at Genno, and in that instant she felt as if she had been transported back in time. Chicago. Eighteen years ago. The hair was still long and dishevelled. The beard still ragged and unkempt. The eyes still cold and intense.

'Hello, Annie,' Genno said softly, after she had pulled up the chair and sat down opposite him. He had been watching her closely ever since she had first entered the room. 'You're looking . . . good. Different, but good. Obviously your new life agrees with you.'

'And you still look like a dinosaur,' she countered icily.

'My life came to a standstill when they put me in here. How can I change my appearance until I've finally managed to put all those ghosts behind me, once and for all?'

'In other words, until you've got your revenge?'

'Revenge?' He sat back without taking his eyes off her face. 'Now what makes you think I'd want revenge?'

'You can cut the crap, Frankie. We both know you sent that bogus priest to the house to try and kill me.'

'I really don't know what you're talking about.' He shook his head sadly to himself. 'And here I thought you'd come to reminisce about the old days. We sure had some good times back in Chicago, didn't we?'

'I'm not wearing a wire, if that's what you're worried about. We can talk freely.'

'That's good to know, Annie,' he said, feigning bewilderment.

'Will you stop calling me Annie!'

'And what should I call you?' came the curious reply.

For a moment she was caught off guard. What if he hadn't hired Klyne to kill her? Then the thought evaporated as quickly as it had entered her mind. No, Frankie had sent him to the house last night. She had no doubts of that. Despite the assurances to boost her own self-confidence, she still chose her reply carefully. 'You know very well what my name is now. How else would you have known where to send your hired gun?'

Genno held her unflinching stare, then the corners of his mouth twitched into a slow smile which was partially concealed underneath the thicket of beard around his lips. 'So, tell me about Lea? She's fifteen now, I believe. Does she look like you? Do you have a picture of her with you?'

'You did send that hired gun to the house last night, didn't you?' she demanded angrily when she realized that he was toying with her.

'*Quid pro quo*, Annie. It's Latin. Means something for something. You'd be amazed at the wealth of information contained in the prison library. It's just a question of digging it out. So what do you say? You tell me something about Lea—'

'Fuck you, Frankie!' she cut in savagely.

'Ah, a bit of the old Annie spirit surfacing again.' A look of mock concern crossed his face. 'I hope you don't speak like that in front of Lea. Hardly the kind of example you'd want to set your daughter, now is it?'

'I thought I could come here and reason with you. Obviously I was wrong.'

Genno frowned thoughtfully and looked slowly round the room, as if pondering the implications of what she had just said, then his eyes settled on her again. 'Tell me, is Lea as good as you?'

'What?' came the quizzical response.

'You used to give great head back in Chicago. I wonder whether Lea also enjoys getting down on her knees in some dimly lit alleyway—'

The rest of his sentence was torn from his lips when she leapt out of her chair and caught him with a hammering punch to the side of the face, snapping his head sideways. His body jerked grotesquely in the chair, restrained by his manacled wrists which tethered him securely to the table. He leaned his head forward to wipe his cheek across his upper arm and smiled faintly to himself on noticing the smear of blood left behind on his overall.

'They say the truth hurts, Annie. Maybe it's too close to the bone for you, not knowing whether your little girl enjoys giving head as much as you did.' He tilted his head back and laughed disdainfully, but kept his eyes on her as she stood beside him, fists clenched tightly at her side. 'You want to take another swing at me, Annie? Hell, why not? It's open season on me today. Go on, it's not as if I can retaliate. Go on. Gimme your best shot.'

Sarah knew that if she'd had a gun in her hand at that moment, she could have ended her misery by shooting him without a second thought. Putting him out of his own misery, that is, because when she thought about it, that's what it ultimately came down to. Eighteen years of interminable frustration, unable to find her to exact his revenge. She finally unclenched her fists, then walked back to her chair and sat down. She didn't feel good about hitting him. And her hand hurt like hell! He'd goaded her, and like a gullible chump she'd retaliated when she should have known better. Now, slipping her hands surreptitiously under the table to gingerly massage her aching knuckles, she had to admit to taking some satisfaction, as she watched a trickle of blood seep from the nick under his right eye and disappear into the tangled mass of hair on his cheek.

'I'm sorry if it's been a wasted visit for you, Annie. But it has been good to see you again after all these years.'

'It's not over yet.' She lifted the attaché case on to the desk, opened it, removed a manila envelope, then replaced the case on the floor beside her chair.

'Don't tell me, you're trying to buy me off?' he said facetiously, indicating the envelope with a nod of his head. 'I'm flattered, Annie, but you couldn't afford my price. Well, at least not financially.'

Sarah removed a set of photographs from the envelope, which she had opened earlier at the airport, then fanned them out across the table in front of him. 'Ma Genno, leaving her house earlier this morning to visit you here. She had no idea that she was being photographed. All the pictures were taken with a telephoto lens. It's very simple, Frankie. Anything happens to me, or to my family, that telephoto lens becomes a telescopic sight. One shot.' She slammed her fist down hard on the table, startling Genno and causing him to look up sharply from the photographs. '*Bang! Dead!* Then who's going to come and visit you in prison? Then who's going to do all your dirty work for you on the outside? Bottom line, you hurt my family and I'll hurt yours. And if you don't believe me, go ahead and call my bluff. *Quid pro quo*, Frankie. Isn't that what you called it?'

'You go near my mother . . .' His voice trailed off, as he struggled with the intensity of the emotions writhing uncontrollably inside him.

'I won't, you can be sure of that,' she retorted, screwing up her face in disgust at the very thought of being in the vicinity of that odious woman. 'The contract's already in place. Whether it's carried out depends entirely on you. It's your call, Frankie.'

'No! No! No!' he screamed in anguish, and tugged furiously on the handcuffs in a desperate attempt to get at her as she stood up and calmly collected the photographs, replacing them in the envelope, which she then dropped back into the attaché case, snapping it shut.

'I can't say it's been a pleasure to see you again, Frankie, and although I dislike your mother intensely, I sincerely hope that she lives to be a hundred. Because by then, Sarah Johnson and her family will have long since vanished into thin air. And I can promise you that you won't find us again.'

'You think you've got it all worked out, don't you?' Genno hissed breathlessly as he glared furiously at her.

'I'm protecting my own, that's all. You'd do well to do the same.' She pressed the buzzer under the table. 'Goodbye, Frankie.'

'Not goodbye, Annie. *A bientôt*.... You should know the difference, coming from New Orleans.' His eyes flickered to D'Amato when the door swung open, then back to Sarah. 'I look forward to renewing this conversation in the near future. You can count on it.'

'You ready to leave?' D'Amato asked her. She nodded, and then followed him from the room.

'It's not over, Annie,' Genno called out after her in a low, menacing voice. 'Believe me, it's not—' He was cut off mid-sentence when the door closed again behind them.

'Are you OK?' D'Amato asked her.

'I've been better. He hasn't changed a bit. That's the scariest part of all.'

'I have to admit that I've never had a problem with him since I've been here, until today.'

'What sort of a problem?' Sarah asked, falling in line beside him as they walked down the corridor.

'I'm afraid I can't divulge that. It's an internal matter.'

'Did it have anything to do with my visit?'

'Indirectly,' was all D'Amato would say on the subject.

'He's never forgiven me for what happened back in Chicago. And he never will either.'

'You mean for testifying against him in court?'

'My testimony didn't put him away,' she replied, shaking her head. 'I wasn't even there when he killed Merill and the two customers during the robbery. I'd already driven off by then, leaving him high and dry. And that's why he'll never forgive me. That, together with the fact that I betrayed him by keeping the police fully informed about the heist all the time he was planning it.'

'I can understand why he could have got sore at you. Tell me, is it true that his mother physically attacked you outside the courthouse? I've heard rumours about it over the years, but I wouldn't have believed it of her. She seems like such a nice old lady.'

'She *tried* to attack me,' Sarah corrected him. 'She would have succeeded as well, had I not been given a police escort. The judge banned her from the courtroom when she started shouting abuse at me as I took the stand.'

'I find that incredible. I've never known her to raise her voice. All the officers in here like her. She brings us freshly baked cookies every week. It's a real treat, I tell you.'

'I'd start checking them for arsenic if I were you,' Sarah told him as they entered the waiting room.

'You don't like her, do you?'

'Whatever gives you that idea, Officer D'Amato?'

'Well, this is as far as I go. The officer who drove you from the airport will be along shortly to take you back again.' D'Amato extended a hand towards her. 'I hope you achieved what you came here for, Mrs Johnson.'

'So do I,' Sarah replied, shaking his hand. She waited until he had left before sitting down on the nearest chair, then added softly to herself, 'So do I . . .'

Eddie Hungate was running scared. After fleeing the house, he had taken a taxi to the French Quarter where he had drawn out a sum of money with his cash card, and then checked into a fleapit of a hotel on Dumaine Street. Under a false name, of course, and paying for the room in cash. He couldn't afford any slip-ups. All he'd had on him was his wallet and the clothes he was wearing. He had since bought himself a pair of jeans, a T-shirt and a pair of sneakers – again paying cash – knowing that any APB put out by the Marshals Service would include a description of the clothes he'd been wearing at the time of his escape from the house.

The hotel was a temporary haven. Nothing more. His only concern was to get out of the city. Except he had no idea where to go. The moment he used his cash card again, or his credit card, the authorities would home in on him. He would have to keep moving. If he could get himself a sum of cash upfront to use on his travels, that would be one more way to avoid detection. Only he didn't have that kind of money in his bank account. He was desperate. But he did have an ace which he had kept in reserve in case of such an emergency. Now it was time to play it and hope it paid off.

He found a payphone on Dauphine Street and dialled a number he had tucked away safely in his wallet. When it was answered he identified himself, and then asked, 'Are you alone?'

'Yes,' came the tentative reply. 'Where are you, Eddie?'

'Where I am isn't important. And don't try and put a trace on the call. It'll only backfire on you.'

'What do you mean?'

'I know about the tape,' Hungate said.

There was a hesitant pause, then, 'Tape? What are you talking about?'

'I didn't think you'd know about it,' Hungate said triumphantly. 'Klyne recorded Lomax's murder on a cassette tape. He even played a part of it back to me when he was drunk. He actually seemed quite proud of himself. Sick bastard.'

'What exactly are you getting at?'

'Lomax told Klyne everything before he died. Your name cropped up quite a few times in his confession.'

'You've lost me. I have no idea what you're talking about.'

Hungate then relayed the information that Klyne had passed on to him while intoxicated.

'That's absurd!' came the disdainful reposte when Hungate had finished.

'The tape exists. I can vouch for that. Do you really want to risk it falling into the wrong hands?'

'OK, so let's say this tape does exist. What do you want from me?'

'I want in on the deal. A percentage of the money you make from selling the contents of the disk.'

'What is this, some kind of shakedown? You're going to have to do a lot better than that—'

'You want to take your chances when Elworthy finds out?' Hungate cut in sharply, 'because if I'm caught, it's every man for himself. It's strange really. I had no idea that you were in on this when we were staking out the Johnsons' house. You sure are a cool customer, partner.'

'We need to talk this over in more detail. One on one. Face to face. What do you say, Eddie?'

'Sounds good. I'll call you and let you know the venue. It'll be in the next twenty-four hours. But if you double-cross me, we'll be doing time together at Oakdale. Klyne tells me it's a real hell-hole. So just bear that in mind before you send in the cavalry.'

'Who's got the tape now? Klyne?'

'He did have, the last I knew.'

'We've got to have a contingency plan in case you're taken in to custody before we can get together.'

'Forget it,' Hungate countered. 'Like I said, every man for himself. Why should I do you any fucking favours?'

'At least hear me out, Eddie. You did say that you wanted in on the action, didn't you?'

Hungate allowed his avarice to get the better of him and fed another quarter into the slot. 'I'm listening. This better be good, partner. Real good.'

An exhausted Sarah arrived back at the safe house shortly after seven o'clock that evening and made straight for Lea's room. She knocked lightly on the door. No reply. Again, slightly louder. Still nothing. She tried the handle. The door was unlocked. She eased it open until there was enough space for her to poke her head into the room. A smile touched her lips when she saw that Lea was asleep on the bed, fully clothed, the portable CD player beside her, the headphones askew on her head. She crossed to the bed, crouched down, and gently removed the headphones. Lea stirred, but no more. Sarah placed the audio set on the bedside table, then retrieved a spare quilt from the closet and laid it carefully over Lea's body. She brushed a loose strand of blonde hair from her daughter's angelic face, and leaned over and kissed her lightly on the forehead.

'You're back, are you?' Bob announced from the doorway.

Sarah swung round, finger to her lips, anger in her eyes. Bob glanced at his slumbering daughter, then turned away and disappeared from view. Sarah switched off the lamp and crossed to the door where she paused to look back with an affectionate smile at Lea, then went out into the hall and closed the door silently behind her.

'You went to see Genno this afternoon, didn't you?' Bob demanded to know.

'You've been drinking,' Sarah countered. She could always tell when he was drunk, or heading in that direction, from the unsightly red blotches on his cheeks and throat. He never slurred his words. And he had to have sunk a skinful before it affected his balance. She noticed that he still appeared to be fairly steady on his feet.

'You never answered my question.'

'Yes, I went to see him. I thought maybe I could try and reason with him.'

'Did you?'

'I think I've given us some breathing space.'

'What d'you mean, breathing space?'

'Just that. Enough time to get our affairs in order before we're given new identities and relocated to another part of the country.'

'What are you talking about? I'm not leaving New Orleans. This is my home. I'm staying right here.'

'Then stay, for all I care. And that bitch can have you all to herself. I'll even throw in a divorce if that's what you want.'

'Divorce?' Bob laughed contemptuously. 'To be honest, I don't even know whether we've been legally married for the last sixteen years.'

'Don't worry, it's all legal,' she assured him. 'I checked with the Marshals Service when our relationship started to get serious. As a precaution.'

'Listen to what we're saying. Divorce? For God's sake, what's happening to us?'

·'I'm not the one who's been unfaithful.'

'And I'm not the one who's been living a lie,' he came back angrily, but held up his hands in apology before she could respond. 'These recriminations aren't getting us anywhere. All we're doing is pushing each other further away. It's not solving anything. We've both made mistakes in the past—'

'Speak for yourself,' she cut in. 'I kept my true identity a secret from you and Lea to hold the family together. I don't regret it.'

'I'm trying to reach out to you, Sarah, only you're not prepared to concede any ground to me at all. I don't know why I'm even bothering to try.'

'Why don't you try when you're not liquored up, then I might be inclined to take you a bit more seriously? It was exactly the same after I'd audited your company's books. The only way you could deal with your partner's fraud was through drink. You turn to the bottle at the first sign of adversity. It doesn't say much for you, does it?'

'I never was good enough for you, was I?' came the resentful riposte.

'That's not true,' she replied testily. Too quickly. Too defensively.

'It's never been easy trying to live up to your idealistic standards, Sarah. Have you ever thought that's why I sought solace in an extramarital affair? At least Renée accepts me for what I am, faults and all. Something you never could.'

'*Accepts*? So it's still in the present tense? And I thought you said it was over between the two of you. Obviously, I was wrong.'

'You want to relocate to another part of the country, go right ahead. It's not as if there's anything left to keep you here any more. Certainly not me.' He levelled a finger of warning at her. 'You walk out, you're going to have to sever all your connections in New Orleans. That includes Lea.'

'Lea goes where I go,' Sarah said matter-of-factly, her eyes narrowing angrily at the very thought of having to leave her daughter behind.

'You're not taking my daughter anywhere. This is a problem entirely of your own making, Sarah. The sooner you face up to that, the better it'll be for all of us. Especially Lea.'

'If I have to relocate under a new identity, do you honestly think Frankie's going to stop looking for me? It'll only spur him on even more, and he'll use any methods at his disposal to draw me back out into the open again. And the first person he'd target would be Lea if she were to remain here with you. Don't you see that?'

'We'll be given the necessary protection,' Bob said.

'The protection *will* be a new identity,' she responded furiously, unable to fathom her husband's dismissive reponse to the problem. 'If you think for one moment that the Marshals Service are going to make an exception and give you twenty-four-hour protection, you'd better think again. I'm not even including Lea in that equation, because I'm not leaving her behind.'

'It's looks like a stalemate then, doesn't it? I'm not about to give her up without one hell of a fight, Sarah, you can be sure of that.'

'If you cared anything for Lea, you'd know she'd be in real danger if she stayed here with you. Only, you're either too stubborn or too stupid to see that.'

'If I cared anything for Lea?' came the incensed reply. 'How dare you! I love Lea more than anything in this whole world, and you know that.'

'And I know that Frankie would use her to get at me if I left her behind with you,' Sarah said in a soft, emotional voice. 'Think about it, Bob. That's all I ask.'

Bob stared at her for several seconds, feeling his own anger evaporating as the tears spilled down her cheeks. She made no attempt to brush them away. 'I need a drink,' he muttered gruffly, then walked off and disappeared into the living room further down the hallway.

She remained motionless after he had gone, staring absently at the spot where he had been standing, then quickly wiped her hand across her cheeks. The tears had come as a complete surprise to her. One moment she was arguing with Bob, imbued with an overwhelming sense of outrage at his apparent selfishness, then the next moment she was overcome by a melancholic despair that had abruptly turned her anger to tears. Was it all the talk of Lea? A mother's frustration at her inability to protect her own daughter's future without having to turn it upside down in the process? Was it Bob? The thought caught her by surprise. Why Bob? Or was it more than just Bob? The marriage? Their future? What future? It certainly didn't appear as if they would remain together. Not after tonight. The chasm between them was widening all the time. There appeared to be no way back.

Was Bob right? Was she a perfectionist? Again she was ambushed by her erratic thought patterns. She'd certainly never consciously striven for perfection. How could she with her sordid past? Admittedly, she was ambitious. Was that such a crime? Bob was a dreamer, with a plethora of grandiose ideas which never got further than the planning stage. Many didn't even get that far. But then that had been part of the initial attraction for her. If anything, she had drawn her own ambition and inspiration from him when they had first met.

His unswerving belief in her had helped to steer her in the right direction. Without him, she would probably still be a secretary in some dead-end job. She owed a lot to Bob. Was this, in fact, her subconscious trying to tell her to fight to save the marriage? Maybe. But was it worth saving? Could it be saved? Not if Bob insisted on remaining behind in New Orleans. If he did, it wouldn't be with Lea. Of that she was certain. She would move heaven and earth to protect her daughter. Heaven, earth and hell, if necessary. A pact with the devil would be a small price to pay to ensure Lea's safety. Then again, she had a sneaking feeling that Frankie had already beaten her to any possible negotiations with the devil. A faint smile touched her lips. What would Ma Genno make of that?

Seven

A 'neutron' was the name given to a non-gang member in Stateville. Most were forced to pay anything up to fifty dollars a month to the gangs just for the privilege of being incarcerated in the same prison as them. Neutrons were sometimes sold, or traded, for sex between the different gangs, but never had any say in the transaction. They were also coerced into smuggling drugs between cellhouses, or hiding weapons from the guards. If caught, they were expected to endure the subsequent punishment, invariably in solitary, in complete silence. Talk, and retribution was both swift and violent. The gangs ruled the prisons with a mixture of fear and terror.

Frankie Genno was regarded a neutron but, unlike his less fortunate colleagues, he had never paid anything to the gangs in all the time he'd been imprisoned at Stateville. He never touched drugs. Never handled a weapon. And he especially prided himself on his enforced celibacy. Self-discipline was all important to him. As was his independence.

Yet his was an exception to the rule and the circumstances, which permitted it, were fortuitous in the extreme. Angelo Cabrerra had been one of the most influential and dangerous gangbangers on the streets of Chicago in the early eighties. He was the leader of the most notorious, and powerful, of the numerous Hispanic gangs of the time, known as the 'Angeles de la Crucifixión' – the 'Crucifixion Angels' – who derived their name from the way they dealt with their enemies by nailing them to crosses, then slowly torturing them to death. Genno had heard of Cabrerra, but had never actually met him before the day he saved his life on Maxwell Street. He had tackled one of Cabrerra's own bodyguards who had surreptitiously drawn a knife behind his leader, intent on stabbing him in the back. It was all part of an internal feud, or so Genno had later discovered. Genno never knew why he had reacted as he did that day. It was just something he had done on the spur of the moment. Cabrerra, who prided himself on being a man of honour despite his distinctly dishonourable lifestyle, had indicated to Genno that, as he owed him his life, he would repay the favour at some point in the future. It was the unspoken law of the street. Then they would be even. A month later, Cabrerra was beginning a life sentence for a triple homicide – the three gang members who had tried to overthrow him as leader of the Crucifixion Angels. As far as Genno was aware, Cabrerra would serve out his sentence at the Pontiac Correctional Center in Livingston County. Little chance of him ever repaying the favour from behind bars. Genno had quickly forgotten about it.

Twelve months later, Genno was starting his own life sentence. He knew the reputation of the gangs in Stateville, and had been genuinely frightened of what awaited him at the prison, while he sat on the correctional bus during the drive from Chicago to Joliet. Yet within an hour of his arrival he received a deputation from the Crucifixion Angels, led by Angelo Cabrerra who, unbeknown to Genno, had been transferred from Pontiac three months earlier. Cabrerra had reiterated his offer of a favour. Unfinished business. It was then that Genno chose to play his trump card – he wanted nothing to do with the gang culture in Stateville. No payments to them; no running errands for them; no interference from them whatsoever. Cabrerra had given him his word that he would be left alone by the gangs. Cabrerra had been true to his word and Genno doubted whether he had spoken more than a dozen times to him in the last eighteen years. Always cordial. Never genial. They had little in common and the stilted conversations had rarely lasted longer than a greeting and a passing enquiry as to each other's general welfare. That kind of limited contact with Cabrerra had always suited Genno, until now . . .

He had made it known shortly after Annie's visit the previous day that he wanted to speak with Cabrerra. These 'audiences', as Cabrerra liked them to be known, could take several days to arrange, depending on your position within the prison hierarchy. Genno had a sneaking feeling that Cabrerra would see him quickly, if only to satisfy his own curiosity. He hadn't been wrong. Shortly before seven o'clock that same day, Genno had received a visit from one of Cabrerra's foot soldiers to inform him that 'the King has graciously agreed to an audience with you at nine o'clock tomorrow morning. Boiler room. Lower ground floor. Cellhouse B. Come alone.' With that, the lackey was gone. The King was the pretentious title

Cabrerra had decreed upon himself some years back. But as he virtually ran Stateville, nobody dared make fun of it. Not even behind his back. Cabrerra had eyes and ears in every corner of the prison.

After breakfast in the mess hall, Genno made his way to Cellhouse B, which had the notorious distinction of being the longest rectangular cellhouse in the world. He was now deep inside Cabrerra's domain. He had to get directions from a couple of inmates along the way, before finally reaching the bowels of the prison. The overhead lighting was sparse, and a cacophony of alien sounds emanated from the thick pipes which ran the length of the low concrete ceilings. It was strangely deserted for that time of the morning. Or so it appeared, but then it was the first time he had been down there.

He'd heard stories about the basement. It was where the junkies scored their regular shit. Any type of drug was available in Stateville – for the right price. It was where murderous plots were hatched in secret, sometimes even against the guards, especially those on the gangs' payroll who'd become too greedy for their own good. Hell, he'd even seen a guard murdered a couple of years back. Not that it had bothered him. One less to worry about. It was also where the newly incarcerated neutrons were regularly initiated by the predatory wolves – the homosexual inmates – most of them lifers or three-time losers, before being handed on to one of the gangs to be used for future trades within the prison community. Then again, most deals in Stateville either involved sex or drugs, even if only indirectly. Stateville was a show house and greenhouse rolled into one, and he was right in the middle of the cesspool. That he neither had sex nor took drugs was even more remarkable under the circumstances . . .

'Genno?'

He froze as a colossus ghosted out from behind a generator twenty yards ahead of him. He wouldn't have looked out of place manning the door at a bouncers' convention. He looked as broad as he was tall. Genno had seen this goon before, shadowing Cabrerra in the exercise yard.

'Did you come alone?'

'No, I brought the whole fucking Bears defensive team with me,' Genno retorted disparagingly. 'What does it look like?'

The goon tilted his head sideways, exposing the sinewy roots of muscles on his trunk of a neck, and looked past Genno to make sure there were no nose tackles or linebackers lurking in the shadows behind him. Satisfied that Genno was by himself, he gestured at him to come forward. 'Face the wall. Assume the position.' Genno did as he was told, and the goon frisked him with the expertise of a man who had done this all too often. 'You're clean.'

'Why d'you think I came here? To assassinate Cabrerra?'

'It's been tried,' was all the goon would say, as he led the way to a large cage further along the concrete bunker. There were another two bodyguards, smaller but still intimidating, standing on either side of the open cage door. 'Frankie Genno,' the goon announced, then he stepped aside and beckoned Genno to enter.

Angelo Cabrerra was seated in an armchair in the corner, smoking a cigar. Although Genno didn't know his exact age, he put Cabrerra somewhere in his early to mid-forties. He was clean-shaven, with short black hair and a crucifix earring dangling from his left ear. The bottom half of a tattooed crucifix was visible below the hem of his multicoloured Hawaiian shirt. A second figure, sitting on the arm of Cabrerra's chair, wouldn't have looked out of place on the fashion catwalks of Europe. Shoulder-length black hair framed an exceptionally pretty face and a slim, willowy figure was outlined underneath a striking, white, ankle-length designer dress. Only this was no woman. It was Cabrerra's bitch. His own personal property. Young enough to be Cabrerra's son . . . or daughter.

'Like what you see?' the transvestite purred seductively in a surprisingly feminine voice and extended the tip of a white stiletto shoe towards him, exposing a glimpse of stockinged ankle.

'Actually, I prefer my women in one piece,' Genno replied. 'Personally, I'm not into detachable breasts that fall off when you unhook the bra. It kinda takes away the enjoyment of it all, don't you think?'

'I think you talk too much,' the transvestite hissed, the voice deepening as the eyes flashed angrily at the insult. 'Maybe I should cut out your tongue.'

'Shut up!' Cabrerra snapped. 'You're here for decoration, bitch. Nothing else. The only time you're required to open your mouth is when you're on your knees. *Entendes?*'

The transvestite stamped a stiletto heel petulantly on the concrete floor and glowered furiously at Genno from under a pair of long false eyelashes.

'You want to sit, Genno?' Cabrerra asked, gesturing to the second armchair in the corner of the cage.

Genno sat down, then slowly rubbed his hands over the cushioned arms. 'Very nice. Real comfortable.'

'Oh, it's nothing.' Cabrerra shrugged, as if getting a set of lounge furniture into Stateville was no big deal. Which it wouldn't have been for him. He got whatever he wanted. Even his own luxury washing machine, which Genno had never actually seen, but had heard about. 'I'm sorry about Carmen. Like any bitch, she can get a little excitable at times.'

'As long as it's at the right times,' Genno said, glancing at the transvestite who continued to scowl back furiously at him.

'Absolutely.' Cabrerra laughed heartily, but then his face became serious and he extended his hands out towards Genno. 'I have to admit, I was surprised when I was told that you wanted to see me. So tell me, my friend, what finally brings you down here after eighteen years?'

'A favour.'

'Frankie Genno wants a favour from me? I am flattered.' The corners of Cabrerra's mouth twitched in a half-smile. 'Unfortunately, favours cost money in here. How much depends on the favour.'

'I'm prepared to pay the asking price.'

'But you don't know the asking price yet. What if it's too much for you?'

'It won't be. And I know that *you* wouldn't try and fuck me over, Cabrerra,' Genno said softly, but there was an underlying tone of menace in his voice.

Cabrerra's smile faltered momentarily as he searched Genno's face, then he laughed again and clapped his hands together. 'You've got balls, Genno, I'll give you that. Most people who come down here are scared as hell. I've seen them shaking with fear. Shit, one guy even pissed his pants. Not you though.' He drew deep on his cigar and expelled the smoke upwards. 'I'm sure we can come to some kind of agreement that would be acceptable to both of us. So tell me, what's this favour you want?'

'To get out of here.'

Cabrerra guffawed loudly. 'You, and every other man in this calaboose.' He sat forward in his chair, his elbows resting on his knees. 'I can get my hands on most things, Genno, but a magic wand isn't one of them. If I could, don't you think I'd have transported myself out of here on to some desert island by now?'

'Don't patronize me, Cabrerra.'

'No, you're the one who's being patronizing.' Cabrerra got to his feet and walked to the opposite side of the cage before turning back to Genno. 'I have an understanding with the guards in here. It's based on give and take. If there's a problem between rival gangs, I act as mediator to try and resolve the situation peacefully. If one gang threatens to cause trouble, I can take the necessary action to prevent it. The guards would probably have to use force against the inmates if I weren't here, which could escalate the situation into a full-blown riot. I am the law here, Genno. And the prison officers, right up to the warden himself, accept that as a small price to pay to keep the peace between rival gangs. What they wouldn't accept, however, is if I started to help prisoners escape. They would revoke my privileges and take away everything that I've built up for myself since I've been here. I *won't* sacrifice that for any amount of money.

'Like you, Genno, I'm a lifer. No chance of ever being paroled. I came to accept that a long time ago. And, to be honest, I thought that you, of all people, had done the same.'

'I'm sure I'd feel the same way if I were in your position. But what if it could be done without any suspicion falling on you?'

'Nothing happens in here without my personal authorization,' Cabrerra replied indignantly.

'Why don't you get off your high horse – or should I say, your *throne* – just for once and look around you through the eyes of the common man. You might actually find it enlightening.' Genno noticed that the goon who'd frisked him was now standing ominously behind him, arms folded across his barrel chest. The other two bodyguards had immediately taken his place in the doorway. 'Go on then, have him beat the shit out of me, if that's what you want,' he said defiantly. 'It won't be the first beating I've had today. And when he's done, tell him to put me out of my misery, because that will be preferable to sitting in here like some dumb fuck after the threat *she* made against me yesterday afternoon. So go on, do it.'

Cabrerra stared at Genno for several seconds, cigar in mouth, before he finally gestured with a flick of his hand for the goon to back off. He returned to his own armchair and sat down. 'You're talking about the woman who testified against you, aren't you?' Genno nodded. 'I thought she went into the Witness Protection Program after the trial?'

'She did, but I've recently discovered her new identity. It's taken me all this time, but I've finally found her again. I hired someone to take her out. Only he fucked up. Badly. She turned up at the prison yesterday and threatened to kill my mother if anything happens to her, or her family. Nobody makes threats against my mother. *Nobody!'*

Cabrerra raised a hand to halt the goon who took a step forward when Genno banged his fist down angrily on the arm of the chair. 'I had no idea that she'd come to see you. My informers must be getting complacent. It must have come as quite a shock to see her again after all this time.'

'I didn't come down here to talk about her visit. I need out, Cabrerra. Not to go sunning myself on some tropical island. All I want to do is isolate my mother and make sure she's safe before I go after that bitch. Hell, I don't give a shit what happens to me after she's dead. That's all that matters to me now. So either you can help me, or I'll find someone else who can.'

'I told you, Genno, nothing goes down in here without my personal say-so.'

'I'm sure that for the right kind of financial incentive, I could persuade one of the other gangs to help me. And the first you'd know about it would be after I was safely on the outside. Is that what you want, Cabrerra, to see your authority undermined like that?'

Cabrerra was aware that his minions were now watching him closely, waiting for his response to Genno's challenge. He took a long drag on his cigar. 'If anyone else had made that kind of threat against me, I'd have killed them myself. But you're different. You don't give a shit about what happens to you, so that would only take away from the enjoyment of the kill. I also have to admit to being just a little intrigued by all this talk of revenge. Eighteen years is a long time to wait.' He removed the cigar from his mouth and pointed it at Genno. 'Maybe we can do business, on the understanding that there will be no comeback whatsoever. And, of course, if you agree to my price which, I have to tell you now, will be exorbitant considering the nature of your request. Cash, upfront. Otherwise we don't take this conversation any further.'

'I told you, it can be done without any suspicion falling on you. As for the money, my mother has an investment portfolio which I told her to cash in yesterday. I don't know exactly how much the policy's worth, but if your offer falls within that framework, we've got ourselves a deal. Take it or leave it.'

'Straight to the point. I like your style, Genno. I assume that you do have a plan in mind to get yourself out of here?'

'Naturally,' Genno replied matter-of-factly.

'Then let's hear it.'

'That's between you and me.' Genno indicated the players around them. 'Get rid of the baggage. Then we'll talk.'

'Baggage?' the transvestite spluttering indignantly.

'Shut up!' Cabrerra snapped tersely without taking his eyes off Genno. 'They stay. No discussion. You take it or leave it.'

Genno noticed a triumphant sneer curl at the corners of the transvestite's red lips. He knew better than to push Cabrerra any further, not in front of his own people. 'Are they trustworthy?'

'If they weren't, they wouldn't be here,' Cabrerra told him, then sat back in his chair and inhaled deeply on his cigar. 'So, Genno, let's hear this plan of yours. It should be interesting, if nothing else.'

Etienne Pascale's years as a cop had prepared him well for life on the wrong side of the law. He still thought like a cop, which gave him a crucial edge when it came to staying one step ahead of the authorities. He always arranged an alibi in advance of any illegal activity so that, should the local cops come knocking on his door, he would be able to prove that he was elsewhere at the time the offence was committed.

Two detectives had been to see him at his apartment that morning. Very early. It had been dark outside. A photograph of Klyne had been thrust under his nose. He had known better than to feign ignorance of the man. After all, they had done time together at Oakdale. And the cops would have known that. Hence the reason for the visit at that unappealing hour of the morning. He had studied the photograph, as if trying to place the face, then agreed that although it was familiar, he couldn't put a name to him. Paul Klyne, he had been told. No, he hadn't seen Klyne since Oakdale. Then he had been asked to account for his movements between eight and midnight two nights earlier. Easy, he had told them. He'd gone to the movies with his girlfriend, Lynne Rodford. Yes, he had bought the tickets at the box office. Cash. Young woman. Late teens. No, he hadn't noticed the name on her tag. No, he had no idea whether she would remember him. That he went to the cinema with his girlfriend was true, except that he had slipped out shortly before the film had started to join up with Klyne. Lynne Rodford had stayed on to watch the film, and outlined the plot to him when she had seen him the following day. She would corroborate his alibi when the cops paid a visit to the bar in the French Quarter where she worked. Lynne Rodford was a three-time divorcée, desperate for love, who would do anything for him, and he, in turn, regularly exploited that weakness to suit his own purposes. The cops had nothing to link him to Klyne. So they had left.

Klyne had left the apartment the previous day. Summoned back to Joliet by Frances Genno, on the specific instructions of her son. Or so he had told Pascale after he had phoned her. That was all Pascale knew, although he had overheard Klyne trying to argue his case to remain on in New Orleans, confident that he could get Sarah Johnson the next time. But it had been obvious that she would have none of it, so he had returned to Joliet. Not that it had bothered Pascale to see the back of him. He had never liked Klyne. A uneasy alliance. He wasn't even sure whether he would see Klyne again. And that didn't bother him either.

The telephone rang on the bedside table, startling him out of his thoughts. He went into the bedroom, sat down on the double bed, and picked up the receiver.

'Mr Pascale, it's Warren.'

Danny Warren. Snitch. Drug addict. One of life's losers. To be exploited.

'What's up, Danny?'

'I got some info that might interest you, Mr Pascale.' Always polite, Danny.

'Go on.'

'Word is there's some serious shit going down at the Marshals Service's district office on Camp Street. One of their agents has gone on the lam. Name of Eddie Hungate. I thought you should know.'

Pascale jumped to his feet, the receiver now gripped tightly in his hand. 'What d'you mean, he's gone on the lam? Why?'

'From what I understand from my sources, he's been on the take for some time. I also heard rumours ... just rumours, you understand ... that maybe you'd done some business with him in the past as well. The guy could be a serious liability to you, Mr Pascale. That's why I called as soon as I heard about it. To warn you.'

'You did well, Danny.'

'Thanks, Mr Pascale.'

'I'll settle up with you tomorrow. Usual place. Usual time. And if you hear anything else tonight, you're to call me right away on this number. I'll be in all night.'

Pascale replaced the handset. He could have done with Klyne to sort out this latest problem. It was his particular area of expertise. Only Klyne wasn't there any more. He would have to do it himself. But first he would have to find Eddie Hungate – before the

authorities did – and then kill him. There was no turning back
now . . .

'How did it go?' Taylor asked, after arriving at the safe house in the
afternoon.

'I think it's given me a bit more time to sort things out before we're
moved on to another location. So, in that sense, it was worth the trip.
Thanks for setting up the meeting with Frankie yesterday at such
short notice, Jack. I appreciate it more than you could ever know.'

'Sure,' Taylor replied with a philosophical smile, thinking back to
the carpeting he had received from Elworthy for not having gone
through the proper channels. He chose not to mention it to her. 'I
checked in with Robideaux before I came out here. He's coordinating
the search for Hungate.'

'Who's Hungate?'

'Eddie Hungate . . .' He trailed off and nodded to himself. 'Of
course, you won't have heard, will you?'

'Heard what?' she asked in exasperation when he fell silent.

Taylor updated her on the latest developments in the investigation.

'An inside man. It makes sense,' she concluded once he'd finished.
'Is he the only one?'

'As far as we're aware, although it's an ongoing investigation.
Nothing can be ruled out until we've had a chance to question him.'

'But first you have to find him.'

'All the local law-enforcement agencies have been alerted. If he's
still in New Orleans, which I'm inclined to believe he is, chances are
he's lying low. He'll know that if he shows his face, word will quickly
get back to us.'

'Or Klyne.'

'Or any of the other names in his little black book,' Taylor added.
'Which is why it's imperative that we get to him first.'

'His arrest may help to strengthen your case against Klyne, and
possibly identify the second man who hijacked the surveillance car,
but it won't do anything to benefit me and my family, will it?'

'Not directly, no,' he admitted.

'It's just as well that I took out my little insurance policy against
Frankie, isn't it?'

'We'll have you and your family safely relocated within the week.
Don't worry, he'll never be able to call your bluff.'

'Who said I was bluffing?'

Taylor's brow knitted in a quizzical frown. 'What are you saying, that you would have his mother killed if anything were to happen to you, or your family?'

'You said that, not me.'

'Sarah?' Taylor grabbed her arm as she was about to turn away from him. 'You make a move against Frances Genno, and I'll see to it personally that you go down for a very long time.'

She shrugged off his hand angrily. 'If my family were dead, d'you honestly think I'd give a shit about what happened to me?'

'I went out on a limb to set up that meeting for you with Genno. It was on the clear understanding that you were bluffing to make him back off long enough for us to safely relocate you and your family.'

'I never gave you any such assurance!' she countered.

'You've used me, haven't you?'

'Call it what you want. As far as I'm concerned, I'm protecting my own. And I will go to any lengths to do that, Jack. Any lengths. *That* I can assure you.'

'To be perfectly honest, I don't believe you've taken out a contract out on Frances Genno,' Taylor said, holding her stare.

'Believe what you want. It doesn't bother me one way or the other,' came the indifferent reply.

'I'd be hard pushed to set up a contract in twenty-four hours. And I've got contacts in the right places. You don't. Which is why I'm not convinced there is a hit man. It is a bluff, isn't it?' He raised a hand before she could issue another rebuttal. 'This is me you're talking to, Sarah. Not Genno. I can understand why you said what you did to him. Hell, I'd probably have done the same thing if I were in your position. I'm prepared to play along with it, even if it means defending your actions to my superiors. But you've got to trust me. I'm on your side. I think I demonstrated that by getting you into Stateville to see Genno yesterday afternoon.'

'You're right, it is a bluff. There's no contract out on Frances Genno,' she conceded. Sarah shook her head slowly to herself. 'If I couldn't even convince you that the contract was real, chances are Frankie wouldn't have believed me either.'

'Not without a name.'

'What do you mean?' she asked hesitantly.

'If the hit man had a name, it would give the contract added credibility.'

'But I've just told you, there is no contract out on Frankie's mother. I don't know any hit men.'

'I do.'

'What exactly are you suggesting?'

'That I spread a little disinformation by putting a name into circulation – call it an anonymous rumour – so that Genno will find out about it when he starts asking questions. Which he will do. That's one thing you can be sure of.'

'I didn't even think of that,' she conceded dejectedly.

'Why do you think I've been trying to get you to level with me? You can't have two names in circulation. That would be as bad as having none at all.'

'I assume you're going to have to use the name of a known hit man?'

'Naturally.'

'But he could easil deny it,' she countered.

'He would anyway, wouldn't he? He's hardly going to admit to it. That's not my main concern, though. I'm more worried about Genno putting out a counter-contract on the hit man to protect his mother.'

'Is there any way round that?'

'Sure, if the hit man disappeared from his usual haunts. That way, it would be much harder for Genno to have him tracked down.'

'And how would you get him to do that without arousing suspicion?'

'Lift him off the streets on a trumped-up charge and keep him out of the way for a few days, until you're safely relocated. I can arrange that with my partner, Keith Yallow, in Washington. Obviously, I'd have to bypass Robideaux. I can't see him going for it, can you?'

'You could lose your job for something like this,' she said uneasily.

'I don't see how. It's not as if there will be any connection between me and the arrest. I trust Keith implicitly. He'll have it done very discreetly. That way, nobody will even know that the guy's off the streets. It'll just look as if he's gone to ground somewhere, waiting for his cue. And that can only add to the credibility of what you've already said to Genno.'

'I don't know what to say.'

'Don't say anything,' he exclaimed, with a look of feigned horror. 'This is strictly between the two of us. Don't breathe a word of it to anyone, otherwise it could all come back on me. Then I would be facing disciplinary action.'

'You can count on my silence.'

'I'll make the call. The hit man I have in mind will be off the streets by midnight. Then Genno can make as many enquiries as he likes, but all he'll do is draw a blank. It'll be very frustrating for him.'

'Why are you doing this?' she asked.

'You said you wanted more time to sort out your affairs. I'm giving you that time. Just make sure you use it productively. You'll have two – at tops three – days. We can't hold the guy any longer than that.'

'Thanks,' she said softly.

'How are Bob and Lea holding up?' he asked, breaking the sudden silence between them.

'Lea's still holed up in her room. Or at least she was when I last looked in on her. As for Bob, he's decided that he's not going to be relocated. He wants to stay in New Orleans. I've tried to talk him out of it, but he's adamant. I can't force him to come with us.'

'If he stays behind here, he's on his own. We can't give him blanket protection. We just don't have the manpower.'

'I've already told him that,' came the exasperated reply.

'Then tell him again. And keep on telling him. It's the only way, Sarah. His life here in New Orleans is over. That's something he has to accept.'

'Perhaps you should try talking some sense into him. Maybe you can get through to him,' she suggested.

'It's best if it comes from you. First thing *you*'ve got to do, though, is come to terms with his extramarital affair. Even if it is just in the short term. I'm not saying you have to accept what he's done. What's happened is between the two of you. Recriminations can come later, after you've safely relocated. But right now, you need to pull together as a family. Otherwise, the family's going to fragment and Lea's going to be the loser.'

'How do you know about Bob's infidelity?'

'Ray Deacon overheard the two of you arguing in the bedroom last night. He wasn't eavesdropping. It's just that voices carry around here.'

'I hope Lea didn't hear us,' she gasped, ashen-faced, and put a hand to her mouth, horrified at the thought of her daughter being further subjected to her parents' lies and deceit.

'From what Ray's told me, Lea never takes off those headphones. Even when she's walking round the house.'

'I hope to God he's right.'

Taylor gave her a reassuring smile. 'It's going to be OK, Sarah. You'll see.'

'I wish I had your confidence.'

'It's not about confidence. This is my job. I've never lost a witness in this program, apart for the occasional felon who's been stupid enough to go back to his old ways after being relocated. Those guys might as well be wearing a target on their chests. Old habits die hard, I guess.'

'I guess.'

Taylor waited until Sarah had gone back to her bedroom and closed the door behind her. He then went into the kitchen and made himself a cup of coffee, before going outside. He walked down to the jetty, looked around to ensure he was alone, then removed his cellphone and dialled a number in Washington. 'Yeah, it's me. How's tricks?'

'Good,' came the reply. 'How about you?'

'I've got a bit of problem down here that needs to be sorted out.' Taylor went on to explain about Sarah's visit to Stateville, and about the 'contract' on Frances Genno.

'She's certainly resilient, if nothing else,' came the bemused reply when he had finished. 'What d'you want me to do?'

'Dave Shephard. Know him?'

'Of him. Ex-Marine. Now a freelance enforcer. Rumour has it he's done some work for the Company in the past.'

'Put out the word that Sarah Johnson's recruited him for the contract. Make sure it reaches a reliable source in Stateville. Then have him picked up and taken to one of the safe houses. Be discreet. Real discreet.'

'This better be worth all the aggro, Jack.'

'It will. Speak to you later.' He barely had time to replace the cellphone in his jacket pocket when a deputy marshal appeared at the back door and shouted to him, beckoning him towards the house. 'What is it?' he demanded, hurrying up from the jetty.'

'Call for you. Inside.'

He entered the kitchen and picked the portable phone off the wooden table in the centre of the room.

'Taylor, it's Robideaux. Chief Deputy Marshal Elworthy asked me to call you. We've got a fix on Hungate. Do you want to be in on the arrest?'

'Damn right I do. Where and when?'

Pascale was lying motionless in bed beside his girlfriend, Lynne Rodford, in his small apartment on Ursulines Street in the French Quarter of the city. She was sound asleep. Which was hardly surprising, since she'd put in a fourteen-hour shift at the bar that day.

He couldn't sleep though, not for worrying about Hungate. If Hungate was on the lam, it meant that the authorities were on to him. And if they did collar him, chances were he'd sing sweeter than a pampered canary to save his own neck. Then it would only be a matter of time before he too was taken into custody. That he hadn't been so far meant the authorities obviously didn't know about his involvement with either Hungate or Klyne. In the meantime, he had put out the word to several of his more reliable snitches that he'd pay handsomely for info on Hungate's present whereabouts. So far the phone beside the bed had remained silent. Not a good omen. The inside man in the Marshals Service was always going to be the weak link as far as he was concerned. He had voiced his doubts to Klyne at the time, but to no avail. Klyne had insisted on an inside man. He'd had dealings with Hungate in the past, which made him the obvious choice. Klyne had paid Hungate in person. In fact, Klyne and Hungate seemed to hit it off right from the start. Drinking buddies. Pascale stayed out of that side of things. His was a purely professional relationship with both men. Now it seemed to have backfired, unless he could get to Hungate before the authorities did. He would have no qualms about killing him, not if it meant avoiding a lengthy jail sentence. As a cop he'd made a lot of enemies over the years, and many of them were now doing time as a direct result of his evidence. He wouldn't last long in a federal penitentiary, and he knew it. That thought didn't help his attempts at sleep either . . .

The telephone rang. He quickly answered it.

'It's Warren, Mr Pascale.'

'What have you got for me, Danny?'

'I've found out where Hungate's holed up, Mr Pascale.'

'Where?' Pascale asked irritably when Warren fell silent.

'The Luneville.'

'On Royal Street?' came the incredulous reply. 'That's less than a hundred yards from here. The son-of-a-bitch's been under my nose all the time.'

'It's a small world, Mr Pascale,' Warren said with a chuckle.

Pascale failed to appreciate anything remotely amusing in the irony of the situation. 'You've done well, Danny. I'll see you right in the morning.'

'Thanks, Mr Pascale.'

Pascale replaced the handset, then glanced at Lynne. She was awake, watching him through bleary eyes. 'I gotta go out,' he announced, throwing back the quilt. 'But as far as you're concerned, I never left the apartment. I've been in all night.'

'What's new? So where are you going?' she asked, struggling to sit up in bed.

'I told you, out.'

'I hate it when you get all mysterious on me, Etienne. Why can't you ever confide in me?'

'Go back to sleep,' he said brusquely as he climbed out of bed, took a cigarette from the pack on the bedside table and lit it. 'I shouldn't be long,' he added absently as he dressed.

'Stop taking me for granted!'

He grabbed the pack of cigarettes off the table as she was reaching for them. 'You don't like it here, you can leave any time you want. I won't stop you.'

'Don't say things like that,' she replied defensively. 'You know I love you.'

'Yeah, so you keep saying.' He went to the closet and, careful to block her view, removed a Beretta from under a pile of T-shirts and deftly palmed it into his jacket pocket.

'At least leave me a cigarette,' she called out, as he headed for the door.

'There's only one left,' came the dismissive reply.

'So buy some more when you're out, but leave me that one.'

'Go and buy some yourself!' A moment later, the front door slammed shut behind him.

'Bastard!' she yelled after him, then slumped back dejectedly on to the mattress.

The Luneville Hotel had seen better days. Now hookers used it mainly to turn tricks by the hour, and the only time of the year that it could sell its full complement of thirty-five rooms was during the Mardi Gras season, when tourists were desperate for accommodation.

Pascale had passed it enough times, but this was the first occasion that he'd ventured inside. The lobby was drab and dimly lit. The front desk was deserted. He tapped twice on the bell. Moments later, the desk clerk appeared, unshaven, and with an expression of complete boredom.

'I'm looking for a man,' Pascale said.

'Yeah, well, to each his own.'

Pascale bit back his anger. 'Mid-thirties. Blond hair. Stocky build. He would have checked in earlier today.'

'Not during my shift.'

'Then check the register. He's definitely here.'

'It's 'gainst the law to give out details . . .' The desk clerk's voice trailed off when Pascale slid two twenty-dollar bills across the desk to him. He slipped them quickly into the breast pocket of his crumpled white shirt. 'There is a guy who fits the description. Saw him earlier this evening. Didn't say nothing to him, mind.'

'What's his room number?' Pascale demanded.

'I don't rightly know.'

'Why doesn't that surprise me?' Pascale pushed another twenty dollars across the desk to him.

'Room thirty-one. Second floor.'

'Name?'

'Smith.'

'How original,' Pascale replied sarcastically, then crossed the threadbare carpet to the elevator. It appeared as decrepit as its surroundings. He chose the stairs instead.

'He's real popular, your Mr Smith,' the desk clerk called out after him.

Pascale froze at the foot of the stairs and looked round. 'What d'you mean?'

'Another guy was asking about him not five minutes ago.'

'Who?'

'Don't remember his name, other than that he was a cop. A federal marshal, I think he said. He did show me a badge, but I didn't take much notice.'

'Why didn't you tell me this before?' Pascale asked angrily.

'You didn't ask. I ain't no mind reader.'

Pascale made his way cautiously up the stairs to the second floor, knowing that he was probably already too late to get at Hungate before the authorities did. His worst fears were realized when he noticed the three men standing outside a door further down the corridor. He knew a cop when he saw one.

'What are you doing here?' a voice demanded behind him.

Pascale looked round at the man. Short hair. Baggy suit. A plain-clothes cop. No doubt about that. Only he had no idea where the guy had materialized from. Had he been watching the stairs from the first-floor landing? It seemed the only logical answer. 'You startled me,' he said, putting his hand to his chest.

'You got business here?'

'Yeah, I'm here to meet someone. On the third floor.' Pascale knew he had to play this right to extricate himself from a potentially dangerous situation.

'A hooker?'

'Oh no, of course not.' Pascale purposely replied too quickly, knowing the cop would realize he was lying. This guy wasn't vice, he was sure of that. They were after Hungate, not some john out to get his rocks off.

The man took a shield from his pocket and held it up towards Pascale. 'United States Marshals Service. You haven't got any business here, if you know what's good for you.'

'No ... no, of course not, officer,' Pascale stammered, feigning anxiety.

'It's deputy, not officer. Now get out of here before I bust you.' The threat was accompanied by a sharp jab of the thumb over the shoulder.

'Thank you, officer ... deputy,' Pascale said apprehensively, before hurrying back down the stairs to the lobby. There was no way he could get to Hungate now. Not with the US Marshals Service crawling all over the hotel. He felt a mixture of anger, frustration and uncertainty. Anger at his apparent helplessness. Frustration that had he been there half an hour earlier he'd have got to Hungate before the authorities. Uncertainty because of what Hungate already had on him. It was the uncertainty which lingered on in his mind as he headed back dejectedly towards the front door.

'Have a good one,' the desk clerk called out cheerily to him.

Pascale shot him a withering look and saw the derisive grin on the desk clerk's face, and the sixty dollars in his hand. The anger and frustration quickly returned as he left the hotel.

'Blane, you ready?'

The marshal, on the opposite side of the door, nodded in response to Robideaux's whispered question, and then his eyes went to Taylor who was standing further down the corridor. Unlike Robideaux and himself, Taylor still had his gun in its holster. Robideaux, determined to play it strictly by the book, didn't want Taylor actively involved in the arrest of Eddie Hungate. That way there could be no comebacks from some slick-talking lawyer. Blane had to admit, he liked Taylor. The guy was unorthodox. Took chances. Which was more than he could say about Robideaux. But Robideaux was his superior, which meant he just had to bite his tongue and follow orders.

'Let's do it,' Robideaux hissed.

Blane slammed the sole of his shoe against the flimsy door. It flew open. Robideaux was first through the door, Beretta extended at arm's length. Blane followed close behind him. Robideaux noticed the movement out the corner of his eye, but wasn't quick enough to react as Hungate lunged at him, deflecting his gun hand and knocking him backwards into Blane who stumbled and fell. Hungate brushed past Robideaux, and then jumped nimbly over Blane, avoiding the grasping hand at his ankle. He burst out into the corridor and saw Taylor in the split second before the punch hammered into his solar plexus, dropping him to his knees. He was still gasping for breath, hands clutched tightly over his stomach, when the deputy marshal watching the fire escape rushed forward and shoved him roughly to the floor. Blane emerged from the room and, between them, they managed to subdue him and snap a pair of handcuffs round his wrists.

Robideaux appeared as Hungate was hauled to his feet. 'Read him his rights, then take him to the car.' He waited until one of the deputy marshals had led Hungate away before turning to Taylor. 'Did you stop him?'

'It was either that, or let him get away.'

'There were men at either end of the corridor. He wouldn't have got away. This will be going in my report.'

'That's what I like about you, Robideaux. You never skimp when it comes to showing your gratitude, do you?'

'I specifically told you not to get involved,' Robideaux replied.

'I wouldn't have needed to, if you'd done your job properly,' Taylor countered.

'I was caught by surprise,' Robideaux bristled.

'Make sure you put that in your report as well. You do know how to spell incompetent, don't you?'

Robideaux noticed the traces of a faint smile twitch at the corners of Blane's mouth. 'You find this funny, do you?'

'No, sir,' Blane replied sombrely, losing the smile.

'I want the room examined thoroughly. Bag anything of relevance and take it downtown. I'll be there for the next few hours should you need to contact me.'

Blane nodded, and then disappeared back into the room.

'Do I get to sit in when you question Hungate?' Taylor asked, falling in step beside Robideaux as they headed towards the stairs.

'Chief Deputy Marshal Elworthy has already said that you'll be permitted to sit in on the questioning.'

The reply left Taylor in no doubt that had it been up to Robideaux, he wouldn't have been allowed anywhere near the building while Hungate was being interrogated. But then it wasn't up to him, and Taylor took great delight in Robideaux's obvious annoyance at being overruled by his superior. He smiled contentedly to himself and followed Robideaux down the stairs.

'Jess Kane's in on it as well, sir.'

Chief Deputy Marshal Elworthy's eyes lingered on Robideaux before he sat back in his wheelchair. 'Hungate told you that?'

'Yes, sir,' Robideaux said.

'What the hell's going on in this department?' Elworthy exploded in frustration. 'I always thought Hungate and Kane were good men. Solid. Reliable. And certainly above corruption. It's fast getting to the point where I don't know who I can trust any more. What else did you find out from questioning Hungate?'

'Not much more than that, sir. He gave up Kane, but refused to cooperate when it came to answering any questions about the names in the book we discovered under the floor in his bedroom. It's been very frustrating trying to get anything out of him.'

'Personally, I think he's out to frame Jess Kane,' Taylor said, entering the conversation for the first time. 'There's no evidence pointing to him being involved. His name wasn't in the book.'

'That book contained Hungate's contacts,' Robideaux said in exasperation. 'Kane was his partner. Why would his name be in the book?'

'And then there's the question of the money that was paid into Kane's account,' Taylor continued, ignoring Robideaux's outburst. 'It was so crudely done, it had to be a set-up.'

'Or maybe that's what the two of them wanted us to think, to make it appear as if Kane was being set up,' Robideaux came back at him.

'So why Kane, and not Hungate as well?' Taylor asked.

'Because if they'd both had identical amounts of money paid into their accounts, that *would* have smacked of a set-up,' Robideaux was quick to reply.

'I'm still not convinced that Kane's in on this. Hungate was very quick to give up Kane at the outset of the interrogation, then he just clammed up altogether after that. I don't like it.'

'You don't have to like it, Taylor. This is an internal inquiry, which means it doesn't fall within the jurisdiction of your investigation.' Robideaux turned to Elworthy. 'I'd like to bring Kane in for questioning, sir.'

Elworthy nodded. 'It's the only way we're going to clear this up. Send a unit to his house. If he's not there, put out an APB to all law-enforcement agencies across the state. Assuming he is involved, he may have already fled the city if he knows that Hungate's now in custody.'

'I'll get on to it right away, sir.' Robideaux got to his feet and left the room.

'You're really not convinced, are you, son?'

Taylor shook his head. 'There's just too many loose ends. The money, for a start. And why would Klyne's accomplice knock out Hungate when he first got into the surveillance car, but not Kane?'

'Perhaps to deflect attention away from the possibility that they were in on it together?'

'Too intricate, sir. No, I don't think Kane's in on it.'

'So then why would Hungate implicate him? They're not only partners, they're also best friends. As are their wives. No, it doesn't make any sense for Hungate to drag Kane down with him, unless he was involved as well.'

'So you agree with Robideaux?' Taylor asked.

'I've known Robert a long time, son. His instincts are rarely wrong.'

'I guess we'll just have to wait and see then, won't we?' Taylor said, making no attempt to mask the uncertainty in his voice.

'I guess we will at that.'

Eddie Hungate was seated in the interview room, his manacled hands resting on the table in front of him. A black coffee in a Styrofoam cup lay untouched close to his elbow. He was alone, although he knew a deputy marshal was standing guard in the corridor, posted there until Robideaux returned to continue questioning him. It had been easy giving up Kane. A lot easier than he had anticipated. Fuck friendship. His only concern now was looking out for number one.

He turned his head towards the door on hearing a muffled thud outside in the corridor. Who was it? Robideaux? Taylor? Then the door opened.

'Well, about fucking time too. Just where the hell have you been, partner?' Hungate said disdainfully. 'I kept to my side of the deal. I didn't tell them anything to incriminate you. Now you gotta get me outta here.' His eyes widened in horror at the sight of the silenced automatic which came into view. 'What the fuck are you . . . wait . . . wait . . . we can—'

The first bullet caught him above the left eye, punching him forward against the table before his body toppled sideways on to the floor. He was already dead when the second bullet was dispatched with clinical precision through the back of his head.

'This is intolerable!' Elworthy entered his office and manoeuvred the wheelchair behind his desk. The paramedics, who'd been summoned as soon as Hungate's body had been found, had confirmed that he was dead, and the interview room had since been sealed off by detectives from the New Orleans Police Department who'd been called in to investigate the homicide.

'We had to call in the NOPD, sir. It's standard procedure in any homicide, irrespective of where it was committed,' Robideaux said, trying to diffuse the tension in the room.

'You'd certainly know all about standard procedure, wouldn't you?' Elworthy's voice was more composed when he continued, 'You're right, of course. But that doesn't mean I have to like these goons prying into our affairs. It makes me real . . . uncomfortable.'

'And embarrassed?' Taylor added from the closed door.

'If you've got nothing constructive—'

'No, he's right,' Elworthy cut across Robideaux's attempted rebuke. 'Of course it's embarrassing. Kane's just allowed to walk in here and execute Hungate in cold blood. Then walk out again and vanish into thin air.'

'Assuming it was Kane,' Taylor said. 'It's not as if anyone actually saw him. The one person who could have made a positive ID was the deputy marshal you had posted outside the door. Only he was slugged from behind. He didn't see, or hear, a thing until he came round and found the body.'

'Nobody saw Kane because he gained access through a door leading into the basement,' Robideaux was quick to point out. 'The cops have already established that as the means of entry.'

'Just what exactly are you getting at, son?' Elworthy hadn't taken his eyes off Taylor since he had first spoken.

'I'm still not convinced that Kane is mixed up in any of this. It's all too convenient.'

'So you're suggesting that Hungate's killer was already in the building, and maybe still is, and staged all this to heap further suspicion on Kane?' Elworthy concluded.

'It has to be a possibility,' Taylor agreed.

'It's preposterous, that's what it is!'

'Is it?' Taylor replied, his eyes moving to Robideaux.

'Then why did Hungate implicate Kane when we questioned him earlier?' Robideaux challenged smugly.

'To divert any suspicion away from his real accomplice? What if his accomplice contacted him before his arrest, or the other way round, and they made some kind of deal in the event of Hungate being taken into custody. He, or she – we can't discount this accomplice being a woman – tells Hungate to finger Kane to give us something to work on. And when we're out of the room, the accomplice will spring him. Only the accomplice kills him instead to cover his, or her, tracks.'

'Ever thought of writing fairy stories, Taylor?' Robideaux asked derisively.

'This isn't getting us anywhere,' Elworthy said, shaking his head at the two men in front of him. 'It's an interesting theory, son, but I'm inclined to agree with Robert. The evidence appears to be over-whelming against Jess Kane.'

'Then I guess we'll just have to wait until Kane's arrested and taken in for questioning before the truth is finally known.' Taylor said, folding his arms defensively across his chest.

'Before the truth is finally *confirmed*,' Robideaux corrected him.

'Let's wait and see, shall we?' Taylor countered.

'At this moment in time, son, it's all we can do.'

Eight

Frankie Genno awoke with a start as his bunk shuddered beneath him. Then the shaking stopped as suddenly as it had begun. For a moment there was silence. Total and utter silence, something he had never experienced in his eighteen years at Stateville. Then a frenzied clamour took hold as inmates rushed to their cell doors, shouting frantically at each other, desperate to ascertain what had woken them so abruptly. Genno could only hear a handful of voices above the chaotic cacophony which now engulfed the entire cellblock.

'What's going on?'

'Fucking earthquake, man.'

'No way. Not in Illinois, asshole.'

'It wasn't no fucking earthquake. Sounded like an explosion to me.'

'Explosion?'

'Could be. Mebbe it's a break-out?'

'No sirens, man. Can't be. I still say it's an earthquake. Small one.'

'Like your brain, motherfucker. I come from LA. That wasn't no earthquake. No way.'

The rest of the dialogue was drowned out by the increasing barrage of inmates as they pounded incessantly on cell doors with any implement which came to hand. They wanted answers. Genno remained motionless in his bunk for some time, listening to the rhythmic beating around him. Then, picking up his mug, he slowly got to his feet and joined in.

The explosion had ripped through a section of the infirmary at the Stateville Correctional Center at 4.54 a.m. Several fires had broken out in close proximity to the storeroom, where the blast had originated, and although the sprinkler system had quickly kicked in, the whole block was soon engulfed in a dense blanket of thick, acrid smoke. The walls of the storeroom had been blown down in the explosion and a section of the roof had collapsed on to the adjoining operating theatre, which had suffered severe structural damage as a result. Several patients in a nearby ward had been injured, two of them seriously, but the fact that nobody had been killed was nothing short of a miracle. The fire department had arrived within minutes and it quickly became evident to the on-scene fire chief that the whole health-care facility was now unsafe and would have to be evacuated. Patients were sent, under armed escort, to several hospitals in and around the Joliet area.

A makeshift clinic was hurriedly set up in one of the administrative wings so that the provision of basic health care for inmates could continue, but the warden had been warned by the senior physician on duty that any serious medical conditions would have to be dealt with in the sterile environment of a civilian hospital.

It was shortly after breakfast that the warden's internal phone rang.

'Sir, it's Officer Baker. We've got a problem. With Genno.'

'Genno? What about him?' the warden replied suspiciously.

'I've already called the medic, sir. Genno's just thrown up his breakfast in his cell.'

'So why call me? I've got enough to worry about as it is,' came the exasperated reply.

'He also appears to be bleeding, sir. Internally.'

'Well?' the warden demanded after the duty physician had emerged from Genno's cell into the range, the area in the corridor outside the cell.

'That he's not,' the doctor said, shaking his head.

'I've no intention of questioning your diagnosis, Doctor, but could this be an elaborate ploy to get himself transferred out of here?'

'It's possible,' the doctor conceded, and then added quickly, 'but in my opinion, given his medical history, I think that's highly unlikely. Tell me, has he been subjected to any kind of stress recently?'

'Yes, you could say that,' the warden replied hesitantly.

'He called for a medic twice during the night, both times complaining of burning pains in his stomach. Now he's thrown up twice in the space of a few minutes, both times with significant traces of blood in the vomit. He also claims to be feeling dizzy and having severe pain in his muscles. These symptoms, together with stress, are indicative of a bleeding peptic ulcer. As he has a history of peptic ulcers, I can't afford to take the chance that this is some kind of ruse to get out of here. If he is bleeding internally, he needs immediate medical treatment.'

'Can't you provide that here?' the warden asked, looking at Genno who was sitting dejectedly on his bunk, head bowed, arms folded across his stomach. A blanket had been wrapped round his shoulders.

'My God, man, I can't even dispense an aspirin from the infirmary at the moment, let alone the possibility of carrying out emergency surgery in there. He has to get to a hospital. And quickly.'

'It's all too convenient for my liking.'

'If he does have internal bleeding and it's not treated properly, he could conceivably die. How will you explain that to the board of governors?'

'I'm sure they'd understand, given the circumstances,' the warden replied caustically.

'I don't give a damn about the circumstances,' the doctor said with equal acerbity. 'My only concern right now is for the well-being of my patient. If you want a dozen armed policemen to watch over him, that's fine by me. That's your department. But he is going to hospital, whether you like it or not. This is one area where I can overrule your decision. I really don't want it to come to that. Now are you going to give permission for Genno to be transferred out of here?'

'Do I have much choice?' the warden replied. 'I'll make the necessary arrangements. You call the ambulance.'

'If it is a ruse, it's certainly a good one,' the doctor admitted as the warden turned away from him, 'and I, for one, would love to know how he's done it.'

With Carberra's help, and a little ingenuity of his own – that was how he'd done it. Once Cabrerra had verified that his contact had collected the money Frances Genno had left at a prearranged location, he had put his part of the plan into action. Shortly before the explosion, one of his more trusted lieutenants, working as an orderly in the infirmary, had gained access to a temporary storeroom beside the operating theatre, and after stacking several boxes of aerosol cans on the shelving units against the wall, he had doused a mound of dusters with liquid polish and placed them directly underneath the bottom shelf. He had then lit the dusters and, once the flames caught, had quickly retreated, locking the door behind him. He was on the other side of the infirmary when the boxes of aerosol cans had ignited in quick succession. There was no incriminating evidence linking either himself, or Cabrerra, to the explosion, as all the items used would normally have been stored in that particular place.

Genno had then put his own part of the plan into action, shortly after returning to his cell after breakfast. He had already been surreptitiously passed two small sachets of blood and half a dozen ipecacuanha tablets in the mess hall by one of Cabrerra's men. The tablets, which had been stolen earlier from the infirmary, could be used as an emetic. He had taken three shortly after returning to his cell. Then, secreting one of the sachets in his cheek, he had bitten down hard on it moments before he threw up, to make it appear as if there was blood in his vomit. He had waited until the doctor was called before palming the remaining tablets and the second sachet of blood into his mouth. He had thrown up again shortly before the doctor arrived. Both sachets had been digested to destroy the incriminating evidence. He hadn't been surprised when the warden had raised his suspicions about the timing of the illness, but he also knew that the doctor would have to take it seriously, considering his history of peptic ulcers. He'd never actually thought he would be grateful one day for all the agony he'd been forced to endure over the years as a result of the recurring ulcers.

Obviously, an internal scan of his stomach at the hospital would reveal the deception and he would be dispatched straight back to prison, but he had every confidence that the rest of his carefully orchestrated scam would go according to plan, leaving him free, after eighteen years of isolated torment, to finally execute his revenge on Annie . . .

A patrol car from the Joliet Police Department escorted the ambulance from Stateville Correctional Centre to the city's Silver Cross Hospital. In addition, a uniformed officer had been assigned to sit with the non-driving paramedic in the back of the ambulance where Genno was secured to the gurney, hands and ankles manacled to the support bars. Both vehicles kept their sirens on, and lights flashing, for the duration of the journey to the hospital.

The patrol car pulled up a short distance beyond the main entrance of the hospital, and then the driver jumped out and hurried round to the rear of the ambulance which had since stopped directly in front of the automatic doors. He hovered in the background as a male nurse opened the rear doors of the ambulance and helped the paramedic lift the gurney out of the vehicle and into the road, where it was wheeled into the reception area by the nurse. The two patrol men flanked the gurney as it was propelled towards the nearest elevator, their brief to keep Genno under close personal guard at all times.

'Where are you taking him?' the older of the two patrolmen asked as the nurse pushed the button for the elevator.

'He's going to the second floor for a series of diagnostic tests, to determine the full extent of the internal bleeding. Blood and urine samples will be taken, then analysed. And his abdomen will be X-rayed as well. If the ulcer is perforated, he'll have to undergo immediate surgery to prevent possible peritonitis.'

'Yeah?' The veteran cop was indifferent.

'What if he's trying to pull a fast one?' the second cop asked, eyeing Genno disdainfully. He was a rookie, fresh out of the academy. 'That would show up on the X-ray, wouldn't it?'

'Well, yes,' the nurse replied hesitantly.

Genno's face was expressionless as he stared at the rookie. He'd mastered the art of concealing his true feelings from an early age. The rookie had accompanied him to the hospital in the back of the ambulance. Had it not been for the presence of the paramedic, he had every reason to believe that the rookie would have used his fists on him. Leaving no telltale marks, of course. He'd taken a bad beating at the precinct shortly after his arrest, but the cops had been careful not to autograph their work. Cops very like these two. The veteran seemed the more reserved of the pair. Experience has its virtues. The rookie, though, was headstrong. Thought he knew how to solve all the world's problems. Fucking little prick was itching for the opportunity to prove himself to his partner. Genno had seen it all before with every intake of new prisoners at Stateville. There wasn't really that much dissimilarity between them and the rookie. Except that the rookie had the law behind him whenever he chose to break the rules. A subtle difference.

The elevator door slid open and the rookie entered first, followed by the nurse who manoeuvred the gurney inside. The veteran stepped in after them, and the nurse was about to push the button when a voice commanded, 'Hold the elevator!'

The veteran cop raised a hand towards the approaching priest. 'Sorry, Father, you can't come in. Police business.' He nodded to the nurse who stabbed the button with his finger.

The priest grabbed the edge of the door and shoved it back forcefully. 'And this is God's business!' he declared resolutely. 'I have a patient on the fourth floor needing the last rites. I got here as quickly as I could. I certainly don't have time to stand here arguing with you. Now step aside and let me in.'

The veteran cop reluctantly gestured for the priest to enter the elevator. 'Second and fourth floors,' he instructed the nurse, indicating the control panel with a nod of his head.

Genno's face remained expressionless as his eyes flickered at the priest. The disguise was good. But then that was Paul Klyne's speciality. The door had barely closed when Klyne drew a silenced automatic from the holster at the back of his trousers, hidden by his black jacket, and shot the veteran cop twice in the chest at close range. He trained the automatic on the rookie, who hadn't even had time to reach for his own holstered weapon. 'Stop the elevator,' he commanded, without taking his eyes off the now terrified rookie who had raised his trembling hands above his head. 'Who's got the keys?'

'I . . . I . . . I've got them,' the rookie stammered fearfully. 'Top . . . top pocket.'

'Take them out *slowly*, then unlock the cuffs,' Klyne told him.

The rookie fumbled nervously with the button of his tunic pocket, then dug his fingers inside and removed the two small keys. He released Genno's right hand. Genno unholstered the rookie's weapon and rattled the other manacle irritably, waiting for him to unlock it. Once unshackled, Genno clambered off the gurney and smiled coldly at the rookie. It was his first facial expression since being loaded into the ambulance back at Stateville. 'You were itching to beat the shit out of me on the way here, weren't you?'

'I . . . I don't . . . know . . . what you're talk . . . talking about,' the rookie stammered apprehensively.

'Genno, we don't have time for this shit!' Klyne barked tersely behind him, his weapon now trained on the nurse who was pressed tightly against the side of the elevator, terror evident on his face.

'You should have done it, kid,' Genno said, ignoring Klyne. 'You should have done it when you had the chance. Only it's too late now. Too late.'

The rookie cried out in pain when Genno lashed the butt of the service revolver across the side of his face, crushing his cheekbone. He was still cradling his shattered cheek when Genno smashed the butt down savagely on to the back of his head. The rookie collapsed across the gurney, arms hanging limply over the side, as the white sheet quickly began to stain a deep crimson around his face.

'It's too fucking late now, isn't it?' Genno repeatedly pounded the butt of the revolver down on to the back of the rookie's blood-soaked head.

'For Christ's sake, that's enough.' Klyne grabbed Genno's raised arm and pulled him away from the blood-spattered gurney. He didn't know whether the rookie was dead, though he had every reason to believe he was, judging by the grotesque crater of gristle and bone at the back of his head and the amount of blood which had already splashed across the walls of the elevator. Klyne applied a *coup de grâce* just the same. 'What the fuck d'you do that for?' he demanded of Genno, staring at the pulped remains of the rookie's skull.

'Because I felt like it,' came the defiant reply.

'You're crazy, Genno, d'you know that?'

'I'm free.'

'Yeah, well not yet,' Klyne said, and then turned to the petrified nurse cowering in the corner of the elevator. 'How do we get out of there without being seen?'

'Please don't kill me,' the nurse pleaded.

Genno grabbed him by the lapels and hauled him roughly to his feet. 'He's not going to kill you. Now answer the question.'

'The basement,' the nurse blurted out. 'It's just pipes and machinery. Only the maintenance guys go down there.'

'Can we get out of the building from the basement?' Klyne asked.

'Yes,' came the fearful reply.

'Which button?' Genno's hand was already poised over the controls.

'Bottom . . . one,' the nurse said.

Genno pressed the button and Klyne trained his silenced automatic on the door when it opened on to the basement. The corridor leading off from the elevator was deserted. Genno tossed the rookie's bloodied revolver under the gurney, out of reach of the nurse, who never had any intention of being a hero anyway, and then snapped his fingers at Klyne. 'Give me your gun.' Klyne handed it to him without a word. Genno shot the nurse through the head and watched as his lifeless body slipped to the floor of the elevator. 'I told you *he* wouldn't kill you,' Genno said. Then, barricading the gurney lengthways in the doorway to prevent the doors from closing, to give themselves a few extra minutes before the bodies were discovered, he ran after Klyne who was already sprinting down the corridor towards the fire exit. Klyne eased open the door and peered out tentatively. A set of concrete steps led up to a slip road which formed part of the car park. Perfect. He took off his tunic to reveal a white shirt underneath, and peeling off the false moustache and pocketing the wire-rimmed glasses, he hurried up the steps and crossed briskly to where he had parked the hired car. Once inside, he slipped on a white overcoat, which carried a laminated lapel badge identifying him as a lab assistant from a neighbouring hospital, then reversed out of the parking space and drove the short distance to where Genno was waiting anxiously for him. Genno scrambled up the steps, doubled over, and slipped unnoticed into the back of the car and closed the door behind him. He lay down on the floor and pulled a plaid blanket over his body. Satisfied that Genno was hidden from view, Klyne engaged the gears and drove to a halt in front of the lowered boom gate. A security guard emerged from the adjacent booth and peered in at him through the open driver's window. He nodded in recognition when he noticed the ID badge. 'You get your samples?' he asked, remembering their earlier conversation.

'Yeah, and I've got to get them back to our own lab for analysis as soon as possible. They've only got a limited incubation period.'

'Then you'd better put your foot down,' the guard said, and activated the barrier. 'You have a nice day now, y'hear?'

Klyne eased the car out into the stream of passing traffic and his mouth creased into a faint smile as he cast a last glance at the security guard in the rearview mirror. 'Yeah, we will.'

Once clear of the hospital, Genno threw back the blanket and reached for the change of clothes that Klyne had earlier stuffed under the passenger seat. Another set of overalls. And a peaked cap. Remaining out of sight of passing vehicles, he proceeded to remove his prison gear before changing into the new set of overalls which were a size too big. But that was of little importance to him, because they were just for the short term. Then, piling his hair on top of his head, he tugged the peaked cap down firmly over his cranium. Only then did he straighten up, and reaching over the passenger seat he pulled down the sun visor to look at himself in the small mirror. 'You did well today, Klyne,' he announced with a satisfied smile, tucking the few remaining strands of loose hair under the cap.

'It's what I was paid to do,' came the matter-of-fact reply.

'But you fucked up in New Orleans.' The smile vanished. Genno's voice was now cold and uncompromising.

'If I hadn't, you wouldn't have your freedom.'

'You think I give a damn about my *freedom*?' Genno countered. 'I didn't do this to get skin cancer on some fucking beach in Acapulco. I'm under no illusions, Klyne. The cops are going to be out in force looking for me as soon as those bodies are discovered at the hospital. And they won't stop searching until they've found me. My only concern is getting to Annie before they relocate her. After that, I couldn't care less what happens to me.'

'Louisiana does carry the death penalty,' Klyne reminded him.

'Good. Assuming, of course, they take me alive. There's no guarantee they will. They're more likely to shoot first, and ask for medals later.'

'You really don't give a damn whether you live or die after you've killed Sarah Johnson, do you?'

'Her name's Annie Stratton,' Genno growled, leaning forward to glare at Klyne behind the wheel. 'My Annie. She'll always be *my* Annie.'

'She might have something to say about that,' Klyne replied, without taking his eyes off the road.

'Oh, I'm sure she will.' Genno laughed, and then slumped back in the seat and smiled thoughtfully to himself. 'She always did like to speak her mind. That much hasn't changed over the years.'

'You're still in love with her, aren't you?' Klyne said in amazement, looking over his shoulder at Genno.

'How far to the motel?' Genno demanded irritably.

'Another few miles.'

'Let's see if you can keep your mouth shut until then. After all, you are still working on my time.'

'Suits me.' Klyne remained silent for the remainder of the journey to the motel.

The Shiller Motel was located off Route 30, close to the Crest Hill Community Park. Small, nondescript, with bland, whitewashed walls and an illuminated neon sign on rusted mountings above the reception area. The parking lot was empty, except for a red Oldsmobile with garish white leather upholstery and a fur-lined dashboard. The last time Genno had seen one of those had been in Chicago, with a black pimp behind the wheel. Eddie 'The Man' Washington. Genno could still visualize the sartorial son-of-a-bitch cruising the streets, constantly checking on his pros and slapping up any who weren't turning enough tricks to satisfy his greed. Washington had even suggested putting Annie on the game as a means of financing her coke habit. Genno's answer had been a knee in the groin. Then he had walked away, leaving Washington writhing in agony at the feet of one of his hookers. Two days later, Washington's body had been found slumped over the wheel of his pimpmobile, throat slit from ear to ear. Suspicion had fallen on Genno when word of the altercation reached the cops, but he'd had an airtight alibi for the time of the murder. The cops soon lost interest, secretly grateful that Washington was off the streets for good. The case was never officially closed. Genno hadn't killed him. But he'd had him killed. A quiet word in the right ear. Why get blood on his hands when he could get someone else to do his dirty work for him?

'What's with the car?' Klyne asked, parking directly in front of his motel room.

'Memories,' came the wistful response.

Klyne stared uncertainly at Genno as he gazed nostalgically at the Oldsmobile, then patted him on the arm. 'Come on, let's go inside.'

Genno got out of the car and followed Klyne to the room. Klyne opened the door and ushered Genno inside. The chintzy furnishings didn't surprise Genno. Neither did the water bed that rippled under Klyne's burly frame when he sat on it. Nor the fact that Klyne had the television set tuned into the pay-per-view porn channel. The picture quality was poor, as were the spurious sounds of feigned passion coming from the screen.

'Why d'you watch this shit?' Genno asked with genuine disgust after turning off the television set. 'It'd be cheaper to pay some hooker for the real thing.'

'I didn't think you'd want me balling some bitch on *your* time,' Klyne replied sarcastically.

'I'm sure it beats the company of Lady Five Fingers. But then to each his own, eh?'

'That's rich coming from someone who's spent the past eighteen years in a state pen',' came the contemptuous response. 'Your only fucking release in there would have been a hand job at the dead of night. Or maybe you got a taste for the sweet kids? The young ones are always the best.'

'If you can discipline the mind, there are any number of ways to stimulate the senses without having to resort to the licentious.

145

Physical pleasure is fundamentally flawed. It's like a drug. The rush only lasts for a short time. It's overrated, Klyne. Take my word for it.'

'What are you saying, Genno? That in all the years you were locked up—'

'That's exactly what I'm saying,' Genno cut in, and then gestured to the door leading into the bathroom. 'Is my stuff in there?'

'Yeah.' Klyne followed Genno to the bathroom and paused in the doorway, leaning his shoulder against the frame. 'I'm intrigued. I can't believe that you've never had any sexual urges in the last eighteen years.'

'I never said that,' Genno replied, looking at Klyne in the reflection of the wall mirror. 'Of course I did. I'm only human. But I was able to control them with the power of thought. It's really not that difficult. You should try it sometime. Now, if you'll excuse me.' He shut the door.

Only then did he turn his attention to the items which had been laid out neatly on the towel at the side of the wash basin. A pair of scissors, a razor and a pack of blades, a canister of shaving foam, a styptic pencil and a cordless hair trimmer – all there. He raised his head and scrutinized his face in the mirror. The long, unkempt hair. The straggly beard. A comfortable familiarity. That was about to change. Picking up the scissors, he first set about the beard, cutting it away in clumps which tumbled to the floor. Then, once the beard had been reduced enough to attack the remainder with the razor, he began on his hair. There was no symmetry to his onslaught. Hacking. Hewing. Chopping. It took several minutes of sustained shearing until he was satisfied with the result. The floor around his feet was covered in offcuts of unwanted hair. He paused again to examine himself in the mirror. Partial transformation. Then he filled the basin with hot water, and as he began to remove the remnants of his patchy beard he realized it was the first time he had actually used a razor. He'd had a beard all his adult life. The results were predictably irksome and he was left with numerous nicks on his skin, particularly across the base of the throat. He used the styptic pencil to stem the bleeding. Then he picked up the hair trimmer, adjusted the blades to the shortest setting and proceeded to run it over his head until he had achieved the uniform length of a Marine cut. He took a step away from the basin and a faint smile of satisfaction played across his lips as he studied his reflection in the mirror. The truth was, he didn't even recognize himself. So what chance would the authorities have?

It was the perfect disguise. He emerged from the bathroom and extended his arms away from him in a theatrical gesture. 'What d'you think?'

'Well, well, so there was a face under all that hair, after all,' Klyne said with a snigger. 'There were times when I did wonder.'

'It makes quite a difference, doesn't it?'

'And some,' Klyne agreed. He indicated the congealed blood round the base of Genno's throat. 'A bit rusty with the old razor, eh?'

'Yeah,' Genno replied absently, then patted the overnight bag lying on the bed. 'Are my clothes in here?'

Klyne nodded. 'Two changes of clothing, as requested by your mother. Toiletries. Some cash in mixed denominations. Which reminds me, I'm still owed the balance of my money.'

'You'll get it,' Genno assured him, as he unzipped the overnight bag and removed a pair of jeans and a white T-shirt.

'When?'

'I'll bring it to you later, after I've been to see my mother. The money's at her house.'

'You're going to your mother's house?' Klyne shook his head in astonishment. 'You're crazy, Genno. The whole area will be swarming with cops, after what happened earlier at the hospital.'

'It's the second time now you've called me that.' Genno levelled a finger of warning at Klyne. 'It doesn't happen again. Understood?'

'Then don't act it,' Klyne countered. 'Your flight ticket from Chicago to New Orleans is in the overnight bag. You've no need to go anywhere near your mother's house. There are other ways to get the money.'

'It's not open to discussion,' Genno told him, discarding the overalls on the bed before stepping into the jeans and zipping them up.

'You've got this far, Genno, why risk everything now? It's so unnecessary.'

'I wouldn't expect you to understand.'

'Try me,' Klyne said.

'You never were that close to your mother, were you?'

'Can't say I was.'

'Which is why I said you wouldn't understand.' Genno pulled on the T-shirt, and then fished out a battered brown leather jacket and a pair of trainers from the overnight bag.

'I ain't driving you out there,' Klyne said defiantly. 'I'm not putting my neck on the block just so that you can play happy families. You want to visit Mommy, you do it on your own. Leave me out of it.'

'Suits me. It's something I have to do myself anyway.' Genno sat on the edge of the bed to put on the trainers, then got to his feet again. 'Give me the keys to the car.'

'You can't use the car in case the licence plates were spotted at the hospital. I was about to go out and dump it anyway.'

'Not *that* car. The back-up car.'

'Back-up car? What are you talking about?' Klyne said in surprise.

'You can cut the act, Klyne. We both know you've got a second car. How else were you going to get back here after you'd dumped the getaway car?' Genno held out a hand. 'Keys.'

Klyne got to his feet and moved to the window where he looked out over the deserted car park. 'That car's my insurance. I was going to use it to drive us to the airport this afternoon. Then leave it there. By the time the cops found the car, we'd have been long gone.'

'Then get another car.' Genno slipped on the leather jacket, retrieved a cellphone from the overnight bag and slid it into the inside pocket of his jacket. 'Now give me the keys.'

'I'll drive you to the other car,' Klyne said, tight-lipped.

'Fine.' Genno held his hands out towards Klyne in a gesture of frustration. 'So, what are we waiting for?'

Genno drove past his mother's house in the Lockport district of the city. The house was exactly as he'd imagined it would be, having built a mental picture from the numerous descriptions she'd given him of the building over the years. Any change to its appearance, whether inside or out, no matter how trivial, had always been recounted to him to ensure that he had the most up-to-date image in his mind.

It was a small, red-bricked bungalow with a compact porch overlooking a picturesque garden, now in full bloom. She had been an avid gardener for as long as he could remember. It was flanked by two larger houses, both with immaculate, whitewashed walls adjoining double garages. The Flints lived to her left. The Kennedys to her right. He knew all about them. Their families, their jobs, their lifestyles. And their peccadilloes. He knew she liked the Flints, who would occasionally invite her round for a sunset barbecue, and that the Kennedys, although always polite to her, were more reserved and preferred to keep to themselves. He had noticed a mountain bike lying on the driveway of the Flints' house, in front of the closed garage door. A present last Christmas for their thirteen-year-old son, Jonathan. It was ironic that he probably knew more about the two families, and about the neighbourhood in general, than many living in the street itself. What he had also noticed was the black BMW parked about twenty yards down the road from his mother's house. Two occupants. A surveillance car. Which was why he had driven straight past the house.

He drove round the block until he was at the back of houses, which were concealed behind a thicket of trees. There didn't appear to be any other surveillance cars in the immediate area. He parked the car on the next block, then got out and walked casually back in the direction of the trees. He was still about a hundred yards from the trees when a patrol car suddenly appeared over the rise in the road directly ahead of him. His first instinct was to hide in the trees, but he quickly checked himself. *Don't attract any unnecessary attention to yourself. The hair's cropped. The beard's gone. Just relax. You won't be recognized.* Yet an unease lingered uncomfortably in his stomach as the patrol car approached. For a split second the driver looked straight at him, but then returned his attention to the road, and moments later the patrol car disappeared from view. He chuckled nervously to himself. *The perfect test and you passed it with flying colours.*

He reached the small woodland where he paused to look around him with a feigned air of indifference, before making his way cautiously through the trees to the edge of the clearing, which bordered on to the back of the houses. No cops in sight. In fact, nobody in sight. He took the cellphone from his pocket and dialled the number of a second cellphone which Klyne had given to his mother earlier in the week, to ensure that his calls to her weren't monitored by the authorities on her own telephone.

'Hello?' a familiar voice answered.

'Is that Mrs Genno?' he enquired politely, knowing there was still a chance that cops could be waiting for him inside the house.

'Francis?' she exclaimed excitedly.

'I take it you're alone in there, Ma?'

'Not for long, I hope. Where are you?'

'Close. Is it safe to come in?'

'There are a couple of federal marshals parked out front. That's all, as far as I know,' she assured him.

'Yeah, I saw them.'

'Nice men. I took them some of my cookies earlier.'

'I'm sure they were thrilled to see you,' he said with a contempt-uous laugh.

'It's a quiet street, Francis. It's hard to blend in when you're sitting in an unmarked police car. But enough of this nonsense. When can I expect you?'

'Soon, Ma. Real soon.'

'Use the back door. I'll leave it off the latch.'

He cut the connection, slipped the phone back into his pocket, and then crossed the clearing. But instead of making for his mother's house, he headed in the direction of the Flints' house. Just a precaution. Both of them would be at work. Kids at school. One dog, always kept indoors while the family were out. Gate leading into the back garden. He knew it all by heart. He unlatched the metal gate and winced when it squeaked as he eased it open. Something his mother hadn't told him. Once inside, he closed the gate behind him, then ducked out of sight behind the wall and smiled to himself when he saw the home-made brick barbecue at the far end of the garden. He could almost smell the meat sizzling on the grill, having heard a number of times about the Flints' famous sunset barbecues. Pushing the thought from his mind, he moved to the interconnecting door built into the wooden fence between the two houses. The Flints had installed it when the fence was erected shortly after they'd moved in, to keep an eye on his mother. Real neighbourly. Unlatching the door, he opened it and peered tentatively into his mother's back garden. Again, it was just as he'd imagined it to be, with the neatly cut rectangular lawn bordered by a blaze of multicoloured blooms. Thick curtains discreetly covered the windows facing out over the garden. He crossed the grass to the back door and tried the handle. It was unlocked. Stepping inside, he closed the door behind him and locked it.

'Francis?'

Genno turned to find his mother standing in the doorway, arms extended towards him. 'In the flesh, Ma,' he said with a grin and hugged her tightly.

'Oh, Francis, I never thought I'd live to see this day.' She drew back from him without releasing his hands. 'Look at you. So handsome without that awful beard.'

'I never knew you didn't like my beard,' he said in surprise.

'You liked it. That's what was important. But I'm glad you've shaved it off, all the same. It makes you look so much younger. You could have left your hair a bit longer, though. It's too short. Makes you look . . . a bit scary.'

'Makes me look different, Ma. That's all that matters.' He helped himself to a chocolate-chip cookie from the jar in the cupboard. Again, it was as if he knew exactly where everything was in the house. He popped the whole cookie into his mouth. 'Am I on the news yet?'

'Don't talk with your mouth full, Francis! That's not the way I raised you,' she chastised him firmly. 'Yes, you have been on the news. In fact, I had a visit from a couple of detectives earlier on.'

'Did they treat you right?'

'Oh, very polite. They did ask me a lot of questions, though.'

'Did they search the house?'

'Yes.'

'Did they show you a search warrant?'

'I wouldn't have let them if they didn't have a search warrant,' came the indignant reply. 'I do know my rights, Francis.'

'I know you do, Ma. They'll be back, though. With reinforcements next time. That's why I can't stay very long. I don't care what happens to me, but I couldn't live with myself if you were arrested for aiding and abetting me. The very thought of you being locked up in a cell . . .' His voice, full of emotion, trailed off.

'You're a good boy, Francis,' she said and kissed him lightly on the cheek. 'Always were. Always will be. And I thank the Lord for that. Every day.'

'You OK, Ma?' he asked anxiously, when she took a hesitant step towards the nearest chair and had to grab the back to support herself.

'I just felt a bit light-headed for a moment. It's the stress of the past few days finally catching up with me. I haven't been sleeping well, Francis. So many different scenarios going through my head. But then I'm a natural worrier anyway.' She smiled gently at him. 'You of all people should know that.'

'I think you should rest up.'

'There'll be plenty of time for rest after you've gone. Right now, I just want to savour our time together. Who knows when I'll see you again?'

'Like I said, I can't stay long. What I'll do is give you a massage if you'll go and lie down in your bedroom. I know you used to like that.'

'Very well,' she agreed, and then let him take her arm and lead her down the hall towards her bedroom. 'How's the Preacher? It can't be easy for him now with his face on every news bulletin across the country.'

'What?' He pulled up sharply as they were about to enter the bedroom. 'The cops know about Klyne's involvement?'

'Of course they do. Surely he's told you?'

'No, he hasn't said a word,' Genno said in a soft, reflective voice. 'Not a word. Son-of-a-bitch!'

'Francis!' came the disapproving response to his outburst.

'Sorry, Ma,' he replied contritely, and then followed her into the bedroom. Heavy curtains were drawn across the windows.

'You still owe him the balance of his money, don't you?' She opened the top drawer of her dresser and removed the envelope, which she handed to him. 'That's the balance of the money I drew from the bank. Pay Klyne out of it. There will still be more than enough left to cover your expenses in New Orleans.'

'Thanks, Ma.' He slipped the bulky envelope into the inside pocket of his leather jacket, then led her to the bed where he crouched down to gently remove her slippers, before easing her down on to the soft mattress. 'You want something to drink? How about some hot milk with a dash of pepper? That's what you always gave me to help me sleep.'

'I don't need anything like that. Not now that you're here.' She pointed to a holdall lying at the foot of the bed. 'I went through your things the other day and put what I thought might be useful to you in there. Don't forget to take it with you when you leave.'

'I won't,' he assured her with a smile, and then indicated for her to lie back on the pillow. 'You close your eyes, Ma. The massage should help you sleep.'

They talked generally. Nothing specific. And no mention of Annie Stratton or of New Orleans. He massaged her neck and shoulders and after a time she fell silent. When he'd finished the massage, she was lying peacefully on the bed, eyes closed, head resting lightly on the pillow, face turned towards him. 'You sleep now, Ma,' he said, tracing his fingers lightly over her cheek. He kissed her on the forehead and got to his feet. 'I won't ever let Annie harm you, Ma. I swear I won't. She'll never hurt you. Never.'

Picking up the holdall at the foot of the bed, he paused at the door to look back at his mother one last time, knowing he would never see her again, but made no attempt to brush away the tears which ran down his cheeks. He left the same way he had come.

*

'So, how's your mother holding up?' Klyne asked when Genno returned to the motel room. He was sitting on the edge of the double bed, a partially consumed take-out beside him.

'Pretty good, all considering,' Genno replied, dropping the holdall on to the floor at his feet.

'You get my money?'

'I got it,' Genno said, and then shook his head in disgust when he saw that Klyne had the porn channel on. 'You watching that shit again?'

'Shh,' Klyne retorted, grinning salaciously as the naked woman responded with enthusiastic moans to the two men on the bed with her.

'Oh, sorry, I'd hate for you to miss the intricacies of the plot,' Genno snorted contemptuously, before transferring the contents of the holdall into the overnight bag.

'She's quite a looker, that one,' Klyne said, pointing to the screen.

'It's kinda hard to tell with her face buried in his groin like that.'

'Yeah, lucky bastard,' Klyne muttered excitedly.

When Genno had finished packing the overnight bag, he zipped it up and carried it to the door. Then he returned to the holdall and removed a sheathed hunting knife. He pulled the knife from its holder, then, without warning, grabbed Klyne's hair and jerked back his head, drawing the serrated blade across the exposed throat from ear to ear. Klyne fell to his knees, his hands clutching at the deep laceration, a mixture of anguish and surprise in his eyes, as the blood pumped through his fingers and down the front of his open-necked shirt.

Genno looked down disdainfully at Klyne. 'You conveniently forgot to tell me that your face has been plastered across every news channel for the past couple of days. That makes you a liability to me. No wonder you were so keen to have the porn channel on whenever I was around. Clever. Pity it didn't work, though.' He discarded the hunting knife on the bed. It didn't bother him that his prints were on the handle. He was a wanted man anyway. Who knows, he might even have made Number One on *America's Most Wanted* by nightfall. He took some satisfaction in that thought. Not that he was finished. He still had so much to do. His eyes went to Klyne lying on the carpet, his body jerking spasmodically in the last throes of death as an ever-widening pool of blood formed on the carpet around his neck. He then crossed to the door where he picked up his overnight bag and left the room, locking the door behind him. He got into the car and drove away from the motel. Destination: Chicago's O'Hare Airport. Final destination: New Orleans.

Nine

'I blame Sarah Johnson for this.'

'What?' Taylor countered in disbelief.

They were sitting with Chief Deputy Marshal Elworthy at the US marshals' district office, in the courthouse building on Camp Street. It was mid afternoon, and the sunlight slanted into the room in luminescent layers through the angle of the partially closed Venetian blinds. Robideaux winced as a stray beam bounced off the glass façade of the opposite building into his face. He got to his feet and rubbed his eyes before answering. 'If she hadn't confronted Genno in prison, none of this would have happened. She forced his hand. Now he's on the lam. This was *so* preventable.'

'That's easy to say with the benefit of hindsight,' Taylor came back. 'She did what she thought was right at the time for her and her family. And let's face it, certain parties who should have been protecting her haven't exactly excelled themselves up to now, have they?'

'Is that another dig at this department?' Robideaux blustered.

'If the shoe fits,' Taylor replied tersely.

'Knock it off, both of you!' Elworthy sat forward in his wheelchair and clasped his hands together on the desk. 'The Illinois police have already circulated an artist's impression to every law-enforcement agency in the country of what he may look like now without the long hair and beard. But even that's pure guesswork. He's had that beard since his late teens.'

'Any early photos of him, before he grew the beard?'

'He grew up in the slums of Chicago,' Elworthy reminded Robideaux. 'The only cameras in those neighbourhoods are stolen and quickly sold on to fences for profit.'

'Chances are he's already here,' Taylor said, directing his assertion to Elworthy. 'It's been too well planned for him to take any unnecessary chances by leading us on a wild-goose chase across the country. His only objective now is to get Sarah. That much is obvious by the series of events in Joliet earlier today. His prints were even on the knife he used to cut Klyne's throat at the motel. He doesn't care what happens to him any more.'

'That's the impression I get as well,' Elworthy agreed.

'A sociopath with a kamikaze mentality. Absolutely nothing to lose. They're the most dangerous of all.' Taylor pursed his lips thoughtfully. 'If the artist's impression doesn't bear a passable likeness to him as he is now, it's going to be like looking for a ghost in the mist.'

'Which means having to wait for him to make the first move,' Elworthy added grimly.

'We can't afford to take that chance.' Robideaux was quick to respond.

'I don't see that we have any choice in the matter,' Elworthy replied.

'Not necessarily,' Robideaux said. 'We could use Sarah Johnson as bait to lure him out into the open.'

'Out of the question!' Elworthy thundered. 'She's a civilian, under our protection. The press would crucify us if anything were to happen to her. And rightly so. We'd be lucky to keep our pensions, never mind our jobs. No, that's a complete nonstarter as far as I'm concerned.'

'What if she agreed to go along with it?'

Elworthy eyed Taylor suspiciously. 'You as well?'

'It sure beats sitting around waiting for him to put the first body in one of your mortuaries. And if that does happen, the press will crucify us anyway. It's a no-win situation, sir. We've got to make the best of what we've got.'

'For once you and I seem to agree on something,' Robideaux said smugly.

'It's not about us agreeing or disagreeing with each other,' Taylor replied angrily. 'It's about us doing what's best for Sarah and her family. Genno's not going to give up until he's tracked her down. We have to act to counter that threat. And a preemptive move on our part seems the most logical strategy right now.'

'You both obviously have strong views on the subject,' Elworthy said at length. 'I'll have to give it some thought.'

'We may not have much time.'

'I'm well aware of that, son,' Elworthy told Taylor. The telephone rang. He scooped up the receiver and his jaw visibly hardened as he listened to the caller. 'I see,' he said at length. 'Where was the body found?' He nodded as he continued to listen, then added, 'I appreciate that it's your investigation, and obviously we'll help in any way we can. I'll send someone to the crime scene. You can brief him more fully. Thanks for letting me know. Appreciate it.' He replaced the receiver. 'Jess Kane's body's been found in his car close to the Lafayette Cemetery over on Washington Avenue. Shot once through the head at close range. A weapon has already been recovered at the scene. It looks like suicide. Robert, I want you to go over there and coordinate with the local homicide detectives assigned to the case. Find out what's going on and whether it was a genuine suicide or not.'

'Suicide?' Taylor said, shaking his head slowly. 'It doesn't make any sense. Not if he *was* Hungate's killer. Why risk breaking into the building, shooting Hungate, and then go away and shoot himself.'

'That's why I want Robert there. It's too damn convenient for my liking.'

'I'll let you know as soon as I have anything positive to go on.' Robideaux got to his feet and left the room.

'To be honest, I can't say I'm particularly surprised that Kane's been found dead,' Elworthy said, breaking the silence which had descended over the room after Robideaux's departure. 'Perhaps he already knew too much and had to be silenced. Assuming, of course, that it wasn't suicide. But I've got my doubts, though.'

'What are you getting at, sir? You think there are others in on it? From this department?'

'I don't know what to think any more, son. As I said before, I thought Jess Kane and Eddie Hungate were straight-up guys. I guess that doesn't make me a very good judge of character. Maybe they were the only two in on it. Maybe not. Thing is, I can't afford to take the chance that there aren't others in on it well. That's why I've already initiated the necessary steps to isolate all members of this department from any further contact with the Johnsons. It's the only way I can be sure of their continued safety. That's why I was dead against using Sarah Johnson as bait for Genno.'

'I don't understand, sir,' Taylor said hesitantly.

'Don't worry, I'll explain it all to you. Then it'll be up to you to sell it to the Johnsons. I've got a feeling that's going to be the hardest part of all.'

*

'We're being moved *again*?' Bob Johnson said incredulously, after Taylor had gathered the family together in the living room at the safe house to break the news to them.

'This has got something to do with Frankie's break-out from Stateville, hasn't it?' Sarah concluded as she studied Taylor's face. 'Does he already know about this place?'

'Not as far as we're aware,' Taylor replied. He took a sip of coffee before leaning forward in his chair and replacing the mug on the table in front him. 'But obviously we can't take any chances, not now that we know Hungate, and possibly Kane as well, was responsible for the breach of security which led to the attempted hit on you at your house.'

'But they're dead. You've told us that already.'

'That's right, but there may be more rotten apples in the barrel. Who's to say that Hungate didn't have another contact in the department? Personally, I think it's very feasible now that Kane's turned up dead. I never bought the idea of Kane breaking into the courthouse building last night to kill Hungate. Why go to these lengths and then commit suicide? It doesn't make any sense.'

'So you think Kane was murdered and it was made to look like suicide?' Bob asked.

'It has to be a possibility,' Taylor told him bluntly.

'But the homicide detectives are treating it as a suicide. You said so yourself,' Bob countered.

'It wouldn't be difficult for a professional to pass off a murder as suicide, given the right circumstances.'

'So where exactly are we going?' Sarah asked. 'Do we have any say in our final destination?'

'That's something you'll have to discuss with Chief Deputy Marshal Elworthy when the situation does arise. Fact of the matter is, you're not actually leaving New Orleans. At least, not for the time being. You're just being moved to a different location, that's all.'

'We're . . . not leaving New Orleans?' Sarah said in bewilderment.

'Not at present, no. The whole idea of this scheme is to relocate you to another safe house in the city without anyone else in the local Marshals Service, apart from the Chief, knowing where you're going. That way, if Genno does have any other contacts in the department, they won't have access to your new location.'

'Will Ray Deacon and his partners still be our protection team?' Sarah asked.

Taylor shook his head. 'Elworthy has already drafted in a team of deputies from out of state to provide twenty-four-hour security at the safe house. They know nothing about the case. That way there can be no comebacks. I'll still be in overall charge of the operation, which will also allow the local deputies to concentrate their attention on finding Genno once he reaches New Orleans.'

'Why not just relocate us to another state until Frankie's caught? Wouldn't that be a lot easier all round?' Sarah wanted to know.

'On the contrary. Any movement between states would involve a lot of paperwork, which could conceivably fall into the wrong hands. It would also mean a lot more deputies being involved in the case, which is exactly what we're trying to avoid.'

'Where is this safe house?' Bob asked.

'To be honest, I don't know. I'll be given further instructions by the Chief once I have you safely out of the bayou. He's determined to play this close to the chest, for obvious reasons.'

'When do we leave here?' Bob asked.

'Whenever you're ready,' Taylor told him. He looked across at Lea who was sitting in an armchair in the corner of the room. Her knees were drawn up tightly to her chest and there was a look of despair in her eyes. 'You OK with this, Lea?' he asked softly.

'Me?' Lea replied with an affected gasp, and clasped a hand to her chest. 'And here I thought you didn't care. After all, I'm just the daughter who's expected to tag along dutifully behind her parents and be grateful for any scraps of attention that they may choose to throw her way.'

'That's not fair, Lea,' Sarah said, biting back her anger.

'No, Mom, I'll tell you what's not fair. That you've been living a lie ever since you first arrived in New Orleans. And as your daughter, I've become a part of that lie. That Dad's started to drink again, because it's the only way he can deal with this. Some role models, eh?'

'That's enough, Lea!' Bob thundered.

'I'll tell you what else is not fair,' Lea continued, ignoring her father's outburst. 'That I've been dragged out of school, in the most important part of the semester, and every day I miss I'm falling that bit further behind in my studies. And when I do finally go back to school, I'm going to have to explain everything to my friends. But, do you know something, I'm actually looking forward to putting across my side of the story. Do you want to know why? Because it'll be the first time that any kind of truth will have emerged from this whole *fucking* fiasco.'

'You mind your language, my girl,' Bob warned, then got to his feet and stepped threateningly towards Lea.

Taylor was on his feet in an instant to block Bob's path towards his daughter. 'Sit down,' he said in a soft, but firm voice.

'This is a family matter, Taylor. It doesn't concern you.'

Taylor grabbed Bob's arm when he tried to get past him. 'Either you sit down voluntarily, or I'll make you. Your choice.'

'Sit down, Bob,' Sarah said brusquely.

Bob held Taylor's stare defiantly for several seconds, then shrugged off his hand and stalked out of the room.

'Feel better now, do you?' Lea said caustically to Taylor, and then got to her feet and followed her father from the room. A short time later came the sound of her bedroom door being slammed shut.

'Bob wouldn't have hit her,' Sarah said softly.

'Maybe not,' Taylor conceded as he sat down again.

'*Definitely* not.' Her voice was now strong and commanding. 'I know Bob. He would never – *never* – lay a finger on Lea.'

'So it's only you he's hit in the past.'

'How dare you!' Sarah yelled and jumped to her feet, face flushed.

'So he's never hit you – is that what you're saying?'

'I'm saying it's none of your goddamn business. You've got some nerve making accusations like that. You really do.'

'I thought as much.'

'And just what's that supposed to mean?' she demanded.

'You didn't deny it, Sarah. That's as good as a confession.' He raised a hand before she could reply. 'That's a private matter between you and Bob, unless he appears threatening towards either you or Lea while you're under my protection. Then I will intercede. I can promise you that.'

She sat down slowly again. 'How did you know he'd hit me before?'

'You get a sense of these things after you've been in this business as long as I have. I've been with a lot of families in similar pressure situations. Maybe not as extreme as this, but then different people react to stress in different ways. It's as if the stress strips away the person's character until you're able to see them for what they really are. And believe me, it's not always pleasant.'

'It hasn't happened ... not very often,' she said awkwardly. 'Twice ... I think. When he'd had a drink.'

'That's something you've got to sort out between yourselves. In fact, it's something you want to sort out before it's too late.'

'I'm going to go and pack my bag.' Sarah stood up and moved to the door, where she paused to look back at him. 'If he ever did lay a hand on Lea, I swear I'd kill him,' she said icily, and then headed off in the direction of the bedroom.

'It's for you,' Lynne Rodford said brusquely, and then pushed the cellphone into Pascale's hand as she passed him on the way out of the living room.

'Charming,' he muttered, then put the telephone to his ear. 'Pascale?'

'Is it a safe line?' the voice demanded.

'Who is this?' Pascale demanded.

'Is it a safe line?' the voice repeated, this time stressing each word in turn.

'Yeah, it's safe,' came the exasperated reply. 'Look, who is this?'

'We had a mutual friend. Paul Klyne. He gave me your name. Now I need a contact here in New Orleans. And I'm prepared to pay good money for the right person.'

'Ah, yes. I know who this is. Enjoying life on the lam? It must be a bit of a culture shock now—'

'I didn't ring to shoot the breeze with you, Pascale,' Genno cut in sharply. 'I told you, I need a contact. You interested, or not?'

'Of course I'm interested,' Pascale assured him.

'Then let's meet.'

'Where and when?'

'An hour. You name the location. I'll be there.'

'How about the Café Pontalba in the French Quarter? Corner of Chartres and St Peter. How will I recognize you, though?'

'Just be there.' The line went dead.

'Who was that?' Lynne Rodford asked, when he entered the bedroom where she was getting ready for work.

'You wouldn't know him.'

'Knowing the company you keep, I probably wouldn't want to know him either,' she replied scornfully as she slipped on her shoes.

'No, you wouldn't,' Pascale replied truthfully. 'Believe me, you wouldn't.'

'Klyne described you well.'

Pascale looked up from the coffee he'd been nursing for the past ten minutes at an isolated table in the corner of the café. 'And how was that?' he asked languidly, and leaned back in his chair as Genno sat down, placing a folded newspaper on the table in front of him.

Genno rested both hands on the newspaper without taking his eyes off Pascale. 'As having the appearance of a shifty, scheming motherfucker.'

Pascale laughed out loud. 'I like it. He described you as a cross between a yeti and a cave man. Can't say I see the resemblance myself.'

'Good.'

'And how is our mutual friend these days?'

'Dead. I cut his throat. Ear to ear.' Genno gave a shrug at Pascale's startled expression. 'No harm in telling you. You'll read about it soon enough in the papers.'

'That was a bit drastic, wasn't it?'

'He knew too much. That made him a liability.'

'Then let's keep our relationship on a need-to-know basis, shall we?' Pascale said with a nervous chuckle, then drank the remainder of his coffee and caught the attention of the waiter standing at the bar. 'You want something to drink?' he asked Genno.

'Coffee's good.'

'Two coffees,' Pascale told the waiter, who nodded and then walked back to the bar. 'So what is it exactly you want me to do for you?'

'For a start, I need accommodation. No hotels or guesthouses. Somewhere out of the way. The more secluded, the better.'

'How about a house on the bayou? There's plenty of them around and it won't cost you much at this time of year.'

'As long as it's isolated.'

'No problem. What else?'

'A rental car. Nondescript. Also, a handgun. Make it an automatic for easier concealment. A silencer. And a couple of spare clips.'

'Any particular model?'

'How about a Beretta?'

'Can do,' Pascale told him.

'I also want you to find out everything you can about Annie . . . Sarah Johnson and her family. Husband, Bob. Daughter, Lea.'

Pascale waited until the waiter had deposited the two coffees on the table then retreated out of earshot, before speaking again. 'You could start with Renée Mercier.'

'Bob's mistress? Yeah, I heard about her. You got an address for her?'

'No, but it won't be too difficult to find that out. Anything else?'

'Yeah. Annie hired someone to take photos of my mother back in Joliet. Chances are it was probably a peeper, possibly working out of New Orleans. I want a name.'

'Who's Annie?'

'Anne Stratton. Sarah Johnson's real name.'

'Gotcha. I'll ask around about the photographer. Shouldn't be a problem coming up with a name. Assuming he is local.'

Genno tapped the folded newspaper. 'There's five grand in an envelope inside here. Two thousand for you. The rest for expenses. There's more should you need it. Just make sure you keep a list of all your expenses, together with the relevant receipts. You try and skim me, and I'll kill you.'

'That's certainly a deterrent if ever I heard one.' Pascale laughed uneasily. Genno's face remained impassive. 'So where can I contact you once I've sorted out your accommodation?'

'You don't. We'll meet again. Tomorrow. Shall we say one o'clock? You'd better have something useful for me by then.' Genno got to his feet, took a five-dollar note from his pocket, and tossed it on to the table. 'That's for the coffees. We wouldn't want you to waste any of your expense money, now would we?'

'Perish the thought,' Pascale muttered facetiously, drawing the newspaper towards him, but Genno was already out of earshot and heading for the exit.

Genno was staying under an assumed name at a nondescript boarding house on Esplanade Avenue, on the edge of the French Quarter. He had paid for two days in advance, although he expected to be out of there by the following day – if Pascale was as efficient as Klyne had made him out to be. An isolated house on the bayou. Sounded good. He could take Annie to the house and there would be nobody to hear . . .

Don't jump the gun, he chided himself. First you have to find her. Which was why Pascale was so important to him while he was in New Orleans. So don't rile him. Give him some leeway. Yeah, like Klyne. And look where that had got him. Then again, he was merely using Pascale as an informer. He sure as hell didn't trust the bastard beyond that. Trust? Wrong word. He didn't trust anybody. Eighteen years at Stateville had only served to reinforce his resolve.

He made his way to Bourbon Street. Night had already descended over the city. He cast his eyes skywards. A full moon. Pale, haunting.

He found himself humming Sting's homage to Bourbon Street as he slowly walked up the sidewalk, hands in his pockets. The street was only just beginning to come to life. Most of the bars were overcrowded and boisterous patrons spilled out on to the sidewalk, shouting to each other above the monotonous thump of the distorted dance beat which blared out from an assortment of indoor speakers. Every bar appeared to be playing the same type of mindless discharge. Certainly not music. For a city steeped in the traditions of jazz, it was noticeably absent from its most famous street. Initially, this surprised him, but then the more he thought about it, the more he came to realize that the youth of New Orleans were no different from the youth of any other American city. And this hideous noise symbolized their culture. He'd certainly heard enough of it at Stateville, together with the rap which was always blaring from ghetto-blasters each day, in every corner of the exercise yard. He pushed the recollection from his mind. Stateville was the past. New Orleans was the present. There was no future.

He found what he was after. A sex shop. He studied the display in the window for some time, marvelling at the catalogue of kinky gear on offer. You've been isolated for too long, he told himself, then pushed open the door and walked up to the counter.

'And what can I do for you, sir?' the male assistant asked. Leather waistcoat. No shirt. Gold sleepers in both ears. A sleeper through the left eyebrow. A stud just below the lower lip.

'Handcuffs.'

'We've got a range of them, sir, if you'd care to see them.'

'I'm after traditional handcuffs.'

The assistant ducked down under the counter and reappeared moments later with a box, which he placed in front of Genno. 'Steel handcuffs. Standard cop issue.'

'Perfect. Give me half a dozen pairs.'

'Half a dozen?' came the surprised reply. 'You planning an orgy?'

'You planning to get them for me, or should I take my business elsewhere?'

Another five boxes were quickly placed on the counter. 'Will that be cash or charge, sir?'

Genno's answer was to remove a wad of notes from his pocket, peel off enough to cover the transaction, and give them to the assistant.

The assistant slipped the six boxes into a plastic carrier bag, then handed over the change. 'Enjoy,' he said with a smile, as Genno plucked the bag from his fingers.

'You can count on it.' Genno left the shop, and headed back towards the boarding house. Like the revellers converging on Bourbon Street in ever increasing numbers, his evening was also only just beginning.

The new safe house couldn't have been more different from the one on the bayou that the Johnson family had vacated less than an hour earlier. Located in the multi-ethnic suburb of Metairie, overlooking the narrow Bonnabel Canal, it was a white and lilac, double-storey mansion dating back to the nineteenth century. It had a spacious garden at the rear, immaculately tended, and a set of swings which appeared to have been recently given a fresh coat of paint. Inside it was tastefully, if inexpensively, furnished. Only it wasn't officially listed as a safe house. It was the home of Chief Deputy Marshal Elworthy. He had taken the drastic step of moving the Johnsons into his own house to ensure that nobody else in the department would know their current whereabouts. He had temporarily moved in with his son and daughter-in-law, who also lived in Metairie. The houses were less than five minutes' drive apart.

'This is neat,' Lea announced, noticing the motorized chair lift secured to the railing at the foot of the stairs. She picked up the remote control unit, then sat in the chair, ready to ascend the stairs in style.

'Lea, get off!' Sarah admonished her curtly.

'Aw, c'mon, Mom,' Lea pleaded. 'Just once.'

'Lea, it's not a toy. Off.' Sarah waited until her daughter had reluctantly climbed out of the chair before asking Taylor, 'Is Elworthy disabled?'

Taylor nodded. 'Took a bullet in the spine. Now he's paralysed from the waist down.'

'How awful.'

'Where are the other deputy marshals?' Bob asked, having returned from a brief exploration of the ground-floor area. 'You said that Elworthy had drafted in three deputies from out of state.'

'I rang them a short time ago. They're on their way over now,' Taylor replied.

'What about the sleeping arrangements?' Sarah asked.

'There's a bedroom downstairs,' Bob said, stabbing his thumb over his shoulder in the general direction of the room.

'That's Chief Deputy Elworthy's bedroom. The deputies will be using that to catch some sleep between shifts,' Taylor told him. 'There are a couple of guest bedrooms upstairs. You'll be using those.'

'I'll take the luggage upstairs,' Bob offered.

'Lea, d'you want to see your bedroom?' Taylor asked her.

'Not particularly,' she replied indifferently.

Sarah sensed that Taylor wanted to speak to her alone. 'Lea, go with your father.'

Bob paused on the stairs, looked at Sarah and Taylor, and then gestured to his daughter. 'Come on, *ange*, we know when we're not wanted.'

Taylor waited until Bob and Lea had disappeared from view before speaking. 'We both want this situation resolved as quickly as possible, don't we?'

'Yes,' Sarah replied hesitantly, waiting for him to continue.

'What if I said there was a chance that you and your family may not have to uproot from New Orleans and relocate in another part of the country?'

'Go on,' Sarah urged, when he fell silent to gauge her reaction.

'If I could draw Genno out into the open, I'd be able to take him out. Quickly. Efficiently. Then he'd be the one leaving New Orleans – in a bodybag.'

'In other words, you'd kill him?' Sarah sat down on the stairs without taking her eyes off him.

'Let's face it, Sarah, as long as Genno's alive he'll always be a threat to you and your family. You know the cliché – you can run, but you can't hide. He'll never stop looking for you. That's for sure.'

'Elworthy would never go for it . . .' Sarah said, then an uncertain frown creased her brow, '. . . would he?'

'He'd have no choice if I was forced to shoot Genno in self-defence.'

'Or made to look like self-defence,' Sarah concluded.

'And if I had a witness to back me up, so much the better.'

'In other words, me?'

'How else are we going to lure Genno out into the open?' Taylor asked.

'So I'd be the tethered goat, is that it?'

'I wouldn't quite put it that way, but you are the one person capable of forcing his hand.'

'So what exactly do you have in mind?'

'You return to your house,' Taylor told her. 'He must have contacts in New Orleans. It wouldn't take long for word to reach him that you were there.'

'Frankie's no fool. He'd know it was a trap.'

'I'm sure he would, but what's he got to lose? There's no way back for him now, not after killing four people in Joliet. His prints were all over the murder weapons. He doesn't care any more, Sarah. He's on a suicide mission. I honestly believe that he'd take the chance and break cover if he thought he had the slightest chance of getting to you. I really do.'

'And what if he were to get to me before you could stop him? It's a pretty sobering thought, isn't it?'

'I can't guarantee that I'd get him first, but I'm pretty confident, all the same. I know that doesn't sound very encouraging, but obviously there's going to be an element of risk involved. This is Genno we're talking about.'

Sarah tugged absently at a loose thread in the carpet on the stairs as she contemplated what Taylor had said to her. She finally nodded thoughtfully, more to herself than to him. 'I'm prepared to do it, on one condition.'

'Which is?' he asked suspiciously.

'That I'm armed as well.'

'You know how to use a gun?'

'Sure. Frankie taught me.'

'Figures,' Taylor replied with a grim smile. 'Do you have a gun at home?'

'Yes.'

'Licensed?'

'Of course,' came the indignant reply.

'I have to ask, Sarah. If you were to shoot Genno with an illegal firearm, even in self-defence, you could end up being prosecuted. That's the last thing you need.'

'I'll show you the licence if you want.' Her voice was challenging.

'That won't be necessary,' he replied, but he made a mental note to run a check on her anyway.

'Now all you have to do is clear the plan with Robideaux.'

'Robideaux won't be the problem,' Taylor said, to her surprise. 'To be honest, I'm more worried about Chief Deputy Marshal Elworthy's reaction.'

'I can't say I like it.'

Taylor wasn't surprised by Elworthy's cautious reply. At least he hadn't refused outright to consider the proposal Taylor had just put to him over the phone. That, in itself, was encouraging.

'I'm still worried about Sarah Johnson's part in it,' Elworthy added after a brief silence. 'If Genno does get to her first, all hell's going to break loose. It's something we have to consider, son.'

'She's agreed to it, sir. Surely that must count for something?'

'Her consent won't count for jack shit if she's lying in a mortuary, unable to back you up,' Elworthy replied testily.

'I hear what you're saying, sir, but the only other alternative is to sit around waiting for Genno to make his move. And we've no way of knowing who he'll move against first. A relative? A friend of the family? A work colleague? A neighbour? We don't have the resources to protect them all. Neither do the local cops.'

There was a heavy silence at the other end of the line, and then Elworthy responded, 'If I were to agree to it, I would want Robideaux in on it as well. Two of you would have a better chance of nailing Genno.'

'I don't want Robideaux anywhere near the house,' Taylor came back sharply and instantly regretted the tone he'd taken with Elworthy. His voice was calm when he spoke again. 'Sir, with all due respect, Robideaux's strength lies in his ability to delegate to others. Not as a field operative. He could turn out to be a liability. Added to which, I doubt Sarah would still agree to go along with it if he was drafted in.'

'I feel as if you're putting me in a corner, son. I don't like that.'

'No, sir, I'm not. I'm being straight up with you, that's all.'

'You can't watch over her twenty-four hours a day.'

'We'd only be at the house during the hours of darkness. If I was him, that's when I'd make my move.'

'*If* you were him,' Elworthy said.

'Wouldn't you?' Taylor countered.

'I need to sleep on it. I'll give you my decision in the morning,' Elworthy told him.

'Yes, sir,' Taylor said through clenched teeth.

'How are the family settling in at my place?'

'Good, sir.'

'Have the other deputies arrived yet?'

'Not yet, sir, but they should be here any time now.'

'Keep me posted on any new developments, son. Day or night, it doesn't matter. You've got my number, haven't you?'

'Yes, sir. Does Robideaux know that the Johnsons left the safe house on the bayou earlier tonight?'

'Uh-huh,' Elworthy replied wearily. 'He's not impressed at being frozen out. Not impressed at all.'

The doorbell rang.

'I have to go, sir. I think the three wise men have just arrived.'

'I'll speak to you again in the morning.'

'You can count on it, sir,' Taylor assured him, but the line had already gone dead. He slipped the cellphone back into his pocket, and after determining the identities of the three deputy marshals on the porch, he unlocked the door to let them into the house.

Bob sat on the edge of the double bed, not even sure where he would be sleeping that night. Sarah had made him sleep on the couch at the last safe house. *Made him.* Why did it make him sound like a wimp? Did she have justifiable cause? OK, so he'd deceived her by having an affair with Renée Mercier. Except that Sarah had been deceiving him ever since they first met. She had been deceiving Lea ever since she was born. Not that Lea knew about Renée. That would really tear her world apart. Yet he was still loath to finally end the affair. At least for the time being. Oh sure, he'd told Sarah it was over. What else could he say when she'd confronted him about it? Damage limitation had been his only means of escape at the time. Whether she'd actually believed him was another matter. It was a stalemate. Each was angry and disappointed with the other, while knowing in their hearts the damage they had caused to the marriage. Did they still have a marriage? Would they stay together for Lea's sake? Under other circumstances, he'd have cited irreconcilable differences as the main factor in the breakdown of their marriage. Some irreconcilable differences! Yet it was the unique nature of their disharmony that could well hold the marriage together. He had no desire to leave New Orleans, but at the same time he knew that as long as Genno was trying to find Sarah, his only real sanctuary was under the protective umbrella of the Marshals Service. Which meant playing by their rules. His threat to stay behind with Lea, if Sarah was relocated, had only been uttered in the heat of argument. He'd go with her, wherever it was, if only to safeguard Lea. The thought of Genno going anywhere near his daughter filled him with revulsion. He felt the same concern for Renée, which was why he had been trying to call her for the past few hours, without success. All he got was her answering machine. He'd thought about leaving a message warning her about Genno, but without the full story it wouldn't have meant anything to her. Which was why he had to speak to her in person.

He dialled her number again. Again, all he got was her answering machine. He tossed the cellphone angrily on to the bed. Where was she? Was he jealous? The thought caught him by surprise. Jealous of what? Another man? Impossible. She would never cheat on him. He knew that. So why was she out? It was so unlike her. She was the quintessential homebody. Picking up the phone again, he redialled her number. Answer machine. He'd try again, after soaking in a hot bath. Maybe then she'd be home. Then he could explain everything to her . . .

Bob Johnson had just stepped into the luxurious foam mountain that completely obscured the hot, steaming water, when Renée Mercier arrived back at her small apartment in the French Quarter. She was harrassed, irritable and downright fed up. That damn car of hers! Why hadn't she listened to Bob when he'd told her to take it to the garage for a service? Before Bob had vanished so abruptly. She'd had one phone call from him since his disappearance. There was a family crisis. Or so he'd told her. Only he wouldn't elaborate further, even though she could tell he was holding back on her. She hadn't pressed him. What good would it have done anyway?

Kicking off her high-heeled shoes, she was about to head for the kitchen to make herself a much-needed coffee when the doorbell rang. She threw up her hands in despair. What now? Crossing to the door, she peered through the spyhole. All she could see were flowers.

'Who is it?' she called out.

'Florist,' came the reply. 'I have a delivery here for a Ms Renée Mercier.'

She unlocked the door and gasped both in surprise and delight at the exquisite arrangement of red roses in the ornate wicker basket. 'They're beautiful. Who are they from? Bob? Bob Johnson?'

'I've no idea, ma'am. There is a card attached, though.'

'May I see it?' she asked excitedly.

'I'll need a signature first. Standard procedure, you understand.'

'Bring them in.' She quickly cleared a space on the hall table. 'Put them here. So, where do you want me to sign?'

The blow caught her viciously across the side of the head. Renée Mercier was unconscious before she hit the floor.

When she came round she found herself lying on her double bed. She had been stripped down to her underwear. Masking tape had been placed over her mouth. Her arms were pinned underneath her back and she could feel the metal handcuffs cutting uncomfortably into her wrists. A pair of stockings had been used to secure her ankles to the wooden bedposts at the foot of the bed, forcing her legs apart in an ungraceful V-shape. She tugged furiously at her tethered ankles, ignoring the throbbing pain that pounded mercilessly through her head, but to no avail. She was completely helpless, totally vulnerable, and very, very scared.

'They're slip knots. So the more you struggle, the tighter they'll become,' a voice announced to the right of the bed, startling her. 'You wouldn't want to cut off the supply of blood to your feet. That could be dangerous.'

She turned her head to look in the direction of the voice. The man who'd delivered the flowers was sitting on the stool in front of her dresser. Not that she'd taken much notice of him before. Now she did. Well-built. Cropped brown hair. Clean-shaven.

He smiled fleetingly at her, then got to his feet. 'You really must excuse my lack of manners. That's what jail does to you, I'm afraid. My name's Frankie Genno. You may have heard of me?' The look of terror that flashed through her eyes was answer enough for him. 'Did Bob tell you about me?' No response. 'Just nod for yes. Shake your head for no. Well, did he?' Still no response. '*Did he tell you about me?*' Genno screamed, his eyes narrowing menacingly as he took a step towards the bed. She shook her head as she desperately tried to shrink away from him. 'Did you hear about me on the news?' he asked, regaining his composure as quickly as he had lost it. This time she nodded her head. Again she tried to pull her feet free of the restraints, as he moved round to the foot of the bed. Again to no avail. He ran his eyes slowly down the length of her semi-naked body and his gaze finally settled on the gentle swell outlined provocatively against the front of her panties. Then his eyes flickered up to her face and he was quick to give her a placatory smile when he noticed the look of stark fear in her eyes. 'Let me assure you right away that I have absolutely no intention of raping you, Renée. You don't mind if I call you Renée, do you? It's just that it's been such a long time since I last saw a woman's body, in the flesh. It was Annie, actually. She was my girl, you know? Then again, she'll always be my Annie. You have met Annie, haven't you?' Uncertainty crossed her face. 'Oh, I'm sorry. You know her as Sarah. Bob's wife. Have you met her?' A nervous nod of the head. He sat down at the foot of the bed. 'The reason I came here tonight was to ask you whether you knew where I could find Bob. I'm sure he must have rung you since he and the family went into hiding. You do know where he is, don't you?' A nervous shake of the head. He placed a hand lightly on her calf and felt her body tense to his touch. 'Renée, it's only right that I'm upfront with you. I am going to kill you, as a personal favour to Annie for all the suffering you've put her through since you started fucking Bob.' For a moment she lay motionless on the bed, as if attempting to comprehend the full impact of his words, then she began to twist her body violently, trying to break free from her bonds. His grip tightened on her leg. 'Listen to me, Renée. Listen . . . to . . . me.' She suddenly stopped struggling, as if realizing the futility of her efforts to try and extricate herself, and a tear trickled from the corner of her eye as she stared fearfully at him. 'You tell me where Annie – Sarah – is and I promise that I'll kill you quickly, and quite painlessly. But if you hold out on me . . .' his voice trailed off and he shrugged, '. . . well, I've got the rest of the night to make you come to your senses. It's your choice, Renée. Now, are you going to tell me where they are?' She tried to say something through the masking tape. He ripped off one side of the tape, allowing her to speak. 'Well?'

'I . . . I . . . don't know . . . where he is. Please, you must—' The rest of the sentence was muffled as he secured the tape back over her mouth.

'Maybe you genuinely don't know where he is. I guess that's something we're going to have to find out, isn't it?'

The telephone rang on the bedside table. The answer machine switched on and her voice asked the caller to leave a message after the tone. There was a hesitant pause from the caller, then the line went dead.

'Could that have been Bob?' Genno asked. She shrugged help-lessly. 'Does he normally leave a message for you if you're out?' More tears began to spill from her eyes as she nodded weakly. 'Then you'd better start praying that he phones again. In the meantime, I'm going to see if I can jog your memory.' He crossed to the dresser where he picked up a dishtowel with several items wrapped inside it. He placed the towel at the foot of the bed, between her legs, and unfolded it, revealing a selection of utensils which he'd collected from the kitchen while she'd been still unconscious. 'Last chance, Renée. Where is Bob?' This time there was no response. Her whole body shook as she sobbed uncontrollably. 'Have it your way. Now, let's see, what shall I use first?'

Ten

'I got here as quickly as I could,' Taylor said, with a hint of apology in his voice. He didn't know his way round New Orleans and Elworthy's directions over the telephone had been vague to say the least. Twice he'd had to stop to ask for help during his drive in the early hours of the morning to Renée Mercier's apartment in the French Quarter.

Elworthy sat in the centre of the living room, alone, his hands resting lightly on the spokes of his wheelchair. 'You'd better go through to the bedroom,' he said, raising his head slowly to acknowledge Taylor for the first time. 'Robideaux's in there. He'll clear it with the local cops for you to see the body. I should warn you, son, it's not a pleasant sight.'

Taylor went out into the hall, but was stopped by a uniformed policeman when he tried to enter the bedroom. 'It's all right, he's with me,' Robideaux called out when he saw Taylor in the doorway. Still the uniformed cop wouldn't admit him and his eyes went to the primary detective for authorization. The detective nodded wearily, and then turning away, he absently beckoned Taylor forward.

As Taylor stepped into the room his attention was drawn to the words which had been finger-written in blood across the blood-spattered wall behind the double bed, where a sheet had been placed discreetly over Renée Mercier's body. The words sent a forbidding shiver tingling down his spine: *I did this for you, Annie.*

'It's what we thought might happen once he hit town. Only we didn't know who he'd target first. Now we do.'

Taylor turned to find a grim-faced Robideaux behind him. For once there was no animosity between them. Just a resigned acceptance of the inevitable. He gestured to the bloodstained sheet. 'May I see the body?'

'Question is, do you want to?'

'That bad, huh?'

'Worse. She's been mutilated. And I don't use the term lightly.' Robideaux crossed to the bed where he pulled back the sheet to her navel. Taylor immediately drew back, his face contorted in disgust. He was grateful that he hadn't eaten recently.

'What the hell did he do to her?' Taylor blurted out, ashen-faced.

'It would probably be easier to tell you what he didn't do to her,' the medical examiner announced, his head suddenly appearing above the outline of the body on the other side of the bed. He spoke briefly to his assistant, who was concealed behind the bed, then straightened up and moved round to where the two men were standing. 'From what I can ascertain so far, it would appear that he tortured her for several hours before she died. He used kitchen utensils, which have already been sent off to forensics for further analysis. Kitchen knives. A pair of scissors. A grater. A corkscrew. The knives were used extensively on her face, abdomen and legs. All superficial lacerations to cause the maximum amount of pain. I'm not sure, as yet, what the scissors were used for. Possibly to remove the earlobes and nipples. The grater was used to shave off the layers of skin from her breasts, abdomen and knees. The corkscrew probably killed her when he pierced her eyeballs, although they were almost certainly removed after death. Then she was disembowelled. I also found red welts round her wrists, which would imply that she'd been handcuffed prior to death. And with her legs tied to the bedposts, she would have been completely at his mercy. This was a ritual killing for him. Very slow, and very deliberate. No question of that.'

'That's not all,' Robideaux said to Taylor after the medical examiner had returned to his work. He led Taylor out into the hallway to where the flowers had been left on the table. He gestured to the card, which had been removed from the envelope and was now sealed protectively inside a plastic evidence bag beside the wicker basket. The message read: *Annie, I hope you appreciate the gesture. Looking forward to seeing you again real soon. Frankie.*

'He's toying with us,' Taylor said frustratingly, 'and what's more, he's enjoying it as well. We're still no closer to finding him than when Klyne sprung him from the hospital in Joliet yesterday morning. No fucking closer!'

'Try telling that to Chief Deputy Marshal Elworthy,' Robideaux suggested, and then added with a trace of bitterness in his voice, 'After all, you two seem to have closed ranks on the rest of us. He might listen to you.'

'It's not a case of closing ranks,' Taylor was quick to point out, 'it's about taking every possible precaution to safeguard the Johnson family. And now more than ever, after what happened here last night.'

'I'd better get back to the crime scene.' Robideaux returned to the bedroom.

Taylor entered the living room. Elworthy hadn't moved. 'Sir, we have to flush him out, otherwise he's going to kill again. Who knows where it's going to stop.'

Elworthy nodded slowly. 'I know. I've still got my doubts about using Sarah Johnson as bait, but, having said that, I don't see that we have much choice any more. Not if we want to avoid this happening again.'

'I'll tell Sarah.'

'I want her to move back into her house later this morning,' Elworthy said.

'I still think it would be better if we left it until nightfall. That way, I can catch a few hours' sleep during the day, then stay awake all night in case Genno does try to make a move against her.'

'Take the night shift by all means. Robert will be at the house during the day.'

'As I said, sir, I don't think she'd agree to work with Robideaux—'

'I'm really not interested whether she agrees or not,' Elworthy cut in sharply. 'We're calling the shots, not her. If she doesn't like it, she can remain in hiding indefinitely while Genno works his way through all her family and friends. Either she plays by our rules, or else she remains under twenty-four-hour protection until Genno's found. It could turn out to be a long wait, leaving a lot of innocent blood on her hands.'

'I'll talk to her, sir.'

'You do that. Let me know her decision as soon as possible.'

'Yes, sir, I will. I'd better get back to the house.'

'Jack?'

Taylor was caught by surprise at Elworthy's use of his first name. He paused at the door to look round at him. 'Sir?'

'If you do get Genno in your sights, kill him.'

Taylor held Elworthy's unremitting stare, then nodded.

'I'm glad we understand each other.'

'Robideaux won't agree to it, sir.'

'I think he might just surprise you, son.'

Taylor was about to express his doubts but thought better of it. He left the room without another word.

Sarah was sitting on the couch in the living room, staring blankly at the television screen. The noise was some comfort to her, and had been since Taylor left the house, after breaking the news to her and Bob that Renée Mercier had been murdered. No details as such, other than that two patrolmen had discovered the body in her apartment in the French Quarter, after the tenant in the apartment below had rung the police on noticing blood seeping through a fissure in the ceiling. Bob hadn't said anything. Just gone upstairs to the main bedroom and closed the door, seeking solace in his own memories.

But that wasn't Sarah's only problem. Unknown to her at the time, Lea had overheard a subsequent conversation between her and Taylor, during which mention was made that Renée Mercier had been Bob's mistress. Or so Lea had told her after Taylor had gone. Lea had been devastated, feeling that both her parents had now betrayed her. Nothing Sarah had said could placate her daughter. Lea had finally fled in tears, locking herself in the spare room. She had yet to emerge. For the time being, Sarah had chosen to leave them both on their own. Nothing she could say would make a damn bit of difference to their individual pain. Hollow words. Nothing more. That had been an hour ago. Perhaps more. She had lost all sense of time while sitting alone in the living room. Time she had spent deep in thought. Not that she'd come to any enlightening conclusions about what to say to Bob, or how to comfort Lea. No magic wand to wave to conjure up answers. Common sense. That's all she had. She only hoped it would be enough.

Getting to her feet, she glanced at the ornate carriage clock on the mantelpiece for the first time that night. It was 4.24 a.m. She stifled a yawn. Not that she had any real chance of getting to sleep; not until she was both physically and mentally exhausted. Physically she was already beyond fatigue, but mentally, she was still wide awake. She made her way silently upstairs, instinctively wincing a couple of times when she stepped on creaking boards, and paused outside the door to the spare bedroom. She tried the handle. The door was locked, though there was a light visible under it. She was about to knock, but then decided against it. If Lea was asleep, the noise would wake her. If she was awake, chances were she would be listening to her music on headphones and wouldn't hear her anyway. She went to the main bedroom. The door was closed. She was suddenly caught in a dilemma. Bob was her husband. Surely she had the right to walk into the room? But if she did, would she be intruding on his grief? Should she knock instead? And then what, once they were face to face? What could she possibly say to him? That she was sorry Frankie had murdered his mistress. No, definitely not. It almost sounded like an apology. Yet she *was* sorry that Renée was dead. Much as she'd despised the woman, she wouldn't have wished that on anybody.

She raised her hand to knock, then let it drop and pushed down the handle. Easing open the door, she peered tentatively into the room. The only light source was the lamp at the side of the bed. Bob was sitting in the armchair at the far side of the room, staring absently at the opposite wall. She wasn't sure whether he was even aware of her presence as she stepped into the room and closed the door behind her. The window was open beside him and a gentle night breeze was teasing the flimsy folds of the diaphanous curtains.

'Bob?' she called out softly.

He turned his head slowly towards her. There was no recognition in his eyes. Only an emptiness that frightened her. She managed a weak smile. There was no response as he continued to stare at her.

'You want . . . something to drink?' She couldn't believe those words had just come out of her mouth. What on earth had possessed her to say that? It had been the first thing that had come into her mind. But why?

'If I start to drink now, I won't stop until I'm unconscious on the floor,' he replied. 'And don't think I haven't thought about it.'

Sarah sat down on the double bed and stared at her hands before speaking again. 'I feel like an outsider right now. I know you're hurting, but, even as your wife, I can't find it in myself to share any of that grief with you. It's difficult to grieve over someone who's caused me as much pain as she did.' She shook her head. 'That didn't come out right. I'm sorry.'

'Blunt as ever.' Bob laughed abruptly, but the sound choked in his throat. 'I wouldn't expect you to grieve, Sarah. Why should you?'

'I don't take any satisfaction in this, Bob. None whatsoever.'

'I know that.' Bob sat forward, elbows resting on his knees. 'I was going to end it. I'd actually come to that decision tonight. While I was in the bath. At the same time that Genno was . . .' His voice trailed off and it took him a few seconds before he was able to continue. 'I couldn't have done it over the phone, though. It had to be in person. I felt I owed her that much. Now I'll never be able to do it. I feel as if the relationship will always be in limbo. Neither together, nor apart. D'you understand what I'm saying?'

'To a point. But you're going to have to sever the connection at some time. You've got to get on with your own life.'

'With, or without, you?'

The question caught Sarah by surprise. 'Let's not get ahead of ourselves. We've both been hurt, albeit in different ways. We have to heal before we can forgive. Only then can we start talking about any future we may still have together.'

'You always were the sensible half of the marriage,' he said with a wry smile.

'Then why are we in hiding like this?' she countered.

'Because you did what you thought was right by not revealing your past to me. I've been thinking a lot about that these last couple of days. I honestly don't know how I'd have reacted if you'd told me that you were in the Witness Protection Program when we first started dating. I'd probably have dumped you, more out of ignorance than anything else. Which vindicates your decision not to tell me in the first place. It's taken a lot of soul-searching, and heartache, to realize that.'

'And if you'd dumped me after our first date, we'd never have had Lea. I couldn't imagine my life without her now.'

'Me neither.' Bob rubbed his hands slowly over his face. 'How am I going to tell her about Renée? She's going to have to know the truth.'

'She already does. She overheard me talking to Jack after you'd left the room. It's cut her deep, Bob. Real deep.'

'Shit!' He got to his feet and began to pace the floor restlessly. 'As if she hasn't been through enough as it is. Now this. She must really hate me.'

'Is that all you're worried about? Whether she hates you or not? Well, if you must know, she seemed more distraught than anything else. She's locked herself in her bedroom and won't come out. Who knows what she'll be like in the morning.'

'Talk to her, Sarah. Please.'

She sprang to her feet, eyes blazing. 'Don't expect me to do your dirty work for you. This is between you and Lea. You have to talk to her. It's about time you started taking some responsibility for your actions, Bob.'

'It's always either your way, or not at all, isn't it?'

'What's that supposed to mean?' she replied in bewilderment.

'I'm reaching out to you, Sarah. I need your support right now. Not your antagonism.'

'I'm not being antagonistic. You're just back on the defensive again. You always do it whenever anyone finds fault with you. Why d'you think you came across so badly during the trial? It was so easy for the defence counsel to rile you on the stand, because you took every little criticism as a personal affront.'

'They were out to get me,' he shot back.

'And you let them.' She threw up her hands in frustration. 'I don't want to go down that road again. We talked about it enough after the trial. And even then, we didn't agree on anything.'

'Then why bring it up again?'

'I was trying to make a point, that's all. Obviously, it didn't work.' She exhaled in exasperation. 'This isn't getting us anywhere. I'm going downstairs.'

'Sarah, wait,' Bob called out after her as she crossed to the door. She paused to look round at him, fingers resting lightly on the handle. 'Please don't go,' he pleaded, even though he could see the doubt lingering in her eyes. 'Please. Just stay for a bit longer.'

'Right now you need to grieve. I can't help you do that. Nobody can.' With that, she left the bedroom and closed the door silently behind her.

'I thought we'd agreed not to involve Robideaux in this?' Sarah demanded. Taylor had returned to the house shortly after five o'clock that morning and explained the latest developments to her.

'It's not up to either of us. Chief Deputy Marshal Elworthy's the senior officer on the case and he calls the shots. He wants Robideaux at your house during the day, and me there at night. He made it quite clear that it wasn't open to discussion. You either accept the compromise, or you remain here with your family until Genno's been tracked down and taken off the streets.'

'Which could take ages.'

'And a body-count which could run into double figures. We can't afford to take that chance, Sarah. We have to find him. Quickly. And you're our only real chance of drawing him out into the open. Chief Deputy Marshal Elworthy has every faith in Robideaux's ability as a field operative. That has to count for something.'

'You don't, do you?' she challenged.

'I don't know Robideaux as well he does.'

'A very diplomatic answer,' she said with a scornful chuckle.

'But true. You have to decide. Are you in or out?'

'You know I'm in. When do I move back into the house?'

'Probably around midday, once Robideaux's had a chance to catch a few hours' sleep. I'd advise you to do the same. I doubt you'll get much sleep once you return home.'

'Sleep? After what happened last night?' she replied incredulously.

'I know how you feel, but try and put your head down for a few hours.'

'I'm not even tired.'

'You keep convincing yourself of that, and you won't sleep.'

She propped a cushion against the arm of the couch, then swung her legs off the ground and stretched out. She yawned and gave him a sheepish grin. 'Maybe I am just a bit tired, after all.'

'Why don't you go to bed? You'll be more comfortable there.'

'Bob's in the bedroom. He needs to be alone right now.' She began to move her head from side to side, trying to release the knots of tension in the back of her neck. 'Anyway, I'll be fine here. Close the door on your way out.'

'See you in a few hours. You sleep well.'

'You too. And Jack . . . thanks.'

'What for?'

'Everything you've done for us.'

'It's not over yet, Sarah.'

'I know. Good night.'

'Yeah, night,' he muttered and left the room.

'Good morning, Mrs Johnson,' Robideaux announced genially, as Sarah climbed out of the car shortly after midday, at the prearranged rendezvous in a parking lot close to the French Market on Decatur Street.

'Is it?' Sarah had never liked Robideaux, and had no intention of putting on any pretence for his benefit.

'Taylor,' Robideaux said, nodding an acknowledgement to the figure who emerged from behind the wheel.

'What's the latest on the Mercier homicide?' Taylor asked.

'Nothing significant. The cops have traced the florist's where the flowers were bought yesterday evening. The sales assistant remembers that the buyer was a white male in his thirties, clean-shaven and wearing a baseball cap. Pretty vague description.'

'It could be Genno, or his accomplice,' Taylor concluded.

'Exactly. Which is why we've already stepped up the search for the accomplice. There's more chance of us finding him than Genno at the moment. It could well be the same man who worked with Klyne during the attack on the Johnsons' house. Which means going back over all the suspects we've already grilled, in case something's been overlooked. They'll all be questioned again. And if we were to apprehend him, chances are he'd sell out Genno if it meant a reduction in jail time.' Robideaux gave Sarah a sceptical look. 'You'll find there really isn't that much honour amongst thieves when there's either money on offer, or their own liberty's at stake.'

'What time d'you want me at the house tonight?' Taylor asked Robideaux.

'Nine o'clock. I'll relieve you at nine tomorrow morning.'

'I'll be there.' Taylor returned to his own car and, as he got in, stifled a yawn of exhaustion. He knew he could easily sleep for the rest of the day, given half a chance. *Half a chance?* Yeah, right . . .

'What's wrong?'

'Nothing,' Pascale replied brusquely, as he pulled on his leather jacket.

'If I didn't know better, I'd say you were spooked,' Lynne Rodford said from the doorway of the bedroom, a mug of hot coffee in her hand. She was wearing a dressing gown, having only woken a few minutes earlier.

'Well, you don't know any fucking better, do you?' Pascale retorted, picking up his wallet from the bedside table and pocketing it.

'Etienne, if something's wrong, please tell me.'

'Don't even think it,' he snapped, when she put the mug down and moved towards him, arms extended to give him a reassuring embrace.

'You really are on edge, aren't you?'

'Get . . . out . . . of . . . my . . . face!' He stabbed a finger at her, stressing each word carefully in a soft, menacing tone.

'Screw you,' came the rasping riposte.

'Yeah, you do. And not very well either. Now get out of my way. I'm going out. Don't expect me back before you leave for work.'

'One day, Etienne Pascale,' she called out after him, as he headed for the front door. 'One day.'

He pulled up abruptly, then turned to face her, his eyes narrowed in anger. She instinctively shrunk back into the doorway when he took a step towards her. 'One day *what?*' he demanded. She said nothing. Another step forward. 'Was that a threat? Well, was it?'

'No,' she replied anxiously, quickly shaking her head.

'You want another beating?'

'No, Etienne, please don't,' she whimpered, raising her hands defensively in front of her face. The last black eye had almost cost her her job and she had been warned in no uncertain terms that the next time she came to work with bruises on her face she would be dismissed. The manager had strongly advised her to leave her partner. But she couldn't. She wouldn't. Etienne loved her. It was all she ever asked of him.

'You can count yourself fortunate that I'm meeting with someone shortly, otherwise I'd have taught you the meaning of respect,' he said menacingly.

'I didn't mean anything by it, Etienne. Honestly. I just get so frustrated when you won't open up to me.'

Pascale left the flat, slamming the front door behind him. He then bounded down the stairs, strode across the foyer and out into the street, where he paused to draw breath. Yes, he was spooked. Yes, he was on edge. It was only natural after reading the lead story which had featured so prominently on the front page of the *Times-Picayune*, the main newspaper serving the greater New Orleans area. The brutal murder of Renée Mercier. He was in no doubt that Genno had killed her. The guy was out of control. His first reaction had been to break off all future contact with Genno. But Genno would have found him before long. That thought really scared him. His second reaction had been to tip off the cops anonymously, tell them Genno would be at the Café Pontalba at one o'clock that afternoon. Except that Genno would know exactly who had grassed him up. And even with Genno behind bars, he would be living in constant fear of his life. That scared him even more. His only chance lay in staying one step ahead of Genno, while keeping him sweet at the same time. Normally, the financial remuneration on offer would have been enough to ease his troubled conscience, but this time it was scant reward.

He arrived at the Café Pontalba with ten minutes to spare. There was no sign of Genno. Despite it being busier than the previous evening, he was able to find an isolated table in the corner of the room. He sat down and a waiter appeared at his elbow. He ordered a lemonade. Still no sign of Genno. Was he already in the vicinity, watching him? The thought unnerved him. He quickly reminded himself that he had nothing to worry about, yet the unease lingered inside him. The waiter brought the ice-cold lemonade to the table, and then withdrew to the bar. Pascale took a sip. It was deeply refreshing, but did nothing to quell his disquiet.

'Punctual. Good.'

Pascale almost dropped the glass, such was the state of his nerves. He looked round to find Genno standing behind him. Face expressionless. Where had he come from? 'Shit, you startled me.' He put a hand to his chest. His heart was pounding feverishly.

'I didn't realize I scared you that much,' Genno said with evident satisfaction, then moved round the table and sat down opposite Pascale.

'Startled, not scared,' Pascale replied, injecting some much-needed bravado into his voice.

'Whatever.' Genno pushed the morning edition of the *Times-Picayune* across the table towards Pascale. 'Have you seen the front page?'

'I've seen it.' Pascale made no attempt to hide the disgust in his voice.

Genno glanced up at the approaching waiter and flicked a hand in the direction of Pascale's glass. 'I'll have the same.'

'How did you find her?' Pascale asked after the waiter was out of earshot.

'Phone book. There was only one Renée Mercier. It was that simple.'

'It says she was tortured before she died.'

'I had to find out whether she knew where Annie was holed up. Seems Bob didn't confide that in her. Unfortunate really. It could have saved her a lot of unnecessary suffering.'

The waiter returned with the lemonade and Pascale waited until he'd retreated again, before leaning his arms on the table and whispering disdainfully, 'You enjoyed it, didn't you?'

'Not particularly,' came the apathetic reply. 'It was a means to an end. No more.'

'You've got to be the most cold-hearted son-of-a-bitch I've ever met in my life,' Pascale hissed repugnantly.

'Considering the drecks that you must mix with every day, I'll take that as a compliment.' Genno smiled contentedly to himself, then took a sip of lemonade. 'Ah, that's refreshing. So, what have you got for me?'

Pascale removed a sealed envelope from the inside pocket of his leather jacket and placed it on the table in front of Genno. 'Three sets of keys. Rental car. Speedboat. House on the bayou. It's been paid upfront for two months. If you want it for longer, I'll arrange it.'

'Two months is good.' Genno slit open the envelope and tilted the keys out on to his palm. 'You'll have to show me exactly where the house is, and the shortest route to get there in the speedboat.'

Pascale nodded. 'Also, I've found out who took the snaps of your mother in Joliet earlier this week. A private dick by the name of Derek Farlowe. Ex-cop. He's got an office on Canal Street. The address is in the envelope.'

'You know him?'

'Of him. But not personally, no.'

'Set up a meeting with him later this afternoon. Somewhere out of the way.'

'You're going to kill him, aren't you?' Pascale said in horror. 'Where does it stop, Genno?'

'Set up the meeting, Pascale. Leave the rest to me.'

'You're asking me to lure a man to his death. Shit, all he did was take a few pictures of your mother.'

Genno clamped a hand tightly round Pascale's arm. 'He violated her rights by taking those pictures.'

'Violated her?' Pascale exclaimed in amazement. 'You make it sound as if he raped her. All he did was take a few long-range photographs. There is a fucking difference, you know.'

'If I'd wanted your opinion, I'd have asked for it.' Genno tapped the newspaper in front of him. 'There's another five grand in there. It's yours. All of it. Just set up a meeting with Farlowe.'

'You think five grand can buy my conscience?' Pascale demanded.

'How can I buy something you don't have? So shut the fuck up and do as you're told. Otherwise, I'll find someone else who'd appreciate the work.'

'I'll set up your meeting,' Pascale retorted tight-lipped. He drew the newspaper towards him, deftly palmed the concealed envelope and slipped it into his pocket. His cellphone rang and he was quick to answer it. His eyes never left Genno's face as he listened to the caller. 'You sure about this, Danny?' Another pause. 'No, don't do anything. You've done well.' He switched off the phone, and turned it round thoughtfully in his hands, a faint smile on his lips. 'That was one of my informers. He's had the Johnsons' house under surveillance since early this morning. Guess who's just moved back in?'

'Who?' Genno retorted in frustration, in no mood to play head games with Pascale.

'Sarah Johnson. Seems that she arrived back at the house about half an hour ago. Suitcase and all.'

'Was she alone?'

'Apparently. It's obviously a trap, though. And a real crude one at that.'

'Maybe,' was all Genno would say.

'You're not honestly thinking about trying get to her at the house, are you?'

'If she is the bait, all I have to do is avoid the hooks.'

'You're crazy. You won't get anywhere near the place. They'll put you down the moment you show your face. There has to be another way.'

'Then find it. That's what I'm paying you for.' Genno drank the rest of his lemonade in one gulp. 'Call me as soon as you've set up the meeting with Farlowe. I'll deal with him first. Then Annie.'

'What's your number?'

'I'm using Klyne's cellphone. You do still have the number?'

'I've got it. You want to see the rental car? It's parked on the next block. I've left the Beretta in the glove compartment, together with the silencer and a couple of spare clips. As requested.'

'Then let's go.'

Pascale took another mouthful of lemonade, left a couple of dollars on the table, got to his feet and followed Genno out into the street.

'The house is being watched.'

'How d'you know?' Sarah asked, as Robideaux entered the study on the second floor, where she was sitting in the leather swivel chair behind the desk, a mug of coffee in her hand.

'There was a car parked further down the road earlier this morning. One occupant. Male. He drove off when challenged. Unfortunately, we lost him.'

'D'you think he knows you're in here with me?'

'He won't have seen me, not with the curtains and blinds drawn. I made sure I wasn't seen coming in the back way. But he'd have to be a real klutz not to realize that it's a set-up. And if he knows you're here, so will Genno. Question is, will he take the bait?'

'And if he does, we will have plenty of warning, won't we?' Sarah asked.

'I've positioned miniature cameras round the house, as well as fitted all the doors and windows with infrared detectors. If a detector beam is broken, it'll set off an alarm and activate a light on this,' Robideaux said, patting a console on the sideboard. 'The light will tell me which detector has been breached. It also contains a small monitor which will trigger the moment the cameras pick up any movement. Obviously, this little baby goes everywhere with me. So don't worry, Mrs Johnson, you're perfectly safe in here.'

'What if he uses a decoy?'

'As I said, I can monitor everything on this screen and, if necessary, I can draft in reinforcements at the flick of a switch. We have a van parked a couple of streets away. Inside are five deputies who would be on the scene within seconds of me raising the alarm.'

'Jack never mentioned the van,' she said in surprise. The thought of those extra deputies on standby gave her added peace of mind.

'It was my idea, in case Genno did decide to launch a commando-style attack on the house. I ran it by Chief Deputy Marshal Elworthy earlier this morning. He was in total agreement with me. Better safe than sorry, Mrs Johnson.'

'You can call me Sarah, you know.'

'I'd prefer to keep this on a purely professional level. But thank you, anyway.'

'As you wish,' she replied with a shrug, as if it didn't bother her one way or the other. To be honest, it didn't. Not with him.

Robideaux eased himself into the armchair in the corner of the room, still within sight of the console. 'You don't like me, do you, Mrs Johnson?'

'Not particularly,' she replied candidly.

'Why?'

She took a sip of coffee as she pondered her response. 'You're very pedantic. Everything has to be done by the book. It's always black and white to you. Never any grey areas. That's scary, especially in your line of work.'

'In other words, I'm not a freethinker like Jack Taylor?' Robideaux countered, but there was no resentment in his voice.

'You two are like chalk and cheese. It's no wonder you don't get on.'

'You may find this hard to believe, Mrs Johnson, but I was once exactly like Jack Taylor.'

'I do find that hard to believe,' she replied, with a sceptical shake of her head.

'I used to be something of a maverick. I'd interpret my superiors' orders to suit my own purposes.' He smiled sadly to himself. 'I never broke the law as such – and I'm sure Taylor hasn't either – but there were times when, like him, I did sail pretty close to the wind.'

'So what changed all that?' Intrigued, she was now sitting forward in the chair, elbows resting on the desk, eyes fixed on his face.

'It happened when I was placed in charge of relocating Luigi Mannetti, a former lieutenant in the New York Mafia. He'd turned supergrass and his evidence had helped to put away several leading members of the most powerful family in New York at the time. He got a whole new identity . . .' Robideaux trailed off with a smile. 'You know the drill. Anyway, he was relocated to Shreveport and, to give him his due, he got a job and kept his nose clean. Obviously, we knew that the Mafia had been looking for him ever since he joined the WITSEC Program, and we took all the usual precautions to protect his new identity. They wouldn't have found him, of that I'm certain, except that someone either inside the Marshals Service, or more likely in the DA's office, tipped them off that I was his case officer. That's all they knew. Two hit men were sent down from Seattle to find him. They snatched my wife from our home, then phoned me at work to offer me a deal. Stella for Mannetti. Well, as soon as my superiors found out, it was out of my hands. At least, officially.

'The cops found their hide-out within twenty-four hours. I heard the news over the police-band radio I'd set up in the basement at home. I knew it would have only been a matter of time before a SWAT team was moved in, and I couldn't risk having her caught up in the crossfire. These guys were professional hitters. So I went to the location myself before the heavy mob got there. I managed to get into the house and I took out one of them when he confronted me. It gave his colleague time to grab Stella and use her as a shield. She struggled with him, and to this day I still don't know whether it was an accident, or deliberate, but the gun went off. She died instantly. The guy knew he had no way out, so he shot himself.' Robideaux lit a cigarette and expelled the smoke through his mouth with a 'whoosh' sound that seemed to come from the back of his throat. 'I was suspended and underwent intensive psychiatric counselling while a thorough investigation was carried out into the incident. I was reprimanded, but no further disciplinary charges were brought against me. Mannetti was relocated to another part of the country and I was taken off active duty and put behind a desk. Where I still am to this day. By choice.' He took a long drag on his cigarette before adding, 'It was my maverick streak that got my wife killed, Mrs Johnson. I may as well have pulled the trigger myself. Had I left it to a trained negotiator to try and initiate her safe release, she might still be alive today. You called me pedantic earlier. You're right. I am. Maybe now you can understand why.'

'I'm sorry, I had no idea,' Sarah said softly, when she finally found her voice to break the heavy, lingering silence between them.

'Why should you? I doubt Taylor knows about it either. It is well documented in my file, but it's not something I talk about any more. There's no point living in the past . . . at least, not publicly. The guilt, though, will remain with me for ever. And rightly so, in my opinion.'

'Don't you think you're being to hard on yourself?'

'I sometimes think that too. Then I visit my wife's tomb in the Lafayette Cemetery. Not only does that put the sense of guilt sharply back in perspective, but also where it belongs.' He put a hand to his chest. 'Right here. Always.'

The first spots of rain began to tap against the windowpane behind the drawn blind. Sarah decided it had to have been divine intervention because, at that awkward moment, she had no idea how to respond to Robideaux's self-condemnation. It was his penance, to carry alone. She wasn't being heartless, only realistic. It's what he wanted. That much was obvious. So any words of comfort from her would be meaningless. Best to stay silent.

'I've always liked the sound of rain,' he announced thoughtfully, stubbing out his cigarette.

'Me too,' she agreed, grateful for the change of subject.

Then they fell silent, each caught up in their own thoughts as they listened to the steady rhythm of the rain. She was grateful for that, too.

Derek Farlowe knew the name Etienne Pascale. Ex-cop from Baton Rouge who'd done time for battery and assault. Now resident in New Orleans, he called himself a private investigator, although Farlowe had never actually heard of anyone ever hiring him. The rumour was that he had close ties with sections of the city's criminal fraternity. So just how he did make his money, Farlowe could only guess. Then again, he wasn't sure he wanted to know. What intrigued him more was why Pascale had set up a meeting with him. He had said over the phone that he wanted to hire him. Good money. Nothing more. Since when do private investigators hire other private investigators? Yeah, real intriguing, to say the least.

Farlowe had suggested an appointment at his office, but Pascale had chosen instead an abandoned steel mill on the outskirts of the city, on the banks of the Mississippi River. All very cloak-and-dagger stuff. But he had no problem with that, as long as Pascale was able to produce the necessary greenbacks upfront. Farlowe drew to a halt in front of the rusted gates which had once been the entrance to a thriving business, until it had been closed down some years earlier after environmentalists had publicly exposed the company for discharging toxicants into the river. He remembered that it had made front-page news at the time. Now, as he got out of his car to push open the gates, it was hard to believe the mill had ever been a threat to the environment. It was a derelict ghost with graffiti-covered walls, smashed window and weed-infested grounds.

He got back behind the wheel and drove inside. Parking close to a rusted, corrugated-iron door which had slipped from its rail and now hung forlornly from one corner of the doorway, he switched off the engine and looked at his watch. It was 3.50 p.m. The meeting was scheduled for four o'clock. He opened the box of chocolate doughnuts on the seat beside him, removed one, and bit it in half. He hadn't yet swallowed it when he pushed the other half into his mouth as well. Wiping his hands together, he opened the door and got out. At least it had stopped raining, although the ground was macerated beneath his feet. He stretched his arms away from him, at the same time taking in his surroundings. Still no sign of Pascale. Hardly surprising. The man didn't strike him as being the punctual type.

'Farlowe?'

He swung round sharply, almost losing his balance in the process, and had to put out a hand to steady himself against the side of the car. He estimated the man to be in his mid-thirties. Clean-shaven. Cropped brown hair. Cold, cobalt-blue eyes. It wasn't Pascale, whom he had seen once on Bourbon Street. 'Fucking hell!' he exclaimed, and then exhaled deeply. 'You could have given me a heart attack creeping up on me like that. I didn't even hear you. Who are you? Where's Pascale? Did he set up this meeting for you?'

'Typical cop. So many questions.'

'Ex-cop,' Farlowe corrected him.

'There's a difference?'

'Look, I've just about had enough of your shit. You want to hire me, let's hear the deal. And let's see some money.'

'I don't want to hire you.'

For the first time since arriving, Farlowe began to feel uneasy. His eyes went to the glove compartment. Why hadn't he taken out his gun before he got out of the car? Complacency, that's why. You've been handling too many divorce cases and eating too many chocolate doughnuts.

'You got a piece in there?' Genno asked, indicating the glove compartment with a nod of his head.

'Who are you?' Farlowe countered hesitantly, a claustrophobic fear now gripping his whole body. A tight, uncompromising fear.

'You took some photos of my mother in Joliet earlier this week.'

'Genno?' Farlowe gasped the name.

'Give the man another doughnut.' Genno pulled the Beretta from the back of his jeans and levelled it at Farlowe's chest. A suppressor was attached to the barrel, which seemed to give it an even more menacing appearance.

'Look, I didn't hurt her,' Farlowe blurted out in terror. 'She didn't even know I was there. You've got to believe me. It was a long-range telephoto lens. She never saw me, Genno. For fuck's sake, she never even saw me!'

'And for that I'm grateful. It would have been very distressing for her. But the fact remains, you violated her. Violated her rights. Violated her privacy. My mother. *She was my mother.*' A look of fury flared up in Genno's eyes. 'Didn't you ever wonder why Annie hired you to take the photos?'

'Who's Annie?' came the anxious reply.

'Annie Stratton. She turned state's evidence against me eighteen years ago, then joined the Witness Protection Program and changed her name to Sarah Johnson. I always swore that I'd find her again. I did, earlier this month. That's why she had you take the photos – to warn me off her, by threatening to exact revenge on my mother if anything happened either to her or her family. Word at Stateville was that she'd already hired someone to do it. I'd have gone after him first, only he seems to have disappeared off the face of the earth. No matter. He won't be a problem any more. Not to me. Or to my mother.'

'I . . . I had no idea why she wanted the photographs,' Farlowe stammered fearfully. 'If . . . if . . . I'd known, I'd never have done it. You've got to believe me, Genno.'

'Why? Scruples?' Genno laughed coarsely. 'It was just another job to you, wasn't it? *Wasn't it?*'

Farlowe stumbled back in terror against the side of the car, his hands raised protectively to his face, when Genno shot out the passenger window. The bullet missed him by a matter of inches. Genno was toying with him. And he was enjoying it. To get his own gun he still had to open the passenger door, as well as the glove compartment. Then he had to turn and get off a shot. What chance did he have when Genno already had his own weapon trained on him? Genno would shoot him even before he'd opened the door. But then Genno was going to shoot him anyway. He had nothing left to lose. Not any more. And a quick death would be preferable to this prolonged psychological torment . . .

He slowly lowered his hands and, carefully shielding his right hand from view behind him, felt for the button through the shattered window. He eased it up and gritted his teeth as the back of his hand brushed against a shard of glass embedded in the frame. Then he lowered his hand, feeling the warm trickle of blood seeping across his skin, and his fingers curled round the handle. Genno still had the Beretta trained on him. It was impossible to read anything into his expression. He had to know what he was doing. The son-of-a-bitch was still playing with him! He jerked open the door and at the same time ducked down behind it, his fingers scrabbling frantically to open the glove compartment. Then he heard the sound of laughter. Mocking laughter. Taunting him. His whole body was tensed, braced for the impact of a bullet. Yet nothing happened. He managed to open the glove compartment, and as his bloodied fingers curled round the butt of his Colt .45 automatic, he felt a searing pain in his ankle and his leg buckled underneath him, dumping him on his backside in the mud. The Colt split from his hand and landed on the passenger seat. He could already feel the blood oozing from the wound, slowly soaking his sock. The pain was unbearable, but he had to concentrate on retrieving the Colt. He was still reaching for it when Genno slammed the passenger door savagely against his body. Farlowe screamed out in agony as he was crushed between the door and the bodywork. Then instant relief, as the door was pulled open again. His ribs were aching, having taken the full brunt of the blow, but he still managed to reach out again for the Colt. The bullet ripped through the back of his hand. He howled in pain and pulled back his hand protectively against his chest. Genno stamped down viciously on to his shattered ankle, and as Farlowe doubled over in excruciating agony, he reached over him, retrieved the Colt and threw it into a patch of undergrowth close to the derelict building.

'Fetch!' Genno lashed out with his foot when Farlowe didn't move, catching him painfully in his injured ribs. 'I said fetch. Crawl on your hands and knees. *Crawl!*'

'Fuck you,' Farlowe hissed through clenched teeth.

Genno kicked him again in the ribs. This time harder. 'Fetch the gun. *Fetch it!*'

'I'm not playing your fucking games. You want to kill me. Go on, do it.'

Genno's response was to put a bullet through the other leg. This time higher. In the back of the calf. 'I'll kill you, when I'm ready. Now fetch the gun.'

'No!' Farlowe yelled back defiantly.

Genno was still deciding where to place the next bullet when his cellphone rang. He cursed furiously and kicked the door viciously against Farlowe. Then, ignoring the anguished howl, he retreated a short distance from the car to answer the call.

'It's Pascale.'

'What the fuck d'you want? I'm busy.'

'I've got some info I thought you might be interested in hearing. But if you're too busy . . .'

'Just get on with it,' Genno snapped irritably without taking his eyes off Farlowe, who now lay in a crumpled heap at the side of the car, whimpering pitifully to himself.

'It's about Lea Johnson.'

'What about her?'

'She's got a boyfriend. Name of Jimmy Boyle. A pusher, who works out of the French Quarter.'

'You know him?'

'Yeah, I've come across him before. Flash bastard. Thinks he's a bad ass, but he's nothing more than a small-time punk. Seems she rang him a couple of days ago. Turns out she's real pissed off with what's going on. She just wants to get some kind of normality back in her life again. Or so he's been telling his friends, even though what she told him was in the strictest confidence. But this is the best bit. Her parents don't know about him. They think she's still an innocent little virgin. That's something else he's been boasting about these past couple of days.'

'You can take that smug tone out of your voice.'

'Hey, chill out. It's not as if she's your daughter.'

'Under different circumstances, who knows?' Genno replied

193

almost wistfully, and then his voice hardened when he continued, 'Have you got someone watching Boyle?'

'Of course.'

'Find out more about him, then call me back.'

'Will do. Did you meet with Farlowe?'

'Yeah.'

'And?'

'You just worry about Boyle.' Genno cut the connection, and then replaced the phone in his pocket. He walked back to the car. Farlowe raised his head slowly to look at him. There was no more fight left in him. Only a look of haunting despair in his eyes. 'Good news,' Genno announced with a knowing smile. 'I don't know about you, but good news always puts me in a good mood. Makes me feel . . . genial. So it looks like it's your lucky day.'

'What . . . do . . . you mean?'

'Floorshow's over. Time to go home.' Genno shot Farlowe through the head, unscrewed the silencer, then slipped it into his pocket before reholstering the Beretta at the back of his trousers. He reached over Farlowe's lifeless body and helped himself to a doughnut from the box. He took a bite, but finding the chocolate filling too sweet for him, he discarded it, and then began to whistle softly to himself as he walked back to where his car was parked beyond the rusted gates, out of sight of the derelict mill. He knew that the US Marshals Service had to be behind Annie's move back home. It was an attempt to flush him out into the open, which smacked of desperation on their part. That gave him immense satisfaction, knowing they were floundering in the dark. It was an option to go after her at the house. Chances were the authorities would ambush him, perhaps even kill him. Not that it bothered him, so long as he got to Annie first. With Annie dead, his life would be meaningless anyway. Only now he had another possible option open to him, which depended entirely on Lea's state of mind. Just how dissatisfied was she with her parents? Enough to seek Boyle's help to get her away from them? He had to believe that was a possibility. And if she did, he would be ready to snatch her. Then the tables would be turned. What better way to entrap Annie than by using her own daughter as bait?

Eleven

Lea had been seeing Jimmy Boyle secretly for the past three months. Seeing, not dating. She felt there was a subtle difference – they had never gone out publicly together. That had been at her request. Insistence, actually. She knew her parents would never have approved of him. He was a dealer: amphetamines, barbiturates, crack, dope. Literally, the A–Z of drugs. If it was available, Jimmy Boyle could get his hands on it. For the right price, of course. He'd been in trouble with the police before, but had, as yet, no convictions to his name. Five years older than her, he was tall, good-looking and always dressed in the latest designer clothes. He prided himself on having never taken drugs. Or so he had assured Lea on any number of occasions. Although she had seen him around – he hustled outside her school – it wasn't until her best friend's fifteenth birthday party that she had first spoken to him and soon discovered that he was as charming as he was handsome. But more than anything else, she found herself attracted to the danger which seemed to surround him. She had lost her virginity to him at the party. He was the classic bad boy and she couldn't get enough of him.

Yet she was under no illusion that this was the right guy for her. No way. She had her own life ahead of her. The hell she was going to visit him in prison when his luck finally did run out. And it would. Sooner, rather than later. But for the moment she was just enjoying the ride, in every sense of the word. She had already rung him from the last safe house, on her father's cellphone, but had stopped short of telling him where they were, other than that the house was on a bayou. She wasn't that stupid. But since then, the situation with her parents had become intolerable. As if it wasn't enough that her mother had lied to her about her past, now she discovered that her father had been secretly screwing his secretary. A double betrayal. She had nobody to turn to for comfort – except Jimmy. He understood her pain. His parents were divorced. Father was doing life for murder. Mother had remarried and both she and his stepfather barely tolerated him. She knew it hurt him. Not that he'd ever told her that. At least, not in so many words. But she could read between the lines. A lot of the bravado was simply a mask to hide his own inner pain.

The first time she had called him, she had been in desperate need of a sympathetic ear. She'd poured out her heart to him. That time, it had been a diatribe of anger and resentment against her mother. She had always been her confidante in the past, which was why the deception had been so hard for her to accept. As for her father, well, she'd never been as close to him as she'd been to her mother, except after her mother had been forced to admit the truth about her past. Then she had turned to her father for support. He'd done his best, but he seemed uneasy around her fragile emotions. Then came the bombshell about his infidelity. That had come as a real blow to her. She remembered thinking at the time that she would have found it more believable if it had been her mother who had been having the affair. Her mother had always been the more adventurous of her parents. Her father had always seemed, well, distant in his affection towards his family, though she knew it didn't mean he loved her any the less. Obviously, there was something fundamentally wrong in the marriage for him to have resorted to an extramarital affair. Well, that's how she interpreted it.

Then, just as she was struggling to come to terms with her father's treachery, her mother had announced that she was going back to the house in another attempt to draw Genno out into the open. Her father had tried to talk her out of it. She had tried to talk her out of it. But her mother had been adamant, saying she had to do something before Genno struck again. Lea had walked out and barricaded herself in the spare room. Her sanctuary. She'd cried. Tears of frustration. Tears of worry. Tears of dread. If anything were to happen to her mother while she was at the house . . .

Her anguish had since turned to anger. Anger at her mother for all the hurt she'd caused her. Anger at her father for all the hurt he'd caused her mother. Anger at Jack Taylor for all the trauma he'd caused the whole family. Anger at herself for feeling all this anger . . .

She needed to get away from them. She *had* to get away from them. If only for her own peace of mind. Which was why she decided to call Jimmy again. Knowing better than to use any of the telephones in the house, she waited until her father went downstairs before sneaking into the master bedroom, where she found his cellphone on the bedside table. She contemplated taking it back to her own room, in case he returned, but realized that if she did, he would certainly notice it missing. However, if she stayed put and he did return unexpectedly, she could quickly switch off the phone and replace it on the bedside table, claiming she was in the room looking for him. He'd buy it. He was gullible, if nothing else. She had always been able to get round him with relative ease. Being Daddy's little girl did have its benefits . . .

She peered into the hallway. It was deserted. Closing the door, she then sat down on the edge of the bed and dialled the number of Boyle's cellphone.

'Yeah?' a languid voice answered.

'Hey, Jimmy, how's it going?' she replied, a grin lighting up her face.

'Who's this?'

'It's Lea.' The smile faltered. 'Is this a bad time?'

'Never for you, baby. How's things on the bayou?'

'We've moved. We're in . . .' She trailed off and realized she was smiling sheepishly to herself. 'I guess it's best if I keep that to myself.'

'No problem. I understand. So how come you moved?' An uneasy pause. 'Or is that also a state secret?'

'Genno broke out of jail. He's in New Orleans.'

'Yeah, I heard on the news he'd escaped. I didn't know he was already in the Big Easy, though.'

'That's what the marshals say,' she replied.

'Is that why they moved you?'

'No, they've got internal problems. A couple of their deputies were playing both sides. We were moved because the head *hombre* doesn't even trust his own troops any more.'

Boyle whistled softly down the line. 'Fucking hell. And these guys are supposed to be protecting you? I could do a better job. I'd hide you where that fucking psycho would never find you. I swear it.'

'It's a tempting offer, especially with everything that's going on here at the moment. My mother's gone back to our house. The marshals are hoping that Genno will hear about it and try to get to her. And as for my father . . . well, let's just say he and I aren't exactly on speaking terms right now. I'm real pissed off with both of them. I feel like I'm a prisoner in here. Everything's on top of me. It's as if I can't breathe any more.'

'I told you, baby, I'll see you right if you want out of there.'

197

'I'd have every cop in the city looking for me if I bailed out of here. And I don't want to get you into any trouble.'

'They won't find you. I guarantee you that.'

'You're on,' she exclaimed in a moment of defiance.

'How are you going to get past the guards?'

'Leave that to me. I'll call you later.'

'I look forward to it, baby.' The line went dead.

She replaced the cellphone on the bedside table and returned to her own room.

'Problems?'

Boyle shook his head as he slipped his cellphone into the inside pocket of his double-breasted suit jacket. The two men seated with him at the table in the alcove of a small, atmospheric restaurant on Bourbon Street were Peruvians. Only one of them could speak English, and had to translate for his colleague. Both were affiliated to a Peruvian drug family who, although not able to compete financially with the more notorious Columbian cartels, were constantly on the lookout for new sources to distribute their product on the streets of America. Negotiations had been going on between the three of them for the past couple of months, and both parties had finally reached an agreement over lunch that afternoon. Boyle felt euphoric. He was finally stepping up into the big time. And he had every confidence that he could make a success of it . . .

'No, no problem,' Boyle mused thoughtfully, breaking the silence. It sounded as if he was talking to himself.

'Your girlfriend?'

'She seems to think so. To me, she's just another fuck, that's all. But now she's starting to become a serious nuisance. I don't need this shit. I really don't.'

'What shit?'

Boyle explained the situation to them, as he understood it. His guests began talking agitatedly between themselves when the Marshals Service was mentioned. 'Hey, it's not a problem,' he was quick to assure them. 'She's been real careful to keep the whole relationship a secret from her parents. Little bitch doesn't think I'm good enough for them. If the Marshals Service did know about me – and why should they? – I'd have been questioned already. It's really nothing to worry about, gentlemen.'

'So why agree to meet with her?'

'Because if I didn't, she'd just keep ringing me. And then it could become a problem.' Boyle lit a cigarette and exhaled the smoke as he slowly looked round the room. Then he turned his attention back to the two men, a faint smile on his lips. 'How about a gesture of goodwill on my part to consummate our new alliance?'

'Go on?'

'I'll give you the girl. Fifteen years old. Great little body. One careful owner. Then when you're through with her . . .' Boyle drew his finger across his throat. 'You're flying back to Lima in the morning. No comebacks for any of us. But if you're not interested, I'll just have to kill her myself. It's up to you.'

The two Peruvians talked at length between themselves, then the translator drank down the last of his coffee before addressing Boyle in English. 'We appreciate your offer, but we have further business to attend to this afternoon.'

'I thought you said I'd be your sole distributor here in New Orleans,' Boyle said suspiciously.

'You are . . . for the moment.'

'What's that supposed to mean?' Boyle demanded, stubbing out his cigarette.

'We have to cover ourselves for every eventuality. If anything were to happen to you, we would need to ensure that our distribution network wasn't compromised. Call it a back-up plan, if you like. We all have to look out for ourselves in this line of business.'

'I told you, the girl is *not* a problem. That's what this is all about, isn't it? You think I could be a liability, don't you?'

'If we thought that, we wouldn't have approached you in the first place. Now, if you'll excuse us, we have another appointment. Thank you for the meal. Quite excellent.'

Boyle shook hands with both men, then lit another cigarette and watched them leave the restaurant. He knew what they were thinking, that he couldn't keep his own house in order. Why else would they suddenly announce that they had another appointment? No mention had been made of it during lunch. Had he appeared too eager to offer Lea to them? Was that it? Did they think he wanted them to do his dirty work for them? It wasn't like that at all. He'd been sincere about it. They'd obviously misunderstood his intentions . . .

He jumped to his feet and hurried to the entrance where he desperately scanned the length of the street for any sign of them. They were nowhere in sight. He cursed furiously and tossed his cigarette out into the road. Little bitch and her fucking problems!

Why couldn't she have rung ten minutes later? By then, the Peruvians would have gone, and he'd have had the deal in the bag. Now everything was up in the air. All he could do now was wait . . .

'Excuse me, sir?'

'What?' Boyle snapped, spinning round to find a waiter hovering behind him, the bill neatly folded on a side plate in his hand.

'Will you be settling this, sir?'

'Do I have any fucking choice?' Boyle retorted bitterly, and then removed his credit card from his wallet and slapped it down on to the plate.

It was an ideal location. A modest wood-framed cabin, raised on stilts above the water level on the banks of the Bayou Bois Picquant, concealed from view at the rear by a row of cypress trees adorned by the grey wisps of Spanish moss, known locally as 'ghost's beard', which hung decoratively from the branches. Further downriver, the bayou intersected with the Louisiana Cypress Lumber Canal before finally merging into the vast Lake Cataouatche. Or so Pascale had told him. Not that Genno could see either – which suited him perfectly. The more isolated the property, the better it was as far as he was concerned.

The whole area seemed to be enveloped in an eerie silence, which was occasionally punctuated by the mating call of an ibis, or the territorial squabbling of a small colony of herons in the lush swamplands, out of sight behind the cypress trees. Yet the tranquillity was something he'd never experienced before, and it left him feeling distinctly edgy. Eighteen years at Stateville and never a moment's silence. Even in the depths of night, there was always some noise in prison. A whisper. A shout. A cry. Sounds which had become a comfort to him. Now he felt as if he'd been transported to another world. Unexplored. Unfathomable. Uneasy.

He knew he would come to terms with the stillness. In time. The main thing was his privacy. He opened the fridge, removed a beer from the six-pack he'd bought earlier in the day, and went out on to the porch where he sat down on the wooden chair. Breaking open the tab, he took a sip, and then looked across at the wooden jetty adjacent to the riverbank at the side of the cabin. A rubber Gemini inflatable, with a detachable outboard motor, was tethered to the side of the jetty, bobbing gently in the water. Pascale had assured him it was easier to pilot than a speedboat. And cheaper to hire. Genno had taken his word for it. Not that it had been difficult to control in the water once he'd mastered the tiller, which was attached to the outboard motor. He took another sip, then wiped his forearm across his face. He still had to acclimatize himself to the stifling heat. Mid-nineties, according to the weather forecast. It was an irritation more than anything else. He had more pressing thoughts to occupy his time.

He'd been all set to try and flush Annie out of her home by starting a fire in a neighbouring house. She would have had to be evacuated. And even with an escort, all he would have needed was a clear shot at her from a good vantage point. But that idea had been shelved when he had heard about Lea's increasing dissatisfaction with her parents. Chances were, she would try and rendezvous with Boyle at some point, possibly in the near future. Not that he was in any hurry to exact his revenge on Annie. After all those years, another few days wouldn't make any difference to him. The prize could be so much greater. First Lea. Then Annie. A smile teased the corners of his mouth. He would have Annie completely at his mercy if he could take Lea hostage. She wouldn't do anything which might put her daughter's life in danger. He could lure Annie out to the cabin as well. Mother and daughter. Who to kill first. What a dilemma! Lea. Yeah, definitely Lea. If only to see the reaction on Annie's face as he drew the blade across Lea's throat. That would totally destroy Annie's life. It would almost be worth letting her go after that, knowing she would have to live with the guilt for the rest of her life. It was a tempting thought. But no, Annie had to die. There was no going back on that. But not necessarily straight after he'd killed Lea. Let her watch Lea die in front of her. Let her sit with the body. Let her think about her treachery, which had ultimately cost him eighteen years of his life. Let her come to realize that by turning state's evidence she had, in effect, become directly responsible for the death of her own daughter. Let her die with that last thought in her mind.

He raised the can in a mock toast. 'Here's to you, Annie. We'll be together again real soon. And this time . . . for ever.'

'Tonight?'

'Sure, baby. What time?'

Lea had sneaked back into the master bedroom after her father had disappeared into the adjoining bathroom to take a shower. The sound of the water drowned out her voice. And as soon as the water was turned off, she'd know to end the conversation and get out before he reappeared. She was seated on the edge of the bed. 'My father always looks in on me before he goes to bed. It'll have to be after that. Could be eleven o'clock. Maybe twelve. I don't know. Is that OK with you, Jimmy?'

'Baby, you call me whenever you're ready. Where do I pick you up?'

'Not from the house. I'll call you from a payphone once I'm clear of the place.' She glanced furtively towards the closed bathroom door. 'Jimmy, thanks.'

'Any time, baby. And I can tell you now, we're going to have some fun tonight.'

'Promise?' she said coyly.

'Oh, yea,' came the knowing reply.

'Can't wait,' she purred.

'All good things come to those who wait. Speak to you later.' The line went dead.

Lea replaced the cellphone on the bedside table, and as she got to her feet, she caught sight of her reflection in the full-length wall mirror and noticed that she was smiling to herself. She had every confidence that she could get out of the house unseen. With that gratifying thought in mind, she left the room and made her way downstairs to the kitchen. Suddenly she was hungry. Very hungry.

'How's it going?' Taylor asked, after unlocking the back door and entering the kitchen to find Sarah and Robideaux seated at the table. The curtains were drawn and the console lay on the table between them. It had been temporarily deactivated to allow him access into the house.

'All quiet,' Sarah replied.

'What are you guys doing in here?' Taylor asked, directing the question at Robideaux. 'If Genno were to toss a stun grenade through the window, you wouldn't have time to react.'

'We came downstairs after you called to say you were on your way. Don't worry, I do know the procedures.' Robideaux drank down the last of his coffee, then pushed back his chair, stifled a yawn, and got to his feet. 'I'll leave you in Taylor's capable hands, Mrs Johnson,' he said to Sarah, and then slipped on his jacket and moved to the door. 'See you both in the morning. Nine o'clock.'

Taylor waited until Robideaux had left, then he locked the door behind him and reactivated the console. 'He's still calling you Mrs Johnson? Doesn't the guy ever chill out?'

'That's just his way.' She decided against telling him about the death of Robideaux's wife. If Robideaux wanted him to know, he'd divulge that information himself. 'And anyway, he's not so bad. Not once you get to know him.'

'Sounds like you two have been cosying up,' Taylor said with a grin.

'Yeah, right.' Sarah gestured to the percolator. 'You want a coffee? Freshly brewed.'

'Sure.'

'Mugs are in the cupbord behind you. Milk's in the fridge. Sugar's on the table. Help yourself.' She noticed his hesitation as he reached for the cupboard door. 'Oh, I'm sorry. Were you expecting me to make it for you?'

The sarcasm wasn't lost on him. He selected a mug from the neat row on the shelf, then looked round at her, a faint smile on his lips. 'Just like Chrissie. You want something, get it yourself.'

'Chrissie?' Sarah asked with a frown.

'My wife.' Taylor added a dash of milk to the coffee, and then replaced the carton in the fridge. 'Let's get out of here. Upstairs, preferably.'

'That where Robideaux and I were sitting for most of the time. In the study.' Sarah refilled her mug, then led the way upstairs and into the study. She sat down behind the desk. 'So, tell me about your wife.'

He took a sip of coffee as he considered his reply. 'What do you want to know? She's a lawyer in Washington. We've been married for five years. No kids.'

'Do you have a picture of her?'

'No!' He gave her an apologetic look. 'I didn't mean to snap at you like that. It's just that, well . . . Chrissie and I aren't really close any more. We pretty much lead separate lives these days.'

'I'm sorry.'

'It happens,' came the philosophical reply.

'Don't I know.'

'You and Bob have got Lea, though. That's a powerful incentive to stay together. Sometimes I think that Chrissie and I only stay together for the sake of the IRS.' He smiled sadly. 'The tax rebates are better for married couples.'

'That's a pretty cynical view, isn't it?'

'We're both pretty cynical people. Maybe that's what drew us together in the first place.' He sat forward in the chair, his eyes fixed on her. 'You think you can turn your marriage round again?'

'I honestly don't know whether we can sort it out. Bob and I are so far apart right now. The recriminations are deep-rooted on both sides.'

'And Lea's caught up in the middle of it,' Taylor said.

'That's what hurts the most. You said just now that she was a powerful incentive for Bob and me to stay together. But if we can't sort out our differences, she's always going to be caught up in the middle of our disharmony. What kind of life would that be for her?'

'And what if you and Bob did decide to separate? She'd still be caught in the middle, wouldn't she? An emotional tug of war.'

'I'd never do that to her,' Sarah was quick to say.

'So, you'd be prepared to give Bob custody of Lea if the two of you did split up?'

'No,' came the defiant reply.

'And I'm sure he feels exactly the same way. That's when the lawyers would be brought in. These guys are character assassins, nothing more. As I said, it would be an emotional tug of war. Whatever happens, Lea's the one who'd ultimately lose out. I've dealt with enough dysfunctional families within the WITSEC Program to know that.'

'You missed your true vocation – you should have been a psychiatrist,' she said, with a hint of disdain in her voice.

'I already am. You have to be in this line of work.'

'I can believe that. I remember how scared I was when I first entered the program. A new identity. A new life. I was just nineteen. Pretty big decisions for a young girl to handle. Especially with my background. Ted Lomax was brilliant, though. I couldn't have asked for a better case officer. He seemed to understand what I was going through.' Sarah finished her coffee, then placed the mug on the coaster and stared thoughtfully at it before looking up at Taylor again. 'Or at least I thought so at the time. Now it turns out he was bent. He sure fooled me.'

'He was under investigation, that's all. Nothing was ever proved against him.'

'There's no smoke without fire, is there?' she countered.

'Except there was no smoke. As I said, there was no specific evidence linking him to any misdemeanours.'

'So why was he murdered and his files stolen? Whoever killed him

must have known about the files. How else would they have known –
unless he'd put out the word that he had them in the first place?'

'It sounds like you missed your true vocation as well – as a
detective. For what it's worth, I agree with you. I think he was bent.
Only I can't prove it. And, to be honest, it's doubtful whether I ever
will. My guess is that Klyne killed him to get the files, and yours in
particular. Now that Klyne's dead as well ... the investigation
appears to be at an impasse.'

'If Klyne did murder him, it's possible that Frankie might know
something that could shed further light on the investigation.'

'It's possible,' he agreed.

'But?' she prompted, when he fell silent.

'What would Genno have to gain by cooperating with the
investigation? That's assuming, of course, he's taken alive. Somehow
I doubt he's going to give up without one hell of a fight. After all,
he's got nothing to lose any more.'

'There might also be something on the files to incriminate Lomax.'

'Assuming Genno even has them. His only interest in all of this
seems to have been in locating you. Why would he want the rest of
the files? What use would they be to him?'

'He could try and sell them on the black market. Surely there
would be a demand for them?'

'A big demand, which is why we're so desperate to retrieve them.
But Genno isn't motivated by money. All he wants is revenge. He's
made no attempt to cover his tracks since he was sprung from
Stateville.'

'So the location of the missing files could have died with Klyne?'

'Possibly, yes.'

'Won't the Marshals Service take the precaution of relocating
everyone on those files anyway?' she asked.

'It's already being done. But it takes time, as you know. What's
more worrying, though, is that there are other names on those files.
Family. Friends. Contacts. Informers. If those files were to fall into
the wrong hands, they'd be the first to be targeted. And we just don't
have the manpower to protect those peripheral players, even
temporarily. It would become a logistical nightmare if we had to
relocate them all. To be honest, I doubt we could do it. Not on our
budget.'

'So they're not being given any protection at present?'

'Not that I'm aware of, no. At least, that was the situation when I
left Washington to come down here. But then I'm not actively

involved in that side of things, so the situation could have changed now that Genno's on the loose. It's unlikely, though. As I said, we just don't have the manpower.' He noticed her put a hand to her mouth to stifle a yawn. 'When did you last get some sleep?'

'I got in a few hours at the safe house this morning.'

'You look exhausted. Go to bed. Get some rest. You need it.'

She looked at her watch. 'It's only nine-thirty.'

'You gotta grab sleep whenever you can. I had six hours earlier today. It did me the world of good. Who knows, back in your own bed, you might even get a good night's sleep.'

She got to her feet and stretched, this time making no attempt to cover the copious yawn. 'I guess it's worth a try. You know where the coffee is—'

'I *can* find my way around a kitchen,' he cut in with a wry grin. 'Now go on, try and get some sleep. Hopefully, the next time I see you will be in the morning.'

'All bright-eyed and bushy-tailed?'

'Well, a little less cynical would be a start.'

She gave him a sheepish grin, then crossed to the door where she paused to look at him. 'Night, Jack.'

He raised his hand in acknowledgement, then waited until she'd closed the door before getting to his feet. He, too, stretched, and then moved to the window where he tweaked aside the edge of the curtain to look down on to the back garden. A security light illuminated the lawn. Nothing moved. He let the curtain fall back into place and sat down in the swivel chair recently vacated by Sarah. The computer, keyboard and printer were all covered by protective dust covers. He flicked absently through the box of diskettes. All were labelled in the same neat handwriting. Small, elegant strokes. Very feminine. He pushed the box away from him and removed the cellphone from his jacket pocket. He rang his partner, Keith Yallow, in Washington.

'Hey, how's tricks?'

'Fuck it, Jack, I've been waiting for your call. What the hell's going on down there?'

'Plenty, as I'm sure you've already heard.'

'You mean about Genno?' Yallow replied.

'Who else? Any problems with Dave Sheppard since you picked him up?'

'You mean apart from being totally pissed off that he's been detained against his will? How much longer do you want me to hold him?'

'That's why I called. We don't need to hold him any more, now that Genno's on the lam.'

'What do you want me to do?'

Taylor sat forward and ran his finger lightly around the rim of Sarah's empty mug. 'Kill him,' he said at length, in soft, emotionless voice. 'Make it look like a contract hit. Who knows, they might even pin it on Genno.' There was an uneasy silence at the other end of the line. 'Keith?' Continued silence. 'Keith, you still there?' he repeated more forcefully.

'I'm still here.'

'It's the only way. You know that as well as I do. But if you've got a better idea, I'm listening.'

'No, I don't,' Yallow replied. His voice was edgy. Uncertain. 'Consider it done.'

'Speak to you soon.' Taylor paused, then added, 'And Keith, it's going to be OK.'

'Don't patronize me. Save that bullshit for the chumps in the program. They seem to appreciate it.' The line went dead.

Taylor replaced the cellphone in his pocket, then got to his feet and, picking up the portable console, went downstairs to the kitchen to refill his mug. He had a feeling it was going to be a long night . . .

It had been an hour since her father had entered the room and whispered 'Sleep tight, *ange*,' then kissed her lightly on the forehead before leaving again and closing the door silently behind him. He did that every night before retiring to bed. Most times she was already asleep. Occasionally she was still awake, but always pretended otherwise. That night she was not only still awake, but fully clothed underneath the bedcovers, apart from her trainers, which she quickly slipped on to her feet after throwing back the sheets. She looked at the illuminated dial of the alarm clock on the bedside table. It was 12.23 a.m. Time to make her move.

Lea stood up and, without switching on the light, moved noiselessly to the door, which she eased open until she had a clear view of the hallway. It was deserted. The door to the master bedroom was closed. She knew that her father not only fell asleep almost as soon as his head hit the pillow, but that he was also a heavy sleeper who rarely woke during the night. She had always envied him that. She took after her mother. Both were light sleepers who rarely fell asleep within the first hour of going to bed. Closing the door again, she crossed to the window and peered down into the street. It appeared to be deserted. At least from where she was standing. Unlatching the window, she pulled it open, and then lifted up the lace curtain. The cool breeze caressed her face and neck as she ducked her head through the opening. She hesitated as she was about to climb out on to the flat roof of the built-on garage. Was she doing the right thing? It was the first time since she'd decided to bail out that she had found herself questioning her motives. Before, she had been consumed with a single-minded determination to get away from her parents, having felt that they had both betrayed her trust. Admittedly, she still felt that way. But was this the answer? They would be beside themselves with worry once she was discovered missing from her room later that morning. A full-scale search would be instigated by the authorities to try and locate her. Was that what she wanted? Yes, if it meant making her mother return to the safe house. Yes, if it meant her parents facing up to their responsibilities. Yes, if it meant they came to realize just how much they had hurt her with their lies. Yes, it was what she wanted. Then, that afternoon – or maybe that night – she would ring them to let them know she was safe. She might even agree to return home. It all depended on their reaction.

Climbing out gingerly on to the roof, she closed the window behind her. She crossed to the front of the house, where she crouched down and surveyed her surroundings. No sign of the deputy marshals who'd been brought in from out of state to baby-sit them. Not surprising. They rarely ventured outside anyway. Their orders were to remain indoors, out of sight of the neighbours. It was essential that everything appeared normal at the house. Or so she had overheard Taylor telling her parents. She didn't like Jack Taylor. Too smooth for his own good. She had an idea that her father felt the same way. As for her mother . . . she seemed to enjoy being around him. Probably made her feel safe, she thought disdainfully to herself. Moving to the corner of the roof, she draped her foot over the side until she could feel the drainpipe. She cast a last look at the closed window. Last chance to change her mind. No, she was determined to go through with it. She locked her legs round the drainpipe, then eased herself over the side of the roof and grabbed gratefully at the cold metal, hugging it tightly to her body. Then slowly, and with infinite care, she manoeuvred herself down. It seemed to take for ever before her feet finally touched the ground. Her heart pounding, she paused in the shadows at the side of the garage to catch her breath. It was the first time she had ever done anything like that. Whenever she had met secretly with Jimmy, she had got her best friend to cover for her by saying they were studying together – either at her friend's house, or at the city library. Her parents had never checked up on her. Too wrapped up in their own world. She knew things would change after this. Not that it bothered her unduly that she would probably never see Jimmy again after tonight. It was time to move on anyway. He had been an experience, nothing more. But an enjoyable one all the same. He'd taught her so much about herself . . .

She snapped back to the moment, and cursing herself for allowing her mind to become distracted, she edged out of the shadows and cast an anxious glance towards the front of the house. Curtains were drawn across all windows. The porch light was off. All clear. She hurried down the driveway to the wrought-iron gates and winced when one of them squeaked as she opened it. Another nervous glance back at the house. Nothing. She slipped through the opening and was about to close the gate behind her when she thought better of it. Don't tempt fate, she chided herself. As she turned away from the house, she was illuminated in the headlights of an oncoming car. Her first thought was to duck back into the driveway, but she managed, with some difficulty, to bridle her sudden rush of fear and stand her ground until the car had driven past and disappeared from view. Then, without looking back, she hurried to the end of the street, where she again paused to catch her breath. She needed to find a payphone to call Jimmy so that he could pick her up. Only this was foreign territory to her. Left? Right? Straight on? She decided to follow the road, hoping to find a payphone before too long.

Three blocks further on, she was rewarded and she hurriedly dialled his number. He told her to stay where she was. He was on his way.

'Did I wake you?'

'Does it matter?' Genno replied gruffly. He'd been sitting on the porch for the past couple of hours listening to the nocturnal sounds of the bayou, having finally adjusted to the tranquillity of his surroundings. The call had shattered that serenity. 'This better be good, Pascale. What have you got for me?'

'How about Lea Johnson?'

Genno, whose chair was on two legs with its back resting against the cabin wall, immediately sat forward, banging the two front legs down on to the wooden floorboards. 'Where?'

'Well, I haven't got her as such. Boyle picked her up at a payphone in Metaire about five minutes ago. I've got somebody on their tail, as we speak. You want me to tell him to grab the girl once they reach their final destination?'

'No!' Genno snapped curtly and was momentarily distracted by a splash in the darkness close to the jetty. He switched on the torch and played the beam across the dark water. All he could see were a succession of ripples fanning out geometrically until they were too weak to continue and were swallowed up by the surrounding water.

'Genno, you still there?' Pascale demanded.

'Yeah, I'm still here.' He switched off the torch. 'Tell your man to follow them to their destination and keep the place under surveillance until we get there.'

'That's what I thought you'd say. I'm already on my way to pick you up. I take it you can find your way back to where I dropped you off earlier? You have got the hang of the inflatable by now, haven't you?'

'You just worry about being there to meet me.'

'What are you going to do about Boyle?' Pascale asked. No reply. 'You're going to kill him, aren't you?'

'Am I?' With that, Genno switched off his cellphone and disappeared into the cabin to get ready.

'Where are we going?'

'Westwego,' Boyle replied, without taking his eyes off the road.

'The first safe house we stayed at was on the Bayou Senette. That's not far from Westwego, is it?' Lea replied.

'No, not far.'

'What's in Westwego?' she asked.

'There's a woodland a couple of miles beyond Westwego. It borders the bayou. There's a cabin in there. It's been derelict for years. Perfect, if you want to remain out of sight. That is what you want, isn't it?'

She nodded. 'Will you be staying with me?'

'I'll stay the night, but I've got business to attend to in the morning.'

'How do you know about this cabin?'

'I was born in Westwego. I used to play in the woods there.'

'I didn't know you were born in Westwego.'

'It's no big deal. And neither is Westwego. Believe me. Fishing community. I couldn't wait to get out of there.'

They both fell silent, and it wasn't until Boyle finally turned off the main road and on to a dirt road leading into the woods that he said,

'The cabin is a couple of hundred yards further on.' He switched the lights on full and carefully negotiated the track until he drew abreast of the cabin, which was partially hidden from view by trees and dense undergrowth. Switching off the engine, he retrieved a torch from a holdall on the back seat. Then he got out and flashed the beam into the car. 'Lea, come on,' he called out brusquely to her.

She climbed out and as she closed the door, she looked around and stared uneasily into the darkness behind her.

'What is it?' He noticed the apprehensive look on her face and followed the direction of her gaze. 'Lea, what is it?'

'I thought I saw something,' she replied, scanning the darkness.

'What?'

'A light of some kind. It could even have been headlights. I don't know.'

Boyle played the beam into the darkness behind them. The road was deserted. The only sounds were the distant nocturnal calls of the bayou. 'There's nothing out there.'

'I guess I was wrong,' she said with a quick shrug.

'Probably just a passing car on the main road.'

'You *are* staying with me tonight?' she asked, looking round anxiously, then she shuddered as she hugged her hands to her arms. 'This place gives me the creeps. It's like something out of a slasher movie.'

'I told you I'll stay with you tonight.' There was a hint of irritation in his voice. 'Now, come on. Follow me.'

She grabbed his hand and he led her through the knee-high undergrowth until the torch beam illuminated the cabin directly ahead of them. She stopped abruptly, momentarily startled by the dilapidated condition of the structure. She gave Boyle a questioning look, as if silently questioning his wisdom in bringing her to such a dump.

'What?' he bristled, when she shook her head in disgust. 'OK, so it's not the fucking Marriott, but I did warn you that it had been abandoned for years. You did want somewhere you could keep your head down without being found. Who the hell's going to look for you out here?'

'Forget it, Jimmy. Look at the place. It's a ruin. God knows what it must be like inside. It's probably full of spiders.'

'That's where you're wrong. It may be a bit dusty, but it's got a bed and a portable stove. I put the bed in there myself.'

'When?' she asked in amazement, allowing him to lead her towards the door.

'Last year. I had to lay low for a while after a business deal went wrong. I stayed out here until the coast was clear.'

'Was that the last time you were here?'

He pushed open the door and scanned the interior with the torch. 'It's the last time *I* was here. Several acquaintances of mine have used it from time to time since then.'

She stepped tentatively through the doorway. A black-and-white striped mattress lay in the corner of the room. The stove, heavy and antiquated, stood in the other corner. Taking the torch from him, she directed the beam upwards. Sturdy timber beams stretched the length and breadth of the ceiling which, from what she could see, appeared to be intact. That was something!

'Put the torch on the stove,' he said behind her.

She crossed to the stove and placed the torch on the dusty surface. 'This is a real shithole, Jimmy. Couldn't you have . . .' Her voice trailed off when she turned back to face him and saw the automatic in his hand. 'What . . . are you doing? Jimmy, what the hell's going on?'

Boyle reached behind him with his free hand and pushed the door closed without taking his eyes off her. 'This has all been one big fucking game to you, hasn't it? In fact, ever since we first met you've been playing games, haven't you?'

'Jimmy, please, you're scaring me,' she said anxiously, her eyes now wide with terror.

'I could handle your games, Lea, because they didn't encroach on business. If anything, you were a distraction from all that. And for a time I enjoyed your company. I really did. Even the sex was good. You were a bit naive, but at least I was able to teach you the way I liked it. Then everything changed when the Marshals Service started swarming all over your family. You became a liability to me, especially when you started calling me on the phone bitching about being cooped up in some safe house.' Boyle took a step towards her. 'I was on the verge of a major deal yesterday afternoon when you called me. You lost me that deal, Lea. You know that? You lost it for me. I'll never get the chance again. Fuck you!'

'Jimmy, please,' Lea begged, and a tear ran down her cheek as she cowered back fearfully against the wall. 'I . . . I . . . was scared. You were . . . the person—'

'I don't want to hear it,' he cut in disdainfully. 'You can lead the authorities to me. And you're fifteen-year-old jailbait. That puts me inside for statutory rape. It's not going to happen, Lea. It's just not going to happen.'

'I . . . I wouldn't . . . tell . . . tell them . . . about us, Jimmy. You . . . you know that.'

'No, Lea, I don't know that. And that's the problem.' Boyle raised the automatic fractionally, until it was level with her forehead. 'Bang!' he shouted, and a faint sneer touched the corners of his mouth when she screamed in terror and clasped her hands to her face, anticipating the bullet. 'Tell me, Lea, what's the one thing you would never do when we were sleeping together?'

She slowly lowered her trembling hands and shook her head on seeing the questioning look on his face. 'No, I won't,' she whimpered.

'Then I may as well kill you right now,' he said and pulled the trigger.

She shrieked as the bullet slammed into the wall, close to her head, and she stumbled off-balance and grabbed desperately at the stove to prevent herself from falling to the floor. The tears were now streaming down her face.

'I won't be so careless next time. Now, what do you say? Are you going to give me that blow job I always wanted, or am I going to blow you away?' He laughed callously. 'Yeah, I like that. Well?' Her whole body was trembling with fear, but when she opened her mouth no words came out. 'You don't have to say anything. Just get on your knees if you're going to do it. Otherwise, I'll kill you. You've got five seconds to decide.'

Lea took a couple of steps away from the stove, her eyes never leaving Boyle's face, then she slowly got down on her knees at his feet.

'I thought you'd see sense in the end.' He approached her, then looked down at her bowed head. 'And in case you're thinking of biting it while you're down there, I wouldn't advise it. I'd kill you very, very slowly. And very, very painfully. Bear it in mind. Now do it!'

Despite her overwhelming fear, Lea also felt a fierce sense of revulsion at the thought of what he wanted her to do. It was something that disgusted her. Always had. Yet she knew that it was her one chance of staying alive long enough to . . . what? It would give her time to think. Survival. That's what it was about now. She had to push the disgust from her mind and concentrate on saving herself. Think, girl. Think. She reached out a hand towards the zip of his trousers.

'*Step away from her!*'

The voice startled Lea and she jerked her hand away from his zipper.

'Don't even think about trying to shoot on the turn, because I'll drop you where you stand,' the voice warned. 'Step away from the girl and drop the gun. Kick it to me. Now!'

Lea leaned her body fractionally to the side to look past Boyle's legs and saw two men standing inside the doorway. She had never seen either of them before. Her eyes settled on the clean-shaven one with the cropped brown hair and mesmerizing blue eyes. She noticed the pair of handcuffs clipped to the side of his belt. Frankie Genno. The name flashed through her head. She didn't know why she had thought that, but she instinctively felt she was right. He was the complete opposite to the way her mother had described him. The sound of the gun clattering to the floor jolted her sharply back to the present.

'Who are you? What do you want?' Boyle demanded. His hands were held away from his sides in a supplicating gesture.

'Frankie Genno,' Lea exclaimed, without taking her eyes off him.

'I'm flattered you recognize me, Lea,' Genno said, and gave her a friendly smile. 'Please, get off your knees. There's no need for you to debase yourself for a shit like Boyle.'

She needed no further encouragement to scramble to her feet. Yet she was well aware that her problems were far from over. She knew that Boyle had had every intention of killing her. What about Genno? Unlikely, otherwise he'd have done it already. More likely he was going to use her as bait to get to her mother. It was at that moment of realization that her fear turned to anger. Not at Genno. Not at Boyle. At herself. She had no idea how Genno had found her, probably by following Boyle – the lights she'd seen when she'd first got out of the car now made sense – but the fact remained she had allowed herself to put her mother's life at risk. Her own selfishness. Her own stupidity. Her own self-importance. Her own damn fault.

No, she wasn't going to allow it to happen. The anger turned to bravado, and she rushed headlong towards Genno. Screaming. Shouting. Arms flailing. She noticed the second man step in front of Genno, who then took a step to the side, his weapon still trained on Boyle. She tried to change direction to get at him. A hand grabbed her arm. She lashed out frantically and felt her hand connect with the side of the man's face. She raked her nails savagely down his cheeks and heard him cry out in pain. But the grip didn't relax. Then she felt a sharp pain in her arm and when she looked down she saw a hypodermic needle being plunged into her skin. She began to feel light-headed, unsteady on her feet. She continued to struggle furiously, but the tranquillizer quickly took hold and the room began to blur around her. She heard a voice. It sounded vague and distorted. Unintelligible. Her legs buckled underneath her. She was vaguely aware of being held under the arms. There was no fight left in her. The room was now out of focus. Light and dark fused together. It became darker. Then complete darkness.

Genno had been caught by surprise when Lea tried to rush him and was grateful when Pascale intervened to sedate her. He had been careful to keep the Beretta trained on Boyle at all times. And keep his distance. The guy may have only been a small-time thug, but he was still a threat all the same.

'She's out,' Pascale told him.

'Take her to the car,' Genno replied, without taking his eyes off Boyle. 'Wait for me there.'

Boyle watched Pascale leave, carrying the unconscious Lea in a fireman's hold over his shoulder, then his eyes flitted back to Genno. 'How did you know about Lea and me? Even her parents didn't know.'

'You've got a big mouth. You like to boast about your conquests to anyone prepared to listen. My colleague has contacts in the city. The sort of contacts who are always prepared to listen to any amount of bullshit, and then pass on what they've heard ... for the right price, of course. You've had a tail for the past ten hours. You didn't know that, did you?' Genno shook his head disdainfully to himself. 'You're so far out of your league it's laughable. You're a punk. Nothing more.'

'Fuck you!' Boyle spat back contemptuously.

Genno lashed out with the Beretta, catching Boyle across the temple. Boyle cried out in pain and fell to his knees, dazed and groggy from the blow. Genno deftly unhooked the handcuffs from his belt and secured Boyle's arms firmly behind his back. Then he picked up the torch and played the beam around the room. A length of rope lay coiled in the corner, close to the mattress. Perfect. He retrieved the rope, and pulling the single chair into the centre of the room, he climbed on to it and looped the rope over a beam. He got off the chair, then made a noose at one end before hauling Boyle roughly to his feet. Blood streamed down the side of Boyle's face from the gash across his temple. His eyes were still glazed and it was only when Genno tried to slip the noose round his neck that he attempted to pull free. Genno hit him again, this time across the back of the neck. He sat Boyle down on the chair and secured the noose round his neck. Then, grabbing the other end, he began to pull at it. Boyle struggled frantically, but was forced to his feet as the noose tightened. Genno continued to pull at the rope until Boyle was standing on tiptoe. Then, climbing back on to the chair, he secured the rope firmly to the beam. He kicked the chair aside and turned to face Boyle, who was swaying uneasily on his toes, still desperately trying to clear his head.

'Fifteen years old. That's all she is. And you took advantage of her.'

'She wanted it,' Boyle hissed, spitting out the blood which had trickled into his mouth.

'Maybe she did, but then you should have known better, shouldn't you? Statutory rape. That's what it was.'

'She enjoyed it, Genno. She fucking enjoyed it. And if you don't believe me, ask her. Go on, ask her.'

'Shut up!'

'You should've heard her moaning. Oh yeah, she enjoyed it, all right.'

Genno noticed a rag on the floor beside the stove and, grabbing it, pushed it firmly into Boyle's mouth. 'That's better. Much better. Now I don't have to listen to your filth any more. Not that I'm going to be hanging around here . . .' He trailed off and chuckled at the unintended pun. 'Hanging around? Geddit?'

There was only hatred in Boyle's eyes. Then, without warning, Genno pressed the automatic against Boyle's left kneecap and pulled the trigger. He was quick to steady Boyle as his body lurched violently to the side and he took a lot satisfaction from the look of excruciating agony in Boyle's eyes.

'You're going to die, Boyle. How long it takes depends entirely on you. You've got one good leg to stand on. But standing on tiptoe on that one good leg is going to become increasingly uncomfortable. Not to mention tiring. And as soon as you lower your foot, and you will after a while, the noose will tighten round your neck. Naturally, you'll try and pull yourself up again on to your toes, but it'll get to the point where you won't have any strength left in your good leg.

Then again, I'd be more worried about the blood loss. After a while you'll start to drift into unconsciousness, and when you do, your body will relax and you'll end up hanging yourself. But don't worry, you won't be alone while you wait to die. You'll have all those memories of Lea to keep you company. I only hope she was worth it.'

Genno picked up the torch and paused again in front of Boyle, the beam focused on his flushed face as he struggled to retain his footing. He was about to say something, decided against it, and then gave a quick shrug before leaving the cabin and closing the door behind him.

Twelve

The first sensation she had on regaining consciousness was a sharp, intense pain echoing deep in the recesses of her head. It felt as if her head was inside a resonating church bell. *Go away. Make it go away.* She tried to reach up a hand to massage her temple. She couldn't move her hands. She tried to move her legs. Same. Only then did she open her eyes and find that she was enveloped in darkness. Pitch-black. She was frightened. Very frightened. She tried to focus her thoughts. Initially they were disorientated. She closed her eyes again and took several deep breaths to try and steady her nerves. Think back. What's the last thing you remember? Suddenly, an image of Genno's face appeared in her mind, as if a light had been switched on, illuminating a mask of evil in front of her. She inhaled sharply, then winced as another shooting pain ricocheted through her head. The cabin. Genno. Jimmy. The other man. It was coming back to her. She had run at Genno. Angry. At herself. The other man . . . had grabbed her before she could get to Genno. The needle prick in her arm. She remembered that. But nothing more. So where was she? Lying on a bed, that much she did know. Comfortable mattress. But she wasn't comfortable. She was lying on her back, her hands pinned underneath her. She opened her eyes again and tried to lift her head off the pillow to look at her feet. The pain was excruciating. Not that she could see anything in the darkness anyway.

'Awake, Sleeping Beauty.'

The voice startled her and she turned her head sharply towards the source. An anguished cry escaped from her lips as a bolt of pain seared through her head. She lay her head back on the pillow, her eyes squeezed shut until it had faded. The voice was both distinctive and familiar. Genno. But she still couldn't see him.

'I'm sorry, I didn't mean to frighten you. Would you like me to put the light on?'

'No,' she hissed through clenched teeth. 'Please . . . don't.'

'OK. How's the head?'

'Like an overworked anvil.'

There was a faint chuckle. 'You want a couple of headache tablets?' No reply. 'Don't worry, they're not doctored. The only reason you were sedated was so that I could bring you here with the minimum amount of fuss. I don't think you'd have come voluntarily.'

'You're right about that. Where's "here"?'

'You needn't worry about that. At least, not yet. I take it you do know who I am, otherwise you'd have asked already, wouldn't you?'

'Genno.'

'Please, call me Frankie,' came the appeal from the darkness. 'So, d'you want those tablets?'

'Yes,' she replied grudgingly.

She sensed a movement from the corner of the room, then the door opened and she saw Genno's silhouette momentarily illuminated in the doorway. The door closed again. She moved the fingers of one hand up her other wrist. She felt something cold, smooth and metallic. Further investigation revealed handcuffs. They weren't manacled tightly round her wrists, but secure enough to ensure she couldn't slip her hands out of them. What about her feet? She tried to pull them apart. It soon became apparent that only her ankles were tied. It felt like flex. The more she struggled to break free, the more the flex bit into her skin. She gave up when the pain intensified. Then the door opened again.

'Leave it open,' she said, as he was about to close it. 'It gives me a bit of light. It's not too bright.'

He crossed to the bed, carrying a couple of tablets and a glass of water. 'Let me help you sit up.'

'Don't touch me,' she shot back, ignoring the piercing pain in her head, and instinctively drew back from his extended hand.

'You want to sit up by yourself, go right ahead.'

She knew she couldn't do it alone and glared furiously at him. 'Just lift my head. That's all.'

'As you wish.' He placed the tablets on her tongue, then put his hand underneath the back of her head and gently raised it until she could reach the glass in his hand. She gulped thirstily at the water, some of which spilt down her chin and on to her T-shirt.

'They're pretty strong. Shouldn't take long to kick in.'

'What did you do to Jimmy?' she demanded, as he carefully laid her head back down on the pillow.

He crossed to the wooden chair in the corner of the room where he had been sitting when she'd first come round. 'Jimmy and I came to an understanding,' he replied casually, easing himself down on to the chair.

'In other words, you killed him.'

'That's my understanding of it,' he said with a satisfied smile. 'Would you like to know how I did it?'

'No,' she replied, the disgust evident in her voice.

'He wasn't your type, Lea. You're better off without him. Hell, the world's better off without him.'

'Who are you, my father?' came the disdainful retort.

'Under different circumstances ... who knows?' he replied reflectively.

She shuddered at the thought. 'Where's the other guy? The bastard who stuck the spike in me?'

'No idea. Probably gone home.'

'So it's just you and me out here?'

'Uh-huh. But don't worry, you're quite safe.'

'I don't doubt it. After all, you still need me as bait to get my mother, don't you?' No reply. 'You're going to kill her, aren't you?' More silence. 'Aren't you, you psycho son-of-a-bitch?'

'I'm not a psycho!' he retorted forcefully, his hands clenched lightly round the arms of the chair.

'You murdered three innocent people in Joliet. You murdered Dad's mistress. You murdered Jimmy. Those are only the ones I know about.'

'All necessary,' was his blunt riposte.

'What did Dad's mistress ever do to you?'

'She caused Annie a lot of psychological pain. I killed her for Annie.'

'Annie? You mean ... my mother?'

'She'll always be Annie to me,' Genno told her.

'You killed her for Mom?' Lea said with a mixture of horror and disbelief. 'You are mad.'

'No,' he yelled, jumping to his feet and knocking over the chair. His breathing was ragged as he stared coldly at her. 'No Lea, I'm not mad. I've spent the last eighteen years in jail because of your mother. She was the only person, apart from my mother, that I ever trusted. And how did she repay that trust? She turned against me. Eighteen years is a long time to sit around thinking about what could have been. And what never can be. A very long time.'

'You killed three people during that robbery,' Lea countered. 'You deserved everything you got.'

'I agree,' he said, much to her surprise. 'I deserved to be locked up for life. And if that's all there had been to it, I'd have gladly accepted my punishment and none of this would have been necessary. But that wasn't all there was to it. The cops knew about the heist from the very start. I told Annie everything. Our relationship was based on mutual trust. Or so I thought. But she chose to pass everything on to the cops. And why? As a trade-off to save herself doing a short stretch in jail for possession. You know something, I wouldn't have done that to her. Never.' Genno shook his head sadly to himself. 'She meant the world to me. She really did.' He righted the chair, and then moved to the door where he paused to look round at her. 'But then Annie's your mother. I wouldn't expect you to understand.'

Lea stared thoughtfully at the shimmering reflection of the moonlit water on the ceiling, after he had left the room. Did she understand? She found herself wondering what she would have done had she been in her mother's position. For a man? Not that she had any real experience of that to guide her, apart from Jimmy. But her relationship with Jimmy had been totally different to the one her mother had had with Genno. Or at least, that's how she saw it. She believed that Genno had genuinely loved her mother. He probably still did, in his own world of trapped memories. But had those feelings been reciprocated at the time? She couldn't be sure. Then again, there had been extenuating circumstances. Her mother had been a junkie. Hooked on drugs supplied to her by Genno. Was that love? Or dependency? What if her only way to break the addiction had been to remove Genno permanently from her life? Had that been her reason for doing what she did? Or was it the fear of going to prison? Both powerful motives. Yeah, she did understand. Only not from Genno's point of view. What her mother had done did make sense to her. A lot of sense . . .

And now her own blinkered stupidity had placed her mother's life in real danger. At a time when she should have been supporting her mother, she'd been consumed by a misplaced sense of her own importance. What had she been thinking about when she turned to Jimmy? Had it been a cry for help? But Jimmy? Why had she got involved with him in the first place? She thought she had all the answers while she was seeing him. Now those answers seemed insignificant excuses for her own selfish lust. But what lay heavy on her troubled conscience were the double standards she had previously used to condemn her parents for shielding the truth from her. Her mother's life before joining the WITSEC Program. Her father's illicit affair. What about her and Jimmy? A cheap, tawdry affair conducted in total secrecy. And, when necessary, using her best friend to lie for her by saying that they had been together when she had been with Jimmy. What kind of friend did that make *her*? At least her mother had a valid reason for keeping her past under wraps all those years. To protect her family. Her father . . . well, that was more of a grey area. But no different from her own circumstances. People in glasshouses . . . and all that. She realized then that she had grown up considerably in the last few hours. But at what price?

'How's the head?'

'Still hurts, but not as bad as before,' she replied, when Genno entered the room again.

'You up to talking to your mother?'

'Go to hell,' came the venomous response.

'I'm sure I will if there is such a place, but not just yet.' Genno picked up the chair and carried it across to the bed, where he sat down. He switched on the bedside lamp.

'Switch it off,' Lea protested, her eyes screwed up against the piercing light.

He removed a pair of sunglasses from his shirt pocket and slipped them over her eyes. 'I'll switch it off just as soon as we've spoken to your mother.'

'And I told you, go to hell. Find yourself another patsy, because I'm damned if I'm going to help you trap my own mother. I've done enough damage as it is.'

'I'd rather you did it voluntarily, Lea. And, believe me, so would you.'

'Is that a threat?' she countered, desperately trying to conceal her inner fear behind a feigned bravado in her voice.

'Considering that I have you immobilized on the bed, I'd take that as read. Don't make me hurt you, Lea. Please. One way or another, you will let your mother know you're here. Would you rather talk to her daughter to mother, as it should be, or let her hear you screaming over the phone? It's your choice.'

'Some choice.'

'So you'll speak to her?'

'I'll speak to her,' Lea replied bitterly through clenched teeth.

'All you need to say is that you're safe. And unharmed. Sure, the authorities will instigate a thorough search for you in and around the New Orleans area. But that will take days and the chances are they won't be any nearer finding you anyway. By then, this will all be over and you'll be released unharmed so that you can get on with your life again.'

'You mean after I've buried my mother? Fuck you, you bastard!'

He flinched at the animosity in her voice. 'I respect your loyalty, Lea, though it's obviously not a characteristic you inherited from your mother. But as I said before, I wouldn't expect you to understand my motives.'

'The only thing I don't understand is what my mother ever saw in a scum sucker like you.'

His hands balled menacingly in his lap and for a horrifying moment she thought she'd pushed him too far. She tensed her body, expecting some form of retribution. Then he relaxed his fists and a fleeting smile touched the corners of his mouth as he nodded thoughtfully to himself. 'You've got guts, kid, I'll give you that. Now that's something you *did* inherit from your mother.'

She was ready with a suitably caustic comeback, but wisely chose to remain silent. The next time she might not be so lucky. She would have to play along with him, at least for the moment. She was in no doubt that he would hurt her if the need arose, and the last thing she wanted was her mother to hear her screams over the telephone. That would tear her apart. And she'd caused her mother enough grief already. Her only hope now lay in the Marshals Service finding Genno's base before he could get his hooks into her mother. And with their track record to date . . . the thought didn't exactly inspire much confidence in her. How desperately she wanted them to prove her wrong.

Genno removed a small black notebook from his pocket and dialled a number that Pascale had listed for him on the first page. The Johnsons' home number. The telephone rang several times before it was answered. A male voice. Genno severed the connection. From what he already knew, Bob Johnson wasn't at the house. It had to have been one of the deputies. He didn't want to speak to them. Only Annie. He redialled the number. This time it was answered by a female voice. One he recognized only too well.

'Hey, Annie. Didn't wake you, did I?'

There was a hesitant pause and he could almost visualize the deputy marshals desperately trying to trace the call, while urging her to keep him on the line for as long as possible. He wasn't about to disappoint them. 'I was wondering when you'd get round to calling, Frankie,' she said finally.

'I thought about putting in a personal appearance, but that's before I found out about Jimmy Boyle. Naughty Lea.'

'What are you talking about?' she asked hesitantly, her voice now laced with fear at the mention of her daughter's name.

'You don't know about Jimmy Boyle, do you? A twenty-year-old drug dealer working out of the French Quarter. Small-time punk. Totally unsuitable for Lea.' There was silence at the other end of the line. 'You think Lea's safely tucked up in bed, don't you? Surprise, Annie. I've got her here with me. You want a word?' Genno placed the receiver close to Lea's face. 'Go on, talk to your mother. Tell her about Jimmy. How you were fucking him on the quiet.'

'Mom?' Lea whispered, as the tears welled up in her eyes. 'Mom, I'm sorry. I'm sorry.'

'Oh my God,' came the gasped response from the other end of the line. 'Lea, are you all right?'

'Yes. Mom, I'm sorry. I never meant . . .' Lea's voice trailed off and she began to sob uncontrollably.

'Looks like I've got the upper hand, Annie. Now we play it my way.'

'Frankie, don't hurt her. Please. Don't hurt her.'

'Why would I want to do that? Don't worry, Annie, she's perfectly safe here with me. I'll take real good care of her.'

'Let me speak to my mother again,' Lea said softly, having regained her composure. 'Please?'

'I'm putting Lea back on,' Genno announced, and leaned forward to listen in to the conversation.

'Mom, I'm all right. Honestly. He hasn't hurt me.'

'Where are you?'

'I don't know,' Lea replied, shaking her head in frustration. Then, before Genno snatched the phone angrily from her, she blurted out, 'I scratched the man's face, Mom. I scratched his face.'

'And here I thought we were all getting along so well,' Genno spoke into the mouthpiece again. 'I'll call you again, Annie. At the house. Soon. Just be there.' He hung up and, getting to his feet, replaced the chair in the corner of the room. Only then did he turn back to Lea. 'You've just killed a man, do you know that? I hope you're proud of yourself.'

'What?' she exclaimed in disbelief.

'Etienne Pascale. The guy whose face you scratched earlier tonight. You've just made him a major liability to me. Now I'll have to kill him. But the blood will be on your hands. You think about that, Lea.' Genno held her horrified stare for a few moments, then left the room.

The Marshals Service had installed a monitoring system on the Johnsons' telephone which would trigger an automatic trace on my incoming call. The first call, which Taylor had answered, hadn't been long enough for the trace to be effective. But the second call, which Sarah had answered, yielded a local number. Chief Deputy Marshal Elworthy, who had been woken by the duty officer as soon as the exact location of the call had been identified, had authorized the use of an assault team covertly to cordon off the area, but not to enter the premises until he had the chance of assessing the situation more fully from the ops centre at the federal building on Camp Street.

Sarah, on the other hand, had rung Bob at the safe house as soon as Genno had hung up, and had him check to see if Lea was in her room. She knew it would prove to be a pointless exercise, but she had to go through the motions to eliminate any false hopes that may still have been lingering at the back of her mind. When he returned to the phone to confirm her worst fears, she hadn't been able to hold back her tears as she told him about the call she had just received from Genno. Bob's distress had also been evident on the phone, and for the first time since being forced to break the news to him about her past, she had felt an affinity with his anguish. Solidarity in the face of adversity. But, under the circumstances, for how long?

Her answer came when Bob arrived at the house. Ignoring her, he rounded furiously on Taylor. 'Who the hell is this Jimmy Boyle? And why didn't your people know about him before now? Dammit, this is all your fault. Do you hear me, your fault. And if anything happens to my daughter because of your incompetence, I'll kill you myself. D'you hear me?'

'I can understand your anger—'

'Don't patronize me!' Bob interjected vehemently. 'You can't begin to understand my anger.' He finally turned to Sarah, who was sitting on the stairs. 'Did Lea ever mention this Jimmy Boyle to you? Did she?'

Sarah got to her feet and when she spoke her voice trembled with emotion. 'Is that all you care about? That we didn't know Lea was seeing some guy on the quiet?'

'He was a twenty-year-old drug dealer, for Christ's sake!' Bob countered. 'Doesn't that bother you in the slightest?'

'Not at the moment, no!' came the emotional response, as a fresh wave of tears ran down her cheeks. 'Right now, I don't care whether Lea's slept with every drug dealer in New Orleans. All I want is to get her back safely.' She put her hand to her mouth and lowered her eyes, her body shaking uncontrollably as she cried. 'I just want her back,' she added softly, her voice now muffled by her hand. 'That's all. I just . . . want her back.'

'I want her back as much as you do,' Bob said, his own voice threatening to break with emotion. 'I'm sorry. I didn't mean to sound insensitive. Lea means the world to me. You know that. It's just . . . such a shock. It's all such a shock.'

The telephone rang and Taylor, standing beside it, scooped up the receiver. He didn't take his eyes off Bob and Sarah Johnson as he listened with a mounting sense of dismay to Elworthy on the other end of the line. 'Yes, sir, I'll tell them. Thanks for letting me know. Goodbye.'

'Well?' Bob prompted, after Taylor had replaced the handset.

'The house where we thought Genno was holding Lea actually belongs to a middle-aged couple. Neither has been in trouble with the law before. The assumption was that Genno was holding them hostage as well. When the assault team raided the house, the couple were fast asleep. No Genno. No Lea. I'm sorry.'

'Oh my God,' Sarah gasped, but the anguish was gone from her voice. And there were no more tears. 'I don't understand. You said the call originated from that house.'

'What I said was, the call originated from a cellphone in that house. That's why the assault team was sent in.'

'So what are you saying?' Bob demanded, irritated by Taylor's apparent ambiguity. 'That the trace was wrong?'

'No. Genno's number definitely coincided with a cellphone in the house.'

'You've lost me,' Bob said with a helpless shrug. 'How did Genno gain access to the phone if he wasn't even there?'

'He didn't. He's used a process known as cellular cloning. Basically, a cellphone with a built-in scanner/decoder. It's nothing more than a microchip that can read existing ESNs – electronic serial numbers, which are unique to each cellphone – so that every time a call is made, the instrument will search out an active number that's not currently in use and clone it. That way it appears as if the call is originating from the clone number. So every call made will use a different clone number. Which makes the original number untrace-able.'

'So, in other words, you've got no way of finding out where he's holding Lea?' Bob asked.

'Not using this, no,' Taylor replied, tapping the scanner. His eyes flickered towards Sarah. 'Remember what Lea said? "I scratched the man's face, Mom. I scratched his face." It's obvious she wasn't talking about Genno.'

'How can you be so sure?'

'Genno may have changed his appearance, but she'll know who he is. Of that I'm certain. If she'd scratched Genno's face, she'd have referred to him by name. I think she was trying to give us a clue. We've always believed that Genno had an accomplice. What if she was referring to him? He may, or may not, be holed up with Genno. My guess is he's not. Chief Deputy Elworthy has already ordered his men to reinterview all the suspects they've spoken to in connection with the case. Chances are, one of them will have scratch marks on his face.'

'Assuming you're right, you're also assuming that this person would know where Genno's holding Lea,' Bob said.

'Oh, I'm certain he will. Genno's never been to New Orleans before. He wouldn't know where to start looking for somewhere to lie low. Which is where his contact would earn his corn. Chances are, he's hiding out somewhere in bayou country. We've already got teams searching the bayous, but it could take days to complete a task like that. And even then, there's no certainty of finding him.'

'If you're right about this, you can be sure that Frankie will be taking measures of his own to cover himself,' Sarah pointed out. 'And if that means killing his contact before the authorities can find him, I'm sure he'd do it.'

'I'm sure he would,' Taylor agreed. 'Which is why we have to get to him first.'

'Assuming it's not already too late,' Sarah said despairingly.

Taylor didn't reply. What could he say? She was right, and he knew it.

Half-asleep, she initially thought the knocking was coming from the street, but when it persisted she realized it was the front door. She squinted through sleepy eyes at the illuminated face of the alarm on the bedside table. It was 3.52 a.m. She cursed furiously when the knocking became pounding, and grabbing her robe, she threw it on before heading down the hallway to the front door. Sliding back the locks, she opened the door on the chain and peered out irritably at the two men standing in the corridor.

'Ms Rodford?'

'Yes,' came the weary reply.

'I'm Deputy Marshal Johnson, US Marshals Service. This is my colleague, Deputy Marshal Ford. We'd like a word with Etienne Pascale.'

'You and me both,' Lynne Rodford retorted caustically.

'Are you saying he's not here?' Johnson enquired.

'You're certainly quick on the uptake.'

'May we come in?' Johnson asked.

'I told you, he's not here.'

'We'd still like to check for ourselves.'

She removed the chain and, opening the door, gestured theatrically inside. 'Help yourselves. The sooner you look, the sooner you'll piss off and let me get back to sleep.'

Johnson remained with Lynne Rodford while Ford began to search the apartment. 'When did you last see Pascale?'

'A couple of hours ago. That's when he got back to the apartment. I've no idea where he'd been, other than it was with a woman. He admitted that much, but when I tried to question him further he stormed out again. I haven't seen him since. Probably gone back to his floozy. He obviously likes it rough, judging from the marks she left on his face. That's not for me, though. We're through. She can have him, as far as I'm concerned. Good riddance!'

'What marks?' Johnson demanded, his interest now stimulated.

'Scratch marks on his cheek.'

'And he didn't have them before tonight?'

'I think I'd have noticed, don't you?' came the sarcastic reply.

'He's not here,' Ford announced, emerging from the door at the end of the hallway.

'Let's go,' Johnson told him, and then turned to Lynne Rodford. 'You've been very helpful. Thank you.'

'If you say so. Now can I go back to sleep?'

'Sure.' Johnson handed her a card. 'And if he does return to the apartment, call that number right away. Day or night. It doesn't matter.'

'What's he done this time?' she asked suspiciously.

'Just call that number if you see him again,' Johnson said. 'There could be a reward in it for you.'

'It'll be reward enough just to see the back of that bastard.'

'Well, this might be your lucky night,' Johnson told her.

She closed the door behind them, then, stifling a yawn, switched off the hall light and went back to bed.

'You in, or not?'

'Don't rush me,' Pascale replied tetchily, studying the cards in his hand. He was seated at a green baize table with three other men in the back room of an all-night bar on Bourbon Street. Cloying smoke hung heavily in the air and a partially consumed bottle of bourbon stood in the middle of the table, beside the latest pot.

One of the men reached for the bottle and poured a generous measure into his empty glass. 'You've been staring at those cards for ages,' he complained, banging the bottle back down on to the table. 'C'mon, Etienne. Your mind's not on the game tonight.'

'He's still thinking about that little fox who scratched his face,' another man piped up, and there was a general chorus of laughter.

'Yeah, tell us more about her,' the third man said with a salacious grin.

'There's nothing to tell. Now shut up and let's play cards.'

'So play, for fuck sake.'

Pascale puffed thoughtfully on his cigarette, then shook his head and tossed the cards down on to the table. 'I'm out.'

'You're out?' the man beside him said in exasperation. 'I thought you must have had a winning hand with the amount of time you took to make your call. Fuck it, Etienne, what's wrong with you? You're not normally like this.'

'I've got things on my mind, OK?' Pascale replied defensively. He sunk the remnants of the bourbon in his glass, stubbed out his cigarette and immediately lit another.

'You in some kind of trouble? You can talk to us, you know.'

'Thank you, Father, I'll be sure to bear that in mind if I ever want to unburden my soul,' Pascale countered sarcastically.

'Fuck you, then. I was only trying to help.'

The door suddenly swung open and two men burst into the room, weapons drawn. 'Don't move!' one of them commanded. 'Hands on the table. Do it now!'

The four astonished men did as they were told. A third man

entered the room. Unarmed. Pascale recognized him even before he identified himself. Deputy Marshal Robert Robideaux.

'What the hell's this all about?' the man beside Pascale demanded. 'We ain't breaking no gambling laws. It's a private game. You've got no right coming in here like this.'

'I've got every right.' Robideaux crossed to Pascale, grabbed him roughly by the chin, and tilted his head to the side. 'How d'you get those marks on your cheek?'

'A woman,' came the surly reply.

'Yeah, I know. Fifteen years old. Tell me, was that before or after you kidnapped her?'

'What are you talking about?' Pascale blurted out, trying to mask the anxiety he was now feeling. How could Robideaux possibly know that the Johnson kid had scratched him? Was he trying to call his bluff? Or had he been released? Had Genno been arrested? Was he dead?

'On your feet and assume the position. You of all people should know how to do that.' Robideaux shoved him forcibly against the wall and one of the other deputies frisked him. When it was established that he was clean, his hands were pulled behind his back and a pair of handcuffs snapped round his wrists. Robideaux read him his Miranda rights, but had to pause several times when Pascale butted in to assert both his disbelief at what was going on and his complete innocence of any kidnapping charges. 'Take him to the car,' Robideaux ordered and Pascale was led from the room, still protesting his innocence. Robideaux picked up Pascale's cards, which lay face down on the table, and shook his head sadly to himself. 'It's just not his night, is it? Enjoy your game, gentlemen.' He tossed the cards back on to the table and left the room.

Genno knew that the deputies who'd been monitoring the phone call may have assumed that Lea had meant she had scratched *his* face. *Assumed*. Not good enough. He couldn't afford to take that chance. But each time he had tried to contact Pascale on his cellphone, he had been met with an engaged signal. He had also rung Pascale's apartment and a sleepy, irritable Lynne Rodford had told him that Pascale wasn't there. Then the receiver had been banged down. When he had tried to call the number a short time later, it had just rung. Either she wasn't answering, or she had disconnected it from the wall. Whatever the reason, he had no way of reaching Pascale. And having no idea where Pascale was, he knew he had to assume the worst: that Pascale could already be in custody. And Pascale was the one person capable of leading the authorities to his hide-out. Which only left him with one option. Move his plan forward . . . and make sure it would still work.

'Sarah, it must be *your* phone,' Bob announced, when they heard the sound of ringing coming from upstairs.

She hurried up to the master bedroom to answer it.

'Hello, Annie. I thought this might be a more private line. Nobody else to listen in to our little conversation.'

'How's Lea? Is she all right?' she asked anxiously, and then looked across at Taylor as he entered the bedroom. Bob followed close behind him.

'Lea's fine. And she'll remain that way as long as you do exactly as I say.'

'It's me you want, Frankie. Not her. Where and when? I'll be there.'

There was a faint chuckle at the other end of the line. 'That's the Annie I remember. No bullshit. Always straight to the point.'

'Only I won't meet with you unless I first know that Lea's safe.'

'I don't think you're in any position to start dictating terms, Annie. Do you?'

'Then we obviously don't have anything more to say to each other, do we?' She abruptly severed the connection and tossed the phone on to the bed.

'What the hell are you doing, Sarah?' Bob exclaimed, staring in disbelief at the discarded phone. 'He's got Lea. You start pissing him off and God knows what he might do to her. Look what happened to . . . Renée.'

'He won't hurt Lea.'

'I'm glad you're so sure of that,' Bob countered angrily.

'She's right,' Taylor said. 'He harms Lea and he doesn't get Sarah. That is what this is all about.'

The phone rang again. Sarah sat down on the bed and answered it.

'Don't you ever hang up on me like that again!' Genno snapped furiously.

'Then you'd better start taking me seriously,' Sarah retorted with equal ferocity.

There was a moment's pause, then Genno spoke again, his voice calm once more. 'OK. Let me tell you what's going to happen. And you try and double-cross me again, Annie, you'll be getting bits of

Lea through the post for the next month. I assume that's not what you want?'

'Just let me speak to her.'

'No. Not yet. This isn't Chicago. You're not calling the shots any more. I am. Which means that you'll either do it my way, or I'll hang up now and send you one of Lea's fingers through the post. It's your call, Annie.'

'Just tell me what you want me to do.'

'I've already told you, I don't know what you're talking about.'

Robideaux ran his hands over his thinning hair, then shook his head sadly. His eyes never left Pascale, who was sitting across from him, on the side of the table. There was nobody else in the room. Pascale's manacled hands were clasped together on the table. A smouldering cigarette was balanced between his fingers.

'So you've never heard of Frankie Genno?'

'Sure I've *heard* of him,' Pascale replied scornfully. 'Christ, he's hardly been out of the news since he escaped from the pen'. He's top of *America's Most Wanted*, isn't he? But that doesn't mean I *know* him.' He raised his manacled hands and took another drag on the cigarette. 'Look, I know my rights. I'm entitled to counsel. So where's my fucking lawyer?'

'You're making this real hard on yourself, Pascale. If anything happens to Lea Johnson while you're sitting here playing dumb, you'll be charged as an accessory to murder. You want to spend the next five years banged up on death row, with nothing else to think about other than the lethal injection with your name on it?'

'I said I want a *fucking* lawyer. What part of that don't you understand?'

'The moment you bring in a lawyer, any chance of a deal with the DA will be out the window.'

'Why would I want to make a deal with the DA when I haven't done anything wrong?'

'You must think we're morons, Pascale,' Chief Deputy Marshal Elworthy said from the doorway. 'Either that, or you're the moron. Which is it?'

Pascale looked round as Elworthy, who had opened the door silently behind him moments earlier, wheeled himself into the room. 'He wants to lawyer up,' Robideaux told Elworthy.

'Right now, I think that would be a pretty good idea,' Elworthy replied.

'But, sir, if he lawyers up, the DA won't deal,' Robideaux said hesitantly.

'I've spoken to the DA. He's already got more than enough evidence to put this shit away for the rest of his life.' Elworthy placed a computer print-out on the table in front of Pascale. 'These are all the numbers you've called on your cellphone in the last week. It makes very interesting reading. We've also carried out a thorough search of your apartment. Ms Rodford has been very cooperative, especially when we explained that we had every reason to believe the scratch marks on your face were made not by another woman, but by a frightened fifteen-year-old girl that you helped to kidnap. She even showed us where you hide your stash. The bills have already been sent to forensics to be dusted for prints. My guess is that we'll find both Klyne and Genno's prints on some of them. And when we do, the DA's office have indicated that they'll be bringing charges against you ranging from kidnapping right through to accessory to murder. To be honest, I don't think you'd get the death sentence, but what you will get is a long stretch inside. Then again, I doubt you'd have to worry about that. Just how long would an ex-cop last in jail? It could be a day. Maybe a week. Perhaps even a month. Before, you had Klyne to watch your back at Oakdale. This time, you'll be on your own. And I'll personally see to it that you're sent back to Oakdale where, I'm reliably informed, there are several lifers who would relish the opportunity to meet up with you again and carry out what they seem to regard as unfinished business. Is that what you want, Pascale? Because if it is, you go right ahead and lawyer up. I'll even have Deputy Marshal Robideaux ring your lawyer for you.'

Pascale sat motionless after Elworthy had finished talking. He was ashen-faced and his eyes were focused on the large column of ash which had accumulated on the end of his cigarette. 'I want to cut a deal with the DA,' he said in a faltering voice. 'I'll cooperate fully. I'll tell him everything he wants to know. Everything.'

'I'll be sure to pass that on to the DA's office,' Elworthy assured him. 'But what I would suggest you do, right now, is prove to the DA that you're sincere about a deal.'

'How?' Pascale asked.

'Tell us where Genno's holding the girl,' Elworthy replied. 'You do know that, don't you?'

'Yeah, I know. I rented the place for him.' The ash finally toppled off the tip of his cigarette and he was quick to buck it off the back of his hand. Only then did he raise his dull, lifeless eyes to look at

Robideaux. 'Give me a pen and pad. I'll tell you exactly where he is. I'll even draw you a map. Then I want you to call the DA and tell him I'm ready to talk.'

'What's the plan, sir?'

Elworthy, back in his office with Robideaux, absently touched the sheet of paper on which Pascale had drawn a map detailing Genno's exact location on the Bayou Bois Piquant. 'I haven't decided that yet. Judging by the diagram, it's going to be impossible to approach the cabin either by air or by water without being seen. That would give Genno enough time to barricade himself inside the cabin, using Lea Johnson as his hostage. That's what I'm desperate to avoid at all costs.'

'He wouldn't be open to negotiation either, would he?' Robideaux added.

'Mother for daughter. That would be his only concession.' Elworthy stared at the map. 'I say we give him what he wants. Or at least, appear to. I don't see how else we're going to get a sniper anywhere near enough to the cabin to take him out.'

'You mean, suggest a trade?' Robideaux said in horror.

'No, we can't get directly involved. Let him make all the moves. It may lull him into a false sense of security.'

'Chances are, he'll have already guessed that Pascale's been arrested. That might force his hand. We may not have much time to put something together.'

'That's where Sarah Johnson comes in. She can stall him until we're ready. After all, she's the one he wants. He won't risk killing the girl. He may be psychotic, but he's no fool.'

'It all depends on whether she agrees to go along with it,' Robideaux said. 'It would put her in the direct line of fire.'

'Never underestimate the maternal instant, Robert. Her immediate concern is to get her daughter back safely. And this may be her only chance.' Elworthy dialled the number of the Johnsons' house. It was answered by Bob Johnson. 'Mr Johnson, it's Chief Deputy Marshal Elworthy. May I speak to Deputy Marshal Taylor, please?'

'He's not here. He and Sarah left the house about ten minutes ago.'

'Where have they gone?' Elworthy asked in surprise.

'To rendezvous with you. They're probably still on their way.'

'To rendezvous with me?' Elworthy replied in bewilderment. 'I don't know what you're talking about.'

'He arranged it with you on the phone before they left the house.'

'I never spoke to him. One moment.' Elworthy placed his hand over the mouthpiece and addressed Robideaux. 'Have you spoken to Taylor in the last half-hour?'

'I've been with Pascale ever since he was arrested.' Robideaux frowned uneasily. 'Why, what is it?'

'Check with the switchboard to see whether Taylor called anyone here in the last hour.' Elworthy removed his hand from the mouthpiece. 'Mr Johnson, did Deputy Marshal Taylor say he'd specifically spoken to me?'

'Yes. Look, what's going on?'

'Did you overhear the conversation?'

'No,' came the indignant reply.

'Tell me what you know.'

'All I know is that Genno rang Sarah on her cellphone. He also spoke to Taylor. He obviously knew Taylor was here at the house. Taylor left the room to talk to him, but he looked pretty shaken up when he came back. Then he called you to arrange a rendezvous.'

'Where?' Elworthy demanded.

'I've no idea. As I said, I didn't overhear the call. He cleared it with the other deputies here, and then he left with Sarah.' There was an uneasy pause. 'What the hell's going on, Elworthy?'

'At this precise moment, Mr Johnson, I have no idea, but I'll call you back as soon I find out.' Elworthy replaced the receiver and looked at Robideaux. 'Well?'

'No calls from Taylor have been logged in the last hour.' Robideaux listened silently as Elworthy briefed him on the conversation with Bob Johnson, then rubbed his chin thoughtfully as he pondered one point in particular. 'I'd love to know what Genno said to Taylor to rattle him like that. Let's face it, Taylor's not the sort of guy who'd spook easily.'

'I think Taylor's made some kind of deal with Genno. It's the only logical explanation I can come up with right now. But it sure as hell wasn't authorized by me.'

'What if he's going to try and take out Genno by himself? Using Sarah Johnson as bait.'

'That's what I'm thinking. Genno's no fool. It's exactly what he'll be expecting. They're going to be walking straight into a trap. Surely Taylor must realize that?'

'Unless he's got a counter-plan of his own,' Robideaux suggested, but there was an edge of uncertainty in his voice.

'Maybe,' came the equally sceptical reply.

'Sir, we've got to intercept them before they reach the cabin. It's the only way we can be sure of preventing any further bloodshed.'

'I just hope we're not too late,' Elworthy replied grimly, as he reached for the phone on his desk.

Thirteen

'D'you think it's going to work?'

'I think it's our . . . or rather, your, once chance of getting Lea back alive,' Taylor replied, casting a sidelong glance at Sarah behind the wheel. 'You're going to have to lull him into a false sense of security, if we're to have any chance of this working. If he thinks for one moment that I'm with you, he'd kill Lea. I'm sure of that.' He noticed the uncertainty etched on her face. It had been obvious that she'd been uneasy about his plan right from the start. 'If I'd told Chief Deputy Marshal Elworthy where we were going, he'd have sent in the cavalry to try and negotiate Lea's release. The last thing we need is a stand-off with Genno. It's not as if he's going to give himself up. He'd rather die first. And he'd take as many people with him as he could in the process. Starting with Lea. Trust me, Sarah. It's the only way.'

'What if he sees you?'

'I keep telling you, he won't see me. That's the whole idea. All I'll need is one shot. But you have to make him believe that you've come alone, as he insisted on the phone. You for Lea. That was the deal he made with you, wasn't it?'

'Yes,' she said in a barely audible voice.

'It's going to be OK, Sarah. I won't let anything happen to Lea. I swear it.'

She said nothing, preferring to keep her eyes fixed on the road ahead. She'd made a decision back at the house to trust Taylor with Lea's life. With her own life. What if she'd made a mistake? But what choice did she have? Tell Elworthy so that he could send in a SWAT team? Lea would be dead the moment Frankie realized he'd been double-crossed. No, she'd made the right choice. If she continued to say that to herself enough times, then she might just begin to believe it . . .

*

Genno stood motionless on the porch, hands in the pockets of his jeans, watching the sun slowly rising over the bayou. As far as he could remember, it was the first sunrise he'd ever watched. It had never been something that had interested him before. Not that it did now – at least, not particularly – except that he thought everyone should witness at least one sunrise before they died. And he was certain he was going to die that day. It didn't bother him. If anything, he would welcome it. He'd finally be at peace with himself after eighteen years of unrelenting torment. But that was in the past. He would kill Annie. Then himself. That way they would never be separated again. As it should be.

He retrieved the binoculars from the chair beside him and slowly scanned his surroundings. Still no sign of Annie. Or Taylor, for that matter. He knew Taylor would be with her after what they had discussed earlier on the phone. He wondered what bullshit Taylor had spun her to conceal the truth. No matter. She'd find out soon enough. He chuckled softly to himself and went back into the cabin.

'McCrory's Boat Hire,' Taylor announced, reading the faded sign on the roof of the general store. 'This is the place Genno told you about, isn't it? Now all we've got to do is get some service.'

He banged loudly on the front door with his fist until an upper-floor window was jerked open and a bleary-eyed, unshaven face poked through the closed curtains. 'What the hell's all that racket down there?' the old man demanded, stifling a yawn.

'Open up,' Taylor demanded.

'We don't open 'til eight. Now clear off.'

'Deputy Marshal.' Taylor held up his shield. 'Open up.'

'What's this about?'

'The sooner you get down here, the sooner you'll find out.'

The old man cursed angrily under his breath. 'I'm coming down.' The window was slammed shut again.

Sarah noticed Taylor glance at his watch, something he'd done several times on the way over. 'What is it?' she asked.

'Chances are Chief Deputy Marshal Elworthy already knows that we're no longer at the house. And if they have already arrested Genno's accomplice – the man Lea scratched on the face – it's only going to be a matter of time before he divulges Genno's location. They'll put two and two together and try to stop us. If they do, the element of surprise will have been lost. And at the moment, that's all we've got going for us.'

'Surely Elworthy must realize that?'

'I'm sure he does, but he still has to play it by the book. That way, if anything were to go wrong, he's covered his own ass.'

Bolts were drawn back from behind the closed door and a moment later it swung open. The man was in his early sixties, with a towelling robe secured round his spindly frame. 'Let's see that shield again.' He remained in the doorway, hand extended. Taylor held it out towards him. 'What about her?' he asked, gesturing towards Sarah with a nod of his head.

'She's with me. That's all you need to know. Are you McCrory?'

'Yeah. Walter McCrory,' the old man replied absently, as his eyes lingered on Sarah. Then he turned his attention back to Taylor. 'What the hell's this 'bout anyway?'

'We need a couple of speedboats.'

'Just like that,' came the disdainful reply.

'Just like that,' Taylor said matter-of-factly, and then put his hand to the window to block out the reflection of the first rays of daylight as he peered into the shop. Wooden beams crisscrossed each other high above dusty wooden floorboards. Dated black-and-white photographs, many faded with age, lined the bleak walls behind the long counter. It reminded him of something out of an episode of *The Waltons*. Some would have called it quaint. He saw it as a potential fire hazard. 'You got those speedboats for us?' he asked, turning round to look at McCrory.

'An' if I don't let you have 'em, you'll shut me down, is that it?'

'I don't have the authority to shut you down. But I'm sure a phone call to the relevant authorities would do the trick.'

'I get the picture,' McCrory muttered angrily. 'An' I suppose you're going to commandeer 'em as well, being as you're a federal marshal.'

'Actually, I was going to hire them. I'll pay cash.'

'Well, why didn't you say that in the first place, G-man? The keys are inside. I'll go an' get 'em for you.'

Taylor followed McCrory into the shop, leaving Sarah on the porch. She descended the wooden steps and crossed to the water's edge, where she watched a solitary figure on the deck of a shrimper casting off its mooring ropes in preparation for a day's trawling beyond the bayou on Lake Cataouatche. He was young. Early twenties, in jeans and a T-shirt. He suddenly noticed Sarah staring at him and she looked away when he raised his hand in greeting and gave her a nicotine-stained grin. She felt angry at herself for allowing her mind to drift away from thoughts of Lea. All that concerned her was getting her daughter back unharmed. The fact that another human life would have to be sacrificed to achieve it was irrelevant. Frankie had put himself up for this. And if he had to die . . . she had no problem with that, not after what he had put her family through these past few days. Especially Lea. No, Sarah had no feelings of guilt about seeing Frankie die, if it meant saving her daughter's life . . .

'You ready?'

She turned to Taylor, his voice snapping her out of her reverie, and nodded. 'I'm ready.'

'You do know how to pilot a speedboat?' he asked cautiously.

'We used to have one, before Bob's partner decided to cook the books. We had to sell it to pay off some of the outstanding creditors.' She took the key he held up to her. 'Where are they?'

'Moored in there,' Taylor said, indicating a weather-beaten boathouse situated a couple of hundred yards further down the riverbank. 'You know what to do?'

'I should do. We went through it enough times on the way over here.'

'Then let's go.'

The directions Frankie had given her over the phone proved to be precise in every detail. She had written them down on a sheet of paper which she now had in her free hand. Her other hand was gripped tightly round the wheel of the speedboat. Taylor was nowhere in sight. That was part of the plan. She was to go in alone. He had given her a few minutes' head start, which gave him more time to study the map of the bayou he'd got from McCrory's store. It was imperative that he wasn't seen from the cabin, which meant finding another route for the last part of the journey. A route which would allow him to approach the cabin unnoticed. The swamplands at the rear of the bayou appeared to be his best bet. At least, that had been his initial conclusion when he'd first consulted the map. She had offered to help him plot the best possible route through the swamplands, but he had been adamant. He would determine the route himself. It was imperative that she set off as soon as possible. Time was of the essence, especially if Elworthy already knew Genno's location. They had to reach him first.

The cabin came into view the moment she turned the speedboat into the mouth of the tributary. But it also meant she could be seen as well. She stopped the speedboat, pretending to look around her, allowing it to drift backwards until it was out of sight of the cabin. Then she dropped the orange buoy into the water. A signal for Taylor. He couldn't proceed further than the buoy without being seen from the cabin. She started up the engine again and continued towards the cabin. There was nobody in sight. It was only as she drew nearer the jetty that she recognized Lea's grey blouson draped over the pillar at the foot of the porch. Tears suddenly welled up in her eyes, but she chided herself angrily for allowing her emotions to surface so easily. She had to be strong. For Lea. For herself. She couldn't afford to let Frankie intimidate her. She manoeuvred the speedboat against the jetty, behind the tethered Gemini inflatable, and grabbed the mooring rope from the stern and secured it round the wooden bollard. Then she stepped on to the jetty.

'That's far enough, Annie,' Genno called out from the cabin. 'Where's Taylor? Hiding in the boat?'

'Taylor isn't here. I came alone. That's what you wanted, wasn't it?'

'No matter,' Genno said, and then the front door opened and he appeared in view, with Lea as a shield in front of him. He was holding a silenced Beretta against her throat. Her hands were manacled behind her and a strip of masking tape had been secured over her mouth. Her eyes were red and puffy.

'Lea,' Sarah cried out and took a step towards the cabin.

'Uh-uh,' Genno said, shaking his head. 'Stay where you are, Annie. Lea and I will come to you.'

'It's me you want, Frankie. That was the deal we made on the phone.'

'It was, wasn't it?' Genno negotiated the steps carefully behind Lea and crossed the lawn to the other end of the jetty. Apart from the Beretta, he also had a hunting knife sheathed at the side of his jeans. On the other side were a pair of handcuffs secured to his belt. The loose cuff was, as always, open. 'What d'you think of my new look, Annie? Pretty trendy, eh?'

She eyed his cropped head disdainfully. 'It's what's inside a person that counts. In your case, evil. Pure evil. But then you always have been, haven't you?'

Genno's eyes narrowed angrily, then he laughed abruptly. 'You never were one to mince your words, Annie. Succinct to the last.'

Where's Taylor? she thought anxiously. All Frankie had to do now was shoot her where she stood. Though she doubted he would. He had eighteen years of animosity stored up inside him. Killing her with a single bullet would be too easy. He would make her suffer. Then he would kill her. She shuddered at the thought. Where the hell was Taylor?

'Let Lea go, Frankie,' Sarah urged anxiously. 'Or doesn't your word count for anything any more?'

'My word?' Genno snorted. 'What about your word, Annie? Do you remember the last thing you said to me before I went into the jeweller's?' He noticed the uncertainty in her eyes. ' "I love you, Frankie." Lies. All fucking lies. So don't talk to me about *my* word.'

She could see he was becoming increasingly agitated as the memories came flooding back to him. His grip tightened on the butt of the Beretta and she had to stop herself from reaching out a placatory hand towards him. Don't play to him, she chided herself. Calm. Stay calm.

·'They weren't lies, Frankie. Not then.'

'You'd already sold me out to the cops by the time we hit the jeweller's. Is that your idea of love? *Is it?*'

'I had no choice, Frankie.'

'What did they have on you, Annie? A second bust for possession? You'd have been looking at six months at the most. Probably less. I'd have willingly done that kind of time for you if the roles had been reversed. You know that. Why? Because I *did* love you. Only you sold me out. You betrayed me. Now it's my turn to settle the score.'

'No!' Sarah yelled in horror when she saw Genno's finger curl round the trigger. Now she was desperate. 'You remember what I said to you at Stateville, Frankie? Whatever you do to my family, I'll have the same done to your mother.'

Genno slowly eased his finger off the trigger and nodded slowly to himself. 'Yeah, I remember. Only you can't hurt my mother. Not any more.'

'You want to bet,' Sarah countered defiantly.

'My mother's beyond harm now. I made sure of that before I left Joliet.' He saw the look of horror flash across Sarah's face as she realized the implication of what he was saying. 'That's right, Annie. I killed her. I broke her neck while I was giving her a massage. It was very quick. Quite painless. She wouldn't have felt a thing. Now you can't hurt her any more. That's what she would have wanted me to do. She wouldn't have wanted me to worry about her. Sorry, Annie, looks like I've just trumped your trump card.' His eyes suddenly flickered past Sarah and he shouted out, 'You must be Deputy Marshal Jack Taylor. Pleased to finally meet you.'

It was only then that Sarah noticed Taylor had emerged from the trees at the back of the cabin. His automatic was drawn, but he was holding it at his side.

'Get in the boat, Lea,' Genno snapped, forcing her to climb into the Gemini inflatable, which was wallowing gently in the waters at the side of the jetty. Then he straightened up and looked across at Taylor, whose automatic was still hanging loosely at his side.

'Shoot him!' Sarah screamed at Taylor. 'For God's sake, Jack, shoot him!'

Genno extended his arms away from his body, offering himself as the perfect target. 'Go on, Jack, do as Annie says. Shoot me. Put me out of her misery once and for all.' He laughed callously at Sarah as she stared in disbelief at Taylor. 'And here you thought he was your protector, out to rescue you and Lea from the clutches of the evil Frankie Genno. Sorry to disappoint you, Annie. He's been in on this right from the start. Haven't you, Jackie boy?'

'Shut up, Genno,' Taylor retorted. 'I brought her, as agreed. Now you keep to your side of the bargain. Give me the disk and the tape.'

'What disk? What tape?' Sarah shouted out in frustration. 'Jack, what's going on?'

'Jack's been a naughty boy,' Genno said scornfully. 'He and his partner, Keith Yallow, were in on the scam with Ted Lomax. All the incriminating evidence is on a tape Klyne made while he was torturing Lomax. Lomax was more than willing to tell him everything he wanted to know. Taylor and his partner were initially brought in to investigate claims that Lomax intended to sell sensitive WITSEC documents on the black market. But then, that's common knowledge anyway.'

'Shut up!' Taylor snarled, his hand tightening on the automatic in his hand.

'She's got a right to know that you've been fucking her over from the very start, Jackie boy.' Genno focused his attention back on Sarah. 'Lomax realized that he was facing a long stretch inside, so he confided his plans to Taylor and Yallow, offering to make them silent partners – a fifty-fifty split – if they told their superiors that there wasn't enough evidence to bring any charges against him. Their avarice got the better of them and they went for it. All charges against Lomax were dropped for "lack of evidence". Lomax was about to start a bidding war on the black market, but Klyne got to him first. He copied all of Lomax's files on to disk, then erased the files on the computer. Klyne was going to sell the disk to the highest bidder after this was all over, except he became too much of a liability to me – so I had to kill him. Now I have both the disk and the tape in my possession. That's what Taylor and I discussed on the phone earlier this morning. He agreed to deliver you to me, and in return I'd give him the disk and the tape. After all, I have no use for them any more.' He tilted his head to one side and gave Sarah a sad smile. 'So you tell me, Annie, who's the bad guy now?'

Sarah stared at Taylor in stunned disbelief, unable to comprehend what Genno had just told her. She wanted to hear Taylor deny it. Tell her it wasn't true. But she knew it wouldn't happen. No wonder he'd been so desperate not to tell Elworthy where they were going. He had brought her to her death. Calmly. Coldly. Detached. A man she had trusted with her life. And the life of her daughter. Now they were both going to die. Despite the overwhelming revulsion she felt for Taylor, she knew she would be partly to blame for Lea's death when it came. What had she done?

'Give me the disk and the tape, Genno,' Taylor said, crossing the lawn towards the jetty. 'Then I'll leave you in peace to play happy families.'

'You'll get them after I've left here,' Genno told him.

'That wasn't the deal!' Taylor retorted angrily.

'If I give them to you now, what's to stop you putting a bullet in me?' Genno shook his head. 'No, you play by my rules. Don't worry, they're in the cabin. Stored away safely. I'll call you on the phone just as soon as the three of us are clear of the area. I can't say fairer than that, can I?'

Taylor raised his hand and trained the automatic on Genno. 'Not good enough. I don't give a shit about Sarah and her kid. You can do what the fuck you want to them. I just want what's mine. The disk. The tape. Where are they?'

'Pull the trigger and you'll never find out, will you?' Genno replied with a knowing smile, but he never took his eyes, or the Beretta, off Sarah.

'I know they're in the cabin. I'll find them.'

'Happy hunting,' Genno retorted. 'I just hope your colleagues don't get here before you've found them. I'm sure the tape would make particularly interesting listening. Life without the possibility of parole. I've been there, Taylor. I wouldn't recommend it. I really wouldn't. Like I said, I'll call you once we're clear of the cabin and let you know where they are. You have my word on that. But if that's not good enough for you, you'd better pull the trigger now.'

Genno turned his head fractionally towards Taylor, but the Beretta remained trained on Sarah. 'Well, are you going to shoot me or not?'

Sarah knew it was her one chance to jump Genno. She also knew that he could just as easily pull the trigger before she could get to him. But what choice did she have? If he handcuffed her as well, both she and Lea would be completely defenceless. She had to risk it. For Lea. For herself . . .

Genno noticed the movement out of the corner of his eye, but before he could get off a shot Sarah slammed into his chest, her momentum knocking him off his feet, and they both tumbled off the jetty. The gun was knocked from Genno's hand as he hit the water and he grunted in pain when she landed heavily on top of him. She lashed out with her fist, catching him painfully in the face. He yelled in fury and shook his head to clear the dizziness which threatened to engulf him. She slammed her feet into his midriff, propelling herself away from him, and then swam with powerful strokes towards the inflatable. And Lea. She was only a matter of feet from it, when an arm was clamped round her throat and her head was shoved roughly under the water. She was suddenly enveloped in darkness, unable to see anything around her. She struggled furiously to try and reach the surface again, but Genno was much stronger than her and was able to keep her head under the water with considerable ease. In desperation she grabbed on to his shirt, trying in vain to pull him down with her. Her lungs were bursting. She could feel herself becoming disorientated from the lack of oxygen. She had to do something in the next few seconds, otherwise she'd lapse into unconsciousness and drown. Leaving Lea to his mercy. This thought seemed to give her renewed strength and, sliding her hand down his stomach until she felt his groin, she clawed with her fingers and crushed his genitals as hard as she could. It had the desired effect, as he pushed her away from him, allowing her to propel herself to the surface, where she gratefully gulped down mouthfuls of air.

Still feeling light-headed, she swam the short distance to a rusting metal ladder at the side of the jetty. But no sooner had she locked an arm round it than Genno grabbed a handful of her wet hair and yanked her backwards, forcing her to release her grip. He thrust her head under the water again, but this time she managed to lock her fingers round his belt, and, looping a leg round the foot of the ladder, she pulled herself downwards, taking him with her. Remembering the sheathed hunting knife on his belt, she felt for it, but instead her fingers brushed lightly against the handcuffs.

She was already struggling to keep her foot round the bottom rung as Genno tried desperately to reach the surface again. Her lungs were once more at bursting point. She doubted she could hold out for much longer. Then an idea came to her. As her eyes slowly adjusted to the murky water and she was able to make out the silhouette of the ladder, she felt for the handcuffs again and used them to pull Genno towards it. With one swift movement she locked the loose cuff round one of the rungs, and then slammed her elbow sharply into Genno's midriff. His grip loosened round her throat and she was able to pull away from him. She propelled herself upwards, broke the surface, and trod water as she again gulped down mouthfuls of air. There was no sign of Genno. Or Taylor, for that matter. She swam to the inflatable and pulled herself aboard. Lea's eyes were filled with tears. She pulled the masking tape off Lea's mouth, and then kissed her lightly on the lips.

'I'll get us out of here, sweetheart. I promise you.'

'Mommy, I'm sorry about—'

'Ssh,' Sarah said softly, placing a finger lightly on her lips. 'First things first, eh? Let's get out of here.'

Sarah discarded the mooring rope, then knelt beside the outboard motor and pulled hard on the cord. It failed to take. She tried a second time, and as the motor started up she glanced towards the cabin, half expecting Taylor to emerge through the front door. He didn't appear. Now to get them as far away from the cabin as possible. She took hold of the tiller and was about to turn the inflatable away from the jetty when Genno burst out from under the water, directly behind Lea, the serrated blade of the hunting knife in his hand glinting menacingly in the first rays of the morning sun. His face was contorted with rage and Sarah had a split second to react as he raised the knife to strike at Lea. She lashed out at Lea, catching her painfully across the face, knocking her sideways just as the blade slashed through the air where she had been kneeling a moment later. Sarah knew that Genno wouldn't miss Lea a second time. He already had an arm wrapped round the side of the inflatable, the knife poised to strike again. Lea, curled in a helpless ball in the middle of the inflatable, was screaming in terror. Sarah knew that if she grabbed at Genno, the chances were he would kill her first. Then Lea. And to reach him, she would have to release her hand from the tiller.

Instead, she jerked the tiller to the right, violently propelling the inflatable sideways. The knife missed Lea by inches and Genno lost his grip on the side of the inflatable. He disappeared under the water only to re-emerge a moment later, this time within striking range of Sarah. He'd played straight into her hands. Now she had to make the advantage pay. It was either her or Genno. That was incentive enough for her . . .

She pivoted the inflatable sharply on its axis. Genno realized at the last moment what she intended to do, but, weighed down by his saturated clothing, he was still trying desperately to pull back from the propeller when she tilted the outboard motor sharply upwards towards him. He screamed in agony when the pitch of the engine faltered as the propeller sliced into his midriff. His body shuddered violently in the water, and blood erupted from his mouth and poured down his chin as the razor-sharp blades effortlessly disembowelled him. She stared defiantly at him with a mixture of contempt and hatred, struggling to hold the outboard motor steady as the water darkened around him. Then the knife slipped from his fingers and he slumped forward, his head lolling on his chest, his lifeless body impaled on the churning blades. Only then did she let go of the outboard motor. His body slipped backwards into the water, and she vomited violently over the side of the inflatable at the sight of the mangled remains of his stomach which, until then, hadn't been visible below the water line. She turned to Lea, anxious that her daughter didn't see Genno's mutilated body. Lea was staring fearfully towards the jetty. Sarah forced herself to follow her daughter's gaze. Taylor was standing at the end of the jetty. Automatic in one hand, computer disk and tape in the other.

'You saved me the job of killing him,' Taylor said coldly. 'I appreciate it. Now all I have to do is kill you and the brat, and blame it on him. Simple really.'

Sarah's mind was racing. With the engine still running, she could try and grab the tiller again. But what chance would she have of getting them out of range before he pulled the trigger? Realistically, none. Chances were, he'd kill her even before she reached the tiller. He took a step forward and raised the automatic. It was aimed at her.

'I'm sorry it has to happen this way, Sarah. I really am. But it's about survival. And I'm the one with the gun.'

Survival. She could certainly identify with that word. She suddenly flung herself backwards, hitting the side of the inflatable with such force that it overturned, catapulting them both into the water. She heard the first bullet as she hit the water. When she surfaced again, close to the upturned inflatable, Lea was nowhere in sight. She panicked as she looked round frantically for her, but didn't dare move from where she was now concealed behind the inflatable. She knew that particular area of the bayou was alligator country, and they would certainly be attracted by the copious amounts of blood now in the water. Yet she didn't fear for her own safety. Only for Lea. Her daughter was a good swimmer. But she was handcuffed. How long could she tread water with her arms manacled behind her back?

'Looking for Lea?' It was Taylor's voice. Patronizing. Contemptuous. 'I think she's under the inflatable. I guess there's only one way to find out.'

A bullet ripped into the side of the inflatable. Sarah screamed in horror and reached underneath the inflatable with her hands. She felt something. Lea's arms. She ducked under the water, pulling Lea down with her, as a second bullet hit the vessel. When she surfaced again, she was holding Lea's arms tightly to keep her afloat. But she had misjudged her position. The inflatable had drifted and they were now both directly in the line of fire. Taylor already had the automatic trained on them. She flinched as the shot rang out, fully expecting to feel the searing pain of the bullet as it hit her. Nothing. Lea? She forced herself to look at her daughter. Lea was staring back at her, a look of bewilderment on her face. She, too, was unharmed.

Taylor was still standing on the jetty, but his gun hand was now hanging limply at his side. He took a hesitant step forward, then dropped to his knees, a look of amazement in his eyes as he toppled forward on to the jetty, the automatic bouncing once on the wooden boards before disappearing into the water.

It was only then that Sarah noticed the man standing at the side of the cabin. Deputy Marshal Robideaux. He lowered his own automatic, snapped his fingers and several other deputies hurried forward to pull Sarah and Lea from the water.

'I'm damned if I know what that was all about, other than that Taylor was trying to kill you,' Robideaux said, approaching Sarah, who now had Lea cocooned tightly in her arms. 'I had no choice but to put him down.'

'That's what it was all about,' Sarah said, indicating the computer disk and the cassette tape lying on the jetty beside Taylor's body. 'Listen to the tape. It's all on there.'

'I will, believe me,' Robideaux said, bagging the two items. 'Where's Genno?'

'Dead,' she said, looking out across the water. There was no sign of the body. Probably taken by an alligator. She shuddered at the thought.

'There's a chopper on its way. It's got a paramedic on board. And blankets. You can take off those wet clothes as soon as it arrives.' Robideaux patted Lea gently on the shoulder. 'We'll get you out of those handcuffs as soon as possible.'

'When did you get here?' Sarah asked. 'Where did you moor your boat?'

'Beside the other one, in the swampland behind the trees. We knew we couldn't come in through the front door. We got there just as Taylor started shooting at you. I was still in the boat at the time. I didn't think I'd get into range before he got off another shot.'

'Well, you did,' Sarah said with a nervous laugh. 'Thank you.'

Robideaux just smiled, and then looked skywards on hearing the first sounds of the helicopter's engine in the distance. A short time later the helicopter came into view and one of the deputy marshals indicated for it to land on the lawn. No sooner had the skids touched the ground than the cabin door was flung open and Bob Johnson jumped out and ran over to where Sarah and Lea were huddled together on the jetty.

'Thank God you're both safe,' he said, hugging them tightly. It was only then he noticed Lea's arms manacled behind her back. 'Hey, can someone get these things off my daughter's wrists,' he yelled to nobody in particular. 'Hey? Hey?'

'It'll be taken care of, Bob,' Sarah was quick to assure him.

'Mommy?' Lea said softly.

'What is it, sweetheart?'

'I've been such a jerk. About . . . you know . . . Jimmy. I never meant to . . .' Her voice trailed off as she began to cry. 'I'm sorry. I'm sorry.'

'It's over, sweetheart. It's all over now. We've all made mistakes, me included, but what matters is that we're still together. Now we have to start looking to the future.'

'As a family?' Lea asked, her eyes flickering between her mother and her father standing on either side of her. Sarah and Bob exchanged glances. Neither of them answered.

A marshal hurried towards them, a miniature key in his hand. 'You think it'll work?' Bob asked Sarah, as they watched the marshal unlock the handcuffs. Sarah shot him a quizzical look. 'Us staying together as a family?' he added.

'I guess it's possible – with a bit of luck, and a hell of a lot of hard work. Question is, are you prepared to give it another try?'

'Mrs Johnson?' Robideaux called out from the helicopter before Bob could reply. 'We've got the blankets here for you and Lea. Come and get changed before you both catch pneumonia.'

'Sarah?' Bob said as she was about to cross to the helicopter. She paused to look back at him. 'Yes, I'm prepared to give it another try. Whatever it takes. What about you?'

Sarah held his stare, but her expression gave nothing away. Then, putting an arm gently around Lea's slender shoulders, she led her towards the helicopter.